Old Glory
and the
Stars and Bars

OLD GLORY

AND THE

STARS AND BARS

Stories of the Civil War

Edited by
George William Koon

University of South Carolina Press

Copyright © 1995 University of South Carolina

Published in Columbia, South Carolina, by the
University of South Carolina Press

Manufactured in the United States of America

99 98 97 96 95   5 4 3 2 1

"**Ambuscade**" is from *The Unvanquished* by William Faulkner. Copyright ©
1934, 1935, 1936, 1938 and renewed © 1962, 1963 by William Faulkner and
1964, 1966 by Estelle Faulkner and Jill Faulkner Summers. Reprinted by
permission of Random House, Inc. "**The War Years**" is from *The Autobiography
of Miss Jane Pittman* by Ernest Gaines. Copyright © 1971 by Ernest J. Gaines.
Used by permission of Doubleday, a division of Bantam Doubleday Dell
Publishing Group, Inc. "**The Forest of the South**" is from *The Collected Stories
of Caroline Gordon*. Copyright © 1945 and copyright renewed © 1972 by
Caroline Gordon. Reprinted by permission of Farrar, Straus, Giroux, Inc.
"**Homemade Yankees**" is printed by permission of Robert Morgan. "**Dragged
Fighting from His Tomb**" is from *Airships* by Barry Hannah. Copyright ©
1978 by Barry Hannah. Reprinted by permission of Alfred A. Knopf, Inc.
"**Ancestors**" is reprinted by permission of Fred Chappell. "**A Late Encounter
with the Enemy**" is from *A Good Man Is Hard to Find and Other Stories*.
Copyright © 1953 by Flannery O'Connor and renewed © 1981 by Regina
O'Connor, reprinted by permission of Harcourt Brace & Company.

Library of Congress Cataloging-in-Publication Data

Old Glory and the Stars and Bars : stories of the Civil War / edited by George
William Koon.
  p. cm.
  ISBN 1-57003-056-1 (cloth : alk. paper). — ISBN 1-57003-057-X
(alk. paper)
  1. United States—History—Civil War, 1861-1865—Fiction. 2. War
stories, American. 3. Short stories, American. 4. American
fiction—20th century. 5. American fiction—19th century.
I. Koon, George William.
PS648.C54043 1995
813'.08108—dc20   95-15222
                                   CIP

CONTENTS

Old Glory
and the
Stars and Bars

INTRODUCTION

The Civil War left a terrible legacy. When it ended in 1865, more than 600,000 people were dead, and part of the country lay ruined. That might have been enough. But more than that, the war left us to ponder stunning ironies—of Americans fighting among themselves, on American soil, about independence and freedom; of Americans actually losing a war and having to adjust not only to the idea of defeat but also to the insult of occupation by American troops; of military colleagues, even classmates and relatives, fighting each other; of incredible gallantry, like that of Lee and Jackson, applied to a lost and questioned cause.

The fight, and the irreconcilable contradictions that it represented, inevitably produced a flood of storytelling that runs nearly as deep and strong today as it did a century ago. While the history has been written and revised and then again revised, the myth has gathered and multiplied itself many times over. Perhaps it takes myth to begin to encompass such astonishing history. Regardless, the blend of the real and the imagined, of truth and our many interpretations of it, has made the Civil War a nearly perfect resource for the American fiction writer. So much history so broadly embellished seems irresistible to the creative mind.

The sixteen stories of this anthology cannot begin to define either the war or the literary responses to it. With them, though, I have tried to present with plain good reading a variety of perspectives and tones in Civil War short fiction. The book includes many "standard" selections, but it avoids much of the sentimentality and partisanship that often comes with such material. In addition, it includes recent work—by writers such as Robert Morgan, Barry Hannah, and Fred Chappell. It includes battle scenes, but it reaches extensively into the home front, and it gathers a few tales about the influences of the war

1

well beyond 1865. And readers will find some comedy winding through the immense tragedy.

The anthology does not have a distinct chronological progression as such. Some readers, I believe, will approach it looking for their favorite stories and authors and will read at random. I hope that their favorites will lead them to some discoveries. I hope that Mark Twain's "The Private History of a Campaign That Failed" might take such a reader into a new piece of work such as Robert Morgan's "Homemade Yankees," that Hamlin Garland's "The Return of a Private" might take such a reader into Fred Chappell's outrageous "Ancestors."

At the same time, however, I hope that the anthology has its own coherence and rhythm. I want the reader who works through the entire book to find some pattern and completeness. Thus I have tried to observe a loose order. To identify a beginning, I have chosen "Ambuscade," the opening section of Faulkner's novel, *The Unvanquished*. With it I have paired "The War Years," the opening section of Ernest Gaines's *The Autobiography of Miss Jane Pittman*. "Ambuscade" focuses on Bayard Sartoris who, with his black friend Ringo, is playing the war game of boys when he discovers that Federal troops are coming and that the Confederacy is losing the war. Before the end of the story, he sees his first Yankee. He begins to see the reality of a war that had been only a game before, and he starts the long process of growing up. Gaines's story works similarly with a slave girl as Federal troops arrive and she begins to realize her freedom.

These two stories do not focus on the actual beginning of the war, obviously. They do focus, however, on the beginning of the war for particular characters, one white and one black. Both of them will have to grow up quickly to deal with a new way of life. Together, the two stories emphasize a sense of beginning, and they note a range of perspective as they deal with Bayard who is losing a way of life and with Ticey, to become Miss Jane, who is gaining a way of life. We leave each character waiting to see what the war will bring.

The nine stories which comprise what I take to be the middle of the anthology range about in Civil War history and among Civil War themes. Mark Twain's "The Private History of a Campaign That Failed" presents one of the most basic themes as it describes a group of Missouri volunteers that goes off to war on a lark and then learns "with a cold suddenness, that here was no jest—we were standing face to face with actual war." "The Reign of the Brute," a chapter of Ellen Glasgow's *The Battle-Ground*, seems to reaffirm that theme by taking a young Confederate soldier off to his first battle, a "glorious victory," and then leaving him to wonder about the glory as he passes a field hospital. Mary Johnston, in "A Woman," from her remarkable 1911 novel, *The Long Roll*, takes us into Richmond just after Federal troops have been turned back for the second time. She offers some fine battle descriptions in the voices of the wounded who have been brought into the army hospital. And she says much about the personal costs of victory.

With the next two stories I attempt to present fresh material from well-known authors. I was pleased to find a Civil War story by Jack London. His "War" efficiently depicts the irony of Americans both helping and killing each other during the conflict. Instead of "An Occurrence at Owl Creek Bridge," an Ambrose Bierce standard, I offer that author's "Killed at Resaca," which gives a unique twist to the familiar story of the soldier and his last letter.

The anthology then turns to more recent work. Caroline Gordon's "The Forest of the South" is a superb and violent piece about romance and treachery across enemy lines. Robert Morgan generates huge suspense in "Homemade Yankees," a tale of renegades plundering the Southern home front while most of the able-bodied are away at war. "Dragged Fighting from His Tomb," from Barry Hannah's collection of short stories *Airships*, follows. Here, in his typically fanciful way, Hannah gives us a new version of the death of Jeb Stuart. Known for his explosive style and his outlandish tales, Hannah, winner of the William Faulkner Prize and a nominee for the National Book Award, gives us perhaps our most contemporary Civil War fiction.

The middle section of the book closes with an old piece (1894) by Thomas Nelson Page. Dramatic and sentimental, "The Burial of the Guns" deals with an officer and his men as they get word of Lee's surrender and then ceremonially and affectionately bury their artillery. I trust that the story brings a conclusion to the battle section. Moreover, I suggest that, taken with the story by Barry Hannah just before it, "The Burial of the Guns" helps us see the broad range of tone and perspective in Civil War fiction.

The five stories of the last part of the anthology function as a kind of epilogue. Set after the war, they take up in a variety of ways the aftermath of the conflict. The first piece, Hamlin Garland's "The Return of a Private," offers a Northern perspective as it depicts Private Ed Smith returning to Wisconsin from Louisiana after the war. Smith finds that his farm is in ruins, that his family barely recognizes him. He finds none of the glory that attended him when he left even though he returns victorious. As Page's Confederates found some glory in their defeat, so Garland's Yankees found much misery in their victory. Such was the irony that inscribed this war.

To acknowledge Stephen Crane, I include in this section his brief story "The Veteran." It concerns Henry Fleming, hero of *The Red Badge of Courage*, in his brave civilian life and death. The two stories which follow suggest that a bit of distance from the war allows some humor. O. Henry tells the tall tale of a Yankee discovered at a Confederate soldiers' convention in "Two Renegades." In "Ancestors," Fred Chappell spoofs Southern fascination with lineage. Set well into the twenty-first century, the story presents technology that can reconstruct in flesh and blood one's ancestors. The discovery, of course, is that, like the war itself, ancestors are more heroic in the imagination than in reality.

The final story is one of the most powerful in the anthology. Flannery O'Connor's "A Late Encounter with the Enemy" focuses on an exploitation of Civil War history in the New South. General Sash, at the age of one hundred four, is a Confederate veteran living in Atlanta with his granddaughter, Sally Poker Sash. At sixty-two, Sally has finally finished college and wants the old man, only a foot-soldier in the war but promoted to the rank of general in the minds of his relatives, to be present in uniform at her graduation to identify her distinguished past. The senile old man agrees, for he is used to such occasions as "parades with floats full of Miss Americas and Miss Daytona Beaches and Miss Queen Cotton Products." In a stunning juxtaposition of old and new Atlanta, we last see the "general" in full regalia, dead in his wheelchair in front of a Coke machine.

I hope that the individual selections, and their arrangement, give this anthology power, variety, and credibility as they survey one of America's most important historical events through one of America's most important literary forms.

This project leaves me in debt to many. I thank in particular Tom Bonner, Hallman Bryant, Mark Charney, Frank Koon, Ron Rash, David Robertson, Mark Steadman, Donna Winchell, and Harold Woodell. I thank Adrienne Ivey for her editorial assistance. And I thank Warren Slesinger, of the University of South Carolina Press, for suggesting the book in the first place and for giving it such good support.

Ambuscade

William Faulkner

Behind the smokehouse that summer, Ringo and I had a living map. Although Vicksburg was just a handful of chips from the woodpile and the River was a trench scraped into the packed earth with the point of a hoe, it (river, city, and terrain) lived, possessing even in miniature that ponderable though passive recalcitrance of topography which outweighs artillery, against which the most brilliant of victories and the most tragic of defeats are but the loud noises of a moment. To Ringo and me it lived, if only because of the fact that the sunimpacted ground drank water faster than we could fetch it from the well, the very setting of the stage for conflict a prolonged and wellnigh hopeless ordeal in which we ran, panting and interminable, with the leaking bucket between wellhouse and battlefield, the two of us needing first to join forces and spend ourselves against a common enemy, time, before we could engender between us and hold intact the pattern of recapitulant mimic furious victory like a cloth, a shield between ourselves and reality, between us and fact and doom. This afternoon it seemed as if we would never get it filled, wet enough, since there had not even been dew in three weeks. But at last it was damp enough, damp-colored enough at least, and we could begin. We were just about to begin. Then suddenly Loosh was standing there, watching us. He was Joby's son and Ringo's uncle; he stood there (we did not know where he had come from; we had not seen him appear, emerge) in the fierce dull early afternoon sunlight, bareheaded, his head slanted a little, tilted a little yet firm

---

"Ambuscade" is an excerpt from Faulkner's novel *The Unvanquished.*

and now askew, like a cannonball (which it resembled) bedded hurriedly and carelessly in concrete, his eyes a little red at the inner corners as negroes' eyes get when they have been drinking, looking down at what Ringo and I called Vicksburg. Then I saw Philadelphy, his wife, over at the woodpile, stooped, with an armful of wood already gathered into the crook of her elbow, watching Loosh's back.

"What's that?" Loosh said.

"Vicksburg," I said.

Loosh laughed. He stood there laughing, not loud, looking at the chips.

"Come on here, Loosh," Philadelphy said from the woodpile. There was something curious in her voice too—urgent, perhaps frightened. "If you wants any supper, you better tote me some wood." But I didn't know which, urgency or fright; I didn't have time to wonder or speculate, because suddenly Loosh stooped before Ringo or I could have moved, and with his hand he swept the chips flat.

"There's your Vicksburg," he said.

"Loosh!" Philadelphy said. But Loosh squatted, looking at me with that expression on his face. I was just twelve then; I didn't know triumph; I didn't even know the word.

"And I tell you nother un you ain't know," he said. "Corinth."

"Corinth?" I said. Philadelphy had dropped the wood and she was coming fast toward us. "That's in Mississippi too. That's not far. I've been there."

"Far don't matter," Loosh said. Now he sounded as if he were about to chant, to sing; squatting there with the fierce dull sun on his iron skull and the flattening slant of his nose, he was not looking at me or Ringo either; it was as if his redcornered eyes had reversed in his skull and it was the blank flat obverses of the balls which we saw. "Far don't matter. Case hit's on the way!"

"On the way? On the way to what?"

"Ask your paw. Ask Marse John."

"He's at Tennessee, fighting. I can't ask him."

"You think he at Tennessee? Ain't no need for him at Tennessee now." Then Philadelphy grabbed him by the arm.

"Hush your mouth, nigger!" she cried, in that tense desperate voice. "Come on here and get me some wood!"

Then they were gone. Ringo and I didn't watch them go. We stood there above our ruined Vicksburg, our tedious hoe-scratch not even damp-colored now, looking at one another quietly. "What?" Ringo said. "What he mean?"

"Nothing," I said. I stooped and set Vicksburg up again. "There it is."

But Ringo didn't move, he just looked at me. "Loosh laughed. He say Corinth too. He laughed at Corinth too. What you reckon he know that we ain't?"

"Nothing!" I said. "Do you reckon Loosh knows anything that Father don't know?"

"Marse John at Tennessee. Maybe he ain't know either."

"Do you reckon he'd be away off at Tennessee if there were Yankees at Corinth? Do you reckon that if there were Yankees at Corinth, Father and General Van Dorn and General Pemberton all three wouldn't be there too?" But I was just talking too, I knew that, because niggers know, they know things; it would have to be something louder, much louder, than words to do any good. So I stooped and caught both hands full of dust and rose; and Ringo still standing there, not moving just looking at me even as I flung the dust. "I'm General Pemberton!" I cried. "Yaaay! Yaay!" stooping and catching up more dust and flinging that too. Still Ringo didn't move. "All right!" I cried. "I'll be Grant this time, then. You can be General Pemberton." Because it was that urgent, since negroes knew. The arrangement was that I would be General Pemberton twice in succession and Ringo would be Grant, then I would have to be Grant once so Ringo could be General Pemberton or he wouldn't play anymore. But now it was that urgent even though Ringo was a nigger too, because Ringo and I had been born in the same month and had both fed at the same breast and had slept together and eaten together for so long that Ringo called Granny 'Granny' just like I did, until maybe he wasn't a nigger anymore or maybe I wasn't a white boy anymore, the two of us neither, not even people any longer; the two supreme undefeated like two moths, two feathers riding above a hurricane. So we were both at it; we didn't see Louvinia, Joby's wife and Ringo's grandmother, at all. We were facing one another at scarcely arms' length, to the other each invisible in the furious slow jerking of the flung dust, yelling "Kill the bastuds! Kill them! Kill them!" when her voice seemed to descend upon us like an enormous hand, flattening the very dust which we had raised, leaving us now visible to one another, dust-colored ourselves to the eyes and still in the act of throwing:

"You, Bayard! You, Ringo!" She stood about ten feet away, her mouth still open with shouting. I noticed that she did not now have on the old hat of Father's which she wore on top of her headrag even when she just stepped out of the kitchen for wood. "What was that word?" she said. "What did I hear you say?" Only she didn't wait to be answered, and then I saw that she had been running too. "Look who coming up the big road!" she said.

We—Ringo and I—ran as one, in midstride out of frozen immobility, across the back yard and around the house, where Granny was standing at the top of the front steps and where Loosh had just come around the house from the other side and stopped, looking down the drive toward the gate. In the spring, when Father came home that time, Ringo and I ran down the drive to meet him and return, I standing in one stirrup with Father's arm around me, and Ringo holding to the other stirrup and running beside the horse. But this time we didn't. I mounted the steps and stood beside Granny, and with Ringo and Loosh on the ground below the gallery we watched the claybank stallion enter the gate which was never closed now, and come up the drive. We watched them—the big gaunt horse almost the color of smoke, lighter in color than the dust which had gathered and caked on his wet hide where they had crossed at the ford three miles away, coming up the drive at a steady gait which was not a walk and not a run, as if he had held it all the way from Tennessee because there was a need to encompass earth which abrogated sleep or rest and relegated to some insulated bourne of perennial and pointless holiday so trivial a thing as galloping; and Father damp too from the ford, his boots dark and dustcaked too, the skirts of his weathered gray coat shades darker than the breast and back and sleeves where the tarnished buttons and the frayed braid of his field officer's rank glinted dully, the sabre hanging loose yet rigid at his side as if it were too heavy to jounce or perhaps were attached to the living thigh itself and took no more motion from the horse than he did. He stopped; he looked at Granny and me on the porch and at Ringo and Loosh on the ground.

"Well, Miss Rosa," he said. "Well, boys."

"Well, John," Granny said. Loosh came and took Jupiter's head; Father dismounted stiffly, the sabre clashing dully and heavily against his wet boot and leg.

"Curry him," Father said. "Give him a good feed, but don't turn him into the pasture. Let him stay in the lot. . . . Go with Loosh," he said, as if Jupiter were a child, slapping him on the flank as Loosh led him on. Then we could see him good. I mean, Father. He was not big; it was just the things he did, that we knew he was doing, had been doing in Virginia and Tennessee, that made him seem big to us. There were others besides him that were doing the things, the same things, but maybe it was because he was the only one we knew, had ever heard snoring at night in a quiet house, had watched eating, had heard when he talked, knew how he liked to sleep and what he liked to eat and how he liked to talk. He was not big, yet somehow he looked even smaller on the horse than off of him, because Jupiter was big and when you thought of Father you thought of him as being big too and so when you thought of Father being on Jupiter it was as if you said, 'Together they will be too big; you won't believe it.' So you didn't believe it and so it wasn't. He came toward the steps and began to mount, the sabre heavy and flat at his side. Then I began to smell it again, like each time he returned, like the day back in the spring when I rode up the drive standing in one of his stirrups—that odor in his clothes and beard and flesh too which I believed was the smell of powder and glory, the elected victorious but know better now; know now to have been only the will to endure, a sardonic and even humorous declining of self-delusion which is not even kin to that optimism which believes that that which is about to happen to us can possibly be the worst which we can suffer. He mounted four of the steps, the sabre (that's how tall he actually was) striking against each one of the steps as he mounted, then he stopped and removed his hat. And that's what I mean; about his doing bigger things than he was. He could have stood on the same level with Granny and he would have only needed to bend his head a little for her to kiss him. But he didn't. He stopped two steps below her, with his head bared and his forehead held for her to touch her lips to, and the fact that Granny had to stoop a little now took nothing from the illusion of height and size which he wore for us at least.

"I've been expecting you," Granny said.

"Ah," Father said. Then he looked at me, who was still looking at him, as Ringo at the foot of the steps beneath still was.

"You rode hard from Tennessee," I said.

"Ah," Father said again.

"Tennessee sho gaunted you," Ringo said. "What does they eat up there, Marse John? Does they eat the same things that folks eat?"

Then I said it, looking him in the face while he looked at me: "Loosh says you haven't been at Tennessee."

"Loosh?" Father said. "Loosh?"

"Come in," Granny said. "Louvinia is putting your dinner on the table. You will just have time to wash."

II

That afternoon we built the stock pen. We built it deep in the creek bottom, where you could not have found it unless you had known where to look, and you could not have seen it until you came to the new sap-sweating, axe-ended rails woven through and into the jungle growth itself. We were all there—Father and Joby and Ringo and Loosh and me—Father in the boots still but with his coat off now, so that we saw for the first time that his trousers were not Confederate ones but were Yankee ones, of new strong blue cloth, which they (he and his troop) had captured, and without the sabre now too. We worked fast, felling the saplings—the willow and pin oak, the swamp maple and chinkapin—and, without even waiting hardly to trim them, dragging them behind the mules and by hand too, through the mud and the briers to where Father waited. And that was it too; Father was everywhere, with a sapling under each arm going through the brush and briers almost faster than the mules; racking the rails into place while Joby and Loosh were still arguing about which end of the rail went where. That was it; not that Father worked faster and harder than anyone else, even though you do look bigger (to twelve, at least, to me and Ringo at twelve, at least) standing still and saying, 'Do this or that' to the ones who are doing; it was the way he did it. When he sat at his old place at the table in the dining room and finished the side meat and greens and the cornbread and milk which Louvinia brought him (and we watching and waiting, Ringo and I at least, waiting for night and the talking, the telling) and wiped his beard and said, "Now we're going to build a new pen. We'll have to cut the rails, too"; when he said that, Ringo and I probably had exactly the same vision. There would be all of us there—Joby and Loosh and Ringo and me on the edge of the bottom and drawn up into a kind of order—an order partaking not of any lusting and sweating for assault or even victory, but rather of that passive yet dynamic affirmation which Napoleon's troops must have felt—and facing us, between us and the bottom, between us and the waiting sap-running boles which were about to be transposed into dead rails, Father. He was on Jupiter now; he wore the frogged gray field-officer's tunic; and while we watched he drew the sabre. Giving us a last embracing and comprehensive glance he drew it, already pivoting Jupiter on the tight snaffle; his hair tossed beneath the cocked hat, the sabre flashed and glinted; he cried, not loud yet stentorian: "Trot! Canter! *Charge!*" Then, without even having to move, we could both watch and follow him—the little man (who in conjunction with the horse looked exactly the right size because that was as big as he needed to look and—to twelve years old—bigger than most folks could hope to look) standing in the stirrups above the smoke-colored diminishing thunderbolt, beneath the arcy and myriad glitter of the sabre from which the chosen saplings, sheared trimmed and lopped, sprang into neat and waiting windrows, requiring only the carrying and the placing to become a fence.

The sun had gone out of the bottom when we finished the fence, that is, left Joby and Loosh with the last three panels to put up, but it was still shining up the slope of the pasture when we rode across it, I behind Father on one of the mules and Ringo on the other one. But it was gone even from the pasture by the time I had left Father at the house and returned to the stable, where Ringo already had a lead rope on the cow. So we went back to the new pen, with the calf following nuzzling and prodding at the cow every time she stopped to snatch a mouthful of grass, and the sow trotting on ahead. She (the sow) was the one who moved slow. She seemed to be moving slower than the cow even while the cow was stopped with Ringo leaned to the taut jerk of the rope and hollering at the cow, so it was dark sure enough when we reached the new pen. But there was still plenty of gap left to drive the stock through. But then, we never had worried about that.

We drove them in—the two mules, the cow and calf, the sow; we put up the last panel by feel, and went back to the house. It was full dark now, even in the pasture; we could see the lamp in the kitchen and the shadow of someone moving across the window. When Ringo and I came in, Louvinia was just closing one of the big trunks from the attic, which hadn't been down stairs since the Christmas four years ago which we spent at Hawkhurst, when there wasn't any war and Uncle Dennison was still alive. It was a big trunk and heavy even when empty; it had not been in the kitchen when we left to build the pen so it had been fetched down some time during the afternoon, while Joby and Loosh were in the bottom and nobody there to carry it down but Granny and Louvinia, and then Father later, after we came back to the house on the mule, so that was a part of the need and urgency too; maybe it was Father who carried the trunk down from the attic too. And when I went in to supper, the table was set with the kitchen knives and forks in place of the silver ones, and the sideboard (on which the silver service had been sitting when I began to remember and where it had been sitting ever since except on each Tuesday afternoon, when Granny and Louvinia and Philadelphy would polish it, why, nobody except Granny maybe knew, since it was never used) was bare.

It didn't take us long to eat. Father had already eaten once early in the afternoon, and besides that was what Ringo and I were waiting for; for after supper, the hour of laxed muscles and full entrails, the talking. In the spring when he came home that time, we waited as we did now, until he was sitting in his old chair with the hickory logs popping and snapping on the hearth and Ringo and I squatting on either side of the hearth, beneath the mantel above which the captured musket which he had brought home from Virginia two years ago rested on two pegs, loaded and oiled for service. Then we listened. We heard: the names—Forrest and Morgan and Barksdale and Van Dorn; the words like Gap and Run which we didn't have in Mississippi even though we did own Barksdale, and Van Dorn until somebody's husband killed him, and one day General Forrest rode down South Street in Oxford where there watched him through a window pane a young girl who scratched her name on it with a diamond ring: Celia Cook.

But we were just twelve; we didn't listen to that. What Ringo and I heard was the cannon and the flags and the anonymous yelling. That's what we intended to hear tonight. Ringo was waiting for me in the hall; we waited until Father was settled in his chair in the room which he and the negroes called the Office—Father because his desk was here in which he kept the seed cotton and corn and in this room he would remove his muddy boots and sit in his stocking feet while the boots dried on the hearth and where the dogs could come and go with impunity, to lie on the rug before the fire or even to sleep there on the cold nights—these whether Mother, who died when I was born, gave him this dispensation before she died or whether Granny carried it on afterward or whether Granny gave him the dispensation herself because Mother died I don't know; and the negroes called the

12

Office because into this room they would be fetched to face the Patroller (sitting in one of the straight hard chairs and smoking one of Father's cigars too but with his hat off) and swear that they could not possibly have been either who or where he (the Patroller) said they were—and which Granny called the library because there was one bookcase in it containing a Coke upon Littleton, a Josephus, a Koran, a volume of Mississippi Reports dated 1848, a Jeremy Taylor, a Napoleon's Maxims, a thousand and ninety-eight page treatise on astrology, a History of Werewolf Men in England, Ireland and Scotland and Including Wales by the Reverend Ptolemy Thorndyke, M.A. (Edinburgh), F.R.S.S., a complete Walter Scott, a complete Fenimore Cooper, a paper-bound Dumas complete, too, save for the volume which Father lost from his pocket at Manassas (retreating, he said).

So Ringo and I squatted again and waited quietly while Granny sewed beside the lamp on the table and Father sat in his old chair in its old place, his muddy boots crossed and lifted into the old heel-marks beside the cold and empty fireplace, chewing the tobacco which Joby had loaned him. Joby was a good deal older than Father. He was too old to have been caught short of tobacco just by a war. He had come to Mississippi from Carolina with Father and he had been Father's body servant all the time that he was raising and training Simon, Ringo's father, to take over when he (Joby) got too old, which was to have been some years yet except for the War. So Simon went with Father; he was still in Tennessee with the army. We waited for Father to begin; we waited so long that we could tell from the sounds that Louvinia was almost through in the kitchen: so I decided Father was waiting for Louvinia to finish and come in to hear too, so I said, "How can you fight in mountains, Father?"

And that's what he was waiting for, though not in the way Ringo and I thought, because he said, "You can't. You just have to. Now you boys run on to bed."

We went up the stairs. But not all the way; we stopped and sat on the top step, just out of the light from the hall lamp, watching the door of the Office, listening; after a while Louvinia crossed the hall without looking up and entered the Office; we could hear Father and her:

"Is the trunk ready?"

"Yes sir. Hit's ready."

"Then tell Loosh to get the lantern and the shovels and wait in the kitchen for me."

"Yes sir," Louvinia said. She came out; she crossed the hall again without even looking up the stairs, who used to follow us up and stand in the bedroom door and scold at us until we were in bed—I in the bed itself, Ringo on the pallet beside it. But this time she not only didn't wonder where we were, she didn't even think about where we might not be.

"I knows what's in that trunk," Ringo whispered. "Hit's the silver. What you reckon—"

"Shhhh," I said. We could hear Father's voice, talking to Granny. After a while Louvinia came back and crossed the hall again. We sat on the top step, listening to Father's voice telling Granny and Louvinia both.

"Vicksburg?" Ringo whispered. We were in the shadow; I couldn't see anything but his eyeballs. "Vicksburg *fell?* Do he mean hit fell off in the River? With Ginrul Pemberton in hit too?"

"Shhhhh!" I said. We sat close together in the shadow, listening to Father. Perhaps it was the dark or perhaps we were the two moths, the two feathers again or perhaps there is a point at which credulity firmly and calmly and irrevocably declines, because suddenly Louvinia was standing over us, shaking us awake. She didn't even scold us. She followed us up stairs and stood in the door to the bedroom and she didn't even light the lamp; she couldn't have told whether or not we had undressed even if she had been paying enough attention to suspect that we had not. She may have been listening as Ringo and I were, to what we thought we heard, though I knew better, just as I knew that we had slept on the stairs for some time; I was telling myself, 'They have already carried it out, they are in the orchard now, digging.' Because there is that point at which credulity declines; somewhere between waking and sleeping I believed I saw or I dreamed that I did see the lantern in the orchard, under the apple trees. But I don't know whether I saw it or not, because then it was morning and it was raining and Father was gone.

III

He must have ridden off in the rain, which was still falling at breakfast and then at dinnertime too, so that it looked as if we wouldn't have to leave the house at all, until at last Granny put the sewing away and said, "Very well. Get the cook book, Marengo." Ringo got the cook book from the kitchen and he and I lay on our stomachs on the floor while Granny opened the book. "What shall we read about today?" she said.

"Read about cake," I said.

"Very well. What kind of cake?" Only she didn't need to say that because Ringo was already answering that before she spoke:

"Cokynut cake, Granny." He said coconut cake every time because we never had been able to decide whether Ringo had ever tasted coconut cake or not. We had had some that Christmas before it started and Ringo had tried to remember whether they had had any of it in the kitchen or not, but he couldn't remember. Now and then I used to try to help him decide, get him to tell me how it tasted and what it looked like and sometimes he would almost decide to risk it before he would change his mind. Because he said that he would rather just maybe have tasted coconut cake without remembering it than to know for certain he had not; that if he were to describe the wrong kind of cake, he would never taste coconut cake as long as he lived.

"I reckon a little more won't hurt us," Granny said.

The rain stopped in the middle of the afternoon; the sun was shining when I stepped out onto the back gallery, with Ringo already saying, "Where we going?" behind me and still saying it after we passed the smokehouse where I could see the stable and the cabins: "Where we going now?" Before we reached the stable Joby and Loosh came into sight beyond the pasture fence, bringing the mules up from the new pen. "What we ghy do now?" Ringo said.

"Watch him," I said.

"Watch him? Watch who?" I looked at Ringo. He was staring at me, his eyeballs white and quiet like last night. "You talking about Loosh. Who tole us to watch him?"

"Nobody. I just know."

"Bayard, did you dream hit?"

"Yes. Last night. It was Father and Louvinia. Father said to watch Loosh, because he knows."

"Knows?" Ringo said. "Knows what?" But he didn't need to ask that either; in the next breath he answered it himself, staring at me with his round quiet eyes, blinking a little: "Yestiddy. Vicksburg. When he knocked hit over. He knowed hit then, already. Like when he said Marse John wasn't at no Tennessee and sho enough Marse John wasn't. Go on; what else did the dream tole you?"

"That's all. To watch him. That he would know before we did.

Father said that Louvinia would have to watch him too, that even if he was her son, she would have to be white a little while longer. Because if we watched him, we could tell by what he did when it was getting ready to happen."

"When what was getting ready to happen?"

"I don't know." Ringo breathed deep, once.

"Then hit's so," he said. "If somebody tole you, hit could be a lie. But if you dremp hit, hit can't be a lie case ain't nobody there to tole hit to you. So we got to watch him."

We followed them when they put the mules to the wagon and went down beyond the pasture to where they had been cutting wood. We watched them for two days, hidden. We realised then what a close watch Louvinia had kept on us all the time. Sometimes while we were hidden watching Loosh and Joby load the wagon we would hear her yelling at us and we would have to sneak away and then run to let Louvinia find us coming from the other direction. Sometimes she would even meet us before we had time to circle, and Ringo hiding behind me then while she scolded at us: "What devilment yawl into now? Yawl up to something. What is it?" But we didn't tell her and we would follow her back to the kitchen while she scolded at us over her shoulder and when she was inside the house we would move quietly until we were out of sight again and then run back to hide and watch Loosh.

So we were outside of his and Philadelphy's cabin that night when he came out. We followed him down to the new pen and heard him catch the mule and ride away. We ran, but when we reached the road too we could only hear the mule loping, dying away. But we had come a good piece, because even Louvinia calling us sounded faint and small. We looked up the road in the starlight, after the mule. "That's where Corinth is," I said.

He didn't get back until after dark the next day. We stayed close to the house and watched the road by turns, to get Louvinia calmed down in case it would be late before he got back. It was late; she had followed us up to bed and we had slipped out again; we were just passing Joby's cabin when the door opened and Loosh kind of surged up out of the darkness right beside us. He was almost close enough for me to have touched him and he did not see us at all; all of a sudden he was just kind of hanging there against the lighted doorway like he had been cut out of tin in the act of running and was inside the cabin and the door shut black again almost before we knew what we had seen. And when we looked in the window he was standing in front of the fire, with his clothes torn and muddy where he had been hiding in swamps and bottoms from the Patrollers and with that look on his face again which resembled drunkenness but was not, as if he had not slept in a long time and did not want to sleep now, and Joby and Philadelphy leaning into the firelight and looking at him and Philadelphy's mouth open too and the same look on her face. Then I saw Louvinia standing in the door. We had not heard her behind us yet there she was, with one hand on the door jamb, looking at Loosh, and again she didn't have on Father's old hat.

"You mean they gwinter free us all?" Philadelphy said. "We gonter all be free?"

"Yes," Loosh said, loud, with his head flung back; he didn't even look at Joby when Joby said, "Hush up, Loosh!"—"Yes!" Loosh said. "Ginral Sherman gonter sweep the earth and the Race gonter all be free!"

Then Louvinia crossed the floor in two steps and hit Loosh across the head hard with her flat hand. "You black fool!" she said. "Do you think there's enough Yankees in the whole world to whip the white folks?"

We ran to the house, we didn't wait for Louvinia; again we didn't know that she was behind us. We ran into the room where Granny was sitting beside the lamp with the bible open on her lap and her neck arched to look at us across her spectacles. "They're coming here!" I said. "They're coming to set us free!"

"What?" she said.

"Loosh saw them! They're just down the road. It's General Sherman and he's going to make us all free!" And we watched her, waiting to see who she would send for to take down the musket: whether it would be Joby because he was the oldest, or Loosh because he had seen them and would know what to shoot at. Then she shouted too, and her voice was strong and loud as Louvinia's:

"You, Bayard Sartoris! Ain't you in bed yet? Louvinia!" she shouted. Louvinia came in. "Take these children up to bed and if you hear another sound out of them tonight you have my permission and my insistence too to whip them both."

It didn't take us long to get to bed. But we couldn't talk even then, because Louvinia was going to bed on the cot in the hall. And Ringo was afraid to come up in the bed with me, so I got down on the pallet with him. "We'll have to watch the road," I said. Ringo whimpered.

"Look like hit haf to be us," he said.

"Are you scared?"

"I ain't very," he said. "I just wish Marse John was here."

"Well he's not," I said. "It'll have to be us."

We watched the road for two days, lying in the cedar copse. Now and then Louvinia hollered at us but we told her where we were and that we were making another map, and besides she could see the cedar copse from the kitchen. It was cool and shady there, and quiet, and Ringo slept most of the time and I slept some too. I was dreaming, it was like I was looking at our place and suddenly the house and stable and cabins and trees and all were gone and I was looking at a place flat and empty as the sideboard and it was growing darker and darker and then all of a sudden I wasn't looking at it, I was there: a sort of frightened drove of little tiny figures moving on it, they were Father and Granny and Joby and Louvinia and Loosh and Philadelphy and Ringo and me and we were wandering around on it lost and it getting darker and darker and we forever more without any home to go to because we were forever free; that's what it was and then Ringo made a choked sound and I was looking at the road and there in the middle of it, sitting on a bright bay horse and looking at the house through a field glass, was a Yankee. For a long time we just lay there looking at him. I don't know what we had expected to see but we knew what he was at once; I remember thinking *He looks just like a man* and then Ringo and I were glaring at one another and then we were crawling backward down the hill without remembering when we started to crawl and then we were running across the pasture toward the house without remembering when we got to our feet. We seemed to run forever, with our heads back and our fists clenched before we reached the fence and fell over it and ran on into the house. Granny's chair was empty beside the table where her sewing lay. "Quick!" I said. "Shove it up here!" But Ringo didn't move; his eyes looked like door knobs while I dragged the chair up and climbed onto it and began to lift down the musket. It weighed about fifteen pounds, though it was not the weight so much as the length; when it came free it and the chair and all went down with a tremendous clatter; we heard Granny sit up in her bed upstairs and then we heard her voice:

"Who is it?"

"Quick!" I said. "Hurry!"

"I'm scared," Ringo said.

"You, Bayard!" Granny said. "Louvinia!"

We held the musket between us like a log of wood. "Do you want to be free?" I said. "Do you want to be free?"

We carried it that way, like a log, one at each end, running. We ran through the grove toward the road and ducked down behind the honeysuckle just as the horse came around the curve. We didn't hear anything else, maybe because of our own breathing or maybe because we were not expecting to hear anything else. We didn't look again either; we were too busy cocking the musket. We had practiced before, once or twice when Granny was not there and Joby would come in to examine it and change the cap on the nipple. Ringo held it up and I took the barrel in both hands, high, and drew myself up and shut my legs about it and slid down over the hammer until it clicked. That's what we were doing, we were too busy to look, the musket was already riding up across Ringo's back as he stooped, his hands on his knees and panting "Shoot the bastud! Shoot him!" and then the sights came level and as I shut my eyes I saw the man and the bright horse vanish in smoke. It sounded like thunder and it made as much smoke as a brushfire and I heard the horse scream but I didn't see anything else; it was Ringo wailing, "Great God, Bayard! Hit's the whole army!"

IV

The house didn't seem to get any nearer, it just hung there in front of us floating and increasing slowly in size like something in a dream, and I could hear Ringo moaning behind me and further back still the shouts and the hooves. But we reached the house at last; Louvinia was just inside the door, with Father's old hat on her headrag and her mouth open, but we didn't stop. We ran on into the room where Granny was standing beside the righted chair, her hand at her chest. "We shot him, Granny!" I cried. "We shot the bastud!"

"What?" She looked at me, her face the same color as her hair almost, her spectacles shining against her hair above her forehead. "Bayard Satoris, what did you say?"

"We killed him, Granny! At the gate. Only there was the whole army too and we never saw them and now they are coming—" She sat down, she dropped into the chair, hard, her hand at her breast. But her voice was strong as ever:

"What's this? You, Marengo! What have you done?"

"We shot the bastud, Granny!" Ringo said. "We kilt him!" Then Louvinia was there too, with her mouth still open too and her face like somebody had thrown ashes at her. Only it didn't need her face; we heard the hooves jerking and sliding in the dirt and one of them hollering, "Get around to the back there, some of you!" and we looked up and saw them ride past the window—the blue coats and the guns. Then we heard the boots and spurs on the porch.

"Granny!" I said. "Granny!" But it seemed like none of us could move at all, we just had to stand there looking at Granny with her hand at her breast and her face looking like she had died and her voice like she had died too:

"Louvinia! What is this? What are they trying to tell me?" That's how it happened, like when once the musket decided to go off, all that was to occur afterward tried to rush into the sound of it all at once. I could still hear it, my ears were still ringing, so that Granny and Ringo and I all seemed to be talking far away. Then she said, "Quick! Here!" and then Ringo and I were squatting with our chins under our knees, on either side of her against her legs, with the hard points of the chair rockers jammed into our backs and her skirts spread over us like a tent, and the heavy feet coming in and (Louvinia told us afterward) the Yankee sergeant shaking the musket at Granny and saying,

"Come on, grandma. Where are they? We saw them run in here."

"We couldn't see, we just squatted in a kind of faint gray light and that smell of Granny that her clothes and bed and room all had and Ringo's eyes looking like two plates of chocolate pudding and maybe both of us thinking how Granny had never whipped us for anything in our lives except lying, and that even when it wasn't even a told lie but just keeping quiet, how she would whip us first and then make us kneel down and kneel down with us herself to ask the Lord to forgive us.

"You are mistaken," she said. "There are no children in this house nor on this place. There is no one here at all except my servant and myself and the people in the quarters."

"You mean you deny ever having seen this gun before?"

"I do." It was that quiet; she didn't move at all, sitting bolt upright and right on the edge of the chair to keep her skirts spread over us. "If you doubt me, you may search the house."

"Don't you worry about that, I'm going to. Send some of the boys upstairs," he said. "If you find any locked doors, you know what to do. And tell them fellows out back to comb and curry the barn and the cabins too."

"You won't find any locked doors," Granny said. "At least let me ask you—"

"Don't you ask anything, grandma. You set still. Better for you if you had done a little asking before you sent them little devils out with this gun."

"Was there. . . . . . ." We could hear her voice die away and then speak again, like she was behind it with a switch, making it talk. "Is he. . . . . . it. . . . . . the one who—"

"Dead? Hell, yes. Broke his back and we had to shoot him."

"Had to—you had—shoot. . . . . . ." I didn't know horrified astonishment either, but Ringo and Granny and I were all three it.

"Yes, by God. Had to shoot him. The best damn horse in the whole army. The whole damn regiment betting on him for next Sunday—" He said some more, but we were not listening. We were not breathing either, glaring at one another in the gray gloom and I was almost shouting too, until Granny said it:

"Didn't—they didn't—Oh, thank God! Thank God!"

"We didn't—" Ringo said.

"Hsh!" I said. Because we didn't have to say it, it was like we had had to hold our breaths for a long time without knowing it, and that now we could let go and breathe again. Maybe that was why we never heard the other man when he came in at all, it was Louvinia that saw that too—a colonel, with a bright short beard and hard bright gray eyes, who looked at Granny sitting in the chair with her hand at her breast and took off his hat. Only he was talking to the sergeant.

"What's this?" he said. "What's going on here, Harrison?"

"This is where they run to," the sergeant said. "I'm searching the house."

"Ah," the colonel said. He didn't sound mad at all. He just sounded cold and short and pleasant. "By whose authority?"

"Well, somebody here fired on United States troops. I guess this is authority enough." We could just hear the sound; it was Louvinia that told us how he shook the musket and banged the butt on the floor.

"And killed one horse," the colonel said.

"It was a United States horse. I heard the general say myself that if he had enough horses, he wouldn't always care whether there was

21

anybody to ride them or not. And so here we are, riding peaceful along the road, not bothering nobody yet, and these two little devils. . . . . . . The best horse in the army, the whole damn regiment betting—"

"Ah," the colonel said. "I see. Well? Have you found them?"

"We ain't yet. But these rebels are like rats when it comes to hiding. She says that there ain't any children here."

"Ah," said the colonel. And Louvinia said how he looked at Granny now for the first time. She said how she could see his eyes going from Granny's face down to where her skirt was spread and looking at her skirt for a whole minute and then going back to her face. And that Granny gave him look for look while she lied. "Do I understand, madam, that there are no children in or about this house?"

"There are none, sir," Granny said.

Louvinia said he looked back at the sergeant. "There are no children here, sergeant. Evidently the shot came from somewhere else. You may call the men in and mount them."

"But, Colonel, we saw them two kids run in here. All of us saw them—"

"Didn't you just hear this lady say there are no children here? Where are your ears, sergeant? Or do you really want the artillery to overtake us, with a creek bottom not five miles away to be got over?"

"Well, sir, you're colonel. But if it was me was colonel—"

"Then doubtless I should be Sergeant Harrison. In which case I think I should be more concerned about getting another horse to protect my wager next Sunday than over a grandchildless old lady—" Louvinia said his eyes just kind of touched Granny now and flicked away "—alone in a house which in all probability (and for her pleasure and satisfaction I am ashamed to say I hope) I shall never see again. Mount your men and get along with you."

We squatted there, not breathing, and heard them leave the house; we heard the sergeant calling the men up from the barn and we heard them ride away. But we did not move yet, because Granny's body had not relaxed at all and so we knew that the colonel was still there even before he spoke:—the voice short, brisk, hard, with that something of laughing behind it: "So you have no grandchildren. What a pity, in a place like this which two boys would enjoy—sports, fishing, game to shoot at, perhaps the most exciting game of all and none the less so for being possibly a little rare this near the house.

And with a gun, a very dependable weapon, I see. . . . . . ." Louvinia said how the sergeant had set the musket in the corner and how the colonel looked at it now, and now we didn't breathe. "—though I understand that this weapon does not belong to you? Which is just as well. Because if it were your weapon (which it is not) and you had two grandsons, or say a grandson and a negro playfellow (which you have not), and if this were the first time, which it is not, someone next time might be seriously hurt. But what am I doing? trying your patience by keeping you in that uncomfortable chair while I waste my time delivering a homily suitable only for a lady with grandchildren—or one grandchild and a negro companion." Now he was about to go too, we could tell it even beneath the skirt; this time it was Granny herself:

"There is little of refreshment I can offer you, sir. But if a glass of cool milk after your ride—"

Only for a long time he didn't answer at all; Louvinia said how he just looked at Granny with his hard bright eyes and that hard bright silence full of laughing. "No, no," he said. "I thank you. You are taxing yourself beyond mere politeness and into sheer bravado."

"Louvinia," Granny said, "conduct the gentleman to the dining-room and serve him with what we have."

He was out of the room now because Granny began to tremble now, trembling and trembling but not relaxing yet; we could hear her panting now. And we breathed too now, looking at one another. "We never killed him!" I whispered. "We never killed him! We haven't killed anybody at all!" So it was Granny's body that told us again, only this time I could almost feel him looking at Granny's spread skirt where we crouched while he thanked her for the milk and told her his name and regiment.

"Perhaps it is just as well that you have no grandchildren," he said. "Since doubtless you wish to live in peace. I have three boys myself, you see. And I have not even had time to become a grandparent." And now there wasn't any laughing behind his voice and Louvinia said he was standing there in the door, with the brass bright on his dark blue and his hat in his hand and his bright beard and hair, looking at Granny without the laughing now: "I wont apologise; fools cry out at wind or fire. But permit me to say and hope that you will never have anything worse than this to remember us by." Then he was gone. We heard his spurs in the hall and on the porch, then the horse, dying away, ceasing, and then Granny let go. She went back into the chair with her hand at her breast and her eyes closed and the sweat on her face in big drops; all of a sudden I began to holler, "Louvinia! Louvinia!" But she opened her eyes then and looked at me; they were looking at me when they opened. Then she looked at Ringo for a moment, but she looked back at me, panting.

"Bayard," she said. "What was that word you used?"

"Word?" I said. "When, Granny?" Then I remembered; I didn't look at her and she lying back in the chair, looking at me and panting.

"Don't repeat it. You cursed. You used obscene language, Bayard."

I didn't look at her. I could see Ringo's feet too. "Ringo did too," I said. She didn't answer, but I could feel her looking at me; I said suddenly: "And you told a lie. You said we were not here."

"I know it," she said. She moved. "Help me up." She got out of the chair, holding to us. We didn't know what she was trying to do. We just stood there while she held to us and to the chair and let herself down to her knees beside it. It was Ringo that knelt first. Then I knelt too while she asked the Lord to forgive her for telling the lie. Then she rose; we didn't have time to help her. "Go to the kitchen and get a pan of water and the soap," she said. "Get the new soap."

V

It was late, as if time had slipped up on us while we were still caught, enmeshed by the sound of the musket and were too busy to notice it; the sun shone almost level into our faces while we stood at the edge of the back gallery, spitting, rinsing the soap from our mouths turn and turn about from the gourd dipper, spitting straight into the sun. For a while, just by breathing we could blow soap bubbles, but soon it was just the taste of the spitting. Then even that began to go away although the impulse to spit did not, while away to the north we could see the cloudbank, faint and blue and faraway at the base and touched with copper sun along the crest. When Father came home in the spring, we tried to understand about mountains. At last he pointed out the cloudbank to tell us what mountains looked like. So ever since then Ringo believed that the cloudbank was Tennessee.

"Yonder they," he said, spitting. "Yonder hit. Tennessee, where Marse John use to fight um at. Looking mighty far, too."

"Too far to go just to fight Yankees," I said, spitting too. But it was gone now—the suds, the glassy weightless iridescent bubbles; even the taste of it.

The War Years

Ernest Gaines

SOLDIERS

It was a day something like right now, dry, hot, and dusty dusty. It might 'a' been July, I'm not too sure, but it was July or August. Burning up. I won't ever forget. The Secesh Army, they came by first. The Officers on their horses, the Troops walking, some of them dragging the guns in the dust they was so tired. The Officers rode up in the yard, and my mistress told them to get down and come in. The colonel said he couldn't come in, he was going somewhere in a hurry, but he would be glad to get down and stretch his legs if the good lady of the house would be so gracious to let him. My mistress said she most graciously did, and after the colonel had got down he told the others to get down too. The colonel was a little man with a gun and a sable. The sable was so long it almost dragged on the ground. Looked like the colonel was a little boy who had got somebody else's sable to play with. My mistress told me stop standing there gaping, go out there in the road and give the Troops some water. I had the water in a barrel under one of the chinaball trees. We knowed the soldiers were coming that way—we had heard the gun fire the day before, and somebody had already passed the house and told us if the soldiers came by be prepared to help in every way we could; so they had put me to hauling water. All morning long I hauled water to that barrel. Now I had to haul the water out the barrel to the Troops out in the road. Buckets after buckets after

---

"The War Years" is an excerpt from Gaines's novel *The Autobiography of Miss Jane Pittman.*

buckets. I can't remember how many buckets I hauled. The Troops was so tired and ragged they didn't even see me. They took the gourd from me when I handed it to them, and that was all. After they had drunk, they just let it hang there in their hands, and I had to reach and get it so I could serve another one. But they didn't even see little old black me. They couldn't tell if I was white or black, a boy or a girl. They didn't even care what I was. One was just griping. He didn't look too much older than me—face just as dirty as it could be. Just griping: "Just left to me I'll turn them niggers loose, just left to me." When I handed him the water he held the gourd a long time before he drank, then after he had drunk he let the gourd hang in his hands while he just sat there gazing down at the ground.

But these was the same ones, mind you, who had told their people they wouldn't be late for supper. That was before—when the war was just getting started—when they thought fighting a war was nothing but another day's work. "Don't put my food up," they said, "Don't put it up and don't give it away. I'm go'n kill me up a few Yankees and I'm coming right on back home. Who they think they is trying to destruck us way of living? We the nobles, not them. God put us here to live the way we want live, that's in the Bible." (I have asked people to find that in the Bible for me, but no one's found it yet.) "And He put niggers here to see us live that way—that's in the Bible, too. John, chapter so and so. Verse, right now I forget. Now, here them Yankees want come and destruck what the Good Lord done said we can have. Keep my supper warm, Mama, I'll be back before breakfast." These was the same ones griping out in the road right now.

Before all them had a chance to get some water, I looked up and saw another one coming down the road on a horse. He was hitting and kicking that horse fast as his arms and feet could move. Hollering far as you could hear him: "Colonel, Colonel, they coming. Colonel, Colonel, they coming." He went right by us, but the Troops was so tired some of them didn't even raise their head. Some of them even laid down on the ground when he went by. "How far?" the colonel asked him. "I don't know for sure," he said. "Maybe three, four miles back there. All I can see is that dust way up in the air." My mistress handed him two biscuits and a cup of water. He looked at that bread and water like he hadn't seen food or water in a long time and he kept bowing and saying, "Thank you, ma'am; thank you, ma'am; thank you, ma'am." The colonel hit his boots together and kissed my mistress on the hand, then he told the others to get on their horses. He hollered for them in the road to get to their feet, too. Some of them did like he said, but many of them just sat there gazing down at the ground. One of the Officers had to come out in the road and call them to attention. Even then they wasn't in any kind of hurry to get on their feet. They started down the road, and I could hear that same one that had been griping before: "Just left to me I'll turn them niggers loose, just left to me." One of the other Troops told him shut up before he got both of them shot. Him for complaining, and him for being his cousin. He told him shut up or cousin or no cousin he liable to shoot him himself. But till they got out hearing distance all I could hear was that little fellow griping: "Yankees want them, let the Yankees have them—just left to me."

After they had made the bend, I went back in the yard with the bucket and the gourd. My mistress was standing on the gallery watching the dust rising over the field, and just crying. "Sweet, precious blood of the South; sweet precious blood of the South." Just watching that dust, wringing her hands and crying. Then she saw me standing there looking up at her. "What you standing there for?" she said. "Go fill that barrel."

"What for, Mistress?" I said. "They gone now."

"Don't you think Yankees drink?" she said. "Go get that water."

"I got to haul water for old Yankees, too?" I said.

"Yes," she said. "You don't want them boiling you in oil and eating you, do you?"

"No, Mistress," I said.

"You better get that water then," she said. "A Yankee like nothing better than cooking a little nigger gal and chewing her up. Where the rest of them no 'count niggers at, I wonder?"

"They went hiding with Master in the swamps," I said, pointing toward the back.

"Stop that pointing," my mistress said. "You can't tell where a Yankee might be. And you watch your tongue when they get here, too. You say anything about your master and the silver, I'll have you skinned."

"Yes, Mistress," I said.

While I was standing there, one of the other slaves bust round the house and said: "Master say come ask that's all?"

"Where your master at?" my mistress asked him.

"Edge of the swamps there," he said. "Peeping round a tree."

"Go back and tell your master that ain't half of them yet," my mistress said.

The slave bust back round the house, running faster than he did coming there. My mistress told me stop standing there and go get that water.

The Yankees didn't show up till late that evening, so that little fellow who had spotted that dust in the air had a keen eye sight or a bad judge of distance. The Yankee Officers rode up in the yard just like the Secesh Officers did; the Yankee troops plopped down side the road just like the other Troops did. I got the bucket and the gourd and went out there to give them water.

"How many Rebs went by here?" one of the Troops asked me.

"I didn't see no Rebs, Master," I said.

"Come now," he said. "Who made all them tracks out there?"

"Just us niggers," I said.

"Wearing shoes?" he said. "Where your shoes?"

"I took mine off," I said. "They hurt my foot."

"Little girl, don't you know you not supposed to lie?" he said.

"I ain't lying, Master," I said.

"What's your name?" he asked me.

"Ticey, Master," I said.

"They ever beat you, Ticey?" he asked.

"No, Master," I said.

The Troop said, "I ain't a master, Ticey. You can be frank with me. They ever beat you?"

I looked back toward the house and I could see my mistress talking with the Officers on the gallery. I knowed she was too far to hear me and the Troop talking. I looked at him again. I waited for him to ask me the same question.

"They do beat you, don't they, Ticey?" he said.

I nodded.

"What they beat you with, Ticey?" he said.

"Cat-o'-nine-tails, Master," I said.

"We'll get them," the Troop said. "Ten'll die for every whipping you ever got."

"Ten houses will burn," another Troop said.

"Ten fields, too," another one said.

"One of y'all sitting there, take that bucket and go haul that water," the first Troop said.

"I better do it, Master," I said. "They whip me if I don't do my work."

"You rest," he said. "Troop Lewis, on your feet."

Troop Lewis got up real slow; he was tired just like all the rest. He was a little fellow and I felt sorry for him because he looked like the kind everybody was always picking on. He took the bucket from me and went in the yard talking to himself. The other Troop had to holler on him to get moving.

"What they whip you for, Ticey?" he asked me.

"I go to sleep when I look after Young Mistress children," I said.

"You nothing but a child yourself," he said. "How old is you right now?"

"I don't know, Master," I said.

"Would you say ten? 'leven?"

"Yes, Master," I said.

"I ain't a master, Ticey," he said. "I'm just a' old ordinary Yankee soldier come down here to beat them Rebs and set y'all free. You want to be free, don't you, Ticey?"

"Yes, Master," I said.

"And what you go'n do when you free?" he asked me.

"Just sleep, Master," I said.

"Ticey, you not the only one go'n just sleep," he said. "But stop calling me master. I'm Corporal Brown. Can you say corporal?"

"No, Master," I said.

"Try," he said.

I started grinning.

"Come on," he said. "Try."

"I can't say that, Master," I said.

"Can you say Brown?"

"Yes, Master."

"Well, just call me Mr. Brown," he said. "And I'm go'n call you something else 'sides Ticey. Ticey is a slave name, and I don't like slavery. I'm go'n call you Jane," he said. "That's right, I'll call you Jane. That's my girl name back there in Ohio. You like for me to call you that?"

I stood there grinning like a little fool. I rubbed my foot with my big toe and just stood there grinning. The other Troops was grinning at me, too.

"Yes," he said, "I think you do like that name. Well, from now on your name is Jane. Not Ticey no more. Jane. Jane Brown. Miss Jane

Brown. When you get older you can change it to what else you want. But till then your name is Jane Brown."

I just stood there grinning, rubbing my foot with my big toe. It was the prettiest name I had ever heard.

"And if any of them ever hit you again, you catch up with me and let me know," he said. "I'll come back here and I'll burn down this place."

The Yankee Officers got on their horses and came out in the road and told the Troops let's go. They got to their feet and marched on. And soon as my mistress thought they couldn't hear her she started calling my name. I just stood there and watched the soldiers go down the road. One of them looked back and waved at me—not Troop Lewis: I reckoned he was still mad at me. I grinned and waved back. After they had made the bend, I stood there and watched the dust high over the field. I was still feeling good because of my new name. Then all of a sudden my mistress was out there and she had grabbed me by the shoulders.

"You little wench, didn't you hear me calling you?" she said. I raised my head high and looked her straight in the face and said: "You called me Ticey. My name ain't no Ticey no more, it's Miss Jane Brown. And Mr. Brown say catch him and tell him if you don't like it."

My mistress face got red, her eyes got wide, and for about half a minute she just stood there gaping at me. Then she gathered up her dress and started running for the house. That night when the master and the rest of them came in from the swamps she told my master I had sassed her in front of the Yankees. My master told two of the other slaves to hold me down. One took my arms, the other one took my legs. My master jerked up my dress and gived my mistress the whip and told her to teach me a lesson. Every time she hit me she asked me what I said my name was. I said Jane Brown. She hit me again: what I said my name was. I said Jane Brown.

My mistress got tired beating me and told my master to beat me some. He told her that was enough, I was already bleeding.

"Sell her," my mistress said.

"Who go'n buy her with them Yankees tramping all over the place?" my master said.

"Take her to the swamps and kill her," my mistress said. "Get her out of my sight."

"Kill her?" my master said. "Brown come back here asking 'bout her, then what? I'll put her in the field and bring another one up here to look after the children."

They put me in the field when I was ten or 'leven. A year after that the Freedom come.

FREEDOM

We was in the field chopping cotton when we heard the bell ringing. We was scared to stop work—the sun was too high in the sky for us to go in yet. But the bell went on ringing and ringing; just ringing and ringing. The driver, a great big old black, round, oily-face nigger kept on looking back over his shoulders toward the house. Every time the bell rang he looked back. He told us to keep on working, he was going in to see what all the ringing was about. I watched him go up to the house, then I saw him coming back waving his arm. We swung our hoes on our shoulders and went across the field. The driver told us the master wanted us all at the house. We didn't ask what he wanted us for, we had no idea, we just went up there. The master was standing on the gallery with a sheet of paper.

"This all y'all?" he asked. "All them children in the quarters, too? I want everybody here who can stand up."

The people said this was all us.

"All right, I got news for y'all," the master said. "Y'all free. Proclamation papers just come to me and they say y'all free as I am. Y'all can stay and work on shares—because I can't pay you nothing, because I ain't got nothing myself since them Yankees went by here last time. Y'all can stay or y'all can go. If y'all stay I promise I'll be fair as I always been with y'all."

Old Mistress and Young Mistress was standing in the door crying, and right behind them the house niggers crying, too. For a while after the master got through reading the Proclamation the people didn't make a sound. Just standing there looking up at him like they was still listening to his words.

"Well, that's that," he said.

Then all a sudden somebody hollered, and everybody started singing. Just singing and dancing and clapping. Old people you didn't think could even walk started hopping round there like game roosters. This what the people was singing:

"We free, we free, we free
We free, we free, we free

31

We free, we free, we free
Oh, Lordy, we free."

Just singing and clapping, just singing and clapping. Just talking to each other, just patting each other on the back.

The driver he never got in the celebration him. Everybody else singing and clapping, he just standing there looking up at the master. Then he moved closer to the gallery and said: "Master, if we free to go, where is we to go?"

Before the master could open his mouth, I said: "Where North at? Point to it. I'll show y'all where to go."

The driver said: "Shut up. You ain't nothing but trouble. I ain't had nothing but trouble out you since you come in that field."

"If I ain't nothing but trouble, you ain't nothing but Nothing," I said.

And the next thing I knowed, my mouth was numb and I was laying down there on the ground. The master looked at me down there and said: "I can't do a thing about it. You free and don't belong to me no more. Got to fight your own battle best you can."

I jumped up from there and sunk my teeth in that nigger's hand. His hand was rough as 'cuda legs. He wrenched his hand out of my mouth and numbed the side of my face. This time when I got up I grabbed that hoe I had brought out the field. An old man we all called Unc Isom stepped in front of me.

"Hold," he said.

"Hold nothing," I said. "Nigger, say your prayers. Maker, here you come."

"Didn't I say hold," Unc Isom said. "When I say hold, I mean just that: hold."

I eased the hoe to the ground, but I kept my eyes on the driver all the time. I touched my lips with my hand, but I couldn't feel a thing. Not bleeding, but numb as it could be.

When Unc Isom seen I wasn't go'n hit that nigger with that hoe, he turned to the master.

"The papers say we can go or we can stay, Master?" he asked him.

"No, they just say y'all free, Isom," the master said. "They don't care what y'all do, where y'all go. I'm the one who saying y'all can stay on if y'all want. If you stay, I got to work you on shares, and you work when you want. You don't have to work on Sundays less you want. Can go to church and stay there and sing all day if you want. You free as I am, Isom."

Unc Isom said, "Master, we can gather down the quarters and talk just between us?"

The master said, "What you go'n be talking 'bout down there, Isom?"

"Just if we ought to go or stay, Master," Unc Isom said.

"Sure, y'all free as I am," the master said. "Y'all can take all the time y'all want to decide. Long as you ain't deciding on burning down the place."

Unc Isom had to grin to himself. "Master, ain't nothing like that," he said.

"Give the children some apples before they go," the mistress said.

"And the men and women cider," the master said. "Celebrate y'all freedom."

"Hold," Unc Isom said. "Apples and cider later. Now, we go in the quarters and talk."

Unc Isom was a kind of advisor to us there in the quarters. Some people said he had been a witch doctor sometime back. I know he knowed a lot about roots and herbs, and the people was always going to him for something to cure colic or the bots or whatever they had. That's why they followed him when he spoke. The young people grumbled because they wanted the apples, but the old people followed him without a word. When we came up to his cabin he told everybody to kneel down and thank God for freedom. I didn't want kneel, I didn't know too much about the Lord then, but I knelt out of respect. When Unc Isom got through praying he stood up and looked at us again. He was an old man, black black, with long white hair. He could have been in his 80s, he could have been in his 90s—I have no idea how old he was.

"Now, I ask the question," he said. "What's we to do?"

"Slavery over, let's get moving," somebody said.

"Let's stay," somebody else said. "See if old Master go'n act different when it's freedom."

"Y'all do like y'all want," I said. "I'm headed North." I turned to leave, but I stopped. "Which way North?"

"Before y'all start out here heading anywhere, what y'all go'n eat?" Unc Isom said. "Where y'all go'n sleep? Who go'n protect you from the patrollers?"

"They got Yankees," I said.

"They got Yankees, they got Yankees," Unc Isom mocked me. I could see he didn't have a tooth in his mouth. "Yankee told you your name was Jane; soon as Old Mistress start beating on you, you can't find Yankee."

"They can't beat me no more," I said. "Them papers say I'm free, free like everybody else."

"They ain't go'n just beat you if they catch you, they kill you if they catch you now," Unc Isom said. "Before now they didn't kill you because you was somebody chattel. Now you ain't owned by nobody but fate. Nobody to protect you now, little Ticey."

"My name is Jane, Unc Isom," I said. "And I'm headed for Ohio. Soon as you point that way."

"I don't know too much 'bout Ohio," Unc Isom said, coming out in the road. "Where it at or where it s'pose to be, I ain't for sure." He turned toward the swamps, then he raised his hand and pointed. "North is that way. Sun on your right in the morning, your left in the evening. North Star point the way at night. If you stay in the swamps, the moss is on the north side of the tree root."

"I'm heading out," I said. "Soon as I get me few of them apples and my other dress. Anybody else going?"

The young people started moving out in the road, but the old people started crying and holding them back. I didn't have a mama or daddy to cry and hold me back. My mama was killed when I was young and I had never knowed my daddy. He belong to another plantation. I never did know his name.

"Hold," Unc Isom said. He raised both of his hands like he was getting ready to wave us back. "This rejoicing time, not crying time. Ain't we done seen enough weeping? Ain't we done seen enough separation? Hold now."

"You telling us to stay here?" somebody young said.

"Them who want stay, stay," he said. "Them who must go, go. But this no time for weeping. Rejoice now."

"We leaving out," somebody young said. "If the old people want stay here, stay. We free, let's move."

"Amen," I said.

"You free from what?" Unc Isom said. "Free to do what—break more hearts?"

"Niggers hearts been broke ever since niggers been in this world," somebody young said. "I done seen babies jecked from mama titty. That was breaking hearts, too."

"That couldn't be helped," Unc Isom said. "This can be helped."

"This can't be helped," somebody young said. "They got blood on this place, and I done stepped all in it. I done waded in it to my waist. You can mend a broken heart, you can't wash blood off your body."

"Hold," Unc Isom said, raising his hands again. "When you talking 'bout mama and papa's heart, hold now."

"Mama and papa's heart can't be pained no more than they been pained already," somebody young said.

"Let's go," somebody else said. "All this arguing ain't putting us no closer North."

"Hold," Unc Isom said. "This wisdom I'm speaking from. Hold now."

"Give your wisdom to the ones staying here with you," somebody young said. "Rest of us moving out."

The boy who spoke to Unc Isom like that started up the quarters toward the big house. Unc Isom let him walk a little piece, then he hollered at him to stop. The boy wouldn't stop. Unc Isom hollered at him again. This time the boy looked back over his shoulder. Unc Isom didn't say a thing, he just stood there pointing his finger at the boy.

Me and some of the other people started toward the big house to get some apples, and one of the women said Unc Isom had put bad mark on the boy. Another woman said Unc Isom didn't have power to put bad mark on you no more, he was too old now. I didn't know how powerful Unc Isom was, so I just listened to the talking and didn't say nothing.

The master had put a barrel of potatoes side the barrel of apples, and he was sitting on the gallery watching the people coming back in the yard. He asked us what we had decided in the quarters. We told him some of us was going, some of us was staying. We asked him could the ones going take anything. He wanted to tell us no, but he nodded toward the barrel and told us to take what we needed and get out. We got all the apples and potatoes we could carry, then we went back to the quarters to get our clothes. In slavery you had two dresses and a pair of pants and an extra shirt, a pair of shoes and a coat. We tied up the apples and potatoes in our extra clothes and started out.

The Private History of a
Campaign That Failed

Mark Twain

You have heard from a great many people who did something in the war; it is not fair and right that you listen a little moment to one who started out to do something in it, but didn't? Thousands entered the war, got just a taste of it, and then stepped out again, permanently. These, by their very numbers, are respectable, and are therefore entitled to a sort of voice—not a loud one, but a modest one; not a boastful one, but an apologetic one. They ought not to be allowed much space among better people—people who did something—I grant that; but they ought at least to be allowed to state why they didn't do anything, and also to explain the process by which they didn't do anything. Surely this kind of light must have a sort of value.

Out West there was a good deal of confusion in men's minds during the first months of the great trouble—a good deal of unsettledness, of leaning first this way, then that, then the other way. It was hard for us to get our bearings. I call to mind an instance of this. I was piloting on the Mississippi when the news came that South Carolina had gone out of the Union on the 20th of December, 1860. My pilot-mate was a New Yorker. He was strong for the Union; so was I. But he would not listen to me with any patience; my loyalty was smirched, to his eye, because my father had owned slaves. I said, in palliation of this dark fact, that I had heard my father say, some years before he died, that slavery was a great wrong, and that he would free the solitary negro he then owned if he could think it right to give away the property of the family when he was so straitened in means. My mate retorted that a mere impulse was

36

nothing—anybody could pretend to a good impulse; and went on decrying my Unionism and libeling my ancestry. A month later the secession atmosphere had considerably thickened on the Lower Mississippi, and I became a rebel; so did he. We were together in New Orleans, the 26th of January, when Louisiana went out of the Union. He did his full share of the rebel shouting, but was bitterly opposed to letting me do mine. He said that I came of bad stock—of a father who had been willing to set slaves free. In the following summer he was piloting a Federal gunboat and shouting for the Union again, and I was in the Confederate army. I held his note for some borrowed money. He was one of the most upright men I ever knew; but he repudiated that note without hesitation, because I was a rebel, and the son of a man who owned slaves.

In that summer— of 1861—the first wash of the wave of war broke upon the shores of Missouri. Our State was invaded by the Union forces. They took possession of St. Louis, Jefferson Barracks, and some other points. The Governor, Claib Jackson, issued his proclamation calling out fifty thousand militia to repel the invader.

I was visiting in the small town where my boyhood had been spent—Hannibal, Marion County. Several of us got together in a secret place by night and formed ourselves into a military company. One Tom Lyman, a young fellow of a good deal of spirit but of no military experience, was made captain; I was made second lieutenant. We had no first lieutenant; I do not know why; it was long ago. There were fifteen of us. By the advice of an innocent connected with the organization, we called ourselves the Marion Rangers. I do not remember that anyone found fault with the name. I did not; I thought it sounded quite well. The young fellow who proposed this title was perhaps a fair sample of the kind of stuff we were made of. He was young, ignorant, good-natured, well-meaning, trivial, full of romance, and given to reading chivalric novels and singing forlorn love-ditties. He had some pathetic little nickel-plated aristocratic instincts, and detested his name, which was Dunlap; detested it, partly because is was nearly as common in that region as Smith, but mainly because it had a plebian sound to his ear. So he tried to ennoble it by writing it in this way: d'Unlap. That contented his eye, but left his ear unsatisfied, for people gave the new name the same old pronunciation—emphasis on the front end of it. He then did the bravest thing that can be imagined,—a thing to make one shiver when one remembers how the world is given to resenting shams and affectations; he began to write his name so: *d'Un Lap*. And he waited patiently through the long storm of mud that was flung at his work of art, and he had his reward at last; for he lived to see that name accepted, and the emphasis put where he wanted it by people who had known him all his life, and to whom the tribe of Dunlaps had been as familiar as the rain and the sunshine for forty years. So sure of victory at last is the courage that can wait. He said he had found, by consulting some ancient French chronicles, that the name was rightly and originally written d'Un Lap; and said that if it were translated into English it would mean Peterson: *Lap*, Latin or Greek, he said, for stone or rock, same as the French *pierre*, that is to say, Peter; *d'*, of or from; *un*, a or one; hence, d'Un Lap, of or from a stone or a Peter; that is to say, one who is the son of a stone, the son of a Peter—Peterson. Our militia company were not learned, and the explanation confused them; so they called him Peterson Dunlap. He proved useful to us in this way; he named our camps for us; and he generally struck a name that was "no slouch," as the boys said.

That is one sample of us. Another was Ed Stevens, son of the town jeweler,—trim-built, handsome, graceful, neat as a cat; bright, educated, but given over entirely to fun. There was nothing serious in life to him. As far as he was concerned, this military expedition of ours was simply a holiday. I should say that about half of us looked upon it in the same way; not consciously, perhaps, but unconsciously. We did not think; we were not capable of it. As for myself, I was full of unreasoning joy to be done with turning out of bed at midnight and four in the morning, for a while; grateful to have a change, new scenes, new occupations, a new interest. In my thoughts that was far as I went; I did not go into the details; as a rule, one doesn't at twenty-four.

Another sample was Smith, the blacksmith's apprentice. This vast donkey had some pluck, of a slow and sluggish nature, but a soft heart; at one time he would knock a horse down for some impropriety, and at another he would get homesick and cry. However, he had one ultimate credit to his account which some of us hadn't; he stuck to the war, and was killed in battle at last.

Jo Bowers, another sample, was a huge, good-natured, flax-headed lubber; lazy, sentimental, full of harmless brag, a grumbler by nature; an experienced, industrious, ambitious, and often quite picturesque liar, and yet not a successful one, for he had had no intelligent training, but was allowed to come up just any way. This life was serious enough to him, and seldom satisfactory. But he was a good fellow anyway, and the boys all liked him. He was made orderly sergeant; Stevens was made corporal.

These samples will answer—and they are quite fair ones. Well, this herd of cattle started for the war. What could you expect of them? They did as well as they knew how; but really what was justly to be expected of them? Nothing, I should say. That is what they did.

We waited for a dark night, for caution and secrecy were necessary; then, toward midnight, we stole in couples and from various directions to the Griffith place, beyond the town; from that point we set out together on foot. Hannibal lies at the extreme southeastern corner of Marion County, on the Mississippi River; our objective point was the hamlet of New London, ten miles away, in Ralls County.

The first hour was all fun, all idle nonsense and laughter. But that could not be kept up. The steady trudging came to be like work; the play had somehow oozed out of it; the stillness of the woods and the somberness of the night began to throw a depressing influence over the spirits of the boys, and presently the talking died out and each person shut himself up in his own thoughts. During the last half of the second hour nobody said a word.

Now we approached a log farm-house where, according to report, there was a guard of five Union soldiers. Lyman called a halt; and there, in the deep gloom of the overhanging branches, he began to whisper a plan of assault upon that house, which made the gloom more depressing than it was before. It was a crucial moment; we realized, with a cold suddenness, that here was no jest—we were standing face to face with actual war. We were equal to the occasion. In our response there was no hesitation, no indecision: we said that if Lyman wanted to meddle with those soldiers, he could go ahead and do it; but if he waited for us to follow him, he would wait a long time.

Lyman urged, pleaded, tried to shame us, but it had no effect. Our course was plain, our minds were made up: we would flank the farmhouse—go out around. And that was what we did.

We struck into the woods and entered upon a rough time, stumbling over roots, getting tangled in vines, and torn by briers. At last we reached an open place in a safe region, and sat down, blown and hot, to cool off and nurse our scratches and bruises. Lyman was annoyed, but the rest of us were cheerful; we had flanked the farmhouse, we had made our first military movement, and it was a success; we had nothing to fret about, we were feeling just the other way. Horse-play and laughing began again; the expedition was become a holiday frolic once more.

Then we had two more hours of dull trudging and ultimate silence and depression; then, about dawn, we straggled into New London, soiled, heel-blistered, fagged with our little march, and all of us except Stevens in a sour and raspy humour and privately down on the war. We stacked our shabby shot-guns in Colonel Rall's barn, and then went in a body and breakfasted with that veteran of the Mexican War. Afterwards he took us to a distant meadow, and there in the shade of a tree we listened to an old-fashioned speech from him, full of gunpowder and glory, full of that adjective-piling, mixed metaphor, and windy declamation which were regarded as eloquence in that ancient time and that remote region; and then he swore us on the Bible to be faithful to the State of Missouri and drive all invaders from her soil, no matter whence they might come or under what flag they might march. This mixed us considerably, and we could not make out just what service we were embarked in; but Colonel Ralls, the practiced politician and phrase-juggler, was not similarly in doubt; he knew quite clearly that he had invested us in the cause of the Southern Confederacy. He closed the solemnities by belting around me the sword which his neighbor, Colonel Brown, had worn at Buena Vista and Molino del Rey; and he accompanied this act with another impressive blast.

Then we formed in line of battle and marched four miles to a shady and pleasant piece of woods on the border of the far-reaching expanses of a flowery prairie. It was an enchanting region for war— our kind of war.

We pierced the forest about half a mile, and took up a strong position, with some low, rocky, and wooded hills behind us, and a purling, limpid creek in front. Straightway half the command were in swimming, and the other half fishing. The ass with the French name gave this position a romantic title, but it was too long, so the boys shortened and simplified it to Camp Ralls.

We occupied an old maple-sugar camp, whose half-rotted troughs were still propped against the trees. A long corn-crib served for sleeping quarters for the battalion. On our left, half a mile away, were Mason's farm and house; and he was a friend to the cause. Shortly after noon the farmers began to arrive from several directions, with mules and horses for our use, and these they lent us for as long as the war might last, which they judged would be about three months. The animals were of all sizes, all colors, and all breeds. They were mainly young and frisky, and nobody in the command could stay on them long at a time; for we were town boys, and ignorant of horsemanship. The creature that fell to my share was a very small mule, and yet so quick and active that it could throw me without difficulty; and it did this whenever I got on it. Then it would bray—stretching its neck out, laying its ears back, and spreading its jaws till you could see down to its works. It was a disagreeable animal, in every way. If I took it by the bridle and tried to lead it off the grounds, it would sit down and brace back, and no one could budge it. However, I was not entirely destitute of military resources, and I did presently manage to spoil this game; for I had seen many a steamboat aground in my time, and knew a trick or two which even a grounded mule would be obliged to respect. There was a well by the corn-crib; so I substituted thirty fathom of rope for the bridle, and fetched him home with the windlass.

I will anticipate here sufficiently to say that we did learn to ride, after some days' practice, but never well. We could not learn to like our animals; there were not choice ones, and most of them had annoying peculiarities of one kind or another. Stevens's horse would carry him, when he was not noticing, under the huge excrescences which form on the trunks of oak-trees, and wipe him out of the saddle; in this way Stevens got several bad hurts. Sergeant Bowers's horse was very large and tall, with slim, long legs, and looked like a railroad bridge. His size enabled him to reach all about, and as far as he wanted to, with his head; so he was always biting Bowers's legs. On the march, in the sun, Bowers slept a good deal; and as soon as the horse recognized that he was asleep he would reach around and bite him on the leg. His legs were black and blue with bites. This was the only thing that could ever make him swear, but this always did; whenever his horse bit him he always swore, and of course Stevens, who laughed at everything, laughed at this, and would even get into such convulsions over it as to lose his balance and fall off his horse; and then Bowers, already irritated by the pain of the horse-bite, would resent the laughter with hard language and there would be a quarrel; so that horse made no end of trouble and bad blood in the command.

However, I will get back to where I was—our first afternoon in the sugar-camp. The sugar-troughs came very handy as horse-troughs, and we had plenty of corn to fill them with. I ordered Sergeant Bowers to feed my mule; but he said that if I reckoned he went to war to be a dry-nurse to a mule, it wouldn't take me very long to find out my mistake. I believed that this was insubordination, but I was full of uncertainties about everything military, and so I let the thing pass, and went and ordered Smith, the blacksmith's apprentice, to feed the mule; but he merely gave me a large, cold, sarcastic grin, such as an ostensibly seven-year-old horse gives you when you lift his lips and find he is fourteen, and turned his back on me. I then went to the captain, and asked if it was not right and proper and military for me to have an orderly. He said it was, but as there was only one orderly in the corps, it was but right that he himself should have Bowers on his staff. Bowers said he wouldn't serve on anybody's staff; and if anybody thought he could make him, let him try it. So, of course, the thing had to be dropped; there was no other way.

Next, nobody would cook; it was considered a degradation; so we had no dinner. We lazied the rest of the pleasant afternoon away, some dozing under the trees, some smoking cob-pipes and talking sweethearts and war, some playing games. By late suppertime all hands were famished; and to meet the difficulty all hands turned to, on an equal footing, and gathered wood, built fires, and cooked the meal. Afterward everything was smooth for a while; then trouble broke out between the corporal and the sergeant, each claiming to rank the other. Nobody knew which was the higher office; so Lyman had to settle the matter by making the rank of both officers equal. The commander of an ignorant crew like that has many troubles and vexations which probably did not occur in the regular army at all. However, with the song-singing and yarn-spinning around the camp-fire, everything presently became serene again; and by and by we raked the corn down level in one end of the crib, and all went to bed on it, tying a horse to the door, so that he would neigh if anyone tried to get in.

We had some horsemanship drill every forenoon; then, afternoons, we rode off here and there in squads a few miles, and visited the farmers' girls, and had a youthful good time, and got an honest good dinner or supper, and then home again to camp, happy and content.

For a time, life was idly delicious, it was perfect; there was nothing to mar it. Then came some farmers with an alarm one day. They said it was rumored that the enemy were advancing in our direction, from over Hyde's prairie. The result was a sharp stir among us, and general consternation. It was a rude awakening from our pleasant trance. The rumor was but a rumor—nothing definite about it; so, in the confusion, we did not know which way to retreat. Lyman was for not retreating at all in these uncertain circumstances; but he found that if he tried to maintain that attitude he would fare badly, for the command were in no humor to put up with insubordination. So he yielded the point and called a council of war—to consist of himself and the three other officers; but the privates made such a fuss about being left out, that we had to allow them to remain, for they were already present, and doing the most of the talking too. The question was, which way to retreat; but all were so flurried that nobody seemed to have even a guess to offer. Except Lyman. He explained in a few calm words, that inasmuch as the enemy were approaching from over Hyde's prairie, our course was simple: all we had to do was not to retreat *toward* him; any other direction would answer our needs perfectly. Everybody saw in a moment how true this was, and how wise; so Lyman got a great many compliments. It was now decided that we should fall back on Mason's farm.

It was after dark by this time, and as we could not know how soon the enemy might arrive, it did not seem best to try to take the horses and things with us; so we only took the guns and ammunition, and started at once. The route was very rough and hilly and rocky, and presently the night grew very black and rain began to fall; so we had a troublesome time of it, struggling and stumbling along in the dark; and soon some person slipped and fell, and then the next person behind stumbled over him and fell, and so did the rest, one after the other; and then Bowers came with the keg of powder in his arms, while the command were all mixed together, arms and legs, on the muddy slope; and so he fell, of course, with the keg, and this started the whole detachment down the hill in a body, and they landed in the brook at the bottom in a pile, and each was undermost pulling the hair and scratching and biting those that were on top of him; and those that were being scratched and bitten scratching and biting the rest in their turn, and all saying they would die before they would ever go to war again if they ever got out of this brook this time, and the invaders might rot for all they cared, and the country along with him—and all such talk as that, which was dismal to hear and take part in, such smothered, low voices, and such a grisly dark place and so wet, and the enemy maybe coming any moment.

The keg of powder was lost, and the guns, too; so the growling and complaining continued straight along whilst the brigade pawed around the pasty hillside and slopped around in the brook hunting for these things; consequently we lost considerable time at this; and then we heard a sound, and held our breath and listened, and it seemed to be the enemy coming, though it could have been a cow, for it had a cough like a cow; but we did not wait, but left a couple of guns behind and struck out for Mason's again as briskly as we could scramble along in the dark. But we got lost presently among the rugged little ravines, and wasted a deal of time finding the way again, so it was after nine when we reached Mason's stile at last; and then before we could open our mouths to give the countersign, several dogs came bounding over the fence, with great riot and noise, and each of them took a soldier by the slack of the trousers and began to back away with him. We could not shoot the dogs without endangering the persons that were attached to; so we had to look on, helpless, at what was perhaps the most mortifying spectacle of the Civil War. There was light enough, and to spare, for the Masons had now run out on the porch with candles in their hands. The old man and his son came and undid the dogs without difficulty, all but Bowers's; but they couldn't undo his dog, they didn't know his combination; he was of the bull kind, and seemed to be set with a Yale time-lock; but they got him loose at last with some scalding water, of which Bowers got his share and returned thanks. Peterson Dunlap afterwards made up a fine name for this engagement, and also for the night march which preceded it, but both have long ago faded out of my memory.

We now went into the house, and they began to ask us a world of questions, whereby it presently came out that we did not know anything concerning who or what we were running from; so the old gentleman made himself very frank, and said we were a curious breed of soldiers, and guessed we could be depended on to end the war in time, because no government could stand the expense of the shoe-leather we should cost it trying to follow us around. "Marion *Rangers!* good name, b'gosh!" said he. And wanted to know why we hadn't had a picket-guard at the place where the road entered the prairie, and why we hadn't sent out a scouting party to spy out the enemy and bring us an account of his strength, and so on, before jumping up and stampeding out of a strong position upon a mere vague rumor—and so forth, till he made us all feel shabbier than the dogs had done, not half so enthusiastically welcome. So we went to bed ashamed and low-spirited; except Stevens. Soon Stevens began to devise a garment for Bowers which could be made to automatically display his battle-scars to the grateful, or conceal them from the envious, according to his occasions; but Bowers was in no humor for this, so there was a fight, and when it was over Stevens had some battle-scars of his own to think about.

Then we got a little sleep. But after all we had gone through, our activities were not over for the night; for about two o'clock in the morning we heard a shout of warning from down the lane, accompanied by a chorus from all the dogs, and in a moment everybody was up and flying around to find out what the alarm was about. The alarmist was a horseman who gave notice that a detachment of Union soldiers was on its way from Hannibal with orders to capture and hang any bands like ours which it could find, and said we had no time to lose. Farmer Mason was in a flurry this time, himself. He hurried us out of the house with all haste, and sent one of his negroes with us to show us where to hide ourselves and our tell-tale guns among the ravines half a mile away. It was raining heavily.

We struck down the lane, then across some rocky pasture-land which offered good advantages for stumbling; consequently we were down in the mud most of the time, and every time a man went down he blackguarded the war, and the people that started it, and everybody connected with it, and gave himself the master dose of all for being so foolish as to go into it. At last we reached the wooded mouth of a ravine, and there we huddled ourselves under the streaming trees, and sent the negro back home. It was a dismal and heartbreaking time. We were like to be drowned with the rain, deafened by the lightning. It was indeed a wild night. The drenching we were getting was misery enough, but a deeper misery still was the reflection that the halter might end us before we were a day older. A death of this shameful sort had not occurred to us as being among the possibilities of war. It took the romance all out of the campaign, and turned our dreams of glory into a repulsive nightmare. As for doubting that so barbarous an order had been given, not one of us did that.

The long night wore itself out at last, and then the negro came to us with the news that the alarm had manifestly been a false one, and that breakfast would soon be ready. Straightway we were lighthearted again and the world was bright, and life as full of hope and promise as ever—for we were young then. How long that was! Twenty-four years.

45

The mongrel child of philology named the night's refuge Camp Devastation, and no soul objected. The Masons gave us a Missouri county breakfast, in Missourian abundance, and we needed it: hot biscuits; hot "wheat-bread," prettily criss-crossed in a lattice pattern on top; hot corn pone; fried chicken; bacon, coffee, eggs, milk, buttermilk, etc.;—and the world may be confidently challenged to furnish the equal of such a breakfast, as it is cooked in the South.

We stayed several days at Mason's; and after all these years the memory of the dullness, and stillness, and lifelessness of that slumberous farmhouse still oppresses my spirit as with a sense of the presence of death and mourning. There was nothing to do, nothing to think about; there was no interest in life. The male part of the household were away in the fields all day, the women were busy and out of our sight; there was no sound but the plaintive wailing of a spinning-wheel, forever moaning out from some distant room,—the most lonesome sound in nature, a sound steeped and sodden with homesickness and the emptiness of life. The family went to bed about dark every night, and as we were not invited to intrude any new customs, we naturally followed theirs. Those nights were a hundred years long to youths accustomed to being up till twelve. We lay awake and miserable till that hour every time, and grew old and decrepit waiting through the still eternities for the clock-strikes. This was no place for town boys. So at last it was with something very like joy that we received news that the enemy were on our track again. With a new birth of the old warrior spirit, we sprang to our places in line of battle and fell back on Camp Ralls.

Captain Lyman had taken a hint from Mason's talk, and he now gave orders that our camp should be guarded against surprise by the posting of pickets. I was ordered to place a picket at the forks of the road in Hyde's prairie. Night shut down black and threatening. I told Sergeant Bowers to go out to that place and stay till midnight; and, just as I was expecting, he said he wouldn't do it. I tried to get others to go, but all refused. Some excused themselves on account of the weather; but the rest were frank enough to say the wouldn't go in any kind of weather. This kind of thing sounds odd now, and impossible, but there was no surprise in it at the time. On the contrary, it seemed a perfectly natural thing to do. There were scores of little camps scattered over Missouri where the same thing was happening. These camps were composed of young men who had been born and reared to a sturdy independence, and who did not know what it meant to be ordered around by Tom, Dick, and Harry, whom they had known familiarly all their lives, in the village or on the farm. It is quite within the probabilities that this same thing was happening all over the South. James Redpath recognized the justice of this assumption, and furnished the following instance in support of it. During a short stay in East Tennessee he was in a citizen colonel's tent one day talking, when a big private appeared at the door, and, without salute or other circumlocution, said the colonel,—

"Say, Jim, I'm a-goin' home for a few days."

"What for?"

"Well, I hain't b'en there for a right smart while, and I'd like to see how things is comin' on."

"How long are you going to be gone?"

" 'Bout two weeks."

"Well, don't be gone longer than that; and get back sooner if you can."

That was all, and the citizen officer resumed his conversation where the private had broken it off. This was in the first months of the war, of course. The camps in our parts of Missouri were under Brigadier-General Thomas H. Harris. He was a townsman of ours, a first-rate fellow, and well liked; but we had all familiarly known him as the sole and modest-salaried operator in our telegraph office, where he had to send about one dispatch a week in ordinary times, and two when there was a rush of business; consequently, when he appeared in our midst one day, on the wing, and delivered a military command of some sort, in a large military fashion, nobody was surprised at the response which he got from the assembled soldiery,—

"Oh, now, what'll you take to *don't*, Tom Harris!"

It was quite the natural thing. One might justly imagine that we were hopeless material for war. And so we seemed, in our ignorant state; but there were those among us who afterward learned the grim trade; learned to obey like machines; became valuable soldiers; fought all through the war, and came out at the end with excellent records. One of the very boys who refused to go out on picket duty that night, and called me an ass for thinking, he would expose himself to danger in such a foolhardy way, had become distinguished for intrepidity before he was a year older.

I did secure my picket that night—not by authority, but by diplomacy. I got Bowers to go by agreeing to exchange ranks with him for the time being, and go along and stand the watch with him as his subordinate. We stayed out there a couple of dreary hours in the pitchy darkness and the rain, with nothing to modify the dreariness but Bowers's monotonous growlings at the war and the weather; then we began to nod, and presently found it next to impossible to stay in the saddle; so we gave up the tedious job, and went back to the camp without waiting for the relief guard. We rode into camp without interruption or objection from anybody, and the enemy could have done the same, for there were no sentries. Everybody was asleep; at midnight there was nobody to send out another picket, so none was sent. We never tried to establish a watch at night again, as far as I remember, but we generally kept a picket out in the daytime.

In that camp the whole command slept on the corn in the big corn-crib; and there was usually a general row before morning, for the place was full of rats, and they would scramble over the boys' bodies and faces, annoying and irritating everybody; and now and then they would bite some one's toe, and the person who owned the toe would start up and magnify his English and begin to throw corn in the dark. The ears were half as heavy as bricks, and when they struck they hurt. The persons struck would respond, and inside of five minutes every man would be locked in a death-grip with his neighbor. There was a grievous deal of blood shed in the corn-crib, but this was all that was spilt while I was in the war. No, that is not quite true. But for one circumstance it would have been all. I will come to that now.

Our scares were frequent. Every few days rumors would come that the enemy were approaching. In these cases we always fell back on some other camp of ours; we never staid where we were. But the rumors always turned out to be false; so at last even we began to grow indifferent to them. One night a negro was sent to our corn-crib with the same old warning: the enemy was hovering in our neighborhood. We all said let him hover. We resolved to stay still and be comfortable. It was a fine warlike resolution, and no doubt we all felt the stir of it in our veins—for a moment. We had been having a very jolly time, that was full of horse-play and school-boy hilarity; but that cooled down now, and presently the fast-waning fire of forced jokes and forced laughs died out altogether, and the company became silent. Silent and nervous. And soon uneasy—worried—apprehensive. We had said we would stay, and we were committed. We could have been persuaded to go, but there was nobody brave enough to suggest it. An almost noiseless movement presently began in the dark, by a general but unvoiced impulse. When the movement was completed, each man knew that he was not the only person who had crept to the front wall and had his eye at a crack between the logs. No, we were all there; all there with our hearts in our throats, and staring out toward the sugar-troughs where the forest footpath came through. It was late, and there was a deep woodsy stillness everywhere. There was a veiled moonlight, which was only just strong enough to enable us to mark the general shape of objects. Presently a muffled sound caught our ears, and we recognized it as the hoof-beats of a horse or horses. And right away a figure appeared in the forest path; it could have been made of smoke, its mass had so little sharpness of outline. It was a man on horseback, and it seemed to me that there were others behind him. I got hold of a gun in the dark, and pushed it through a crack between the logs, hardly knowing what I was doing, I was so dazed with fright. Somebody said, "Fire!" I pulled the trigger. I seemed to see a hundred flashes and hear a hundred reports; then I saw the man fall down out of the saddle. My first feeling was of surprised gratification; my first impulse was an apprentice-sportsman's impulse to run and pick up his game. Somebody said, hardly audibly, "Good—we've got him!—wait for the rest." But the rest did not come. We waited—listened—still no more came. There was not a sound, not the whisper of a leaf; just perfect stillness, an uncanny kind of stillness, which was all the more uncanny on account of the damp, earthy late-night smells now rising and pervading it. Then, wondering, we crept stealthily out, and approached the man. When we got to him the moon revealed him distinctly. He was lying on his back with his arms abroad; his mouth was open and his chest heaving with long gasps, and his white shirt-front was all splashed with blood. The thought shot through me that I was a murderer; that I had killed a man—a man who had never done me any harm. That was the coldest sensation that ever went through my marrow. I was down by him in a moment, helplessly stroking his forehead; and I would have given anything then—my own life freely—to make him again what he had been five minutes before. And all the boys seemed to be feeling in the same way; they hung over him, full of pitying interest, and tried all they could to help him, and said all sorts of regretful things. They had forgotten all about the enemy; they thought only of this one forlorn unit of the foe. Once my imagination persuaded me that the dying man gave me a reproachful look out of his shadowy eyes, and it seemed to me that

I could rather he had stabbed me than done that. He muttered and mumbled like a dreamer in his sleep, about his wife and his child; and I thought with a new despair, "This thing that I have done does not end with him; it falls upon *them* too, and they never did me any harm, any more than he."

In a little while the man was dead. He was killed in war; killed in fair and legitimate war; killed in battle, as you may say; and yet he was as sincerely mourned by the opposing force as if he had been their brother. The boys stood there a half hour sorrowing over him, and recalling the details of the tragedy, and wondering who he might be, and if he were a spy, and saying that if it were to do over again they would not hurt him unless he attacked them first. It soon came out that mine was not the only shot fired; there were five others,—a division of guilt which was a great relief to me, since it in some degree lightened and diminished the burden I was carrying. There were six shots fired at once; but I was not in my right mind at the time, and my heated imagination had magnified my one shot into a volley.

The man was not in uniform, and was not armed. He was a stranger in the country; that was all we ever found out about him. The thought of him got to preying upon me every night; I could not get rid of it. I could not drive it away, the taking of that unoffending life seemed such a wanton thing. And it seemed an epitome of war; that all war must be just that—the killing of strangers against whom you feel no personal animosity; strangers whom, in other circumstances, you would help if you found them in trouble, and who would help you if you needed it. My campaign was spoiled. It seemed to me that I was not rightly equipped for this awful business; that war was intended for men, and I for a child's nurse. I resolved to retire from this avocation of sham soldiership while I could save some remnant of my self-respect. These morbid thoughts clung to me against reason; for at bottom I did not believe I had touched that man. The law of probabilities decreed me guiltless of his blood; for in all my small experience with guns I had never hit anything I had tried to hit, and I knew I had done my best to hit him. Yet there was no solace in the thought. Against a diseased imagination demonstration goes for nothing.

The rest of my war experience was a piece with what I have already told of it. We kept monotonously falling back upon one camp or another, and eating up the country. I marvel now at the patience of the farmers and their families. They ought to have shot us; on the contrary, they were as hospitably kind and courteous to us as if we had deserved it. In one of these camps we found Ab Grimes, an Upper Mississippi pilot, who afterwards became famous as a daredevil rebel spy, whose career bristled with desperate adventures. The look and style of his comrades suggested that they had not come into war to play, and their deeds made good the conjecture later. They were fine horsemen and good revolver-shots; but their favorite arm was the lasso. Each had one at his pommel, and could snatch a man out of the saddle with it every time, on a full gallop, at any reasonable distance.

In another camp the chief was a fierce and profane old blacksmith of sixty, and he had furnished his twenty recruits with gigantic home-made bowie-knives, to be swung with two hands, like the *machetes* of the Isthmus. It was a grisly spectacle to see that earnest band practicing their murderous cuts and slashes under the eye of that remorseless old fanatic.

The last camp which we fell back upon was in a hollow near the village of Florida, where I was born—in Monroe County. Here we were warned, one day, that a Union colonel was sweeping down on us with a whole regiment at his heels. This looked decidedly serious. Our boys went apart and consulted; then we went back and told the other companies present that the war was a disappointment to us, and we were going to disband. They were getting ready, themselves, to fall back on some place or other, and were only waiting for General Tom Harris, who was expected to arrive at any moment; so they tried to persuade us to wait a little while, but the majority of us said no, we were accustomed to falling back, and didn't need any of Tom Harris's help; we could get along perfectly well without him—and save time too. So about half of our fifteen, including myself, mounted and left on the instant; the others yielded to persuasion and staid— staid through the war.

An hour later we met General Harris on the road, with two or three people in his company—his staff, probably, but we could not tell; none of them were in uniform; uniforms had not come into vogue among us yet. Harris ordered us back; but we told him there was a Union colonel coming with a whole regiment in his wake, and it looked as if there was going to be a disturbance; so we had concluded to go home. He raged a little, but it was of no use; our minds were made up. We had done our share; had killed one man, exterminated

51

one army, such as it was; let him go and kill the rest, and that would end the war. I did not see that brisk young general again until last year; then he was wearing white hair and whiskers.

In time I came to know that Union colonel whose coming frightened me out of the war and crippled the Southern cause to that extent—General Grant. I came within a few hours of seeing him when he was an unknown as I was myself; at a time when anybody could have said, "Grant?—Ulysses S. Grant? I do not remember hearing the name before." It seems difficult to realize that there was once a time when such a remark could be rationally made; but there *was,* and I was within a few miles of the place and the occasion too, though proceeding in the other direction.

The thoughtful will not throw this war-paper of mine lightly aside as being valueless. It has this value: it is a not unfair picture of what went on in many and many a militia camp in the first month of the rebellion, when the green recruits were without discipline, without the steadying and heartening influence of trained leaders; when all their circumstances were new and strange, and charged with exaggerated terror, and before the invaluable experience of actual collision in the field had turned them from rabbits into soldiers. If this side of the picture of that early day has not before been put into history, then history has been to that degree incomplete, for it had and has its rightful place there. There was more Bull Run material scattered through the early camps of this country than exhibited itself at Bull Run. And yet it learned its trade presently, and helped to fight the great battles later. I could have become a soldier myself, if I had waited. I had got part of it learned; I knew more about retreating than the man that invented retreating.

THE REIGN OF THE BRUTE

ELLEN GLASGOW

The noise of the guns rolled over the green hills into the little valley where the regiment had halted before a wayside spring, which lay hidden beneath a clump of rank pokeberry. As each company filled its canteens, it filed across the sunny road, from which the dust rose like steam, and stood resting in an open meadow that swept down into a hollow between two gently rising hills. From the spring a thin stream trickled, bordered by short grass, and the water, dashed from it by the thirsty men, gathered in shining puddles in the red clay road. By one of these puddles a man had knelt to wash his face, and as Dan passed, draining his canteen, he looked up with a sprinkling of brown drops on his forehead. Near him, unharmed by the tramping feet, a little purple flower was blooming in the mud.

Dan gazed thoughtfully down upon him and upon the little purple flower in its dangerous spot. What did mud or dust matter, he questioned grimly, when in a breathing space they would be in the midst of the smoke that hung close above the hill-top? The sound of the cannon ceased suddenly, as abruptly as if the battery had sunk into the ground, and through the sunny air he heard a long rattle that reminded him of the fall of hail on the shingled roof at Chericoke. As his canteen struck against his side, it seemed to him that it met the resistance of a leaden weight. There was a lump in his throat and his lips felt parched, though the moisture from the fresh spring water was hardly dried. When he moved he was conscious of stepping high

---

"The Reign of the Brute" is an excerpt from Glasgow's novel *The Battle-Ground*.

53

above the earth, as he had done once at college after an overmerry night and many wines.

Straight ahead the sunshine lay hot and still over the smooth fields and the little hollow where a brook ran between marshy banks. High above he saw it flashing on the gray smoke that hung in tatters from the tree-tops on the hill.

An ambulance, drawn by a white and a bay horse, turned gayly from the road into the meadow, and he saw, with surprise, that one of the surgeons was trimming his finger nails wtih a small penknife. The surgeon was a slight young man, with pointed yellow whiskers, and light blue eyes that squinted in the sunshine. As he passed he stifled a yawn with an elaborate affectation of unconcern.

A man on horseback, with a white handkerchief tied above his collar, galloped up and spoke in a low voice to the Colonel. Then, as his horse reared, he glanced nervously about, grew embarrassed, and, with a sharp jerk of the bridle, galloped off again across the field. Presently other men rode back and forth along the road; there were so many of them that Dan wondered, bewildered, if anybody was left to make the battle beyond the hill.

The regiment formed into line and started at "double quick" across the broad meadow powdered white with daisies. As it went into the ravine, skirting the hillside, a stream of men came toward it and passed slowly to the rear. Some were on stretchers, some were stumbling in the arms of slightly wounded comrades, some were merely warm and dirty and very much afraid. One and all advised the fresh regiment to "go home and finish ploughing." "The Yankees have got us on the hip," they declared emphatically. "Whoopee! it's as hot as hell where you're going." Then a boy, with a blood-stained sleeve, waved his shattered arm in the air and laughed deliriously. "Don't believe them, friends, it's glorious!" he cried, in the voice of the far South, and lurched forward upon the grass.

The sight of the soaked shirt and the smell of blood turned Dan faint. He felt a sudden tremor in his limbs, and his arteries throbbed dully in his ears. "I didn't know it was like this," he muttered thickly. "Why, they're no better than mangled rabbits—I didn't know it was like this."

They wound through the little ravine, climbed a hillside planted in thin corn, and were ordered to "load and lie down" in a strip of woodland. Dan tore at his cartridge with set teeth; then as he drove his ramrod home, a shell, thrown from a distant gun, burst in the trees above him, and a red flame ran, for an instant, along the barrel of his musket. He dodged quickly, and a rain of young pine needles fell in scattered showers from the smoked boughs overhead. Somewhere beside him a man was groaning in terror or in pain. "I'm hit, boys, by God, I'm hit this time." The groans changed promptly into a laugh. "Bless my soul! the plagued thing went right into the earth beneath me."

"Damn you, it went into my leg," retorted a hoarse voice that fell suddenly silent.

With a shiver Dan lay down on the carpet of rotted pine-cones and peered, like a squirrel, through the meshes of the brushwood. At first he saw only gray smoke and a long sweep of briers and broom-sedge, standing out dimly from an obscurity that was thick as dusk. Then came a clatter near at hand, and a battery swept at a long gallop across the thinned edge of the pines. So close it came that he saw the flashing white eyeballs and the spreading sorrel manes of the horses, and almost felt their hot breath upon his cheek. He heard the shouts of the outriders, the crack of the stout whips, the rattle of the caissons, and, before it passed, he had caught the excited gestures of the men upon the guns. The battery unlimbered, as he watched it, shot a few rounds from the summit of the hill, and retreated rapidly to a new position. When the wind scattered the heavy smoke, he saw only the broom-sedge and several ridges of poor corn; some of the gaunt stalks blackened and beaten to the ground, some still flaunting their brave tassels beneath the whistling bullets. It was all in sunlight, and the gray smoke swept ceaselessly to and fro over the smiling face of the field.

Then, as he turned a little in his shelter, he saw that there was a single Confederate battery in position under a slight swell on his left. Beyond it he knew that the long slope sank gently into a marshy stream and the broad turnpike, but the brow of the hill went up against the sky, and hidden in the brushwood he could see only the darkened line of the horizon. Against it the guns stood there in the sunlight, unsupported, solitary, majestic, while around them the earth was tossed up in the air as if a loose plough had run wild across the field. A handful of artillerymen moved back and forth, like dim outlines, serving the guns in a group of fallen horses that showed in dark mounds upon the hill. From time to time he saw a rammer waved excitedly as a shot went home, or heard, in a lull, the hoarse voices of the gunners when they called for "grape!"

As he lay there, with is eyes on the solitary battery, he forgot, for an instant, his own part in the coming work. A bullet cut the air above him, and a branch, clipped by a razor's stroke, fell upon his head; but his nerves had grown steady and his thoughts were not of himself; he was watching, with breathless interest, for another of the gray shadows at the guns to go down among the fallen horses.

Then, while he watched, he saw other batteries come out upon the hill; saw the cannon thrown into position and heard the call change from "grape!" to "canister!" On the edge of the pines a voice was speaking, and beyond the voice a man on horseback was riding quietly back and forth in the open. Behind him Jack Powell called out suddenly, "We're ready, Colonel Burwell!" and his voice was easy, familiar, almost affectionate.

"I know it, boys!" replied the Colonel in the same tone, and Dan felt a quick sympathy spring up within him. At that instant he knew that he loved every man in the regiment beside him—loved the affectionate Colonel, with the sleepy voice, loved Pinetop, loved the lieutenant whose nose he had broken after drill.

At a word he had leaped, with the others, to his feet, and stood drawn up for battle against the wood. Then it was that he saw the General of the day riding beside fluttering colours across the waste land to the crest of the hill. He was rallying the scattered brigades about the flag—so the fight had gone against them and gone badly, after all.

Around him the men drifted back, frightened, straggling, defeated, and the broken ranks closed up slowly. The standards dipped for a moment before a sharp fire, and then, as the colour bearers shook out the bright folds, soared like great red birds' wings above the smoke.

It seemed to Dan that he stood for hours motionless there against the pines. For a time the fight passed away from him, and he remembered a mountain storm which had caught him as a boy in the woods at Chericoke. He heard again the cloud burst overhead, the soughing of the pines and the crackling of dried branches as they came drifting down through interlacing boughs. The old childish terror returned to him, and he recalled his mad rush for light and space when he had doubled like a hare in the wooded twilight among the dim bodies of the trees. Then as now it was not the open that he feared, but the unseen horror of the shelter.

Again the affectionate voice came from the sunlight and he gripped his musket as he started forward. He had caught only the last words, and he repeated them half mechanically, as he stepped out from the brushwood. Once again, when he stood on the trampled broom-sedge, he said them over with a nervous jerk, "Wait until they come within fifty yards—and, for God's sake, boys, shoot at the knees!"

He thought of the jolly Colonel, and laughed hysterically. Why, he had been at that man's wedding—had kissed the bride—and now he was begging him to shoot at people's knees!

With a cheer, the regiment broke from cover and swept forward toward the summit of the hill. Dan's foot caught in a blackberry vine, and he stumbled blindly. As he regained himself a shell ripped up the ground before him, flinging the warm clods of earth into his face. A "worm" fence at a little distance scattered beneath the fire, and as he looked up he saw the long rails flying across the field. For an instant he hesitated; then something that was like a nervous spasm shook his heart, and he was no more afraid. Over the blackberries and the broom-sedge, on he went toward the swirls of golden dust that swept upward from the bright green slope. If this was a battle, what was the old engraving? Where were the prancing horses and the uplifted swords?

Something whistled in his ears and the air was filled with sharp sounds that set his teeth on edge. A man went down beside him and clutched at his boots as he ran past; but the smell of the battle—a smell of oil and smoke, of blood and sweat—was in his nostrils, and he could have kicked the stiff hands grasping at his feet. The hot old blood of his fathers had stirred again and the dead had rallied to the call of their descendant. He was not afraid, for he had been here long before.

Behind him, and beside him, row after row of gray men leaped from the shadow—the very hill seemed rising to his support—and it was almost gayly, as the dead fighters lived again, that he went straight onward over the sunny field. He saw the golden dust float nearer up the slope, saw the brave flags unfurling in the breeze—saw, at last, man after man emerge from the yellow cloud. As he bent to fire, the fury of the game swept over him and aroused the sleeping brute within him. All the primeval instincts, throttled by the restraint of centuries—the instincts of bloodguiltiness, of hot pursuit, of the fierce exhilaration of the chase, of the death grapple with a resisting foe—these awoke suddenly to life and turned the battle scarlet to his eyes.

Two hours later, when the heavy clouds were smothering the sunset, he came slowly back across the field. A gripping nausea had seized upon him—a nausea such as he had known before after that merry night at college. His head throbbed, and as he walked he staggered like a drunken man. The revulsion of his overwrought emotions had thrown him into a state of sensibility almost hysterical.

The battle-field stretched grimly round him, and as the sunset was blotted out, a gray mist crept slowly from the west. Here and there he saw men looking for the wounded, and he heard one utter an impatient, "Pshaw!" as he lifted a half-cold body and let it fall. Rude stretchers went by him on either side, and still the field seemed as thickly sown as before; on the left, where a regiment of Zouaves had been cut down, there was a flash of white and scarlet, as if the loose grass was strewn with great tropical flowers. Among them he saw the reproachful eyes of dead and dying horses.

Before him, on the gradual slope of the hill, stood a group of abandoned guns, and there was something almost human in the pathos of their utter isolation. Around them the ground was scorched and blackened, and scattered over the broken trails lay the men who had fallen at their post. He saw them lying there in the fading daylight, with the sponges and the rammers still in their hands, and he saw upon each man's face the look with which he had met and recognized the end. Some were smiling, some staring, and one lay grinning as if at a ghastly joke. Near him a boy, with the hair still damp on his forehead, had fallen upon an uprooted blackberry vine, and the purple stain of the berries was on his mouth. As Dan looked down upon him, the smell of powder and burned grass came to him with a wave of sickness, and turning he stumbled on across the field. At the first step his foot struck upon something hard, and, picking it up, he saw that it was a Minie ball, which, in passing through a man's spine, had been transformed into a mass of mingled bone and lead. With a gesture of disgust he dropped it and went on rapidly. A stretcher moved beside him, and the man on it, shot through the waist, was saying in a whisper, "It is cold—cold—so cold." Against his will, Dan, found, he had fallen into step with the men who bore the stretcher, and together they kept time to the words of the wounded soldier who cried out ceaselessly that it was cold. On their way they passed a group on horseback and, standing near it, a handsome artilleryman, who wore a red flannel shirt with one sleeve missing. As Dan went on he discovered that he was thinking of the handsome man in the red and wondering how he had lost his missing sleeve. He pondered the question as if it were a puzzle, and, finally, yielded it up in doubt.

Beyond the base of the hill they came into the small ravine which had been turned into a rude field hospital. Here the stretcher was put down, and a tired-looking surgeon, wiping his hands upon a soiled towel, came and knelt down beside the wounded man.

"Bring a light—I can't see—bring a light!" he exclaimed irritably, as he cut away the clothes with gentle fingers.

Dan was passing on, when he heard his name called from behind, and turning quickly found Governor Ambler anxiously regarding him.

"You're not hurt, my boy?" asked the Governor, and from his tone he might have parted from the younger man only the day before.

"Hurt? Oh, no, I'm not hurt," replied Dan a little bitterly, "but there's a whole field of them back there, Colonel."

"Well, I suppose so—I suppose so," returned the other absently. "I'm looking after my men now, poor fellows. A victory doesn't come cheap, you know, and thank God, it was a glorious victory."

"A glorious victory," repeated Dan, looking at the surgeons who were working by the light of tallow candles.

The Governor followed his gaze. "It's your first fight," he said, "and you haven't learned your lesson as I learned mine in Mexico. The best, or the worst of it, is that after the first fight it comes easy, my boy, it comes too easy."

There was hot blood in him also, thought Dan, as he looked at him—and yet of all the men that he had ever known he would have called the Governor the most humane.

"I dare say—I'll get used to it, sir," he answered. "Yes, it was a glorious victory."

He broke away and went off into the twilight over the wide meadow to the little wayside spring. Across the road there was a field of clover, where a few campfires twinkled, and he hastened toward it eager to lie down in the darkness and fall asleep. As his feet sank in the moist earth, he looked down and saw that the little purple flower was still blooming in the mud.

A Woman

MARY JOHNSTON

Allan Gold, lying in a corner of the Stonewall Hospital, turned his head toward the high window. It showed him little, merely a long strip of blue sky above housetops. The window was open, and the noises of the street came in. He knew them, checked them off in his mind. He was doing well. A body, superbly healthful, might stand out boldly against a minie ball or two, just as calm nerves, courage and serene judgment were of service in a war hospital such as this. If he was restless now, it was because he was wondering about Christianna. It was an hour past her time for coming.

The ward was fearfully crowded. This, however, was the end by the stair, and he had a little cut-off place to himself. Many in the ward yet lay on the floor, on a blanket as he had done that first morning. In the afternoon of that day a wide bench had been brought into his corner, a thin flock mattress laid upon it, and he himself lifted from the floor. He had protested that others needed a bed much more, that he was used to lying on the earth—but Christianna had been firm. He wondered why she did not come.

Chickahominy, Gaines's Mill, Garnett's and Golding's farms, Peach Orchard, Savage Station, White Oak Swamp, Frayser's Farm, Malvern Hill—dire echoes of the Seven Days' fighting had thronged into this hospital as into all others, as into the houses of wounded soldiers told the story—ever so many soldiers and ever so many variants of the story. The dead bore witness, and the wailing of women which was now and then heard in the streets; not often, for

---

"A Woman" is an excerpt from Johnston's novel *The Long Roll*.

the women were mostly silent, with pressed lips. And the ambulances jolting by—and the sound of funerals—and the church bells tolling, tolling—all these bore witness. And day and night there was the thunder of the cannon. From Mechanicsville and Gaines's Mill it had rolled near and loud, from Savage Station somewhat less so; White Oak Swamp and Frayser's Farm had carried the sound yet further off, and from Malvern Hill it came but distantly. But loud or low, near or far, day by day and into each night, Richmond heard the cannon. At first the vibration played on the town's heart, like a giant hand on giant strings. But at last the tune grew old and the town went about its business. There was so much to do! one could not stop to listen to cannon. Richmond was a vast hospital; pain and fever in all places, and, around, the shadow of death. Hardly a house but mourned a kinsman or kinsmen; early and late the dirges wailed through the streets. So breathlessly filled were the days, that often the dead were buried at night. The weather was hot—days and nights hot, close and still. Men and women went swiftly through them, swift and direct as weavers' shuttles. Privation, early comrade of the South, was here; scant room, scant supplies, not too much of wholesome food for the crowded town, few medicines or alleviatives, much to be done and done at once with the inadequatest means. There was little time in which to think in general terms; all effort must go toward getting done the immediate thing. The lift and tension of the time sloughed off the immaterial weak act or thought. There were present a heroic simplicity, a naked verity, a full cup of service, a high and noble altruism. The plane was epic, and the people did well.

The sky within Allan's range of vision was deep blue; the old brick gable-ends of houses, mellow and old, against it. A soldier with a broken leg and a great sabre cut over the head, just brought into the ward, brought with him the latest news. He talked loudly and all down the long room, crowded to suffocation, the less desperately wounded raised themselves on their elbows to hear. Others, shot through stomach or bowels, or fearfully torn by shells, or with the stumps of amputated limbs not doing well, raved on in delirium or kept up their pitiful moaning. The soldier raised his voice higher, and those leaning on elbows listened with avidity. "Evelington Heights? Where's Evelington Heights?"—"Between Westover and Rawling's millpond, near Malvern Hill!"—"Malvern Hill! That was ghastly!"—"Go on, sergeant-major! We're been pining for a newspaper."

"Were any of you boys at Malvern Hill?"

"Yes,—only those who were there ain't in a fix to tell about it! That man over there—and that one—and that one—oh, a middling lot! They're pretty badly off—poor boys!"

From a pallet came a hollow voice. "I was at Malvern Hill, and I ain't never going there again—I ain't never going there again—I ain't never. . . . Who's that singing? I kin sing, too—

'The years creep slowly by, Lorena;
The snow is on the grass again;
The sun's low down the sky, Lorena;
The frost gleams where the flowers have been—' "

"Don't mind him," said the soldiers on elbows. "Poor fellow! he ain't got any voice anyhow. We know about Malvern Hill. Malvern Hill was pretty bad. And we heard there'd been a cavalry rumpus— Jeb Stuart and Sweeney playing their tricks! We didn't know the name of the place. Evelington Heights! Pretty name."

The sergeant-major would not be cheated of Malvern Hill. " 'Pretty bad!' I should say 't was pretty bad! Malvern Hill was *awful*. If anything could induce me to be a damn Yankee 't would be them guns of their'n! Yes, sirree, bob! we fought and fought, and ten o'clock came and there wasn't any moon, and we stopped. And in the night-time the damn Yankees continued to retreat away. There was an awful noise of gun-wheels all the night long—so the sentries said, and the surgeons and the wounded and, I reckon, the generals. The rest of us, we were asleep. I don't reckon there ever was men any more tired. Malvern Hill was—I can't swear because there are ladies nursing us, but Malvern Hill was—Well, dawn blew at reveille—No, doctor, I ain't getting light-headed. I just get my words a little twisted. Reveille blew at dawn, and there were sheets of cold pouring rain, and everywhere there were dead men, dead men, dead men lying there in the wet, and the ambulances were wandering round like ghosts of wagons, and the wood was too dripping to make a fire, and three men out of my mess were killed, and one was a boy that we'd all adopted, and it was awful discouraging. Yes, we were right tired, damn Yankees and all of us. . . . Doctor, if I was you I wouldn't bother about that leg. It's all right as it is, and you might hurt me. . . . Oh, all right! Kin I smoke? . . . Yuugh! Well, boys, the damn Yankees continued their retreat to Harrison's Landing, where their hell-fire gunboats could stand picket for them. . . . Say, ma'am, would you kindly tell me why that four-post bed over there is all hung with wreaths of roses?—'Isn't any bed there?' But there is! I see it. . . . Evelington Heights—and Stuart dropping shells into the damn Yankees' camp. . . . They *are* roses, the old Giants of Battle by the beehive. . . . Evelington Heights. Eveling—Well, the damn Yankees dragged their guns up there, too. . . . If the beehive's there, then the apple tree's here—Grandma, if you'll ask him not to whip me I'll never take them again, and I'll hold your yarn every time you want me to—"

The ward heard no more about Evelington Heights. It knew, however, that it had been no great affair; it knew that McClellan with his exhausted army, less many thousand dead, wounded, and prisoners, less fifty-two guns and thirty-five thousand small arms, less enormous stores captured or destroyed, less some confidence at Washington, rested down the James by Westover, in the shadow of gunboats. The ward guessed that, for a time at least, Richmond was freed from the Northern embrace. It knew that Lee and his exhausted army, less even more of dead and wounded than had fallen on the other side, rested between that enemy and Richmond. Lee was watching; the enemy would come no nearer for this while. For all its pain, for all the heat, the blood, the fever, thirst and woe, the ward, the hospital, all the hospitals, experienced to-day a sense of triumph. It was so with the whole city. Allan knew this, lying, looking with sea-blue eyes at the blue summer sky and the old and mellow roofs. The city mourned, but also it rejoiced. There stretched the black thread, but twisted with it was the gold. A pæan sounded as well as a dirge. Seven days and nights of smoke and glare upon the horizon, of the heart-shaking cannon roar, of the pouring in of the wounded, of processions to Hollywood, of anguish, ceaseless labour, sick waiting, dizzy hope, descending despair. . . . Now, at last, above it all the bells rang for victory. A young girl, coming through the ward, had an armful of flowers—white lilies, citron aloes, mignonette, and phlox—She gave her posies to all who stretched out a hand, and went out with her smiling face. Allan held a great stalk of garden phlox, white and sweet. It carried him back to the tollgate and to the log schoolhouse by Thunder Run. . . . Twelve o'clock. Was not Christianna coming at all?

This was not Judith Cary's ward, but now she entered it. Allan, watching the narrow path between the wounded, saw her coming from the far door. He did not know who she was; he only looked from the flower in his hand and had a sense of strength and sweetness, of something noble approaching nearer. She paused to ask a question of one of the women; answered, she came straight on. He saw that she was coming to the cut-off corner by the stair, and instinctively he straightened a little the covering over him. In a moment she was standing beside him, in her cool hospital dress, with her dark hair knotted low, with a flower at her breast. "You are Allan Gold?" she said.

"Yes."

"My name is Judith Cary. Perhaps you have heard of me. I have been to Lauderdale and to Three Oaks."

"Yes," said Allan. "I have heard of you. I—"

There was an empty box beside the wall. Judith drew it nearer to his bed and sat down. "You have been looking for Christianna? I came to tell you about poor little Christianna—and—and other things. Christianna's father has been killed."

Allan uttered an exclamation. "Isham Maydew! I never thought of his going! . . . Poor child!"

"So she thought she ought not to come to-day. Had there been strong reason, many people dependent upon her, she would have come."

"Poor Christianna—poor wild rose! . . . It's ghastly, this war! There is nothing too small and harmless for its grist."

"I agree with you. Nothing too great; nothing too small. Nothing too base, as there is nothing too noble."

"Isham Maydew! He was lean and tough and still, like Death in a picture. Where was he killed?"

"It was at White Oak Swamp. At White Oak Swamp, the day before Malvern Hill."

Allan looked at her. There was more in her voice than the non-coming of Christianna, than the death of Isham Maydew. She had spoken in a clear, low, bell-like tone that held somehow the ache of the world. He was simple and direct, and he spoke at once out of his thought. He knew that all the men of her house were at the front. "You have had a loss of your own?—"

She shook her head. "I? No. I have had no loss."

"Now," thought Allan, "there's something proud in it." He looked at her with his kindly, sea-blue eyes. In some chamber of the brain there flashed out a picture—the day of the Botetourt Resolutions,

winter dusk after winter sunset and Cleave and himself going homeward over the long hilltop—with talk, among other things, of visitors
at Lauderdale. This was "the beautiful one." He remembered the lift
of Cleve's head and his voice. Judith's large dark eyes had been
raised; transparent, showing always the soul within as did his own,
they now met Allan's. "The 65th," she said, "was cut to pieces."

The words, dragged out as they were, left a shocked silence. Here,
in the corner by the stair, the arch of wood partially obscuring the
ward, with the still blue sky and the still brick gables, they seemed
for the moment cut away from the world, met on desert sands to tell
and hear a dreadful thing. "Cut to pieces," breathed Allan. "The
65th cut to pieces!"

The movement which he made displaced the bandage about his
shoulder. She left the box, kneeled by him and straightened matters,
then went back to her seat. "It was this way," she said,—and told
him the story as she had heard it from her father and from Fauquier
Cary. She spoke with simplicity, in the low, bell-like tone that held
the ache of the world. Allan listened, with his hand over his eyes.
His regiment that he loved! . . . all the old, familiar faces.

"Yes, he was killed—Hairston Breckinridge was killed, fighting
gallantly. He died, they say, before he knew the trap they were
caught in. And Christianna's father was killed, and others of the
Thunder Run men, and very many from the county and from other
counties. I do not know how many. Fauquier called it slaughter, said
no worse thing has happened to any single command. Richard got
what was left back across the swamp."

Allan groaned. "The 65th! General Jackson himself called it 'the
fighting 65th!' Just a remnant of it left—left of the 65th!"

"Yes. The roll was called, and so many did not answer. They say
other Stonewall regiments wept."

Allan raised himself upon the bench. She started forward. "Don't
do that!" and with her hand pressed him gently down again. "I
knew," she said, "that you were here, and I have heard Richard
speak of you and say how good and likable you were. And I have
worked hard all morning, and just now I thought, 'I must speak to
some one who knows and loves him or I will die.' And so I came. I
knew that the ward might hear of the 65th any moment now and
begin to talk of it, so I was not afraid of hurting you. But you must
lie quiet."

"Very well, I will. I want to know about Richard Cleave—about my colonel."

Her dark eyes met the sea-blue ones fully. "He is under arrest," she said. "General Jackson has preferred charges against him."

"Charges of what?"

"Of disobedience to orders—of sacrificing the regiment—of—of retreating at last when he should not have done so and leaving his men to perish—of—of—. I have seen a copy of the charge. *Whereas the said colonel of the 65th did shamefully—*"

Her voice broke. "Oh, if I were God—"

There was a moment's silence—silence here in the corner by the stair, though none beyond in the painful, moaning ward. A bird sailed across the strip of blue sky; the stalk of phlox on the soldier's narrow bed lay withering in the light. Allan spoke. "General Jackson is very stern with failure. He may believe that charge. I don't see how he can; but if he made it he believes it. But you—you don't believe it?—"

"Believe it?" she said. "No more than God believes it! The question is now, how to help Richard."

"Have you heard from him?"

She took from her dress a folded leaf torn from a pocket-book. "You are his friend. You may read it. Wait, I will hold it." She laid it before him, holding it in her slight, fine, strong fingers.

He read. *Judith: You will hear of the fate of the 65th. How it happened I do not yet understand. It is like death on my heart. You will hear, too, of my own trouble. As to me, believe only that I could sit beside you and talk to-day as we talked awhile ago, in the sunset. Richard.*

She refolded the paper and put it back. "The evidence will clear him," said Allan. "It must. The very doubt is absurd."

Her face lightened. "General Jackson will see that he was hasty—unjust. I can understand such anger at first, but later, when he reflects—Richard will be declared innocent—"

"Yes. An honourable acquittal. It will surely be so."

"I am glad I came. You have always known him and been his friend."

"Let me tell you the kind of things I know of Richard Cleave. No, it doesn't hurt me to talk."

"I can stay a little longer. Yes, tell me."

Allan spoke at some length, in his frank, quiet voice. She sat beside him, with her cheek on her hand, the blue sky and old house roofs above her. When he ceased her eyes were full of tears. She would not let them fall. "If I began to cry I should never stop," she said, and smiled them away. Presently she rose. "I must go now. Christianna will be back to-morrow."

She went away, passing up the narrow path between the wounded and out at the further door. Allan watched her going, then turned a little on the flock bed, and lifting his unbandaged arm laid it across his eyes. *The 65th cut to pieces—The 65th cut to pieces—*

At sunset Judith went home. The small room up in the branches of the tulip tree—she hardly knew how many months or years she had inhabited it. There had passed, of course, only weeks—but Time had widened its measure. To all intents and purposes she had been a long while in Richmond. This high, quiet niche was familiar, familiar! familiar the old, slender, inlaid dressing-table and the long, thin curtains and the engraving of Charlotte Corday; familiar the cool, green tree without the window and the next upon a bough; familiar the far view and wide horizon, by day smoke-veiled, by night red-lit. The smoke was lifted now; the eye saw further than it had seen for days. The room seemed as quiet as a tomb. For a moment the silence oppressed her, and then she remembered that it was because the cannon had stopped.

She sat beside the window, through the dusk, until the stars came out; then went downstairs and took her part at the table, about which the soldier sons of the house were gathering. They brought comrades with them. The wounded eldest son was doing well, the army was victorious, the siege was lifted, the house must be made gay for "the boys." No house was ever less bright for Judith. Now she smiled and listened, and the young men thought she did not realize the seriousness of the army talk about the 65th. They themselves were careful not to mention the matter. They talked of a thousand hero-isms, a thousand incidents of the Seven Days; but they turned the talk—if any one, unwary, drew it that way—from White Oak Swamp. They mistook her feeling; she would rather they had spoken out. Her comfort was when, afterwards, she went for a moment into the "chamber" to see the wounded eldest. He was a warm-hearted, rough diamond, fond of his cousin.

"What's this damned stuff I hear about Richard Cleave and a court-martial? What—nonsense! I beg your pardon, Judith." Judith kissed him, and finding "Le Vicomte de Bragelonne" face down on the counterpane offered to read to him.

67

"You would rather talk about Richard," he said. "I know you would. So should I. It's all the damnedest nonsense! Such a charge as that!—Tell you what, Judith. D'ye remember 'Woodstock' and Cromwell in it? Well, Stonewall Jackson's like Cromwell—of course, a better man, and a greater general, and a nobler cause, but still he's like him! Don't you fret! Cromwell had to listen to the truth. He did it, and so will Stonewall Jackson. Such damned stuff and nonsense! It hurts me worse than that old bayonet jab ever could! I'd like to hear what Edward says."

"He says, 'Duck your head and let it go by. The grass'll grow as green to-morrow.' "

"You aren't crying, are you, Judith?—I thought not. You aren't the crying kind. Don't do it. War's the stupidest beast."

"Yes, it is."

"Cousin Margaret's with Richard, isn't she?"

"Not with him—that couldn't be, they said. But she and Miriam have gone to Merry Mount. It's in the lines. I have had a note from her."

"What did she say?—You don't mind, Judith?"

"No, Rob, I don't mind. It was just a verse from a psalm. She said, *I had fainted unless I had believed to see the goodness of the Lord in the land of the living. . . . Be of good courage and He shall strengthen thy heart.*"

Later, in her room again, she sat by the window through the greater part of the night. The stars were large and soft, the airs faint, the jasmine in the garden below smelled sweet. The hospital day stretched before her; she must sleep so that she could work. She never thought—in that city and time no woman thought—of ceasing from service because of private grief. Moreover, work was her salvation. She would be betimes at the hospital to-morrow, and she would leave it late. She bent once more a long look upon the east, where were the camp-fires of Lee and Stonewall Jackson. In imagination she passed the sentries; she moved among the sleeping brigades. She found one tent, or perhaps it would be instead a rude cabin. . . . She stretched her arms upon the window-sill, and they and her thick fallen hair were wet at last with her tears.

Three days passed. On the third afternoon she left the hospital early and went to St. Paul's. She chose again the dusk beneath the gallery, and she prayed dumbly, fiercely, "O God. . . . O God—"

The church was fairly filled. The grey army was not but a little way without the city; it had come back to the seven hills after the seven days. It had come back the hero, the darling. Richmond took the cypress from her doors; put off the purple pall and tragic mask. Last July Richmond was to fall, and this July Richmond was to fall, and lo! she sat secure on her seven hills and her sons did her honour, and for them she would have made herself a waste place. She yet toiled and watched, yet mourned for the dead and hung over the beds of the wounded, and more and more she wondered whence were to appear the next day's yard of cloth and measure of flour. But in these days she overlaid her life with gladness and made her house pleasant for her sons. The service at St. Paul's this afternoon was one of thankfulness; the hymns rang triumphantly. There were many soldiers. Two officers came in together. Judith knew General Lee, but the other? . . . in a moment she saw that it was General Jackson. Her heart beat to suffocation. She sank down in the gold dusk of her corner. "O God, let him see the truth. O God, let him see the truth—"

Outside, as she went homeward in the red sunset, she paused for a moment to speak to an old free negro who was begging for alms. She gave him something, and when he had shambled on she stood still a moment here at the corner of the street, with her eyes upon the beautiful rosy west. There was a garden wall behind her and a tall crape myrtle. As she stood, with the light upon her face, Maury Stafford rode by. He saw her as she saw him. His brooding face flushed; he made as if to check his horse, but did not so. He lifted his hat high and rode on, out of the town, back to the encamped army. Judith had made no answering motion; she stood with lifted face and unchanged look, the rosy light flooding her, the rosy tree behind her. When he was gone she shivered a little. "It is not Happiness that hates; it is Misery," she thought. "When I was happy I never felt like this. I hate him. He is *glad* of Richard's peril."

That night she did not sleep at all but sat bowed together in the window, her arms about her knees, her forehead upon them, and her dark hair loose about her. She sat like a sibyl till the dawn, then rose and bathed and dressed, and was at the hospital earliest of all the workers of that day. In the evening again, just at dusk, she reentered the room, and presently again took her seat by the window. The red light of the camp-fires was beginning to show.

There was a knock at the door. Judith rose and opened to a turbaned coloured girl. "Yes, Dilsey?"

"Miss Judith, de gin'ral air downstairs. He say, ax you kin he come up to yo' room?"

"Yes, yes, Dilsey! Tell him to come."

When her father came he found her standing against the wall, her hands, outstretched behind her, resting on it. The last soft bloom of day was upon her; indefinably, with her hands so, the wall behind her and her lifted head, she looked a soldier facing a firing party. "Tell me quickly," she said, "the exact truth."

Warwick Cary closed the door behind him and came toward her. "The court found him guilty, Judith."

As she still stood, the light from without upon her face, he took her in his arms, drew her from the wall and made her sit in the chair by the window, then placed himself beside her, and leaning over took her hands in his strong clasp. "Many a court has found many a man guilty, Judith, whom his own soul cleared."

"That is true," she answered. "Your own judgment has not changed?"

"No, Judith, no."

She lifted his hand and kissed it. "Just a moment, and then you'll tell me—"

They sat still in the soft summer air. The stars were coming out. Off to the east showed the long red light where was the army. Judith's eyes rested here. He saw it, and saw, presently, courage lift into her face. It came steady, with a deathless look. "Now," she said, and loosed her hands.

"It is very bad," he answered slowly. "The evidence was more adverse than I could have dreamed. Only on the last count was there acquittal."

"The last count?—"

"The charge of personal cowardice."

Her eyelids trembled a little. "I am glad," she said, "that they had a gleam of reason."

The other uttered a short laugh, proud and troubled. "Yes. It would not have occurred to me—just that accusation. . . . Well, he stood cleared of that. But the other charges, Judith, the others—" He rested his hands on his sword hilt and gazed broodingly into the deepening night. "The court could only find as it did. I myself, sitting there, listening to that testimony. . . . It is inexplicable!"

"Tell me all."

"General Jackson's order was plain. A staff officer carried it to General Winder with perfect correctness. Winder repeated it to the court, and word for word Jackson corroborated it. The same officer, carrying it on from Winder to the 65th came up with a courier belonging to the regiment. To this man, an educated, reliable, trusted soldier, he gave the order."

"He should not have done so?"

"It is easy to say that—to blame because this time there's a snarl to unravel! The thing is done often enough. It should not be done, but it is. Staff service with us is far too irregular. The officer stands to receive a severe reprimand—but there is no reason to believe that he did not give the order to the courier with all the accuracy with which he had already delivered it to Winder. He testified that he did so give it, repeated it word for word to the court. He entrusted it to the courier, taking the precaution to make the latter say it over to him, and then he returned to General Jackson, down the stream, before the bridge they were building. That closed his testimony. He received the censure of the court, but what he did has been done before."

"The courier testified—"

"No. That is the link that drops out. The courier was killed. A Thunder Run man—Steven Dagg—testified that he had been separated from the regiment. Returning to it along the wooded bank of the creek, he arrived just behind the courier. He heard him give the order to the colonel. 'Could he repeat it?' 'Yes.' He did so, and it was, accurately, Jackson's order."

"Richard—what did Richard say?"

"He said the man lied."

"Ah!"

"The courier fell before the first volley from the troops in the woods. He died almost at once, but two men testified as to the only thing he had said. It was, 'We ought never all of us to have crossed. Tell Old Jack I carried the order straight.' "

He rose and with a restless sigh began to pace the little room. "I see a tangle—something not understood—some stumbling-block laid by laws beyond our vision. We cannot even define it, cannot even find its edges. We do not know its nature. Things happen so sometimes in this strange world. I do not think that Richard himself understands how the thing chanced. He testified—"

"Yes, oh, yes—"

"He repeated to the court the order he had received. It was not the order that Jackson had given and that Winder had sent on to him, though it differed in only two points. And neither—and there, Judith, there is a trouble!—neither was it with entire explicitness an order to

71

do that which he did do. He acknowledged that, quite simply. He had found at the time an ambiguity—he had thought of sending again for confirmation to Winder. And then—unfortunate man! something happened to strengthen the interpretation which, when all is said, he preferred to receive, and upon which he acted. Time pressed. He took the risk, if there was a risk, and crossed the stream."

"Father, do you blame him?"

"He blames himself, Judith, somewhat cruelly. But I think it is because, just now, of the agony of memory. He loved his regiment.—No. What sense in blaming where, had there followed success, you would have praised? Then it would have been proper daring; now—I could say that he had been wiser to wait, but I do not know that in his place I should have waited. He was rash, perhaps, but who is there to tell? Had he chosen another interpretation and delayed, and been mistaken, then, too, commination would have fallen. No. I blame him less than he blames himself, Judith. But the fact remains. Even by his own showing there was a doubt. Even accepting his statement of the order he received, he took it upon himself to decide."

"They did not accept his statement—"

"No, Judith. They judged that he had received General Jackson's order and had disobeyed it.—I know—I know! To us it is monstrous. But the court must judge by the evidence—and the verdict was to be expected. It was his sole word, and where his own safety was at stake. 'Had not the dead courier a reputation for reliability, for accuracy?' 'He had, and he would not lay the blame there, besmirching a brave man's name.' 'Where then?' 'He did not know. It was so that he had received the order'—Judith, Judith! I have rarely seen truth so helpless as in this case."

She drew a difficult breath. "No help. And they said—"

"He was pronounced guilty of the first charge. That carried with it the verdict as to the second—the sacrifice of the regiment. There, too—guilty. Only the third there was no sustaining. The loss was fearful, but there were men enough left to clear him from that charge. He struggled with desperation to retrieve his error, if error it were; he escaped death himself as a miracle, and he brought off a remnant of the command which, in weaker hands, might have been utterly swallowed up. On that count he is clear. But on the others—guilty, and without mitigation."

He came back to the woman by the window. "Judith, I would

rather put the sword in my own heart than put it thus in yours. War is a key, child, that unlocks to all dreadful things, to all mistakes, to every sorrow!"

"I want every worst drop of it," she said. "Afterward I'll look for comfort. Do not be afraid for me; I feel as strong as the hills, the air, the sea—anything. What is the sentence?"

"Dismissal from the army."

Judith rose and, with her hands on the window-sill, leaned out into the night. Her gaze went straight to the red light in the eastern sky. There was an effect as though the force, impalpable, real, which was herself, had gone too, flown from the window straight toward that horizon, leaving here but a fair ivory shell. It was but momentary; the chains held and she turned back to the shadowed room. "You have seen him?"

"Yes."

"How—"

"He has much of his mother in him, Judith. Eventually he will, I think, take it that way. But now it is his father that shows. He is very silent—grey and hard and silent."

"Where is he?"

"At present yet under guard. To-morrow it will all be over."

"He will be set free, you mean?"

"Yes, he will be free."

She came and put her arm around her father's neck. "Father, you know what I want to do then? To do just as soon as I shall have seen him and made him realize that it is for my happiness. I want to marry him. . . . Ah, don't look at me so, saying nothing!" She withdrew herself a little, standing with her clasped hands against his breast. "You expected that, did you not? Why, what else. . . . Father, I am not afraid of you. You will let me do it."

He regarded her with a grave, compassionate face. "No. You need not fear me, Judith. It is hardly father and child with you and me. It is soul and soul, and I trust your soul with its own concerns. Moreover, if it is pain to consider what you would do, the pang would be greater to find you not capable. . . . Yes, I would let you do it. But I do not think that Richard will."

War

Jack London

He was a young man, not more than twenty-four or five, and he might have sat his horse with the careless grace of his youth had he not been so catlike and tense. His black eyes roved everywhere, catching the movements of twigs and branches where small birds hopped, questing ever onward through the changing vistas of trees and brush, and returning always to the clumps of undergrowth on either side. And as he watched, so did he listen, though he rode on in silence, save for the boom of heavy guns from far to the west. This had been sounding monotonously in his ears for hours, and only its cessation would have aroused his notice. For he had business closer to hand. Across his saddle-bow was balanced a carbine.

So tensely was he strung, that a bunch of quail, exploding into flight from under his horse's nose, startled him to such an extent that automatically, instantly, he had reined in and fetched the carbine halfway to his shoulder. He grinned sheepishly, recovered himself, and rode on. So tense was he, so bent upon the work he had to do, that the sweat stung his eyes unwiped, and unheeded rolled down his nose and spattered his saddle pommel. The band of his cavalryman's hat was fresh-stained with sweat. The roan horse under him was likewise wet. It was high noon of a breathless day of heat. Even the birds and squirrels did not dare the sun, but sheltered in shady hiding places among the trees.

Man and horse were littered with leaves and dusted with yellow pollen, for the open was ventured no more than was compulsory. They kept to the brush and trees, and invariably the man halted and peered out before crossing a dry glade or naked stretch of upland pasturage. He worked always to the north, though his way was

74

devious, and it was from the north that he seemed most to apprehend that for which he was looking. He was no coward, but his courage was only that of the average civilized man, and he was looking to live, not die.

Up a small hillside he followed a cowpath through such dense scrub that he was forced to dismount and lead his horse. But when the path swung around to the west, he abandoned it and headed to the north again along the oak-covered top of the ridge.

The ridge ended in a steep descent—so steep that he zigzagged back and forth across the face of the slope, sliding and stumbling among the dead leaves and matted vines and keeping a watchful eye on the horse above that threatened to fall down upon him. The sweat ran from him, and the pollen-dust, settling pungently in mouth and nostrils, increased his thirst. Try as he would, nevertheless the descent was noisy, and frequently he stopped, panting in the dry heat and listening for any warning from beneath.

At the bottom he came out on a flat, so densely forested that he could not make out its extent. Here the character of the woods changed, and he was able to remount. Instead of the twisted hillside oaks, tall straight trees, big-trunked and prosperous, rose from the damp fat soil. Only here and there were thickets, easily avoided, while he encountered winding, park-like glades where the cattle had pastured in the days before war had run them off.

His progress was more rapid now, as he came down into the valley, and at the end of half an hour he halted at an ancient rail fence on the edge of a clearing. He did not like the openness of it, yet his path lay across to the fringe of trees that marked the banks of the stream. It was a mere quarter of a mile across that open, but the thought of venturing out in it was repugnant. A rifle, a score of them, a thousand, might lurk in that fringe by the stream.

Twice he essayed to start, and twice he paused. He was appalled by his own loneliness. The pulse of war that beat from the West suggested the companionship of battling thousands; here was naught but silence, and himself, and possible death-dealing bullets from a myriad ambushes. And yet his task was to find what he feared to find. He must go on, and on, till somewhere, some time, he encountered another man, or other men, from the other side, scouting, as he was scouting, to make report, as he must make report, of having come in touch.

Changing his mind, he skirted inside the woods for a distance, and again peeped forth. This time, in the middle of the clearing, he saw a small farmhouse. There were no signs of life. No smoke curled from the chimney, not a barnyard fowl clucked and strutted. The kitchen door stood open, and he gazed so long and hard into the black aperture that it seemed almost that a farmer's wife must emerge at any moment.

He licked the pollen and dust from his dry lips, stiffened himself, mind and body, and rode out into the blazing sunshine. Nothing stirred. He went on past the house, and approached the wall of trees and bushes by the river's bank. One thought persisted maddeningly. It was of the crash into his body of a high-velocity bullet. It made him feel very fragile and defenseless, and he crouched lower in the saddle.

Tethering his horse in the edge of the wood, he continued a hundred yards on foot till he came to the stream. Twenty feet wide it was, without perceptible current, cool and inviting, and he was very thirsty. But he waited inside his screen of leafage, his eyes fixed on the screen on the opposite side. To make the wait endurable, he sat down, his carbine resting on his knees. The minutes passed, and slowly his tenseness relaxed. At last he decided there was no danger; but just as he prepared to part the bushes and bend down to the water, a movement among the opposite bushes caught his eye.

It might be a bird. But he waited. Again there was an agitation of the bushes, and then, so suddenly that it almost startled a cry from him, the bushes parted and a face peered out. It was a face covered with several weeks' growth of ginger-colored beard. The eyes were blue and wide apart, with laughter-wrinkles in the corners that showed despite the tired and anxious expression of the whole face.

All this he could see with microscopic clearness, for the distance was no more than twenty feet. And all this he saw in such brief time, that he saw it as he lifted his carbine to his shoulder. He glanced along the sights, and knew that he was gazing upon a man who was as good as dead. It was impossible to miss at such point blank range.

But he did not shoot. Slowly he lowered the carbine and watched. A hand, clutching a water-bottle, became visible and the ginger beard bent downward to fill the bottle. He could hear the gurgle of the water. Then arm and bottle and ginger beard disappeared behind the closing bushes. A long time he waited, when, with thirst unslaked, he crept back to his horse, rode slowly across the sun-washed clearing, and passed into the shelter of the woods beyond.

II

Another day, hot and breathless. A deserted farmhouse, large, with many outbuildings and an orchard, standing in a clearing. From the woods, on a roan horse, carbine across pommel, rode the young man with the quick black eyes. He breathed with relief as he gained the house. That a fight had taken place here earlier in the season was evident. Chips and empty cartridges, tarnished with verdigris, lay on the ground, which, while wet, had been torn up by the hoofs of horses. Hard by the kitchen garden were graves, tagged and numbered. From the oak tree by the kitchen door, in tattered, weather-beaten garments, hung the bodies of two men. The faces, shriveled and defaced, bore no likeness to the faces of men. The roan horse snorted beneath them, and the rider caressed and soothed it and tied it farther away.

Entering the house, he found the interior a wreck. He trod on empty cartridges as he walked from room to room to reconnoiter from the windows. Men had camped and slept everywhere, and on the floor of one room he came upon stains unmistakable where the wounded had been laid down.

Again outside, he led the horse around behind the barn and invaded the orchard. A dozen trees were burdened with ripe apples. He filled his pockets, eating while he picked. Then a thought came to him, and he glanced at the sun, calculating the time of his return to camp. He pulled off his shirt, tying the sleeves and making a bag. This he proceeded to fill with apples.

As he was about to mount his horse, the animal suddenly pricked up its ears. The man, too, listened, and heard, faintly, the thud of hoofs on soft earth. He crept to the corner of the barn and peered out. A dozen mounted men, strung out loosely, approaching from the opposite side of the clearing, were only a matter of a hundred yards or so away. They rode on to the house. Some dismounted, while others remained in the saddle as an earnest that their stay would be short. They seemed to be holding a council, for he could hear them talking excitedly in the detested tongue of the alien invader. The time passed, but they seemed unable to reach a decision. He put the carbine away in its boot, mounted, and waited impatiently, balancing the shirt of apples on the pommel.

He heard footsteps approaching, and drove his spurs so fiercely into the roan as to force a surprise groan from the animal as it leaped forward. At the corner of the barn he saw the intruder, a mere boy of nineteen or twenty for all of his uniform, jump back to escape being run down. At the same moment the roan swerved, and its rider caught a glimpse of the aroused men by the house. Some were springing from their horses, and he could see the rifles going to their shoulders. He passed the kitchen door and the dried corpses swinging in the shade, compelling his foes to run around the front of the house. A rifle cracked, and a second, but he was going fast, leaning forward, low in the saddle, one hand clutching the shirt of apples, the other guiding the horse.

The top bar of the fence was four feet high, but he knew his roan and leaped it at full career to the accompaniment of several scattered shots. Eight hundred yards straight away were the woods, and the roan was covering the distance with mighty strides. Every man was now firing. They were pumping their guns so rapidly that he no longer heard individual shots. A bullet went through his hat, but he was unaware, though he did know when another tore through the apples on the pommel. And he winced and ducked even lower when a third bullet, fired low, struck a stone between his horse's leg and ricochetted off through the air, buzzing and humming like some incredible insect.

The shots died down as the magazines were emptied, until, quickly, there was no more shooting. The young man was elated. Through that astonishing fusillade he had come unscathed. He glanced back. Yes, they had emptied their magazines. He could see several reloading. Others were running back behind the house for their horses. As he looked, two already mounted, came back into view around the corner, riding hard. And at the same moment, he saw the man with the unmistakable ginger beard kneel down on the ground, level his gun, and coolly take his time for the long shot.

The young man threw his spurs into the horse, crouched very low, and swerved in his flight in order to distract the other's aim. And still the shot did not come. With each jump of the horse, the woods sprang nearer. They were only two hundred yards away, and still the shot was delayed.

And then he heard it, the last thing he was to hear, for he was dead ere he hit the ground in the long crashing fall from the saddle. And they, watching at the house, saw him fall, saw his body bounce when it struck the earth, and saw the burst of red-cheeked apples that rolled about him. They laughed at the unexpected eruption of apples, and clapped their hands in applause of the long shot by the man with the ginger beard.

KILLED AT RESACA

AMBROSE BIERCE

The best soldier of our staff was Lieutenant Herman Brayle, one of the two aides-de-camp. I don't remember where the general picked him up; from some Ohio regiment, I think; none of us had previously known him, and it would have been strange if we had, for no two of us came from the same State, nor even from adjoining States. The general seemed to think that a position on his staff was a distinction that should be so judiciously conferred as not to beget any sectional jealousies and imperil the integrity of that part of the country which was still an integer. He would not even choose officers from his own command, but by some jugglery at department headquarters obtained them from other brigades. Under such circumstances, a man's services had to be very distinguished indeed to be heard of by his family and the friends of his youth; and "the speaking trump of fame" was a trifle hoarse from loquacity, anyhow.

Lieutenant Brayle was more than six feet in height and of splendid proportions, with the light hair and gray-blue eyes which men so gifted usually find associated with a high order of courage. As he was commonly in full uniform, especially in action, when most officers are content to be less flamboyantly attired, he was a very striking and conspicuous figure. As to the rest, he had a gentleman's manners, a scholar's head, and a lion's heart. His age was about thirty.

We all soon came to like Brayle as much as we admired him, and it was with sincere concern that in the engagement at Stone's River— our first action after he joined us—we observed that he had one most objectionable and unsoldierly quality: he was vain of his courage. During all the vicissitudes and mutations of that hideous encounter, whether our troops were fighting in the open cotton fields, in the cedar thickets, or behind the railway embankment, he did not once take cover, except when sternly commanded to do so by the general, who usually had other things to think of than the lives of his staff officers—or those of his men, for that matter.

In every later engagement while Brayle was with us it was the same way. He would sit his horse like an equestrian statue, in a storm of bullets and grape, in the most exposed places—wherever, in fact, duty, requiring him to go, permitted him to remain—when, without trouble and with distinct advantage to his reputation for common sense, he might have been in such security as is possible on a battlefield in the brief intervals of personal inaction.

On foot, from necessity or in deference to his dismounted commander or associates, his conduct was the same. He would stand like a rock in the open when officers and men alike had taken to cover; while men older in service and years, higher in rank and of unquestionable intrepidity, were loyally preserving behind the crest of a hill lives infinitely precious to their country, this fellow would stand, equally idle, on the ridge, facing in the direction of the sharpest fire.

When battles are going on in open ground it frequently occurs that the opposing lines, confronting each other within a stone's throw for hours, hug the earth as closely as if they loved it. The line officers in their proper places flatten themselves no less, and the field officers, their horses all killed or sent to the rear, crouch beneath the infernal canopy of hissing lead and screaming iron without a thought of personal dignity.

In such circumstances the life of a staff officer of a brigade is distinctly "not a happy one," mainly because of its precarious tenure and the unnerving alternations of emotion to which he is exposed. From a position of that comparative security from which a civilian would ascribe his escape to a "miracle," he may be despatched with an order to some commander of a prone regiment in the front line—a person for the moment inconspicuous and not always easy to find without a deal of search among men somewhat preoccupied, and in a din in which question and answer alike must be imparted in the sign language. It is customary in such cases to duck the head and scuttle away on a keen run, an object of lively interest to some thousands of admiring marksmen. In returning—well, it is not customary to return.

Brayle's practice was different. He would consign his horse to the care of an orderly,—he loved his horse,—and walk quietly away on his perilous errand with never a stoop of the back, his splendid figure, accentuated by his uniform, holding the eye with a strange fascination. We watched him with suspended breath, our hearts in our mouths. On one occasion of this kind, indeed, one of our number, an impetuous stammerer, was so possessed by his emotion that he shouted at me:

"I'll b-b-bet you t-two d-d-dollars they d-drop him b-b-before he g-gets to that d-d-ditch!"

I did not accept the brutal wager; I thought they would.

Let me do justice to a brave man's memory; in all these needless exposures of life there was no visible bravado nor subsequent narration. In the few instances when some of us had ventured to remonstrate, Brayle had smiled pleasantly and made some light reply, which, however, had not encouraged a further pursuit of the subject. Once he said:

"Captain, if ever I come to grief by forgetting your advice, I hope my last moments will be cheered by the sound of your beloved voice breathing into my ear the blessed words, 'I told you so.' "

We laughed at the captain—just why we could probably not have explained—and that afternoon when he was shot to rags from an ambuscade Brayle remained by the body for some time, adjusting the limbs with needless care—there in the middle of a road swept by gusts of grape and canister! It is easy to condemn this kind of thing, and not very difficult to refrain from imitation, but it is impossible not to respect, and Brayle was liked none the less for the weakness which had so heroic an expression. We wished he were not a fool, but he went on that way to the end, sometimes hard hit, but always returning to duty about as good as new.

Of course, it came at last; he who ignores the law of probabilities challenges an adversary that is seldom beaten. It was at Resaca, in Georgia, during the movement that resulted in the taking of Atlanta. In front of our brigade the enemy's line of earthworks ran through open fields along a slight crest. At each end of this open ground we were close up to him in the woods, but the clear ground we could not hope to occupy until night, when darkness would enable us to burrow like moles and throw up earth. At this point our line was a quarter-mile away in the edge of a wood. Roughly, we formed a semicircle, the enemy's fortified line being the chord of the arc.

"Lieutenant, go tell Colonel Ward to work up as close as he can get cover, and not to waste much ammunition in unnecessary firing. You may leave your horse."

When the general gave this direction we were in the fringe of the forest, near the right extremity of the arc. Colonel Ward was at the left. The suggestion to leave the horse obviously enough meant that Brayle was to take the longer line, through the woods and among the men. Indeed, the suggestion was needless; to go by the short route meant absolutely certain failure to deliver the message. Before anybody could interpose, Brayle had cantered lightly into the field and the enemy's works were in crackling conflagration.

"Stop that damned fool!" shouted the general.

A private of the escort, with more ambition than brains, spurred forward to obey, and within ten yards left himself and his horse dead on the field of honor.

Brayle was beyond recall, galloping easily along, parallel to the enemy and less than two hundred yards distant. He was a picture to see! His hat had been blown or shot from his head, and his long, blond hair rose and fell with the motion of his horse. He sat erect in the saddle, holding the reins lightly in his left hand, his right hanging carelessly at his side. An occasional glimpse of his handsome profile as he turned his head one way or the other proved that the interest which he took in what was going on was natural and without affectation.

The picture was intensely dramatic, but in no degree theatrical. Successive scores of rifles spat at him viciously as he came within range, and our own line in the edge of the timber broke out in visible and audible defense. No longer regardful of themselves or their orders, our fellows sprang to their feet, and swarming into the open sent broad sheets of bullets against the blazing crest of the offending works, which poured an answering fire into their unprotected groups with deadly effect. The artillery on both sides joined the battle, punctuating the rattle and roar with deep, earth-shaking explosions and tearing the air with storms of screaming grape, which from the enemy's side splintered the trees and spattered them with blood, and from ours defiled the smoke of his arms with banks and clouds of dust from his parapet.

My attention had been for a moment drawn to the general combat, but now, glancing down the unobscured avenue between these two thunderclouds, I saw Brayle, the cause of the carnage. Invisible now from either side, and equally doomed by friend and foe, he stood in the shot-swept space, motionless, his face toward the enemy. At some little distance lay his horse. I instantly saw what had stopped him.

As topographical engineer I had, early in the day, made a hasty examination of the ground, and now remembered that at that point was a deep and sinuous gully, crossing half the field from the enemy's line, its general course at right angles to it. From where we now were it was invisible, and Brayle had evidently not known about it. Clearly, it was impassable. Its salient angles would have afforded him absolute security if he had chosen to be satisfied with the miracle already wrought in his favor and leapt into it. He could not go forward, he would not turn back; he stood awaiting death. It did not keep him long waiting.

By some mysterious coincidence, almost instantaneously as he fell, the firing ceased, a few desultory shots at long intervals serving rather to accentuate than break the silence. It was as if both sides had suddenly repented of their profitless crime. Four stretcher-bearers of ours, following a sergeant with a white flag, soon afterward moved unmolested into the field, and made straight for Brayle's body. Several Confederate officers and men came out to meet them, and with uncovered heads assisted them to take up their sacred burden. As it was borne toward us we heard beyond the hostile works fifes and a muffled drum—a dirge. A generous enemy honored the fallen brave.

Amongst the dead man's effects was a soiled Russia-leather pocketbook. In the distribution of mementoes of our friend, which the general, as administrator, decreed, this fell to me.

A year after the close of the war, on my way to California, I opened and idly inspected it. Out of an overlooked compartment fell a letter without envelope or address. It was in a woman's handwriting, and began with words of endearment, but no name.

It had the following dateline: "San Francisco, Cal., July 9, 1862." The signature was "Darling," in marks of quotation. Incidentally, in the body of the text, the writer's full name was given—Marian Mendenhall.

The letter showed evidence of cultivation and good breeding, but it was an ordinary love letter, if a love letter can be ordinary. There was not much in it, but there was something. It was this:

"Mr. Winters, whom I shall always hate for it, has been telling that at some battle in Virginia, where he got his hurt, you were seen crouching behind a tree. I think he wants to injure you in my regard, which he knows the story would do if I believed it. I could bear to hear of my soldier lover's death, but not of his cowardice."

These were the words which on that sunny afternoon, in a distant region, had slain a hundred men. Is woman weak?

One evening I called on Miss Mendenhall to return the letter to her. I intended, also, to tell her what she had done—but not that she did it. I found her in a handsome dwelling on Rincon Hill. She was beautiful, well bred—in a word, charming.

"You knew Lieutenant Herman Brayle," I said, rather abruptly. "You know, doubtless, that he fell in battle. Among his effects was found this letter from you. My errand here is to place it in your hands."

She mechanically took the letter, glanced through it with deepening color, and then, looking at me with a smile, said:

"It is very good of you, though I am sure it was hardly worth while." She started suddenly and changed color. "This stain," she said, "is it—surely it is not—"

"Madam," I said, "pardon me, but that is the blood of the truest and bravest heart that ever beat."

She hastily flung the letter on the blazing coals. "Uh! I cannot bear the sight of blood!" she said. "How did he die?"

I had involuntarily risen to rescue that scrap of paper, sacred even to me, and now stood partly behind her. As she asked the question she turned her face about and slightly upward. The light of the burning letter was reflected in her eyes and touched her cheek with a tinge of crimson like the stain upon its page. I had never seen anything so beautiful as this detestable creature.

"He was bitten by a snake," I replied.

THE FOREST OF THE SOUTH

CAROLINE GORDON

I

Major Reilly and Lieutenant Munford stood on the upper gallery of Villa Rose and watched the blowing up of Clifton. They knew the time it was to happen, knew the hour, even the minute. An orderly had ridden out from Natchez that morning with the news. A fort was to be built. Its line would cut through the mansion of Clifton. The house and its garden were to be blown up within the hour.

Major Reilly and Lieutenant Manford were in the major's office at Villa Rose, making our reports—there had been a brush with Confederate cavalry over near Lake St. John the night before. One of Reilly's men had been killed, another wounded. He was glad to be back at this old house with the rest of his squadron safe.

He read the papers the orderly brought. When the soldier had left the room he turned to John Munford. His dark mustache lifted to disclose gleaming teeth.

"Mr. Surget of Clifton would never make a diplomat."

John Munford turned serious blue eyes on his chief. "A diplomat?"

The major leaned back in his chair. "Mr. Surget of Clifton has given a series of dinners for Federal officers. But he has never had the wit to invite the Chief Engineer."

John Munford said, "Ah!" and tried to look knowing. But he still did not understand. "Do you mean, sir, that the Chief Engineer is going to blow the place up because he was not invited to dinner?"

"He is going to blow it clean to hell," the major said. He looked at his watch. "In about three minutes, I should say. Come on, boy, we might as well see the explosion."

They went out through the hall and up the winding stairway into an upper hall and then up another short flight of steps and emerged on a balcony. John Munford had stepped out on this balcony before and always with astonishment. Villa Rose, a squat house built in the old manorial style, stood on a hill high for that part of the country. Below them on the right lay the Mississippi and four or five miles away as the crow flies was the town. Munford's eyes sought and found the tall spire of St. Mary's Cathedral, white in the morning sun, then moved on. There was the river again and, dark against it, masses of green: the famous gardens of Clifton. His eye roved on. More white. That would be the columns of the house or perhaps one of the pavilions. It was hard to tell at this distance just where the house stood.

He summoned up the picture of the house as he had seen it two days before when he had gone in to town with a message from Major Reilly. The Indiana colonel whom he was seeking was an ardent botanist. He had been told to look for him in the gardens of Clifton. He had traversed graveled walks, between box hedges, through scented arbors, and at last had found the colonel standing with Mr. Surget beside a great star-shaped flower bed. There had been an expanse of placid water beyond them with, as he lived, swans floating upon it. Returning through a vine-hung pavilion he had had to put up his hand to brush away masses of bloom. He had made a mental note of the lake, of the swans, of the oleanders for the letter he wrote home each week.

Major Reilly drew in his breath with a whistle. "There she goes!"

A great column of smoke rose and wavered over the trees. A few seconds later they heard the detonation. It jarred the earth beneath them and rattled against the distant woods. Reilly was turning away. John Munford followed him down the stairs. In his mind was a dull wonder. The flowers and the fountains he had seen two days before, the camellias, the Cape jessamines, the late roses, the marble of the grottoes and the pavilions—all those shining, rose-colored things had vanished in that plume of dull smoke!

In the hall below, the two men faced each other a second, then crossed the gallery and went out into the garden. Major Reilly was breathing hard as if to clear his lungs. "A great pity, Munford. As handsome a gentleman's estate as I've seen, here or in the old country." He had found his cigars at last and was offering Munford one. He drew on his cigar and suddenly was himself again. He remembered an engagement in town. "I'll let you finish up those requisitions by yourself, boy. You can manage, eh?"

John said that he could. The major motioned to an orderly to bring his horse, and strode toward the gate. Halfway there he turned. "You'd better look in on the old lady. See if she wants anything."

John said, "Yes, sir," again. After the major had ridden off he stood there a few minutes, the unlit cigar in his hand. There was an acrid smell of smoke in the air but the garden—this garden in which he stood—was just as it had been when he came out on the gallery into the fresh morning air an hour ago. The walks, branching out from the graveled circular drive, straggled off into dense greenery. The greenery was starred here and there with the pink of japonicas and off to the right a low hedge of Cape jessamine was popcorn-white with bloom.

His thoughts went to his Connecticut home. He had had a letter that morning from his sister, Eunice. She reported that the first big snow of the winter had come the night before. She was driving in to Danbury that afternoon, but she would have to go by sleigh, and over the winter road. Snow was drifted five feet deep between their house and the Robinsons'.

A hummingbird was hovering over a vine nearby. Munford watched the tiny wings which never for a second stopped their beating, then raised his eyes. Everywhere about him light fell, on glossy green leaves, on a scarlet flower, on the scarlet of the bird's breast. The fancy came to him that this light might have been filtered through the wings of birds, so shimmering it was, so iridescent. Off toward the stables some men were shouting to each other but their distant voices only served to emphasize the quiet of the garden. He had never known it so quiet before. But the stillness was oppressive and the landscape, he thought suddenly, too bright. This shining air held a menace.

A soldier came down the steps and made off toward the stables. Munford, recalled to his duty, followed the man around to the back of the house. A wide gallery ran the length of the ell. At the end of the ell up a short flight of steps there was a little room. It had been the overseer's room, originally. Now Mrs. Mazereau and her daughter, the owners of the house, lived in it.

In the shadow of one of the columns a soldier sat in a low, split-bottomed chair picking a chicken. Munford paused beside him a second to watch how deftly he was pulling the pinfeathers out from the wings. A good forager, Bill Morehouse. A good man at everything. Munford wished that Morehouse had the job of looking after the old lady instead of himself.

He went up the short flight of steps and knocked at the door. There was the sound of footsteps. The door opened a little way. He put the palm of his hand against it and pushed. It opened a little wider. He stepped inside the room. The blinds were drawn and the air was oppressive with stale odors. A young woman confronted him. She stood erect at first, then shrank a little back. Her hands came up in front of her face. She did not speak.

Impatience and embarrassment made his voice brusque. He said: "It is Lieutenant Munford, Miss Mazereau. Major Reilly's compliments. He wants to known how your mother is this morning."

The girl, still moving backwards, let her hands drop to her sides. "She didn't sleep," she said in a low voice.

He glanced toward the closed blinds. "Perhaps if you had more light . . ."

She halted at that. "I had the blinds open when we first got up but she saw some men going by. . . ." Suddenly she was coming toward him. He could not be sure in that half light but he thought that there was a smile on her face. "She thinks she's a girl," she said. "And I'm another girl. We're on our way to her old home . . . to the Green Springs, in Virginia. . . ." Damn it, she was laughing! Laughing at her old mother for being crazy. He would have to tell Reilly that.

A harsh voice came from the bed in the corner. "Eugénie!"

"Yes, Mama!"

The old woman was out of the bed and was coming toward them. A fierce, incredibly fat white cockatoo. The quilt from the bed was half hanging from her shoulders. She wore a nightgown which he, John Munford, had bought for her in a shop in Natchez-under-the-Hill. Clutching the quilt about her as if it had been a bed gown, she fixed him with her bloodshot blue eyes. "Young man, where are you going?"

Munford bowed his fair head. He said patiently, "I wasn't going anywhere this morning, ma'am. Major Reilly has gone to town and has left me in command."

She said, *"Major!"* She closed her eyes, pursed her lips. *"Soldiers,"* she whispered. She leaned forward, so close that her foul breath fanned his check. She went on whispering. "Two women in distress. . . . Trying to find our way home. . . . I knew this country well once

88

but it has changed. . . . So many roads . . . and the people . . ." Her voice sank lower. Her lower lip was wry with cunning. "I will give you a barrel of flour if you will conduct us to our home. It is in the Green Springs. . . ."

"We haven't any barrel of flour, Mama!"

Munford felt the girl's eyes upon him. He bowed and said, "I am sorry, ma'am, but I don't know the country. I can't conduct you to your home." He went out, shutting the door behind him.

As he reached the foot of the stairs a cur pup, the soldiers' pet, came scampering toward him, then fell on her back with her habitual gesture of outstretched paws. He thrust out his toe to poke her gently in the belly and then withdrew his foot, frowning. "Get up!" he said harshly.

He walked the length of the gallery and entered the wide front hall. At the far end the open door disclosed vistas of green. Patches of quivering light fell on the broad boards. There was one place where the oak was discolored in a great splotch. Munford, as he approached it, slowed his steps. Always when he passed this spot he had to stop and look down. Colonel Mazereau's blood, gushing from his cloven chest, had made that dark, greasy-looking place there by the newel post.

Munford's thoughts went to that night. He had had the story from Major Reilly, who in turn had had it from Eugénie Mazereau. Reilly, when he told it to Munford, had used what must have been the girl's words.

"The Negroes all ran away. Then the soldiers came. Mama said not to worry. She talked to the captain and she said he was a gentleman. But he rode off somewhere. He left three or four soldiers. There was one kept walking through the house. He came and looked in the library where we were. Mama said not to notice. We worked on our embroidery.

"Then we heard somebody step up on the porch, Mama said, 'Eugénie, it's your father.'

"I went to the door. I could see the soldier hiding there by the post and I could see Papa. He had on a long cloak and he was all splashed with mud. He stood there and he kept calling: 'Josephine! Eugénie! Josephine!'

"I went back into the room. I said, 'Mama, Papa is there and he keeps calling.'

"She went to the door. She said, 'Arsène, for God's sake . . . Arsène,' she said, 'I beg of you. For God's sake, go away!'

"He didn't listen. He started toward her. He got as far as the post. The soldier came up from behind. He had the axe in his hand." Major Reilly, telling the story, would put his hand on his breast. "It was like felling an ox. He went back, very slow, on his heels. Then he was standing straight and then he fell over. The blood was on the floor even before he fell."

John Munford had wanted to know what the women did then.

Colonel Mazereau, the major reported, had lived for several hours, until nearly sundown. "The thing that worried the girl most was that her mother kept trying to get the cloth out of the wound. The cloth of his uniform, Munford, was driven down into his breastbone and he was spouting blood like a whale. Unconscious, of course, from the moment of the blow. Finally, toward sundown, they were convinced that he was dead. The old lady was all for getting him buried before the soldiers came back. She made the girl go out and dig the grave. The girl said she dug over the garden, but the ground was too hard. At last she persuaded the old lady to bury him temporarily under a pile of rotting leaves. Just as they finished Slocomb's men came back. The women ran and hid in the overseer's room and stayed there till those damned Dutchmen set the house on fire.

"I found them wandering around in the yard after the fire was put out and Slocomb's men had gone. The old lady was perfectly quiet then. It was the girl that was hard to handle. She kept coming up to me and saying they wouldn't do any harm and when I said I didn't expect them to she kept thanking me. I said, 'My God, madam, the exigencies of war have made it necessary for me to commandeer your house but you needn't be grateful to me. . . .' A queer girl, Munford. I wonder what she'd be like in other circumstances."

It was a subject that Major Reilly often speculated on: the character and personality of Miss Eugénie Mazereau. "In my opinion she's loonier than the old lady." Or "She's still scared out of her wits. You ought to do something about that, Munford. Take her for a buggy ride. Convince her we're not ogres."

John Munford, following the major's suggestion, had invited Miss Mazereau to walk with him in the garden and had even taken her driving several times in a trap that had been found in the stables. She came with him whenever he invited her, wearing always the same black dress and a voluminous black shawl that must have been her mother's. She never wore a bonnet. She had been bareheaded when she escaped from the house.

She talked to him as they drove along the river road. "Yes, Lieutenant Munford, the weather has been delightful for the past week . . . You say your home is in Connecticut . . . No, I have never been farther north than Memphis . . ."

Once he halted his horse before a gate set in a tall hedge. He motioned with his whip. "All those people who lived here. What has become of them?"

"They have all gone away, Lieutenant Munford."

But as they drove on she had turned to look back at the gate. "The Macrae place," she said. "That is the Macrae place." Her tone struck Munford as strange. It was the tone that might have been used by a traveler returning to his old haunts after years of absence.

He went now through the hall and turned right, into the great room that was used as an office for the cavalry squadron. It was barely furnished: two field desks, six or seven pine chairs, and an old sofa in one corner where Major Reilly sometimes napped. The major had a grudge against the officer whom he had relieved. Once, walking in the garden with Munford, Reilly had kicked at the charred pieces of a mahogany dining table. "Those damned Dutchmen! They might at least have left that for the officers to eat on."

Young Slater was pushing a sheaf of requisition blanks toward Munford. He took them and began signing them mechanically. They worked for two hours. At twelve o'clock Munford put his pen down and went out on the gallery. Young Slater stood with him for a few minutes, then went back into the house. Munford began pacing up and down the gallery. Once he stopped to stare into the windows that ran on each side of the doorway. The glass was full of imperfections; some of the whorls had opalescent tints. When he was a child he used to press his nose against just such cloudy panes of glass—in his grandfather's house at Danbury. A white house with a steep, gabled roof, twin "bride" trees—elms—on each side of the stoop. He could see it all clearly but it seemed unreal, like something he had seen in a picture rather than something he remembered. He fell to pacing again and as he went was conscious of greenery pressing in there beyond the graveled walks, of sunshine on the gravel, of pink and white blossoms. And yet it was a hushed landscape. Moving about these grounds he had sometimes the feeling that he imagined a man might have on a desert island. Here in this smiling land he was lonely. It came to him that there was one person lonelier than he. That girl in the little back room. There was not, he supposed, anybody in the world lonelier than she. Colonel Mazereau, before he was killed, had quarreled with all his relations, Reilly said. The girl's mother, her companion in misfortune, had deserted her to wander in memory along the road that led to the Green Springs in Virginia. Yes, she was quite alone, that girl.

The call for mess sounded. Young Slater spoke to him from the doorway. He told the boy that he was coming, but before he went into the mess hall he turned back into the office. Sitting down at his desk, he drew a sheet of paper toward him and wrote a note. It presented Lieutenant Munford's compliments to Miss Mazereau and inquired if she would drive with him that afternoon.

II

At three o'clock Lieutenant Munford and Miss Mazereau were driving north along the river road. She sat with her hands folded, one over the other, in her lap. She was wearing a pair of gloves, lace gloves or rather mitts, for they left the tips of her fingers bare. Munford wondered where in the world she had got them. Some old trunk, probably, that had escaped Slocomb's men.

He stared ahead of him. The bit of road visible between the horse's forward-picked ears was not unlike a stretch of road on the way to Gaylordsville with the dark trees and that old rail fence riding against the skyline. He had driven young ladies along that road often enough—in sleighs at this time of year. That New Year's party at the Robinsons'. He had escorted Jane Scoville, and Sam Dillon and Roberta Jennings had been in the back seat. He was not in love with Jane Scoville now but he would like to have her beside him with her furs and her perfume and her chatter. Well, he was on pleasure bent this afternoon, with a pretty girl beside him. He had always flattered himself that he could keep a pretty girl entertained, but how could you make yourself agreeable to a girl when you were occupying the house that by rights should have been hers?

By rights? His thoughts went, as they often did these days, to the conflict in which he was engaged. Major Reilly said that he himself was not opposed to slavery. Certain types of civilization, he said, were always founded on slavery, and he had cited ancient Athens and God knows what other countries—the major was a graduate of the University of Dublin. Well, he, John Munford, was not a highly educated man. But he knew right from wrong. He would do it all over again, to strike the shackles from the wrists of slaves. And yet it was all so different from what he had pictured.

The girl was turning toward him. Her eyes—unusually large, luminous eyes—were the color of the chestnuts that used to fall from the great tree in his grandfather's yard. The lids were heavy, so heavy that they dimmed the brilliance of her glance. And the lids themselves had a peculiar pallor. Wax-white, like the petals of the magnolia blossom. When he had first come into this country he had gathered one of those creamy blossoms only to see it turn brown in his grasp. She was saying something about a letter. ". . . It may be we can leave."

He said, "*Leave* Villa Rose?"

She nodded, still with those large strange-colored eyes fixed on his. "My cousin in Kentucky says we can come there."

He said, "I should not think you would want to go to Kentucky, Miss Mazereau. They are fighting there too."

She did not answer. As they drove on he considered what she had said. If he or Major Reilly went away—and they might be ordered away at any time—what would become of this girl and her mother? He turned to her abruptly. "Perhaps you would be better advised to go to Kentucky—if you can get through the lines."

She looked up at him, then suddenly shrank back as, he thought savagely, she might have done if he had menaced her with the whip he held in his hand. "I don't want to go where they're fighting."

He compressed his lips, feeling the angry blood surge to his forehead. "I don't know where you'll go then," he said curtly.

She did not answer.

They were at the top of a little rise, descending toward a stream. The horse's hooves splashed little drops of water in their faces as they crossed it. And now they were on a rise again. He looked at the pines crowding close on each side of the road and wondered if they would come to any hilltop which would command a view. "What is the name of that stream we have just crossed?" he asked.

"Sand Creek," she said.

He checked the horse. Before them was the tall hedge and the gate where they had paused the other day. She was looking about her with more animation than he had ever seen her display. On an impulse he pulled the horse up short and motioned with his whip at the gate. "Shall we go in there?"

"Yes," she said.

He got down and opened the gate; then, as she did not pick up the reins from where he had hung them over the dashboard, he led the horse through. He closed the gate and went up to the trap. "Shall we hitch the horse and walk for a little?"

"Yes," she said.

He assisted her down, then turned the trap about and hitched the horse to one of the bars of the gate. They started up the avenue. It was broader than the one at Villa Rose and lined on each side with live oaks. At the end of the avenue a square gray structure with a dilapidated double gallery was visible through the drooping wreaths of Spanish moss. They paused beside the carriage block to look up at it.

"A dreary place," Munford said.

She did not say anything.

"What is the name of the family that lived here?"

"Macrae," she said dreamily. Suddenly she took a few steps away from him, then looked back over her shoulder. "There is a fountain over here in the shrubbery," she said.

He followed her silently between the unclipped hedges into an abandoned garden. Once she had to stand aside while he dragged away a great, fallen branch. Suddenly the path widened and they emerged into what had once been a circle of flower beds. In the center was a fountain, a great basin, and standing beside it the marble figure of a woman. The woman was bending a little forward. Water from the pitcher which she carried had once run into the basin but no water had run there for a long time now. The basin was green with moss up to its rim.

The girl had walked over and was standing beside the fountain in much the same attitude as that of the marble figure. He studied the pale, down-bent face, wondering wherein lay its attraction. For it had come to that. She was the most attractive woman he had ever seen. The conviction had been growing on him for months. He remembered now his first sight of her, the day after he had been transferred to Reilly's squadron. A small figure in black, hurrying around the corner of the house—she had been gathering chips and was carrying them in her upturned skirt. He had thought that she must be the wife of one of the soldiers or perhaps a camp follower—Reilly was lenient with them. Then he had seen slim ankles swinging out from under a ragged petticoat and the thought had come to him that she might be a lady. A lady! He had not seen a woman—a respectable woman—in weeks. He hurried on and caught up with her. She had looked up at him just as she had looked at him a moment ago, but he had insisted on gathering some more wood for her and had carried it up to the little room. He had followed her at first because he had been attracted by the sight of a woman. After he caught up with her he was repelled by her manner—the slight favor he proposed doing her did not deserve such effusive thanks. He had gone on, however, finding the wood for her, showing her all the courtesy he would have shown any respectable woman. He might never have thought of her again if Reilly had not told him her story that night.

He had seen her often since, and though he felt that he understood her better he still found her manner strange. He thought of another girl, a girl he had seen for one brief evening only, in Tennessee. When she was asked to play the piano for some Federal officers she had asked to be excused for a moment and had returned to the parlor with an axe. She had hurled it high above her head and had brought it down on the keyboard, saying she would make matchwood of the instrument before it should play a tune for despised "Yankees." The word "Yankee" was never on Eugénie Mazereau's lips. She seemed to have no concern for the Confederate cause, and yet, he thought, she might be patriotic, and proud too, in other circumstances. . . .

She had put out her hand and with the tip of her index finger was tracking the rim of the basin. Her head, with its smoothly banded black hair, was still down-bent. There was a faint, mysterious smile on her lips.

Munford found this smile maddening. He took two steps and was beside her. "Why are you doing that?"

She looked up. Her eyes were blue! He had thought them brown. That was because of the stain of light brown about the iris but the eye itself was blue. Blue, that is, if you stood there and looked into her eyes but if you stepped back a few paces you would say, "This girl's eyes are brown, pale brown," and you would say, too, "She looks at me but she never sees me." Why should an eye look out and not see? Does it look within? Has it seen something it cannot look away from?

She had not spoken. He laid his finger on that part of the marble her finger had touched.

She smiled. "The fountain? You mean why did I touch the fountain?"

He said hoarsely, "Miss Mazereau . . . Eugénie . . . you must know my sentiments."

She gazed at him, still smiling. He could not tell whether she had heard what he said.

A sudden thought turned him scarlet. He took a turn around the fountain and came back. He bowed. "I have the honor to ask for your hand in marriage."

She said, "My hand!" and moved a little away so that a tuft of long grass she had been standing on sprang up between them.

"I would have spoken to your mother," he said stiffly, "if circumstances had been different."

"No," she whispered. "Don't speak to my mother."

"I understand that," he said. "The point is . . . will you marry me? I . . . Is the prospect agreeable to you, Miss Mazereau?"

"Agreeable?" she said.

He stammered, "Eugénie. *Look* at me!"

She put on a hand and fearfully touched his face. He seized her. He kissed her lips, her brow, her throat, her lips again. "I will send you home," he whispered. "To my people. To Connecticut."

She drew back at that. "Connecticut? Is it a long way?"

"Yes," he said impatiently, and went on to tell her that his mother would welcome her as a daughter. His sister, Eunice, would be a sister to her, for there was a special bond of affection between him and his sister. In place of the family she had lost she should have his family. He swore that he would make her so happy that she would forget everything that had happened.

She did not say anything, only put up her hand again and touched his check. They went over and sat down on a bench near the fountain. Munford's arm was about her waist. She allowed her head to rest on his shoulder. All around them was a tangle of green but they could see rising about the hedge of a slanting roof, a red chimney.

"What is that?" he asked.

"The old schoolhouse."

"Did you go to school there?"

"Yes, with the Macrae children."

He had been thinking that very soon, in a few days at most, he would have to send her North. Yes, three days at most, and he did not know how she had looked as a child, what nickname she had had, what paths she had taken when she came here to school. He was even curious about the Macraes, the departed owners of this place. "How many children were there?" he asked.

"Mary and Ellen. And there was Frank."

Some impulse made him repeat the name he was never afterwards to forget. "Frank . . . ?"

She tilted her head away from his caressing hand. The strange eyes gleamed under the heavy lids. "Frank . . . He was always playing jokes. He put Cousin Maria's crinoline on that statue there and he put a bonnet on it and painted its face with pokeberry juice and put a prayer book in its hand. He said she was going to church."

He laughed. "Where is Frank now?"

"He joined the army. . . ."

The shadows were getting longer. He roused himself and said that they must go back. They walked slowly along the path past the fountain. Munford smiled, seeing a mischievous boy coming through the hedge, his arms heaped with women's wear. The boy's eyes were gray and lively. He was laughing as he went up to the statue. Suddenly Munford was jealous of that boy who had played here in this garden. He stopped and, taking Eugénie's face between his hands, looked deep into her eyes before he kissed her.

"Say you love me."

"I love you," she said.

III

Major Reilly was silent when Munford told him of his engagement. Finally he shook his head. "You are a rash man. You seem to forget that Miss Mazereau's father was killed here in this hall. Her brothers, if she has any, certainly many of her cousins, are in the Confederate service."

"I shall be able to answer for my wife's loyalty," Munford said stiffly.

The major's brown face broke up into crisscross lines as it did when he laughed, and yet he wasn't laughing. "I wasn't thinking of her loyalty," he said.

Munford left the room. Later that night, lying on his cot in the officers' quarters, he thought of the expression that had been on Reilly's face. Yet Reilly, on the whole, had been as sympathetic, as considerate as a man could be. Munford and Eugénie Mazereau were to be married in Reilly's office tomorrow afternoon at four o'clock—Reilly had already sent a message to the chaplain. It would be all right for Eugénie to stay at Villa Rose a few days, Reilly said, but it could be only a few days. She and her mother ought to be on their way north as soon as the trip could be arranged for. Munford wondered what his mother and sister would think when they were confronted with the old woman and had to listen to her ravings. Would it not perhaps be better to let the two women stay in the South; if not at Villa Rose, at some safe quarters nearby?

His head felt hot. There was little air in the room. He got up and went to the open window. There was a full moon over the garden. In its light every leaf, every twig stood out as bright as if in noonday light. "Too bright, too light," he thought irritably. He stayed at the window long enough to smoke a cigar, then went back to bed and finally slept.

Major Reilly rode off to town early the next morning and Munford was again left in command. He was engaged with Ralph Slater in making out company reports when the guard at the door suddenly advanced into the room and told him that Miss Mazereau wanted to see him on business.

He told young Slater he would be gone for a little while and went, half smiling at the word "business," through the hall and out onto the back gallery. Eugénie Mazereau was waiting for him there. She had her black shawl drawn close about her shoulders. Her face was pale. Her eyes had a curious, intent look.

She came up to him, whispering, "Could you come with me a minute?"

He had given a cautious glance over his shoulder and, seeing that no one was in sight, was about to lean over to kiss her when something in her expression checked him. "Yes," he said quietly, and followed her down the steps and out through the yard. They passed through a side gate and took a path through the woods. They had progressed some distance along it before Munford saw the gray outline of a house through the trees and realized that this was a shortcut to the Macrae place.

The girl walked on before him in silence. And yet when they had stopped there in the woods a moment ago she had yielded herself to his embraces more freely than at any time yesterday. She had even put her arm up about his neck to draw his head down to hers. He had thought when they first started out that she had changed her mind about their engagement and was bringing him back to the same place they had visited yesterday to tell him she would not marry him. He smiled. If that was the case he would be able to persuade her to change her mind back to what it had been yesterday. They were entering the ground by a side entrance. She did not go toward the garden but walked instead toward the house. On the gallery she paused a moment, then slipped quietly inside the half-open door, motioning to him to follow her. He hesitated a second. He was armed but he was only one man. But he put the thought of ambush away from him and walked resolutely after her.

The hall smelled musty. The blinds at both ends were drawn. What light there was came from a window high on the landing. Munford's eyes went to this window and then to the stairs below. The steps were thick with dust. He stiffened suddenly as he saw places where that dust had been disturbed, by boot soles. At the same moment there was the sound of steps above him. A face appeared over the railing.

Munford drew back, his hand on his revolver. But the girl was already starting up the steps. She looked back at him over her shoulder. "You can come," she said, "he's alone."

Munford drew his revolver. He pushed past her and went up, taking the stairs two at a time. The best way, he told himself mechanically. To rush the man was the only chance now. He came to the landing, made the turn, and stopped dead still. A man in a Federal uniform stood at the head of the stairs.

Eugénie had come up behind him. She stretched out her hand. "Lieutenant Munford, this is my cousin, Captain Macrae," she said, calmly, as if she were making an introduction in a drawing room.

Frank Macrae stood on the top step, staring down at them. He looked exactly as Munford had pictured him. Blond, with a handsome, well-fleshed face, made red by exposure to wind and weather, an aquiline nose, steady gray eyes set under fair brows.

He did not seem to see Munford. He was staring at the girl.

"Eugénie," he said in a low voice, "have you gone crazy?"

Her laugh rang out. "It's Mama . . . She thinks she's a girl and she thinks she's back in the Green Springs. . . . Ever since Papa was killed."

Munford said stiffly, "I regret to say that Mrs. Mazereau suffers from hallucinations . . ."

Eugénie interrupted him. "He came in the hall and a soldier killed him, with an axe." She looked at her cousin. "The blood was all over everything, Frank."

Frank Macrae, as if suddenly recollecting himself, took a step backwards. He looked at Munford, then stood aside while the other two ascended the stairs. Munford, his revolver cocked, went up to Macrae, laid his hand on his arm. "Captain Macrae, you are my prisoner," he said sternly. He paused a moment, then added, "It is unfortunate that you are in Federal uniform."

Frank Macrae laughed. "It is indeed unfortunate," he said. But he did not start down the stairs. Instead he turned into one of the great dim rooms opening off the upper hall. Munford, a little bewildered, followed him. The girl came too. She advanced toward her cousin but he motioned her back. "Go over there and stand by the window, Eugénie," he said curtly.

She went obediently and stood in the place he had indicated. The two men confronted each other. Macrae was very pale and his brows were drawn. He had been staring at the girl and now he still kept glancing at her though he had turned to Munford. Absent-mindedly, in the manner of a man making conversation, he asked Munford some questions about recent movements of the Federal squadron. Munford answered them. But he was conscious that time was passing. Perhaps he was in a trap. The Confederate officer might be trying to delay him until help came. He was about to speak when Macrae gave a long sigh.

"Well, we had better get on with it . . . Lieutenant, before your court meets there is a matter I must attend to."

Munford bowed. "I am at your service, Captain."

"Will you secure for me a license and the services of a chaplain? I want to go through a marriage ceremony with my cousin. I . . . there is certain property that will then be automatically at her disposal!"

Munford lifted his fair head haughtily. "That is impossible, Captain. Your cousin has promised to marry me."

Macrae stared. "You are engaged to marry my cousin?"

Munford bowed again.

There was a long silence. The girl laughed suddenly, left the window, and started toward the two men. Macrae lifted his hand, gently, in the gesture he might have used to a child or a puppy.

"Stay where you are, Eugénie." He turned to Munford. "Lieutenant Munford, I know you by reputation. I believe you to be a man of honor. I do not envy you the privilege of marrying my cousin. . . . Do you fully understand the responsibilities you assume?"

The two men gazed at each other. Macrae's eyes were gray and hard as steel. It came to Munford that in a few hours this man would be dead, hanged as a spy. He looked away, to where the girl was standing beside the open window. Her strange, incurious eyes were fixed upon him, Munford. There was a smile on her lips. It was the smile that had so wrought upon him in the garden. It was not mysterious now. He averted his gaze. The window frame was dark and gauzy with cobwebs that beyond stretched a green meadow. Light played everywhere upon it, the same luminous, quivering light that yesterday at this hour had struck through the leaves at Villa Rose.

He withdrew his eyes from the scene. When he lifted them it was to meet the prisoner's hard, victorious glance.

"Yes," he said dully, "I understand."

HOMEMADE YANKEES

ROBERT MORGAN

How come I was so determined to put in the pumplogs and lead water all the way from the spring on the hill across the pasture to the house was the night of the bushwhackers. Josie and me was caught inside with just a little bit of water in a bucket and that was on the back porch. Josie was thirteen, and I was going on fifteen myself. We was doing for ourselves after Pa left for the army. A boy that's fourteen can do whatever he has to. And I had to look after the place as well as Josie. The day he left Pa said, "Now you look after things same as I would, and I'll be back to see how you done." And then he lit out across the mountains to Tennessee.

Why toward Tennessee? 'Cause that's where the Union army was, over there in Kentucky and Tennessee. He'd heard it was around the Cumberland Gap. He didn't hold with the rebellion and he headed out soon as he knowed he'd be drafted. Nearly every family around here was split, some in one army and some in the other. Truth is almost nobody wanted to join the rebellion, but they was scared not to go, once the draft started.

The night the bushwhackers come was up in November. I had gathered in all the corn and put taters and pumpkins in the hole under leaves. We had what you'd call a harvest moon. It was the kind of weather that would have been perfect for coon hunting back in peaceful times. Not too cold, but with a needle of frost in the air. Might be a skim of ice in the morning on water in a bucket. I fed the stock and come in before dark where Josie was fixing hoecakes and baking sweet taters. I'd learned her to do some of the cooking. I was wishing I had some coffee, but coffee was all gone from the moun-

102

tains by then. You could pay ten dollars a pound for coffee over in Asheville, but most folks parched bran and made a kind of brew.

Just before I come in and closed the door I heard men talking down the valley, and the sound of horses. It was just enough light to see the ridge tops, and the valleys was all in shadow. But I thought I could see the riders crossing the branch just beyond the chinquapin thicket. They was riding fast and talking loud, like they didn't need to worry about being seen. They must have been eight or ten at least.

"Close the door, you're making the fireplace smoke," Josie said.

I stood there looking and listening to see which way they went. I thought they climbed on up the hill toward Flat Rock.

"Close the door," Josie hollered at me. She never did have a bad temper, like Ma had.

"Shhhh," I said. "Them's bushwhackers riding up Chinquapin Hill."

She turned around quick to see if I was scaring her. But I closed the door and dropped down the latch bar. "I think they went on toward Flat Rock," I said. "They're after richer pickings than what little stuff we've got." Josie dropped a hoecake and I near burned my hand to pick it up and brush the ashes off.

All that third year of the war we kept hearing about the outliers. They was several gangs of them, holed up in caves and camps in the high mountains, and in the Dark Corner of South Carolina. They was deserters from both armies we heard, though most was from the Union side it was said. They was draft dodgers and deserters that had become regular outlaws and blackguards. And some was just ordinary local trash that took advantage of the war to steal from neighbors, to raid any houseplace and take what they wanted.

But nobody had been able to stop the bushwhacking. The Home Guard was just a few old men and boys too young to fight. Mostly all they was good for was scaring a few deserters, men that had come home to put in a crop for their families and to get fed up a little after starving in the Confederate army. They wasn't no way the Home Guard could stop the gangs that rode wherever they wanted to and hit whoever they wanted to, and took whatever they wanted. They stole cows and horses. They broke into smokehouses and took whatever meat they was. They stole chickens and guineas, lead and powder, and whatever guns they found.

Scarcest things in those days besides coffee was salt and lead, and they took whatever they could find. Rumor was they abused the women they caught too, though nobody ever talked much about that to me. I was just fourteen, and when people whispered about the bushwhackers they implied more than they would say. That's why Josie was so shook when I mentioned the men on horses. She had heard they done things to women.

After I latched the front door I went to secure the back one too. If we was lucky the bushwhackers would continue on to Flat Rock and we wouldn't see then no more. Pa's gun was up on the rack but they wasn't more than a dust of powder in the house, and I had only two shots left in the bag. I was hoping to save them for killing a deer at Christmas time. But the gun was already loaded.

"We ain't got no water in here," Josie said.

"They's some on the back porch," I said. I was going to unbolt the back door and get the bucket when a horse whinnied up on the hill. And then I heard the men talking. They was coming by the spring down the pasture hill. Instead of going on to Flat Rock they must have circled back.

"Hey you all," somebody hollered. "You got any supper ready?"

I blowed out the lamp on the table and seen the terror on Josie's face in the firelight. I knowed I had to act growed-up and sure of what I was doing. "Only thing we ain't got inside is water," I said. And for some reason I suddenly felt thirsty.

"Anybody home?" the man hollered again.

Ever since Pa had built the house he meant to bring water closer. The spring was almost a quarter of a mile around the pasture hill, in a holler of hemlocks. It was the best spring in this end of the county, a yard across and fed by at least three outlets. The old cabin built by my grandpa when he come to these parts stood just on the other side where the white pines is now.

But Pa had found the perfect place for his house further down toward the creek. He said he picked the house place one day when he was coming back from Greenville after selling furs. When he seen the sun breaking through the clouds it lighted up this spot of ground.

Neighbors told him he could dig a well; but he didn't want a well. He wanted to drink from the family spring, which had the best water he'd ever tasted, and he carried drinking water all the way across the pasture, but took milk and butter to the branch to stay cold. Water for washing he carried from the branch down here too. A well, he said, is liable to get typhoid in it. And maybe he was afraid a well would get tainted from all the pasture land above it. All our folks had had springs, and he'd heard stories about wells struck by lightning, and babies falling into wells, and men poisoned by gas while digging wells. Wells was something flatlanders had, and people in town.

I'd heard of pumplogs, but never seen them made nor used. I just knowed you could holler out logs and stick them together like pipes, but I didn't begin to study on them till after the war was over. I had to think and think about what I was going to do.

I was in Greenville, where I had took a wagonload of hams and wild honey, and after I sold my load, peddling door to door, I went up to the big Miller's store to do my trading. I got some cloth for Josie and a bag of coffee, needles and gunpowder. I was thinking about buying a new knife when I seen this long shiny auger. It looked like it was three feet long and two inches wide.

"What is that thing for?" I asked the clerk.

"That's for boring pumplogs," he said. And you know how it is when something drops into place, something you've been studying on and wondering about just comes out into the open and you see it clear, and you know what you're going to do.

"Must be short logs," I said. "Just three feet long."

"Six foot logs," the clerk said. "You bore from both ends."

That showed me how much I had to learn. I always liked making things, working with wood or stone, or even metal. But I seen instantly how much work it would take, how much care and study, to bring water to the house across the pasture. I seen it would take most of the winter. I had planned to split rails and clear more new ground that year, but that time would have to be give to the pipelogs.

After I traded for all we had to have I had just enough left over for the big bit. It was a yard long and shiny as a doctor's tool. It come to a point in a silver screw, and it was heavy.

"Do you have a brace?" the clerk said.

"Sure I've got a brace."

"It might not be big enough to fit this auger," he said. "You may need one with a bigger chuck." And he showed me a regular brace and how the neck of the big auger wouldn't fit in it, and then a heavy brace with a chuck the size of a hen's egg that swallowed the neck of the big drill and clamped tight when you screwed it down.

Well I had spent my money. The three dollars for the bit was the last I had and I didn't have nothing else to trade. I stood around trying to think what to do. Other customers was waiting and I was embarrassed in that big store to be out of money and needing something else. I looked out the window, and at the clerk, and then at the big brace. And I knowed I had to get out of there. I grabbed my packages and the big auger. "I'll be back," I said to the clerk over my shoulder.

All the way back to the mountains I burned with embarrassment. I never did feel easy in stores, and I never did like to talk about money. And to be caught without enough money was like being seen naked. In the time after the war they wasn't no money to be found. Most trading was by barter, paying in kind, paying in labor. All the way back to the mountains I made up my mind what I was going to do.

"What's that thing for?" Josie said when she seen the big shiny auger. But I didn't tell her. I didn't open my packages. I unhitched the horse and took it to the pasture and then I got my extra number-two trap and carried it down to the branch. I knowed where they was a mink using and I set the trap in the water at the bottom of a little slide, where the mink would drown before it could gnaw off its foot in the trap. I reset all my other traps up and down the branch. Before Christmas I had five mink pelts, and I took them down to Greenville and traded for the brace. I wanted to show that clerk I had the money. I slapped the silver dollars down on the counter and I said "Keep the change," when I took the brace from his hand.

"Could you spare a hot biscuit?" the man called in front of the house. The bushwhackers was circling on their horses. One knocked on the chicken coop and I could hear the pullets start to fuss. If chickens get riled up after dark it's hard to quiet them down. And they won't lay eggs next day neither.

"They's somebody in there," the man said. "I can see smoke from the chimney."

"Hell I can see light through the cracks," another man said.

"I don't think they're going to invite us in," a third voice said.

"People has forgot their manners," the first man said. "They's no Southern hospitality anymore."

"Open up, Reb," the second voice said.

I got the gun from the rack and made sure it was loaded. I had exactly enough powder and shot for two more loads. If I used them up I wouldn't have nothing to kill game that winter. They wasn't nowhere to get lead this side of Greenville even if you had money.

Josie had froze with fear. She stood by the fire and looked at me to do something. I don't think it was the surprise of the bushwhackers showing up as much as it was the tales she had heard that scared her. It was like we had been dreading this, half expecting it, ever since Pa left for Tennessee and Kentucky. And where a fear has been built up that way the ground has been prepared for pure terror.

Josie had not really got over Ma's death before the war broke out. I knowed it was hard on a young girl to lose her mama, and to have the housework fall on her at an early age. A girl needs her mama to show her things and to talk to. And when she's about to become a woman it's hard to learn about female things with just a man around the house.

She hadn't no more than got over the shock of Ma's death and the strain of growing to a woman, than the war come and Pa was talking of joining.

"You ain't gonna leave us?" Josie said, her face white as she set at the table.

"I ain't gonna be drafted to fight my own government," Pa said. His face was burned by cold wind from where he'd been up on the ridge clearing new ground.

"They're calling them that join the Union 'homemade Yankees,' " I said. I knowed I couldn't go to school no more if Pa joined the Union. And we couldn't go to church neither.

"That's what I guess I am," Pa said. "A homemade Yankee."

But Josie didn't say nothing else. That was the biggest sign of how scared she was when Pa took his sack of clothes and rations and lit out over the mountains to Tennessee.

"They can't get in," I said to Josie, "But they may try to smoke us out."

"You mean by setting fire to the house?"

"No, by stuffing the chimney. That's why we've got to put the fire out."

It was a cold night to do without a fire, but I seen right quick they could stop the chimney with sacks or a couple of boards and smoke us out in a few minutes. Problem was we didn't have any water to throw on the fire. And we had a good blaze going, of oak and chestnut wood, to cook supper and drive away the chill, and it was going to keep burning for another half hour. They wasn't nothing to smother it with that wouldn't catch fire itself. I looked at what we had, a half pitcher of buttermilk, a jug of whiskey on the medicine shelf, a jug of vinegar that had a mother in it. They was a chamber pot but it didn't have no pee in it. Josie had emptied the pot and washed it out that morning.

The whiskey would feed the fire, not put it out. And I didn't know what the vinegar would do. I hated to waste buttermilk, and knowed split milk would stink awful in a few hours. I tried to think if they was some way I could take the sticks out of the fire and put them out one by one, maybe by pushing their ends in the ashes. But the logs had burned down too far to catch hold of. We didn't have no dirt to throw on the flames, for all our flowerpots was on the porch.

I thought maybe it was best to let the fire burn, till I looked at Josie's face again. Sweat stood out on her forehead, and her cheeks was white as a linen handkerchief. Something banged on the roof, and I wondered if somebody was climbing up there. But it was just a rock, for next I heard it rolling on the cedar shingles.

"Ain't you folks friendly," a man called. "Having supper and not inviting us in."

"One good turn deserves another," a second voice said.

"Trick or treat," a young voice said.

I grabbed the pitcher of buttermilk and dashed about half of it on the fire. The flames hissed and sputtered in the middle, turning to thick blue smoke. Little flames blazed up in separate places, and I splashed more milk on them. Another fire started from under a chestnut log and I poured the rest of the milk on it.

It was completely dark in the house. I couldn't even see Josie, or the table where I'd picked up the pitcher. The dark swirled and crowded in on me. "Where are you?" I said to Josie.

"Here," she said. I felt my way to the table and set the pitcher down.

"Let's be quiet," I said, "and see what they do."

Suddenly I smelled the smoke that come from the drenched fire. It was a wet sour smoke, like smoke from green white oak, except it smelled like scorched milk too. It had that burnt sugar sharpness to it. I coughed before I could stop myself.

"Let's move back away," I said, "till the smoke thins out." I bumped against the table trying to get away from the fireplace. Josie hit against some pots and banged the medicine shelf. But we worked our way to the other end of the room where Ma's spinning wheel was. It was already cold at that end. I seen how cold it was going to get. Josie's teeth was chattering.

"Get a quilt out of the chest," I said. The smell of the buttermilk clung to my nose and skin like burned vomit. I didn't think we would ever get rid of that smell. It was like some mixture of chemicals and something rotten. It was like a wicked spirit in the air.

Josie lifted the top of the cedar chest, but they was something on the lid that slid crashing off, a vase or pewter pot.

"What's you'uns doing in there?" somebody called from the yard. Steps mounted the porch and a stick or gunstock banged on the door. "I believe their fire's gone out," he said.

"Smell's like somebody's gut-sick," another man said.

"We didn't mean to scare you," the first voice said.

"You all are going to get cold," the second man said. They rapped on the door again.

Josie and me wrapped ourselves in a quilt. We was both beginning to shake with the cold, and maybe from fear. It occurred to me they could dump some smoking rags down the chimney and still drive us out. Wasn't nothing I could do to stop them. I had to think what to do.

"You can't run water through logs all the way from the spring," Josie said when I showed her the auger. "It'll every bit leak out in the dirt."

I had thought of that myself, and I knowed I'd have to join the logs tight to make them hold water, and I'd have to cut them just right to make them fit. It was near Christmas, and I had to go back into the Flat Woods to kill us a deer. Seemed a luxury to be able to get shot and powder and to buy salt whenever you wanted it. During the war we dug up the dirt of the smokehouse floor and boiled it for salt, but we didn't get more than a cup or two. It seemed almost a sin to go down to the store and buy a bag of salt for a dime to sprinkle on deer meat and rub into hams and shoulder meat.

I killed me a deer and carried it back on the horse and hung the meat up in the smokehouse. And then I went out and got Christmas greens for the house, a cedar tee for Josie to decorate with popcorn and shiny paper stars and candles, some holly and some turkey's paw from the north side of the pasture hill, and some mistletoe from our oaks above the spring. I was hoping Susan Johnson would come if we had a play party or candy pulling. I always did like to brighten up the house at Christmas time. But after I got it all done, and after I got in galax leaves for Josie to thread into streamers, and after I hung a sprig of mistletoe from the ceiling over the door, I got out my shiny new brace and bit. What I wanted for Christmas most was to get to work on the pumplogs.

"Ain't you gonna rest now and enjoy yourself?" Josie said. But she was just teasing. Sundays and holidays make me feel empty if I can't do nothing. The fences needed more rails, and the new ground up on the ridge still wasn't cleared. Pa had left it when he went off to Kentucky and never did come back. They was no end of work to do. I never could study on just sitting around. To feel good I had to be doing something. If I wasn't doing nothing I started listening to gossip and worrying about the church quarrels, and what all people was saying about each other. Mean talk always made me feel dirty, and only work made me feel clean.

First thing I done was saw me out a pile of six-foot pine logs. I figured I'd need better than two hundred of them. I went up on the hill where the pine grove was, beyond the pasture. Pines grow up where an old field has been. They grow up thick and straight where they crowd together. I wanted them small as possible to still have a two-inch hole down the middle. I figured about four inches through was the least I could do with. That left a shell an inch thick around the hole. All through Christmas I cut and piled up logs. I sawed almost two hundred and fifty sections and sledded them to the pasture. Josie had her party at New Year's and all her friends come. I kissed Susan Johnson under the sprig of mistletoe, and folks noticed it and started talking. I was tickled myself.

Mr. Johnson come by to see what I was doing. I reckon he'd heard about my project. Maybe he wanted to see what my intentions was with Susan. He looked at the pine logs I was piling up across the pasture and he looked at the auger in the woodshed. "Water won't be fit to drink," he said, "after it gets so much pine rosin in it."

I had thought of that, but decided the cold water would harden the rosin and neither the taste nor the smell would amount to much after the water run a little. But I didn't say nothing. Wouldn't do no good to argue. And besides, he was Susan's Pa.

"The water will all leak out between the logs if you don't tar the joints," he said.

"I'm hoping the wood will swell tight at the joints," I said. "Like the wood in a barrel does."

He studied the logs like he could find a clue there. "Reckon they will rot in three or four years anyway," he said.

"Hope not," I said.

He left without telling me what he come for. Maybe he wanted to enlist my vote for the new organ in the church. Or more likely he just wanted me to know he had his eye on me, after he heard I had kissed his girl at the play party. I wasn't but sixteen, but I was big for my age and had worked like a man since I was twelve.

I had thought the hardest job would be to drill out the logs. But after I fixed a platform so I could stand above the logs and bore down the ends I seen it wasn't all that hard. Of course nothing's hard once you get into it, not if you do it a careful step at a time. Only problem was my chest got sore from leaning on the knob of the brace. You had to do that to bear down, but after a few hours my ribs got sore. Drilling with a brace has a funny rhythm, round and round, and round and round, as the wood shavings boil up in crumbs around the auger. It's harder drilling with the grain of the wood than against it. For sawing and slicing it's always better to cut across the grain. But I had no choice; I had to bore lengthwise. And I had to worry about aiming the auger straight so it would stay in the middle of the log, and so I could meet the hole that would be coming from the other end.

I was slow the first few logs, and I ruined several, drilling at a tilt, or drilling a slightly curved log. But after a while I got the habit of it. You don't learn nothing except by doing it. I bent over on that platform for hours, turning the brace and smelling the new pine shavings. Pine sap is like spice from the East. Every wood has its own scent, and pine is the most fragrant, except for cedar and Balm of Gilead trees.

When my chest got too sore I'd go off and do my other work. Turned out the hardest part of the job was something that seemed so easy I hadn't hardly thought about it.

I cleared away brush below the spring where I figured the pipelogs would go, and then I started to mark out the path around the pasture hill where I would dig the ditch. It looked simple; it would go right toward the house.

"How you know water will run in your pipe?" Josie said.

" 'Cause it will be downhill," I said. But I seen immediately how much care it would take to make sure it *was* downhill all the way. It would have to be downhill at just the right steady grade with no dips and peaks. That was the hard job.

It was getting cold in the room fast. I could feel the warmth from my clothes being soaked up by the dark air. The pain of fear was a kind of heat, but we was already shivering. I seen we would freeze if we just stood there. I had an old sheepskin coat, but it was up in the loft. My machinaw jacket was hung on a peg by the door.

The room was dark except for streaks of moonlight coming through cracks. I had been meaning to daub mud between the logs, but hadn't done it yet. The moonlight looked like silver strings once our eyes got used to the dark. I felt my way across the room and got the wool jacket off the nail. It was slick with cold and wear, but I felt better with it on. I hunkered down to a crack and tried to see what the outliers was doing.

Two of the men was walking along the porch looking at the stuff we had hung up there. Whatever they saw and didn't want they throwed away.

"Why looky here," one said, carrying something out into the moonlight. "It's a gourd full of nails." He throwed the gourd out into the yard and you could hear the nails ringing as they scattered on the hard ground.

"What's all this mess?" the other one said. He grabbed something off the wall. It was the strings of leather britches Josie had put on threads. He gathered up a handful and tossed them in the yard. Then he come back and got the rest, combing them off pegs with his fingers. "Ain't nothing but some damn beans," and said, and flung them like vines to the dirt.

They was a box of apples I had picked, red Winter Johns, from the tree out beyond the smokehouse. I had left them on the porch to be wrapped in newspapers and put in the potato hole. The first man picked up a handful of apples. "Hey Skag," he hollered, and when a man in the yard turned around he throwed an apple that hit him right in the neck.

"You cut that out," the man called Skag said. "These people will think we ain't civilized." He picked up a rock and hurled it at the apple thrower. The rock missed and banged on the wall of the cabin. The men started laughing and chasing each other around the yard, throwing apples and rocks. It was like they knowed we was watching them. And they was showing out. They wanted us to see how free they was on our place. How they wasn't afraid at all of the law or us. Wasn't nobody could do a thing about them. One picked up a flowerpot and throwed it at the other, and then the other throwed another flowerpot. They run among their horses like little boys, giggling and hollering, "I'm gonna pay you back for that."

Our pullets was still in the coop but the older hens roosted in the arborvitae tree. The Dominicker rooster and Josie's banties and all the other laying hens roosted way up in that tree. When the men got to running around and hollering and throwing things I guess something landed up in the trace because suddenly the hens started cackling and squawking. They sounded like a fox or weasel had got among them. You never heard such a racket. When chickens get scared they just go crazy with cackling and crowing. They sould like they're drowning and have the hiccups at the same time.

"Now look what you done," one of the them hollered, and throwed another rock up into the arborvitae. That made the chickens cackle even louder.

The man who seemed to be the leader rode back from the barn. He was carrying a pine torch and he looked into the arborvitae where all the squawking was coming from. "You boys ain't even polite," he said. "You're going to wake everybody up."

"We want us some chicken," one of the younger men said.

"And some guineas," another said.

"We don't want no guineas," Skag said. "Guinea is hard and stringy. We want white tender meat. Fair and tender as a little girl." And he shoved his companion and they both laughed like he had told the biggest joke.

"Let's us have some tender white meat," his buddy said.

The leader looked toward the house. He knowed we was listening to him. "If they don't invite us in to their feast, we'll invite them to ours," he said.

They got wood from the woodpile and stacked it right in front of the porch steps. After they started the bonfire I couldn't see nothing in the yard except what was around the fire. It ruined my night eyes, though I could see the moon above like a chalky face that looked down but wasn't paying no attention to the goings on.

They clumb up in the arborvitae and grabbed the chickens. And when one got away they chased it all over the yard. They run the chickens around the fire and under the horses and out into the dark. "Get him Kyle, get him Kyle," one would call.

"That ain't no chicken, that's a crow."

"Catch that damn buzzard and wring his neck."

Finally they seemed to have caught all the chickens. Two of the men come toting the washpot from the branch and put it on the fire.

"We ain't got no water," one of the men said.

"They's half a bucket on the backporch."

"You can't scald these chickens with half a bucket."

"Hey, where is you'uns's spring?" the leader called. He seemed to know just where I was looking at him from, like he could see through the dark wall. I could tell from the way he talked he wasn't no Yankee deserter like most of the rest of them. I almost thought I recognized him. He reminded me of the Wheelers from up on the mountain. He was Lester Price's Uncle Hiram Wheeler, that's who he was.

"Ain't you got no spring?" he hollered. "Ain't you gonna offer us some water? We was thirsty and you offered us no drink. We was tired and you took us not in. We was hungry and you offered us no meat for succor."

"That's what I want, some succor," the one called Kyle said.

"We'll have to go to the branch for water."

"Branch water ain't fit to drink."

"Not less it's mixed with liquor."

"We're gonna boil it."

"We'll boil it and mix it with liquor."

I turned around and couldn't see nothing at first. And then I seen Josie standing behind me like something you see deep under water so vague you're not sure you see it. Her face was like something white you see way through smoke. And then I seen her eyes, how wide they was, like a little kid's that has seen a haint.

"We ain't forgot you," the leader called from out in the yard. "We'll eat first and then call on you. We ain't forgot our manners."

How many times I've found a job that looked the easiest to be a trial. I got all my pumplogs bored out and I still hadn't started on the ditch. I walked the likely route back and forth and tramped down weeds and cleaned away brush. But every time I put off the actual digging. I wanted to study it some more, and they was so much else to do to get ready. I knowed real surveyors and engineers used transits and levelers to lay off roads and building sites, and with a telescope and marking pole they could tell how far downhill a right of way run. But I didn't have such instruments. I did have a carpenter's level and plumb bob, and I thought I could make a sighting tool without a telescope. But I wondered how accurate it might be. I would have loved to learn about surveying, how you start with a corner and run a line at an angle with a compass, or even at an angle with the north star to be really accurate. It was an art I wished I knowed, setting all fences and springs in relation to the north pole, or even a star. But it was the middle of January, and I had to finish the job before plowing time. I thought of Susan Johnson and I thought how I'd make a great fool of myself if I drilled all those pumplogs and didn't bring water to the house. People would talk about me "boring with a big auger" for years.

It come a snow past the middle of the month and while the ground was covered I studied on the problem of joining and fitting the logs. They had to be coupled like male and female and they had to stay tight and not leak out the water before it reached the house. I figured if the joints was made with care they would swell in place and wouldn't need much cement to seal them. I set in the woodshed whittling and studying the problem.

Lester Price stopped by and asked was I going to vote against the organ at the next church meeting. Lester and me had just been baptized the year before, after they let me go back to the church. I told him the deacons would do the voting. Wasn't no need for me and him to worry about it.

"They want to bring the devil right into the church," he said. He'd heard his pa and uncles say it. I don't think he cared much one way or another.

"They try to bring that instrument into the church they'll be some blood spilled," he said.

"Surely not," I said.

"People is ready to fight," he said.

"I don't want no fight," I said.

"Only homemade Yankees would want an organ in the church," he said. I kept whittling before I looked up. I wondered should I remind him his uncle had been one of the bushwhackers in the war, when they thought he was off in the Confederate army. I was still trying to decide when I looked up and seen he was gone.

But just then it come to me what I had to do to join the logs. I needed to take my one-inch auger and bore holes in six-inch sections of saplings, then sharpen each end of the section and drive one into the hole of one log and the other into another log. When the sections swole up the connections would be tight. It took me some practice to make the sections the right size, but after the first half dozen I seen exactly how it was to be done. I turned out two hundred and forty of them before the snow melted. I whittled the ends of the sections at night by the fireplace.

"I don't like the looks of them things," Josie said.

"You won't never see them again," I said. I liked the idea that nobody would see what I was making once it was in place. They would only see the cool water that went in at the spring and come out at the house. Everything I was making would be hid, as long as it was working right. I was going to string a vein of water around the hill where nobody could see anything but pasture once the grass had growed back.

Once I finished with the holler connecting pegs, and the snow had melted, I figured out how to do the ditch. It would be the simplest way of all, but I seen it would work. I'd start digging at the spring and let a little water into the ditch every so often as I went along. As long as the water was flowing the ditch was going right. If I got off course I could redo it right there, before I had gone too far. And once I got to the bank above the smokehouse I could run it right downhill to the place where I would build the springhouse. It all come clear in my mind at once.

Of course that's how you do any job. You go one tiny step at a time.

I've always liked to dig in the dirt, with a hoe or plow, a shovel or a pick. And once I seen how it was to be done I started right in. The ground was froze in places, but I chopped through it like a bark or crust. The ground below the spring was all leafmold and quartz rock. I dug there for about a hundred feet before letting in any water, because I seen how it had to go, out from the branch and around the hill. I was digging a little canal. I chopped through roots and pried big rocks out. But the mold and humus itself was soft and easy, and it wasn't till I got almost to the pasture that I touched into clay and subsoil.

By the second day I had to try out my plan. When I let a little water into the ditch it run right down, feeling its way steady around crumbs and little rocks, ponding up in places and then rushing on till it reached the end of my digging. There it swelled up into a little pool, and I closed off the intake. I seen I'd swung too far uphill with the last ten feet, trying to aim too straight for the house. I dug that section over, dropping the ditch about a foot at the end, and started out again. Ditching in the pasture was easy as eating pudding. I had to slice through the turf and roots of grass, right through the inch or so of topsoil. And then I was into mealy yellow soil full of gravel. It was a place the Indians had chipped arrowheads, and they was thousands of little pieces of flint and quartz. My shovel rung on the rocks, grinding as I cut through the spoil. I dug down about a foot to bury the logs. But where they was a kind of hump I had to go deeper. By the end of the second day I had shoveled a hundred feet around the pasture hill, and when I opened the new section water run all the way to the end.

The smell of scorched milk will always make me think of that gang of outliers hollering and running around our yard. The burned stench seemed like the end of the world. It reminds me to this day of the doom we felt. That fried vomit odor is my sense of the way hell would stink. Everything goes wrong and just keeps going wrong I smell that smell. When the bottom falls out and emptiness washes over me like a flashflood that stink comes back on me.

The gang of bushwhackers caught every single one of our chickens and wrung their necks. They carried water from the branch in the milk bucket and boiled it in front of the steps. Then they scalded the dead chickens and plucked out all their feathers. Me and Josie watched them in the firelight. They pulled out feathers and throwed them at each other. The wet feathers stuck to their hands and they flung them off and wiped their hands on their clothes and on each other's clothes. Feathers was floating and flying all over the yard.

"My fine feathered friend," one would say and laugh like he was drunk.

"I heard your Ma rode out of town wearing feathers," another said. They flung feathers around the porch and on each other's heads until it looked like the sky had snowed feathers. And the smell of the hot wet feathers was almost as bad as the stink of burned buttermilk.

After they plucked all the chickens they cut off their heads and feet with big knives and begun to gut them. You would have thought they would get the bucket to put the guts in, and something to put the liver and craws in. But oh no, they just flung the guts and giblets all over the place. Along with all the other stinks, I could soon smell the chicken guts they throwed on the porch. One of the boys said, "Where's your manners, Kyle? We don't throw guts on people's doorsteps."

"Here's my manners," Kyle said, and throwed a handful of guts at the man teasing him. The guts stuck to his face and hat. He tried to claw them away, and then him and Kyle started pushing each other and hitting each other with their chickens till their leader come up.

"Stop that!" he hollered. "We got no time for foolishness." He held a jug up in the firelight. I guess they had brought it with them 'cause it didn't look like any of our jugs. The men wiped their hands on their pants and drunk from the jug as it was passed around. They wanted to take a second drink but the leader grabbed the jug back. "Save some for dessert," he said.

"Yahooo," Kyle said. "They's a rebel woman inside this house."

"Rebel women is good as any women," the man called Skag said.

"All women is the same where it counts," Kyle said.

Josie shivered and wrapped the quilt tighter on her shoulders. Sometimes I thought her mind hadn't been perfect since Ma died. And she hadn't got no better after Pa left for Tennessee. But she didn't talk much, and I couldn't be sure. Maybe she was just getting older and that made her talk less.

"I ain't gonna let them come in," I said.

"What if they burn down the house?" she said. The bonfire was leaping high, not too many yards from the roof of the porch. It would be easy for them to throw a burning stick on the roof and catch the cedar shingles.

"They won't burn the house," I said. "They want to eat theirselves full and steal all they can and leave before daylight."

I had no way to judge what time it was. Usually I could tell time just by feeling how long it had been. But when hard and surprising things happen that feeling gets wrenched and stretched out of shape. It could have been long after midnight, but I couldn't tell.

I tried to see where the moon was. I thought I could see its light on the floor at the end of the porch. If so it was way after midnight. I hoped it was that late. I hoped the night would pass quick for I was sure the outlaws would leave by sunup. They always done their doings in the dark. Even though they was no law to go after them they didn't like to be seen in the light of day. I guess they was afraid somebody would take a shot at them from the thickets if they rode around in daylight.

"We want us some chicken meat," the man called Kyle hollered.

"You got plenty of chicken meat," Skag said.

"We want some tender Rebel meat," another man said.

118

"I don't think them Rebels is going to come out," Skag said.

"Smoke them out," one said. "We got some wet feathers and pine needles to poke down the chimney. They'll come out coughing and puking."

"Don't want no pretty Rebel girl to get sick," Kyle said.

I had to think of something. Josie was trembling and her teeth was clicking. I was shaking myself so I could hardly make my tongue work. "Josie," I said, "you do what I tell you. When the time comes you do just what I say."

The bushwhackers brought some more water up from the branch and boiled the chickens they had plucked and cleaned. I knowed that would keep them busy for at least one hour, boiling and eating the hot chickens right out of the pot. They passed the jug around and eat with their fingers. They flung bones at the house and up on the roof. They wiped their hands on their pants and coats and passed the jug again. Some went back to the washpot for another chicken.

"Ain't you gonna offer us no salt?" the leader hollered at the house.

Every so often the one named Kyle would walk up on the porch and kick the door. "You are sleeping?" he'd call. Then he'd go back to the fire and eat some more and have a drink. "Ain't you going to entertain your guests?" he would holler.

"They ain't showed us no welcome," Skag said. "Here we've come all this way and they won't show us no welcome."

"This may make them open their door," the leader said. It looked like he had some rags and feathers and pine needles. "Take this up on the roof and drop it down the chimney and see if that don't make them a little friendlier," he said.

One of the men got up on his horse to climb on the porch roof, and Kyle handed him a burning stick from the fire. I knowed it was time to move. I was so stiff with cold and weak with dread I couldn't hardly raise the latch on the door. It slipped out of my hands a time or two, but I finally got it up. I didn't take Pa's gun or a stick or anything. I just slipped out the door and closed it behind me.

"Look who woke up," Kyle hollered when I stepped into the firelight.

"He smells like misery wrapped up in vomit," Skag said.

"Much obliged for your welcome," the leader said.

* * *

119

My plan for testing the ditch as I shoveled along worked better than I had hoped. Every time I dug another hundred feet I let in a little more water and watched it crawl along the furrow. Where it stopped and started to swell into a puddle I knowed had to be dug deeper. I never did like to see water penned up. Every time I see a puddle I want to cut a drain for it. I want to see water on its way downhill toward the ocean. Standing water gets foul and moving water is clean. Even if I see standing water around the barn I'll get a shovel or pitchfork and rake out a drain for it to go away in.

I had got my ditch about halfway dug around the pasture hill when Mr. Johnson come by again. He had been to his traps down on the river and he was carrying a couple of muskrats. "Ain't been cold enough this year for prime fur," he said.

" 'Been cold enough for work," I said.

"Has to stay colder just to kill the bugs," he said. "Stays this warm they'll be all kinds of flies and skeeters next summer."

But I knowed he had not stopped by to talk about bugs and the weather. He looked up and down the ditch I had dug, and at the piles of bored out logs. "How you going to couple your pumplogs?" he said.

"I made some holler pegs to pin them together," I said. I thought he might be going to mention the church quarrel. I was not going to say nothing about the organ one way or another.

"Did your daddy leave you title to the place?" he said.

Now I seen his line of thought. I didn't like to answer such questions, so I kept on digging. "Pa went off to the army when I was fourteen," I said.

"So the place will go to both you and Josie?" he said.

"Might be," I said.

"Even if Josie marries she'll still get half the property?" he said.

"I want to do the fair thing," I said.

"A lot of folks just give their girl a little money or a cow when she marries," he said. "And they leave their land to the oldest son. It's the old way of doing things."

I didn't answer him. Wasn't any of his business how we divided up the place when Josie got married, if she got married. Not even if I had asked Susan Johnson to marry me, which I hadn't, though I had kissed her under the mistletoe. I kept on digging the pasture turf with the mattock, right along the line around the hill where I knowed it should go. I dug right through the shiny cover of broomsedge.

"Did your pa leave you any money?" Mr. Johnson said.

"When Pa went off to fight he had to outfit hisself," I said. I didn't answer his question. I didn't want to be disrespectful, but I didn't answer his question. I seen Mr. Johnson was trying to take advantage of me because I was only sixteen.

"I heard your pa buried a jar of money before he left," he said.

"Pa had to buy his own uniform and knapsack and cooking kit," I said. I was working along fast in my anger. I was digging the ditch through clay and broomsedge maybe a foot a minute. The dirt was just opening up for the mattock with every lick and coming loose in great mealy chunks.

"Did you ever find the money?" Mr. Johnson said. "Or was it lost like so much stuff buried before the war?"

"The bushwhackers took near everything we had," I said. "They cleaned us out." I knowed it was time to shovel out the loose dirt I had dug up with the mattock and then test the ditch with more water. But I didn't want to stop while I was working so fast, and while Mr. Johnson was pestering me. I was afraid of what I might do if I stopped and looked him in the eye. I'd have to trust my judgment about the grade of the ditch.

"What I want to know is, was the money Yankee money?" Mr. Johnson said. "Or was it no count war bonds and Confederate money?"

I stopped digging and stood up and looked at Mr. Johnson. I had just enough breath to talk and not holler. "They's another custom from olden times I've heard," I said.

"What's that?" he said.

"Used to when a girl got married she had to bring her husband a dowry," I said.

"That ain't been practiced since ancient times," he said, and leaned over to blow his nose on the grass, pressing one nostril closed. "That was a heathen practice," he said.

"The dowry could be money, or land, or cattle, or some other kind of property," I said. "But it had to be equal to the value of the property the man had."

"No dowry I ever heard was equal to more than a hundred dollars or a good horse," Mr. Johnson said.

I went back to working and only after he left with his skinny muskrats did I stop to see how far I had come. I must have dug out another fifty feet while he was talking. I shoveled out the loose dirt and let a stream of water in. The water come like a shiny snake darting its head and tongue this way and that. It swelled up in little pools like a snake swallering something where I had dug too deep, but it kept coming on until about fifteen feet from where I had stopped. There it ponded up and I could see I'd swung too high. I had to redig that end, shifting slightly downhill.

"Much obliged to you," the leader said. He knowed I knowed who he was. The other fellers was deserters and draft dodgers from all over, but the leader was from up on the mountain. I had seen him at Shepherd's store in town when Pa and me went to trade. I knowed he was Lester's uncle.

"It's called a Rebel welcome," the man named Skag said.

Their faces was greasy from all the chicken they had eat.

"This ain't no Rebel," the leader said.

"He looks like a Rebel," Kyle said.

"No sir, this is a homemade Yankee," the leader said.

"Well praise the Lord," Kyle said and took a drink from the jug.

They all seemed a little groggy from the night of eating and drinking. I looked at the sky beyond the rim of Painter Mountain and it seemed to be lighting up. The moon was low over Cicero Mountain. They would have to leave before too long.

"Ain't you going to invite us in?" the leader said.

"He don't want us to meet his womenfolks," Skag said.

"That ain't no hospitality at all," Kyle said. "A man needs to fill his gut, and then he's ready for other kinds of comfort." He stumbled up on the porch and looked me close in the face. He looked me hard in the eyes, and his breath smelled like rotten corn. I stepped back against the door.

"You smell worser than a sick polecat," Kyle said.

"Maybe he got scared," another man said.

"Ain't no need to be scared of us," Kyle said. "We're neighbors, and neighbors got to share what they got." He turned around to the other man. "Everything they got." The others laughed.

"Step aside boy," the leader said. "Now that you've invited us in."

I pressed against the door. I knowed whatever happened it was going to be bad.

"Look in his pockets," the leader said. "He might have a key to the door."

"Or the key to his sister," Kyle said. They all laughed again.

I must have reached out a hand to push them away for Kyle hit me across the side of the head, and then he hit me in the belly and chest. I felt sick in my belly as they slammed me against the door. They wasn't nothing in my pockets but my knife and Kyle took that.

"Knife like this will get a boy into meanness," Kyle said.

"You all will fry in hell like lard fat," I said, trying to find my breath.

"What you say?" the leader said.

"You'll fry in hell," I gulped.

The leader hit me with his gun butt and when I was on the floor they kicked me several times. Somebody stood over me while Kyle lifted the latch on the door. Josie had not slid the bolt back in place.

"Wasn't locked at all," Kyle said. "Anybody home. Yahoo?" It was dark and silent inside.

"This whole house smells like a heap of gut-sick," Skag said.

"Bring me a light," the leader said.

They brought some lighted sticks from the fire, and I could hear them stomping around inside, kicking things over. The leader come back to the door. "Where's your gun, boy?" he said.

"Ain't got no gun," I said. "Ain't got no powder and shot neither."

"But he's got a sister," Skag said.

"Where's your sister?" the leader said.

"Ain't got no sister," I said. My mouth was full of blood but I didn't know where the blood was coming from.

They pushed me inside and made me stand with my back to the dead fireplace.

"Hey, little sister," Kyle sung in a high voice. "Where you hiding, little sister?" He lifted clothes off pegs and throwed them on the floor.

One of the men was looking through the bottles on the medicine shelf. "Look at this," he said and held up the jug of liquor.

"Give me that," the leader said. He took the jug and sniffed it. He pulled out the cob and took a swaller. "Damn, that's good liquor," he said.

"Little sister, we know you're here," Kyle said. He looked around with his torch like he was playing hide and seek. Then he seen the cedar chest.

"No!" I hollered. "Them's Ma's quilts."

"Ah ha!" Kyle said, and flung back the lid of the chest. He throwed aside one quilt, and then he carefully lifted another. He throwed aside Ma's woolen shawl and throwed out a counterpane Ma had been give when she was married. He flung away a tablecloth Ma had always saved. The chest was empty.

"Aint no use to hide, little sister," Kyle said. He took the jug and give hisself a long swaller.

The leader looked up toward the loft, and Kyle follered his gaze. "You hid your little sister up there," he said.

"Ain't nothing in the loft," I said. Quick as a cat Kyle clumb up the ladder to the loft. He raised his torch and looked around up there. It was just a shelf with some straw on it where I slept when I was little. Pa had left some tobacco up there and Kyle throwed down the four or five hands of it. He got my sheepskin jacket and throwed that down. He poked his rifle through the hay until he hit the wall, and then he clumb back down.

"You gonna tell us where she is, boy?" he said.

"Nobody can disappear," Skag said. "Except witches."

"Is you folks witches?" Kyle said. "You know what the Bible says to do with witches." He took out my knife and opened the blade. I had honed it on a creek rock the day before and it was sharp enough to shave with. He held the blade right up to my face. "You're old enough to shave," he said. "I'm going to show you how to shave."

"Kyle," the leader said. "It's time to go."

"Ain't time to go yet," Kyle said. "Not till we teach him a lesson."

"It's time to go," the leader said, and drawed his gun on Kyle. "It's daylight near about."

Quick as you could blink Kyle cut my suspenders with the knife and jerked my pants down to my knees. "I want to expose all these traitors and witches," he said. All the men laughed. I pulled my pants back up.

Before they left they took everything in the cabin they wanted, the tobacco, the quilts, the liquor, a few pans and pewter cups, my sheepskin coat. The rest they knocked down and trampled on. We had just about half a cup of saleratus and they spilt that in front of the fireplace. One of the men relieved hisself right in the floor by the door.

"Much obliged," the leader said again as they got on their horses. It was getting light and the bonfire was dying down to powdery sticks and ashes.

When they was gone I shut the door and clumb up the ladder to the loft. The room below looked like a buffalo herd had stomped through it. I pushed the straw aside and pulled away the big board in the eave. Josie laid behind it with the gun in her hands. Her hair was stuck to her face with sweat and all the tears she had cried.

Once I got the ditch cut all the way to the house I had to build a springhouse. I've heard of water being run right into a house. But we didn't have room for that. I had to build something close by but separate.

"You're gonna turn this yard into a mud hole," Josie said when she seen the water I run through the ditch to show that it worked. She sounded like Ma when she talked like that. She always said the worst thing that come to mind.

"You won't see no mud when I'm finished," I said.

"I don't see nothing but mud," she said.

About thirty feet from the corner of the house I dug a hole, right at the end of the ditch. I shoveled out a basin in the clay and lined it with white branch sand. And every time I seen a pretty rock of quartz or glittering with mica I carried it to the hole and added it to the sand. I'd always liked to look into springs, and here I was making my own. I got shiny pebbles from the branch and from the sandbar down on the creek.

I built a lip of flagstone for the pool and lined the overflow ditch with fieldstone. I cut the ditch for runoff straight down the side of the yard toward the branch. The walls of the spring I lined with drystone. It was the first masonry I'd ever done, and I worked for days getting the rocks to set on top of each other straight before I filled in the dirt behind them.

Over the pit I built a little house. I hewed poplar logs and dovetailed them. And I split cedar for the shingles. When I finished it was dark inside the building as in a little church. I pegged shelves to the walls and made a door that creaked on leather hinges.

Lester come by the day I started to put the pumplogs together. "What you gonna do if one of your logs freezes?" he said. "It'll split right open and then all the rest will freeze and bust."

"Maybe they won't freeze," I said. "If they're buried a foot down and the water keeps moving in them."

"But what if they was to freeze?" he said.

I didn't answer. Wasn't no use to argue if somebody wanted to pick flaws with your work. Arguing was always a waste.

"Them logs look like organ pipes," Lester said. "Stacked up like that. Bet a feller could make his own organ if he tried."

The argument over the organ had got so hot at church the week before men had started to bring their guns to meeting. Both sides was threatening to shoot the other. I had decided to stay away from church for a while.

"Feller has got to take a stand," Lester said before he left. "Unless he wants to be a mugwump or a scalawag." I just kept on working.

It was harder to fit the logs together than I had thought. A lot of the pegs had to be whittled some more to stick into the pumplogs. Several of the pins cracked when I joined the logs together and I had to bore new ones. It took twice as long as I had figured. It was getting up toward time for spring plowing.

Not all the logs was perfectly shaped and sometimes the hole in one would not line up with the hole in the other. I had to keep switching logs around and boring out extra ones. I had to even go back to the hill and cut a few more pines before I was through.

But the logs had seasoned nice while they laid out in the winter sun. White pine gets light and hard when it dries out a little. The logs was easier to lift now, and they smelled like Christmas spice from the Holy Land. I hoped the bark would keep them from rotting.

It took me almost a week to fit the logs together, and only a day to cover them up. I raked the dirt right over the ditch and smoothed it so the grass would come back same as before. The log reaching into the spring I put in last. I didn't want to get any muddy water in the pumplogs if possible. But in the end I did stir up the sand and mud a little to dig out a place for the intake. But I had plugged up the first log until the spring had settled clear. I didn't want any mud to get in those logs to taint the taste.

It takes a bold spring about fifteen minutes to clear itself. The mud in the water will fall out like dust after a wind. The trash will hang longest in the pockets where eddies spin around. But most of the dirt will settle on the bottom like fog and snow flurries, or find its way to the overflow. I set there watching the clouds clear out of the spring, and felt sad as I always do when a job is about done. I had that empty feeling like everything was wrong and nothing could be done about it. It was too late to start all over again. The church was all tore up and Mr. Johnson and Lester had made me feel bad. They didn't seem anything more that could be done. I had about come to the end.

Finally the spring was clear as it ever had been. It was a bright winter day and steam rose a little bit off the pool. The spring bubbled like it was boiling. It was sad, and they was nothing else to do but

126

try out my pumplogs. I pulled the plug out and heard water pouring into the first log. The pipelogs couldn't carry all the runoff from the spring, but they could carry most of it. I listened, and could hear water running through the logs under the ground. I started walking along to see if I could hear water going all the way through for the first time, and to see how fast it would go.

At the fence I had to pause to climb over while the water run right underneath. I fancied I could hear the water tinkling under my feet. It sounded like the water was talking down there. I thought of it shiny and flashing through the dark holes like through a flute. I run along the new-covered ground wondering if I was ahead of the water or behind it. I stopped to see if I could hear it again, but crows was cawing on the hill and a dog was barking somewhere. I run on another hundred yards to where the pumplogs passed the molasses furnace. They was no sign of the ground wet or water leaking.

Whatever was happening under the ground, it was a secret and a mystery that you never would have guessed from the way the pasture looked. I started running along the line, no longer trying to hear the water in the vein beneath. I did not see Josie and her friends until I come around the corner of the springhouse. There they stood watching through the door. Josie must have told them what I was doing. They was Susan Johnson, and Mary Petillo, and Falby Jones, and Lee Ellen Hartwick. Their hair sparkled in the late winter sun. They all looked pretty in different ways.

"Has it come?" I said.

"Don't see a thing yet," Josie said. They all stepped aside so I could look through the door. I leaned into the building and at first I couldn't see nothing or hear nothing except my own breathing. And then my eyes got used to the gloom a little and I seen this tongue of water jump from the spout log into the basin. The water was clear and come out like it was talking, and like it would go on talking. I hollered, "Here it is!" The water was filling up the basin of bright sand and rocks and it was like the hill was saying some secret from way up inside and the voice was coming out cold and clear down here by the house. Already the basin was full and running over.

Knowing they was all watching me, I said, "Sure beats carrying water from the branch." But I didn't turn around. I could feel their eyes on me.

DRAGGED FIGHTING
FROM HIS TOMB

BARRY HANNAH

It was a rout.

We hit them, but they were ready this time.

His great idea was to erupt in the middle of the loungers. Stuart was a profound laugher. His banjo-nigger was with him almost all the time, a man who could make a ballad instantly after an ambush. We had very funny songs about the wide-eyed loungers and pickets, the people of negligent spine leisuring around the depots and warehouses, straightening their cuffs and holding their guns as if they were fishing poles. Jeb loved to break out of cover in the clearing in front of these guards. He offered them first shot if they were ready, but they never were. It was us and the dirty gray, sabers out, and a bunch of fleeing boys in blue.

Except the last time, at Two Roads Junction in Pennsylvania.

These boys had repeaters and they were waiting for us. Maybe they had better scouts than the others. We'd surprised a couple of their pickets and shot them down. But I suppose there were others who got back. This was my fault. My talent was supposed to be circling behind the pickets and slaying every one of them. So I blame myself for the rout, though there are always uncertainties in an ambush. This time it was us that were routed.

We rode in. They were ready with the repeating rifles, and we were blown apart. I myself took a bullet through the throat. It didn't take me off my mount, but I rode about a hundred yards out under a big shade tree and readied myself to die. I offered my prayers.

"Christ, I am dead. Comfort me in the valley of the shadow. Take

128

me through it with honor. Don't let me make the banshee noises I've heard so many times in the field. You and I know I am worth more than that."

I heard the repeating rifles behind me and the shrieks, but my head was a calm green church. I was prepared to accept the big shadow. But I didn't seem to be dying. I felt my neck. I thrust my forefinger in the hole. It was to the right of my windpipe and there was blood on the rear of my neck. The thing had passed clean through the muscle of my right neck. In truth, it didn't even hurt.

I had been thinking: Death does not especially hurt. Then I was merely asleep on the neck of my horse, a red-haired genius for me and a steady one. I'd named him Mount Auburn. We took him from a big farm outside Gettysburg. He wanted me as I wanted him. He was mine. He was the Confederacy.

As I slept on him, he was curious but stable as a rock. The great beast felt my need to lie against his neck and suffered me. He lay the neck out there for my comfort and stood his front heels.

A very old cavalryman in blue woke me up. He was touching me with a flagstaff. He didn't even have a weapon out.

"Eh, boy, you're a pretty dead one, ain't you? Got your hoss's head all bloody. Did you think Jeb was gonna surprise us forever?"

We were alone.

He was amazed when I stood up in the saddle. I could see beyond him through the hanging limbs. A few men in blue were picking things up. It was very quiet. Without a thought, I already had my pistol on his thin chest. I could not see him for a moment for the snout of my pistol.

He went to quivering, of course, the old fool. I saw he had a bardlike face.

What I began was half sport and half earnest.

"Say wise things to me or die, patriot," I said.

"But but but but but but," he said.

"Shhh!" I said. "Let nobody else hear. Only me. Tell the most exquisite truths you know."

He paled and squirmed.

"What's wrong?" I asked.

A stream of water came out the cuff of his pants.

I don't laugh. I've seen pretty much all of it. Nothing a body does

129

disgusts me. After you've seen them burst in the field in two days of sun, you are not surprised by much that the mortal torso can do.

"I've soiled myself, you gray motherfucker," said the old guy.

"Get on with it. No profanity necessary," I said.

"I believe in Jehovah, the Lord; in Jesus Christ, his son; and in the Holy Ghost. I believe in the Trinity of God's bride, the church. To be honest. To be square with your neighbor. To be American and free," he said.

"I asked for the truths, not beliefs," I said.

"But I don't understand what you mean," said the shivering home guard. "Give me an example."

"You're thrice as old as I. You should give *me* the examples. For instance: Where is the angry machine of all of us? Why is God such a blurred magician? Why are you begging for your life if you believe other things? Prove to me that you're better than the rabbits we ate last night."

"I'm better because I know I'm better," he said.

I said, "I've read Darwin and floundered in him. You give me aid, old man. Find your way out of this forest. Earn your life back for your trouble."

"Don't shoot me. They'll hear the shot down there and come blow you over. All the boys got Winchester repeaters," he said.

By this time he'd dropped the regiment flag into a steaming pile of turd from his horse. I noticed that his mount was scared too. The layman does not know how the currents of the rider affect that dumb beast he bestrides. *I've seen a thoroughbred horse refuse to move at all under a man well known as an idiot with a plume. It happened in the early days in the streets of Richmond with Wailing Ott, a colonel too quick if I've ever seen one. His horse just wouldn't move when Ott's boys paraded out to Manassas. He screamed and there were guffaws. He even cut the beast with his saber. The horse sat right down on the ground like a deaf beggar of a darky. Later, in fact during the battle of Manassas, Colonel Ott, loaded with pistols, sabers and even a Prussian dagger, used a rotten outhouse and fell through the aperture (or split it by his outlandish weight in iron) and drowned head down in night soil. I saw his horse roaming. It took to me. I loved it and its name (I christened it afresh) was Black Answer, because a mare had just died under me and here this other beast ran into my arms. It ran for me. I had to rein Black Answer to keep him behind General Stuart himself. (Though Jeb was just another colonel then.) I am saying that a good animal knows his man. I was riding Black Answer on a bluff over the York when a puff went out of a little boat we were harassing with Pelham's cannon from the shore. I said to Black Answer, "Look at McClellan's little sailors playing war down there, boy." The horse gave a sporty little snort in appreciation. He knew what I was saying.*

It wasn't a full fifteen minutes before a cannon ball took him right out from under me. I was standing on the ground and really not even stunned, my boots solid in the dust. But over to my right Black Answer was rolling up in the vines, broken in two. That moment is what raised my anger about the war. I recalled it as I held the pistol on the old makeshift soldier. I pulled back the hammer. I recalled the eyes of the horse were still bright when I went to comfort it. I picked up the great head of Black Answer and it came away from the body very easily. What a deliberate and pure expression Black Answer retained, even in death.

What a bog and labyrinth the human essence is, in comparison. We are all overbrained and overemotioned. No wonder my professor at the University of Virginia pointed out to us the horses of that great fantast Jonathan Swift and his Gulliver book. Compared with horses, we are all a dizzy and smelly face. An old man cannot tell you the truth. An old man, even inspired by death, simply foams and is addled like a crab.

"Tell me," I said, "do you hate me because I hold niggers in bondage? Because I do not hold niggers in bondage. I can't afford it. You know what I'm fighting for? I asked you a question."

"What're you fighting for?"

"For the North to keep off."

"But you're here in Pennsylvania, boy. You attacked *us*. This time we were ready. I'm sorry it made you mad. I'm grievous sorry about your neck, son."

"You never told me any truths. Not one. Look at that head. Look at all those gray hairs spilling out of your cap. Say something wise. I'm about to kill you," I said.

"I have daughters and sons who look up to me," he said.

"Say I am one of your sons. Why do I look up to you?" I said.

"Because I've tried to know the world and have tried to pass it on to the others." He jumped off the horse right into the droppings. He looked as if he were venturing to run. "We're not simple animals. There's a god in every one of us, if we find him," he said.

"Don't try to run. I'd kill you before I even thought," I said.

His horse ran away. It didn't like him.

131

On the ground, below my big horse Mount Auburn, the old man was a little earthling in an overbig uniform. He kept chattering.

"I want a single important truth from you," I said.

"My mouth can't do it," he said. "But there's something here!" He struck his chest at the heart place. Then he started running back to the depot, slapping hanging limbs out of his way. I turned Mount Auburn and rode after. We hit the clearing and Mount Auburn was in an easy prance. The old man was about ten yards ahead, too breathless to warn the troops.

In an idle way I watched their progress too. Captain Swain had been killed during our ambush. I saw the blueboys had put his body up on a pole with a rope around his neck, a target in dirty gray. His body was turning around as they tried out the repeaters on him. But ahead of me the old man bounced like a snowtail in front of Mount Auburn. We were in a harrowed field. The next time I looked up, a stand of repeaters was under my left hand three strides ahead. I was into their camp. Mount Auburn stopped for me as I picked up a handful of the rifles by the muzzles.

The old man finally let out something.

"It's a secesh!" he shouted.

Only a couple looked back. I noticed a crock of whiskey on a stool where the brave ones were reloading to shoot at Captain Swain again. I jumped off Mount Auburn and went in the back door of the staff house. I kicked the old man through the half-open door and pulled Mount Auburn into the room with me, got his big sweaty withers inside. When I looked around I saw their captain standing up and trying to get out his horse pistol. He was about my age, maybe twenty-five, and he had spectacles. My piece was already cocked and I shot him square in the chest. He backed up and died in another little off-room behind his desk. A woman ran out of the room. She threw open the front door and bullets smacked into the space all around her. She shut the door. A couple of bullets broke wood.

"Lay down," I said.

She had a little Derringer double-shot pistol hanging in her hand. The old man was lying flat on the floor behind the desk with me.

The woman was a painted type, lips like blood. "Get down," I told her. She was ugly, just lips, tan hair, and a huge bottom under a petticoat. I wondered what she was going to try with the little pistol. She lay down flat on the floor. I asked her to throw me the pistol. She wouldn't. Then she wormed it across to us behind the big desk.

She looked me over, her face grimy from the floor. She had no underwear and her petticoat was hiked up around her middle. The old man and I were looking at her organ.

"Wha? War again?" she said. "I thought we already won."

The woman and the old man laid themselves out like a carpet. I knew the blueboys thought they had me down and were about ready to come in. I was in that position at Chancellorsville. There should be about six fools, I thought. I made it to the open window. Then I moved into the window. With the repeater, I killed four, and the other two limped off. Some histrionic plumehead was raising his saber up and down on the top of a pyramid of crossties. I shot him just for fun. Then I brought up another repeater and sprayed the yard.

This brought on a silence. Nothing was moving. Nobody was shooting. I knew what they were about to do. I had five minutes to live, until they brought the cannon up. It would be canister or the straight big ball. Then the firing started again. The bullets were nicking the wall in back of me. I saw Mount Auburn behind the desk. He was just standing there, my friend, my legs. Christ, how could I have forgotten him? "Roll down, Auburn!" I shouted. He lay down quick. He lay down behind the thick oak desk alongside the slut and the old man.

Then what do you think? With nothing to do but have patience until they got the cannon up, somebody's hero came in the back door with a flambeau and a pistol, his eyes closed, shooting everywhere. Mount Auburn whinnied. The moron had shot Auburn. This man I overmurdered. I hit him four times in the face, and his torch flew out the back door with one of the bullets.

I was looking at the hole in Auburn when the roof of the house disappeared. It was a canister blast. The sound was deafening. Auburn was hurting but he was keeping it in. His breaths were deeper, the huge bold eyes waiting on me. I had done a lead-out once before on a corporal who was shot in the buttocks. He screamed the whole time, but he lives now, with a trifling scar on his arse, now the war is over. You put your stiletto very hard to one side of the hole until you feel metal—the bullet—and then you twist. The bullet comes out of the hole by this coiling motion and may even jump up in your hand.

So it was with the lead in Auburn's flank. It hopped right out. The thing to do then is get a sanitary piece of paper and stuff it into the wound. I took a leaf from the middle of the pile of stationery on the captain's table, spun it, and rammed it down.

Auburn never made a complaint. It was I who was mad. I mean, angry beyond myself.

When I went out the front door with the two repeaters, firing and levering, through a dream of revenge—fire from my right hand and fire from my left—the cannoneers did not expect it. I knocked down five of them. Then I knelt and started shooting to kill. I let the maimed go by. But I saw the little team of blue screeching and trying to shoot me, and I killed four of them. Then they all ran off.

There was nothing to shoot at.

I turned around and walked back toward the shack I'd been in. The roof was blown off. The roof was in the backyard lying on the toilet. A Yank with a broken leg had squirmed out from under it.

"Don't kill me," he said.

"Lay still and leave me alone," I said. "I won't kill you."

Mount Auburn had got out of the house and was standing with no expression in the bare dirt. I saw the paper sticking out of his wound. He made an alarmed sound. I turned. The Yank with a broken leg had found that slut's double-barreled Derringer. I suppose she threw it up in the air about the time the roof was blown over.

He shot at me with both barrels. One shot hit my boot and the other hit me right in the chin, but did nothing. It had been misloaded or maybe it wasn't ever a good pistol to begin with. The bullet hit me and just fell off.

"Leave me along," I said. "Come here, Auburn," I called to the big horse. "Hurt him."

I went back in the house while Mount Auburn ran back and forth over the Yank. I cast aside some of the rafters and paper in search of the old man and the slut. They were unscathed. They were under the big desk in a carnal act. I was out of ammunition or I would have slaughtered them too. I went out to the yard and called Mount Auburn off the Yank, who was hollering and running on one leg.

By the time the old man and the slut got through, I had reloaded. They came out the back slot that used to be the door.

"Tell me something. Tell me something wise!" I screamed.

He was a much braver man than I'd seen when I'd seen him in the shade of the tree.

"Tell me *something*. Tell me *something wise!*" I screamed.

"There is no wisdom, Johnny Reb," the old man said. "There's only tomorrow if you're lucky. Don't kill us. Let us have tomorrow."

I spared them. They wandered out through the corpses into the plowed rows. I couldn't see them very far because of the dirty moon. I was petting Mount Auburn when Jeb and fifteen others of the cavalry rode up. Jeb has the great beard to hide his weak chin and his basic ugliness. He's shy. I'm standing here and we've got this whole depot to plunder and burn. So he starts being chums with me. Damned if I don't think he was jealous.

"You stayed and won it, Howard, all on your own?" he says.

"Yes, sir. I did."

"There's lots of dead Christians in the ground," he said. "You've got blood all over your shirt. You're a stout fellow, aren't you?"

"You remember what you said to me when you came back and I was holding Black Answer's head in my hands when he'd been shot out from under me?"

"I recall the time but not what I said," said Jeb Stuart.

"You said, 'Use your weeping on people, not on animals,' " I said.

"I think I'd hold by that," said Stuart.

"You shit! What are we doing killing people in Pennsylvania?" I screamed.

"Showing them that we can, Captain Howard!"

They arrested me and I was taken back (by the nightways) to a detention room in North Carolina. But that was easy to break out of.

I rode my horse, another steed that knew me, named Vermont Nose.

I made it across the Mason-Dixon.

Then I went down with Grant when he had them at Cold Harbor and in the Wilderness. My uniform was blue.

I did not care if it was violet.

I knew how Stuart moved. We were equal Virginia boys. All I needed was twenty cavalry.

I saw him on the road, still dashing around and stroking his beard.

"Stuarrrrrrrrt!" I yelled.

He trotted over on his big gray horse.

"Don't I know this voice?" he said.

"It's Howard," I said.

"But I sent you away. What uniform are you wearing?"

"Of your enemy," I said.

They had furnished me with a shotgun. But I preferred the old Colt. I shot him right in the brow, so that not another thought would pass about me or about himself or about the South, before death. I knew I was killing a man with wife and children.

I never looked at what the body did on its big horse.

Then Booth shot Lincoln, issuing in the graft of the Grant administration.

I am dying from emphysema in a Miami hotel, from a twenty-five-year routine of cigars and whiskey. I can't raise my arm without gasping.

I know I am not going to make it through 1901. I am the old guy in a blue uniform. I want a woman to lie down for me. I am still functional. I believe we must eradicate all the old soldiers and all their assemblies. My lusts surpass my frame. I don't dare show my pale ribs on the beach. I hire a woman who breast-feeds me and lets me moil over her body. I've got twenty thousand left in the till from the Feds.

The only friends of the human sort I have are the ghosts that I killed. They speak when I am really drunk.

"Welcome," they say. Then I enter a large gray hall, and Stuart comes up.

"Awwww!" he groans. "Treason."

"That's right," I say.

In 1900 they had a convention of Confederate veterans at the hotel, this lonely tall thing on the barbarous waves. I was well into my third stewed mango, wearing my grays merely to be decorous. I heard a group of old coots of about my age hissing at a nearby table. It became clear that I was the object of distaste.

I stood up.

"What is it?" I asked them.

I was answered by a bearded high-mannered coot struck half dead by Parkinson's disease. He was nodding like a reed in wind. He rose in his colonel's cape. Beside him his cane clattered to the floor.

"I say I saw you in the road, dog. I'm a Virginian, and I saw it by these good eyes. You killed Jeb Stuart. *You!* Your presence is a mockery to us of the Old Cause."

"Leave me alone, you old toy," I said.

I raised my freckled fists. His companions brought him down.

When the convention left, I dressed in my grays again and walked to the beach. Presently Charlie came out of the little corral over the dune, walking Mount Auburn's grandchild. If President Grant lied to me, I don't want to know. I have proof positive that it came from a Pennsylvania farm in the region where we foraged and ambushed.

It was an exquisitely shouldered red horse, the good look in its eye.

Charlie let me have the rein and I led the animal down to the hard sand next to the water. It took me some time to mount. My overcoat fell over his withers.

"You need any help, Captain Howard?" Charlie asked.

"I don't need a goddamned thing except privacy," I said.

There was nothing on the beach, only the waves, the hard sand, and the spray. The beauty I sat on ran to the verge of his heartburst. I had never given the horse a name. I suppose I was waiting for him to say what he wanted, to talk.

But Christ is his name, this muscle and heart striding under me.

THE BURIAL OF THE GUNS

THOMAS NELSON PAGE

Lee surrendered the remnant of his army at Appomattox, April 9, 1965, and yet a couple of days later the old Colonel's battery lay intrenched right in the mountain-pass where it had halted three days before. Two weeks previously it had been detailed with a light division sent to meet and repel a force which it was understood was coming in by way of the south-west valley to strike Lee in the rear of his long line from Richmond to Petersburg. It had done its work. The mountain-pass had been seized and held, and the Federal force had not gotten by that road within the blue rampart which guarded on that side the heart of Virginia. This pass, which was the key to the main line of passage over the mountains, had been assigned by the commander of the division to the old Colonel and his old battery, and they had held it. The position taken by the battery had been chosen with a soldier's eye. A better place could not have been selected to hold the pass. It was its highest point, just where the road crawled over the shoulder of the mountain along the limestone cliff, a hundred feet sheer above the deep river, where its waters had cut their way in ages past, and now lay deep and silent, as if resting after their arduous toil before they began to boil over the great boulders which filled the bed a hundred or more yards below.

The little plateau at the top guarded the descending road on either side for nearly a mile, and the mountain on the other side of the river was the center of a clump of rocky, heavily timbered spurs, so inaccessible that no feet but those of wild animals or of the hardiest hunter had ever climbed it. On the side of the river on which the road lay, the only path out over the mountain except the road itself was a charcoal-burner's track, dwindling at times to a footway known only to the mountain-folk, which a picket at the top could hold against an army. The position, well defended, was impregnable, and it was well defended. This the general of the division knew when he detailed the old Colonel and gave him his order to hold the pass until relieved, and not let his guns fall into the hands of the enemy. He knew both the Colonel and his battery. The battery was one of the oldest in the army. It had been in the service since April, 1861, and its commander had come to be known as "The Wheel Horse of his division." He was, perhaps, the oldest officer of his rank in his branch of the service. Although he had bitterly opposed secession, and was many years past the age of service when the war came on, yet as soon as the President called on the State for her quota of troops to coerce South Carolina, he had raised and uniformed an artillery company, and offered it, not to the President of the United States, but to the Governor of Virginia.

It is just at this point that he suddenly looms up to me as a soldier; the relation he never wholly lost to me afterward, though I knew him for many, many years of peace. His gray coat with the red facing and the bars on the collar; his military cap; his gray flannel shirt—it was the first time I ever saw him wear anything but immaculate linen—his high boots; his horse caparisoned with a black, high-peaked saddle, with crupper and breast-girth, instead of the light English hunting-saddle to which I had been accustomed, all come before me now as if it were but the other day. I remember but little beyond it, yet I remember, as if it were yesterday, his leaving home, and the scenes which immediately preceded it; the excitement created by the news of the President's call for troops; the unanimous judgment that it meant war; the immediate determination of the old Colonel, who had hitherto opposed secession, that it must be met; the suppressed agitation on the plantation attendant upon the tender of his services and the governor's acceptance of them. The prompt and continuous work incident to the enlistment of the men, the bustle of preparation, and all the scenes of that time, come before me now. It turned the calm current of the life of an old and placid country neighborhood, far from any city or center, and stirred it into a boiling torrent, strong enough, or fierce enough to cut its way and join the general torrent which was bearing down and sweeping everything before it. It seemed but a minute before the quiet old plantation, in which the harvest, the corn-shucking, and the Christmas holidays alone marked the passage of the quiet seasons, and where a strange carriage or a single horseman coming down the big road was an event in life, was turned into a depot of war-supplies, and the neighborhood became a parade-ground. The old Colonel, not a colonel yet, nor even a captain, except by brevet, was on his horse by daybreak and off on his rounds through the plantations and the pines enlisting his company. The office in the yard, heretofore one in name only, became one now in reality, and a table was set out piled with papers, pens, ink, books of tactics and regulations, at which men were accepted and enrolled. Soldiers seemed to spring from the ground, as they did from the sowing of the dragon's teeth in the days of Cadmus. Men came up the high road or down the paths across the fields, sometimes singly, but oftener in little parties of two or three, and, asking for the Captain, entered the office as private citizens and came out soldiers enlisted for the war. There was nothing heard of on the plantation except fighting; white and black, all were at work, and all were eager; the servants contended for the honor of going with their master; the women flocked to the house to assist in the work of preparation, cutting out and making underclothes, knitting socks, picking lint, preparing bandages, and sewing on uniforms; for many of the men who had enlisted were of the poorest class, far too poor to furnish anything themselves, and their equipment had to be contributed mainly by wealthier neighbors. The work was carried on at night as well as by day, for the occasion was urgent. Meantime the men were being drilled by the Captain and his lieutenants, who had been militia officers of old. We were carried to see the drill at the cross-roads, and a brave sight it seemed to us: the lines marching and countermarching in the field, with the horses galloping as they wheeled amid clouds of dust, at the hoarse commands of the excited officers, and the roadside lined with spectators of every age and condition. I recall the arrival of the messenger one night, with the telegraphic order to the Captain to report with his company at "Camp Lee" immediately; the hush in the parlor that attended its reading; then the forced beginning of the conversation afterward in a somewhat strained and unnatural key, and the Captain's quick and decisive outlining of his plans.

Within the hour a dozen messengers were on their way in various directions to notify the members of the command of the summons, and to deliver the order for their attendance at a given point next day. It seemed that a sudden and great change had come. It was the actual appearance of what had hitherto only been theoretical—war.

The next morning the Captain, in full uniform, took leave of the assembled plantation, with a few solemn words commending all he left behind to God, and galloped away up the big road to join and lead his battery to the war, and to be gone just four years.

Within a month he was on "the Peninsula" with Magruder, guarding Virginia on the east against the first attack. His camp was first at Yorktown and then on Jamestown Island, the honor having been assigned his battery of guarding the oldest cradle of the race on this continent. It was at "Little Bethel" that his guns were first trained on the enemy, and that the battery first saw what they had to do, and from this time until the middle of April, 1865, they were in service, and no battery saw more service or suffered more in it. Its story was a part of the story of the Southern army in Virginia. The Captain was a rigid disciplinarian, and his company had more work to do than most new companies. A pious churchman, of the old puritanical type not uncommon to Virginia, he looked after the spiritual as well as the physical welfare of his men, and his chaplain or he read prayers at the head of his company every morning during the war. At first he was not popular with the men; he made the duties of camp life so onerous to them, it was "nothing but drilling and praying all the time," they said. But he had not commanded very long before they came to know the stuff that was in him. He had not been in service a year before he had had four horses shot under him, and when later on he was offered the command of a battalion, the old company petitioned to be one of his batteries, and still remained under his command. Before the first year was out the battery had, through its own elements, and the discipline of the Captain, become a cohesive force, and a distinct integer in the Army of Northern Virginia. Young farmer recruits knew of its prestige and expressed preference for it over many batteries of rapidly growing or grown reputation. Owing to its high stand, the old and clumsy guns with which it had started out were taken from it, and in their place was presented a battery of four fine, brass, twelve-pound Napoleons of the newest and most approved kind, and two three-inch Parrotts, all captured. The men were as pleased with them as children with new toys. The care and attention needed to keep them in prime order broke the monotony of camp life. They soon had abundant opportunities to test their power. They worked admirably, carried far, and were extraordinarily accurate in their aim. The men from admiration of their guns grew to have first a pride in, and then an affection for, them, and gave them

141

nicknames as they did their comrades; the four Napoleons being dubbed "The Evangelists," and the two rifles being "The Eagle," because of its scream and force, and "The Cat," because when it became hot from rapid firing "it jumped," they said, "like a cat." From many a hill-top in Virginia, Maryland, and Pennsylvania "The Evangelists" spoke their hoarse message of battle and death, "The Eagle" screamed her terrible note, and "The Cat" jumped as she spat her deadly shot from her hot throat. In the Valley of Virginia; on the levels of Henrico and Hanover; on the slopes of Manassas; in the woods of Chancellorsville; on the heights of Fredericksburg; at Antietam and Gettysburg; in the Spottsylvania wilderness, and again on the Hanover levels and on the lines before Petersburg, the old guns through nearly four years roared from fiery throats their deadly messages. The history of the battery was bound up with the history of Lee's army. A rivalry sprang up among the detachments of the different guns, and their several records were jealously kept. The number of duels each gun was in was carefully counted, every scar got in battle was treasured, and the men around their campfires, at their scanty messes, or on the march, bragged of them among themselves and avouched them as witnesses. New recruits coming in to fill the gaps made by the killed and disabled, readily fell in with the common mood and caught the spirit like a contagion. It was not an uncommon thing for a wheel to be smashed in by a shell, but if it happened to one gun oftener than to another there was envy. Two of the Evangelists seemed to be especially favored in this line, while the Cat was so exempt as to become the subject of some derision. The men stood by the guns till they were knocked to pieces, and when the fortune of the day went against them, had with their own hands oftener than once saved them after most of their horses were killed.

This had happened in turn to every gun, the men at times working like beavers in mud up to their thighs and under a murderous fire to get their guns out. Many a man had been killed tugging at trail or wheel when the day was against them; but not a gun had ever been lost. At last the evil day arrived. At Winchester a sudden and impetuous charge for a while swept everything before it, and carried the knoll where the old battery was posted; but all the guns were got out by the toiling and rapidly dropping men, except the Cat, which was captured with its entire detachment working at it until they were surrounded and knocked from the piece by cavalrymen. Most of the men who were not killed were retaken before the day was over, with many guns; but the Cat was lost. She remained in the enemy's hands and probably was being turned against her old comrades and lovers. The company was inconsolable. The death of comrades was too natural and common a thing to depress the men beyond what such occurrences necessarily did; but to lose a gun! It was like losing the old Colonel; it was worse: a gun was ranked as a brigadier; and the Cat was equal to a major-general. The other guns seemed lost without her; the Eagle especially, which generally went next to her, appeared to the men to have a lonely and subdued air. The battery was no longer the same: it seemed broken and depleted, shrunken to a mere section. It was worse than Cold Harbor, where over half the men were killed or wounded. The old Captain, now Colonel of the battalion, appreciated the loss and apprehended its effect on the men as much as they themselves did, and application was made for a gun to take the place of the lost piece; but there was none to be had, as the men said they had known all along. It was added—perhaps by a departmental clerk—that if they wanted a gun to take the place of the one they had lost, they had better capture it. "By—, we will," they said—adding epithets, intended for the department clerk in his "bomb-proof," not to be printed in this record—and they did. For some time afterward in every engagement into which they got there used to be speculation among them as to whether the Cat were not there on the other side; some of the men swearing they could tell her report, and even going to the rash length of offering bets on her presence.

By one of those curious coincidences, as strange as anything in fiction, a new general had, in 1864, come down across the Rapidan to take Richmond, and the old battery had found a hill-top in the line in which Lee's army lay stretched across "the Wilderness" country to stop him. The day, though early in May, was a hot one, and the old battery, like most others, had suffered fearfully. Two of the guns had had wheels cut down by shells and the men had been badly cut up; but the fortune of the day had been with Lee, and a little before nightfall, after a terrible fight, there was a rapid advance, Lee's infantry sweeping everything before it, and the artillery, after opening the way for the charge, pushing along with it; now unlimbering as some vantage-ground was gained, and using canister with deadly effect; now driving ahead again so rapidly that it was mixed up with the muskets when the long line of breastworks was carried with a rush, and a line of guns were caught still hot from their rapid work.

As the old battery, with lathered horses and smoke-grimed men, swung up the crest and unlimbered on the captured breastwork, a cheer went up which was heard even above the long general yell of the advancing line, and for a moment half the men in the battery crowded together around some object on the edge of the redoubt, yelling like madmen. The next instant they divided, and there was the Cat, smoke-grimed and blood-stained and still sweating hot from her last fire, being dragged from her muddy ditch by as many men as could get hold of trailrope or wheel, and rushed into her old place beside the Eagle, in time to be double-shotted with canister to the muzzle, and to pour it from among her old comrades into her now retiring former masters. Still, she had a new carriage, and her record was lost, while those of the other guns had been faithfully kept by the men. This made a difference in her position for which even the bullets in her wheels did not wholly atone; even Harris, the sergeant of her detachment, felt that.

It was only a few days later, however, that abundant atonement was made. The new general did not retire across the Rapidan after his first defeat, and a new battle had to be fought: a battle, if anything, more furious, more terrible than the first, when the dead filled the trenches and covered the fields. He simply marched by the left flank, and Lee marching by the right flank to head him, flung himself upon him again at Spottsylvania Court-House. That day the Cat, standing in her place behind the new and temporary breastwork thrown up when the battery was posted, had the felloes of her wheels, which showed above the top of the bank, entirely cut away by Minie-bullets, so that when she jumped in the recoil her wheels smashed and let her down. This covered all old scores. The other guns had been cut down by shells or solid shot; but never before had one been gnawed down by musketballs. From this time all through the campaign the Cat held her own beside her brazen and bloody sisters, and in the cold trenches before Petersburg that winter, when the new general—Starvation—had joined the one already there, she made her bloody mark as often as any gun on the long lines.

Thus the old battery had come to be known, as its old commander, now colonel of a battalion, had come to be known by those in yet higher command. And when in the opening spring of 1865 it became apparent to the leaders of both armies that the long line could not longer be held if a force should enter behind it, and, sweeping the one partially unswept portion of Virginia, cut the railways in the

144

south-west, and a man was wanted to command the artillery in the expedition sent to meet this force, it was not remarkable that the old Colonel and his battalion should be selected for the work. The force sent out was but small; for the long line was worn on a thin one in those days, and great changes were taking place, the consequences of which were known only to the commanders. In a few days the commander of the expedition found that he must divide his small force for a time, at least, to accomplish his purpose, and sending the old Colonel with one battery of artillery to guard one pass, must push on over the mountain by another way to meet the expected force, if possible, and repel it before it crossed the farther range. Thus, the old battery, on an April evening of 1865, found itself toiling along up the steep mountain road which leads above the river to the gap, which formed the chief pass in that part of the Blue Ridge. Both men and horses looked, in the dim and waning light of the gray April day, rather like shadows of the beings they represented than the actual beings themselves. And any one seeing them as they toiled painfully up, the thin horses floundering in the mud, and the men, often up to their knees, tugging at the sinking wheels, now stopping to rest, and always moving so slowly that they seemed scarcely to advance at all, might have thought them the ghosts of some old battery lost from some long gone and forgotten war on that deep and desolate mountain road. Often, when they stopped, the blowing of the horses and the murmuring of the river in its bed below were the only sounds heard, and the tired voices of the men when they spoke among themselves seemed hardly more articulate sounds than they. Then the voice of the mounted figure on the roan horse half hidden in the mist would cut in, clear and inspiring, in a tone of encouragement more than of command, and everything would wake up: the drivers would shout and crack their whips; the horses would bend themselves on the collars and flounder in the mud; the men would spring once more to the mud-clogged wheels, and the slow ascent would begin again.

The orders to the Colonel, as has been said, were brief: To hold the pass until he received further instructions, and not to lose his guns. To be ordered, with him, was to obey. The last streak of twilight brought them to the top of the pass; his soldier's instinct and a brief reconnoissance made earlier in the day told him that this was his place, and before daybreak next morning the point was as well fortified as a night's work by weary and supperless men could make it. A prettier spot could not have been found for the purpose; a small plateau, something over an acre in extent, where a charcoal-burner's hut had once stood, lay right at the top of the pass. It was a little higher on either side than in the middle, where a small brook, along which the charcoal-burner's track was yet visible, came down from the wooded mountain above, thus giving a natural crest to aid the fortification on either side, with open space for the guns, while the edge of the wood coming down from the mountain afforded shelter for the camp.

As the battery was unsupported it had to rely on itself for everything, a condition which most soldiers by this time were accustomed to. A dozen or so of rifles were in the camp, and with these pickets were armed and posted. The pass had been seized none too soon; a scout brought in the information before nightfall that the invading force had crossed the further range before that sent to meet it could get there, and taking the nearest road had avoided the main body opposing it, and been met only by a rapidly moving detachment, nothing more than a scouting party, and now was advancing rapidly on the road on which they were posted, evidently meaning to seize the pass and cross the mountain at this point. The day was Sunday; a beautiful spring Sunday; but it was no Sabbath for the old battery. All day the men worked, making and strengthening their redoubt to guard the pass, and by the next morning, with the old battery at the top, it was impregnable. They were just in time. Before noon their vedettes brought in word that the enemy were ascending the mountain, and the sun had hardly turned when the advance guard rode up, came within range of the picket, and were fired on.

It was apparent that they supposed the force there only a small one, for they retired and soon came up again reinforced in some numbers, and a sharp little skirmish ensued, not enough to make them more prudent afterward, though the picket retired up the mountain. This gave them encouragement and probably misled them, for they now advanced boldly. They saw the redoubt on the crest as they came on, and unlimbering a section or two, flung a few shells up at it, which neither fell short or passed over without doing material damage. None of the guns was allowed to respond, as the distance was too great with the ammunition the battery had, and, indifferent as it was, it was too precious to be wasted in a duel at an ineffectual range. Doubtless deceived by this, the enemy came on in force, being obliged by the character of the ground to keep almost

146

entirely to the road, which really made them advance in column. The battery waited. Under orders of the Colonel the guns standing in line were double-shotted with canister, and, loaded to the muzzle, were trained down to sweep the road at from four to five hundred yards' distance. And when the column reached this point the six guns, aimed by old and skillful gunners, at a given word swept road and mountain-side with a storm of leaden hail. It was a fire no mortal man could stand up against, and the practiced gunners rammed their pieces full again, and before the smoke had cleared or the reverberation had died away among the mountains, had fired the guns again and yet again. The road was cleared of living things when the draught setting down the river drew the smoke away; but it was no discredit to the other force; for no army that was ever uniformed could stand against that battery in that pass. Again and again the attempt was made to get a body of men up under cover of the woods and rocks on the mountain-side, while the guns below utilized their better ammunition from longer range; but it was useless. Although one of the lieutenants and several men were killed in the skirmish, and a number more were wounded, though not severely, the old battery commanded the mountain-side, and its skilful gunners swept it at every point the foot of man could scale. The sun went down flinging his last flame on a victorious battery still crowning the mountain pass. The dead were buried by night in a corner of the little plateau, borne to their last bivouac on the old gun-carriages which they had stood by so often—which the men said would "sort of ease their minds."

The next day the fight was renewed, and with the same result. The old battery in its position was unconquerable. Only one fear now faced them: their ammunition was getting as low as their rations; another such day or half-day would exhaust it. A sergeant was sent back down the mountain to try to get more, or, if not, to get tidings. The next day it was supposed the fight would be renewed; and the men waited, alert, eager, vigilant, their spirits high, their appetite for victory whetted by success. The men were at their breakfast, or what went for breakfast, scanty at all times, now doubly so, hardly deserving the title of a meal, so poor and small were the portions of corn-meal, cooked in their frying-pans, which went for their rations, when the sound of artillery below broke on the quiet air. They were on their feet in an instant and at the guns, crowding upon the breastwork to look or to listen; for the road, as far as could be seen down the mountain, was empty except for their own picket, and lay as quiet as if sleeping in the balmy air. And yet volley after volley of artillery came rolling up the mountain. What could it mean? That the rest of their force had come up and was engaged with that at the foot of the mountain? The Colonel decided to be ready to go and help them; to fall on the enemy in the rear; perhaps they might capture the entire force. It seemed the natural thing to do, and the guns were limbered up in an incredibly short time, and a roadway made through the intrenchment, the men working like beavers under the excitement. Before they had left the redoubt, however, the vedettes sent out returned and reported that there was no engagement going on, and the firing below seemed to be only practicing. There was quite a stir in the camp below; but they had not even broken camp. This was mysterious. Perhaps it meant that they had received reinforcements, but it was a queer way of showing it. The old Colonel sighed as he thought of the good ammunition they could throw away down there, and of his empty limber-chests. It was necessary to be on the alert, however; the guns were run back into their old places, and the horses picketed once more back among the trees. Meantime he sent another messenger back, this time a courier, for he had but one commissioned officer left, and the picket below was strengthened.

The morning passed and no one came; the day wore on and still no advance was made by the force below. It was suggested that the enemy had left; he had, at least, gotten enough of that battery. A reconnoissance, however, showed that he was still encamped at the foot of the mountain. It was conjectured that he was trying to find a way around to take them in the rear, or to cross the ridge by the foot-path. Preparation was made to guard more closely the mountain-path across the spur, and a detachment was sent up to strengthen the picket there. The waiting told on the men and they grew bored and restless. They gathered about the guns in groups and talked; talked of each piece some, but not with the old spirit and vim; the loneliness of the mountain seemed to oppress them; the mountains stretching up so brown and gray on one side of them, and so brown and gray on the other, with their bare, dark forests soughing from time to time as the wind swept up the pass. The minds of the men seemed to go back to the time when they were not so alone, but were part of a great and busy army, and some of them fell to talking of the past, and the battles they had figured in, and of the comrades they had lost. They told them off in a slow and colorless way, as it if were all part of the past as much as the dead they named. One hundred and nineteen times they had been in action. Only seventeen men were left of the eighty odd who had first enlisted in the battery, and of these four were at home crippled for life. Two of the oldest men had been among the half-dozen who had fallen in the skirmish just the day before. It looked tolerably hard to be killed that way after passing for four years through such battles as they had been in; and both had wives and children at home, too, and not a cent to leave them to their names. They agreed calmly that they'd have to "sort of look after them a little" if they ever got home. These were some of the things they talked about as they pulled their old worn coats about them, stuffed their thin, weather-stained hands in their ragged pockets to warm them, and squatted down under the breastwork to keep a little out of the wind. One thing they talked about a good deal was something to eat. They described meals they had had at one time or another as personal adventures, and discussed the chances of securing others in the future as if they were prizes of fortune. One listening and seeing their thin, worn faces and their wasted frames might have supposed they were starving, and they were, but they did not say so.

Toward the middle of the afternoon there was a sudden excitement in the camp. A dozen men saw them at the same time: a squad of three men down the road at the farthest turn, past their picket; but an advancing column could not have created as much excitement, for the middle man carried a white flag. In a minute every man in the battery was on the breastwork. What could it mean! It was a long way off, nearly half a mile, and the flag was small: possibly only a pocket-handkerchief or a napkin; but it was held aloft as a flag unmistakably. A hundred conjectures were indulged in. Was it a summons to surrender? A request for an armistice for some purpose? Or was it a trick to ascertain their number and position? Some held one view, some another. Some extreme ones thought a shot ought to be fired over them to warn them not to come on; no flags of truce were wanted. The old Colonel, who had walked to the edge of the plateau outside the redoubt and taken his position where he could study the advancing figures with his field-glass, had not spoken. The lieutenant who was next in command to him had walked out after him, and stood near him, from time to time dropping a word or two of conjecture in a half-audible tone; but the Colonel had not answered a word; perhaps none was expected. Suddenly he took his glass down, and gave an order to the lieutenant: "Take two men and meet them at the turn yonder; learn their business; and act as your best judgment advises. If necessary to bring the messenger farther, bring only the officer who has the flag, and halt him at that rock yonder, where I will join him." The tone was as placid as if such an occurrence came every day. Two minutes later the lieutenant was on his way down the mountain and the Colonel had the men in ranks. His face was as grave and his manner as quiet as usual, neither more nor less so. The men were in a state of suppressed excitement. Having put them in charge of the second sergeant, the Colonel returned to the breastwork. The two officers were slowly ascending the hill, side by side, the bearer of the flag, now easily distinguishable in his jaunty uniform as a captain of cavalry, talking, and the lieutenant in faded gray, faced with yet more faded red, walking beside him with a face white even at that distance, and lips shut as though they would never open again. They halted at the big boulder which the Colonel had indicated, and the lieutenant, having saluted ceremoniously, turned to come up to the camp; the Colonel, however, went down to meet him. The two men met, but there was no spoken question; if the Colonel inquired it was only with the eyes. The lieutenant spoke, however. "He says," he began and stopped, then began again—"he says, General Lee—" again he choked, then he blurted out, "I believe it is all a lie—a damned lie."

"Not dead? Not killed?" said the Colonel, quickly.

"No, not so bad as that; surrendered: surrendered his entire army at Appomattox day before yesterday. I believe it is all a damned lie," he broke out again, as if the hot denial relieved him. The Colonel simply turned away his face and stepped a pace or two off, and the two men stood motionless back to back for more than a minute. Then the Colonel stirred.

"Shall I go back with you?" the lieutenant asked, huskily.

The Colonel did not answer immediately. Then he said: "No, go back to camp and await my return." He said nothing about not speaking of the report. He knew it was not needed. Then he went down the hill slowly alone, while the lieutenant went up to the camp.

The interview between the two officers beside the boulder was not a long one. It consisted of a brief statement by the Federal envoy of the fact of Lee's surrender two days before near Appomattox Court-House, with the sources of his information, coupled with a formal demand on the Colonel for his surrender. To this the Colonel replied that he had been detached and put under command of another officer for a specific purpose, and that his orders were to hold that pass, which he should do until he was instructed otherwise by his superior in command. With that they parted, ceremoniously, the Federal captain returning to where he had left his horse in charge of his companions a little below, and the old Colonel coming slowly up the hill to camp. The men were at once set to work to meet any attack which might be made. They knew that the message was of grave import, but not of how grave. They thought it meant that another attack would be made immediately, and they sprang to their work with renewed vigor, and a zeal as fresh as if it were but the beginning and not the end.

The time wore on, however, and there was no demonstration below, though hour after hour it was expected and even hoped for. Just as the sun sank into a bed of blue cloud a horseman was seen coming up the darkened mountain from the eastward side, and in a little while practiced eyes reported him one of their own men—the sergeant who had been sent back the day before for ammunition. He was alone, and had something white before him on his horse—it could not be the ammunition; but perhaps that might be coming on behind. Every step of his jaded horse was anxiously watched. As he drew near, the lieutenant, after a word with the Colonel, walked down to meet him, and there was a short colloquy in the muddy road; then they came back together and slowly entered the camp, the sergeant handing down a bag of corn which he had got somewhere below, with the grim remark to his comrades, "There's your rations," and going at once to the Colonel's camp-fire, a little to one side among the trees, where the Colonel awaited him. A long conference was held, and then the sergeant left to take his luck with his mess, who were already parching the corn he had brought for their supper, while the lieutenant made the round of the camp; leaving the Colonel seated alone on a log by his camp-fire. He sat without moving, hardly stirring until the lieutenant returned from his round. A minute later the men were called from the guns and made to fall into line. They were silent, tremulous with suppressed excitement; the most sun-burned and weather-stained of them a little pale; the meanest, raggedest, and most insignificant not unimpressive in the deep and solemn silence with which they stood, their eyes fastened on the Colonel, waiting for him to speak. He stepped out in front of them, slowly ran his eye along the irregular line, up and down, taking in every man in his glance, resting on some longer than on others, the older men, then dropped them to the ground, and then suddenly, as if with an effort, began to speak. His voice had a somewhat metallic sound, as if it were restrained; but it was otherwise the ordinary tone of command. It was not much that he said: simply that it had become his duty to acquaint them with the information which he had received: that General Lee had surrendered two days before at Appomattox Court-House, yielding to overwhelming numbers; that this afternoon when he had first heard the report he had questioned its truth, but that it had been confirmed by one of their own men, and no longer admitted of doubt; that the rest of their own force, it was learned, had been captured, or had disbanded, and the enemy was now on both sides of the mountain; that a demand had been made on him that morning to surrender too; but that he had orders which he felt held good until they were countermanded, and he had declined. Later intelligence satisfied him that to attempt to hold out further would be useless, and would involve needless waste of life; he had determined, therefore, not to attempt to hold their position longer; but to lead them out, if possible, so as to avoid being made prisoners and enable them to reach home sooner and aid their families. His orders were not to let his guns fall into the enemy's hands, and he should take the only step possible to prevent it. In fifty minutes he should call the battery into line once more, and roll the guns over the cliff into the river, and immediately afterward, leaving the wagons there, he would try to lead them across the mountain, and as far as they could go in a body without being liable to capture, and then he should disband them, and his responsibility for them would end. As it was necessary to make some preparations, he would now dismiss them to prepare any rations they might have and get ready to march.

All this was in the formal manner of a common order of the day; and the old Colonel had spoken in measured sentences, with little feeling in his voice. Not a man in the line had uttered a word after the first sound, half exclamation, half groan, which had burst from them at the announcement of Lee's surrender. After that they had stood in their tracks like rooted trees, as motionless as those on the mountain behind them, their eyes fixed on their commander, and only the quick heaving up and down the dark line, as of horses over-laboring, told of the emotion which was shaking them. The Colonel, as he ended, half turned to his subordinate officer at the end of the dim line, as though he were about to turn the company over to him to be dismissed; then faced the line again, and taking a step nearer, with a sudden movement of his hands toward the men as though he would have stretched them out to them, began again:

"Men," he said, and his voice changed at the word, and sounded like a father's or a brother's, "my men, I cannot let you go so. We were neighbors when the war began—many of us, and some not here to-night; we have been more since then—comrades, brothers in arms; we have all stood for one thing—for Virginia and the South; we have all done our duty—tried to do our duty; we have fought a good fight, and now it seems to be over, and we have been overwhelmed by numbers, not whipped—and we are going home. We have the future before us—we don't know just what it will bring, but we can stand a good deal. We have proved it. Upon us depends the South in the future as in the past. You have done your duty in the past, you will not fail in the future. Go home and be honest, brave, self-sacrificing, God-fearing citizens, as you have been soldiers, and you need not fear for Virginia and the South. The war may be over; but you will ever be ready to serve your country. The end may not be as we wanted it, prayed for it, fought for it; but we can trust God; the end in the end will be the best that could be; even if the South is not free she will be better and stronger that she fought as she did. Go home and bring up your children to love her, and though you may have nothing else to leave them, you can leave them the heritage that they are sons of men who were in Lee's army."

He stopped, looked up and down the ranks again, which had instinctively crowded together and drawn around him in a half-circle; made a sign to the lieutenant to take charge, and turned abruptly on his heel to walk away. But as he did so, the long pent-up emotion burst forth. With a wild cheer the men seized him, crowding around and hugging him, as with protestations, prayers, sobs, oaths—broken, incoherent, inarticulate—they swore to be faithful, to live loyal forever to the South, to him, to Lee. Many of them cried like children; others offered to go down and have one more battle on the plain. The old Colonel soothed them, and quieted their excitement, and then gave a command about the preparations to be made. This called them to order at once; and in a few minutes the camp was as orderly and quiet as usual: the fires were replenished; the scanty stores were being overhauled; the place was selected, and being got ready to roll the guns over the cliff; the camp was being ransacked

153

for such articles as could be carried, and all preparations were being hastily made for their march.

The old Colonel, having completed his arrangements, sat down by his camp-fire with paper and pencil, and began to write; and as the men finished their work they gathered about in groups, at first around their campfires, but shortly strolled over to where the guns still stood at the breastwork, black and vague in the darkness. Soon they were all assembled about the guns. One after another they visited, closing around it and handling it from muzzle to trail as a man might a horse to try its sinew and bone, or a child to feel its fineness and warmth. They were for the most part silent, and when any sound came through the dusk from them to the officers at their fire, it was murmurous and fitful as of men speaking low and brokenly. There was no sound of the noisy controversy which was generally heard, the give-and-take of the camp-fire, the firing backward and forward that went on on the march; if a compliment was paid a gun by one of its special detachment, it was accepted by the others; in fact, those who had generally run it down now seemed most anxious to accord the piece praise. Presently a small number of the men returned to a camp-fire, and, building it up, seated themselves about it, gathering closer and closer together until they were in a little knot. One of them appeared to be writing, while two or three took up flaming chunks from the fire and held them as torches for him to see by. In time the entire company assembled about them, standing in respectful silence, broken only occasionally by a reply from one or another to some question from the scribe. After a little there was a sound of a roll-call, and reading and a short colloquy followed, and then two men, one with a paper in his hand, approached the fire beside which the officers sat still engaged.

"What is it, Harris?" said the Colonel to the man with the paper, who bore remnants of the chevrons of a sergeant on his stained and faded jacket.

"If you please, sir," he said, with a salute, "we have been talking it over, and we'd like this paper to go in along with that you're writing." He held it out to the lieutenant, who was the nearer and had reached forward to take it. "We s'pose you're a-goin' to bury it with the guns," he said, hesitatingly, as he handed it over.

"What is it?" asked the Colonel, shading his eyes with his hands.

"It's just a little list we made out in and among us," he said, "with a few things we'd like to put in, so's if any one ever hauls 'em out they'll find it there to tell what the old battery was, and if they don't, it'll be in one of 'em down thar till judgment, an' it'll sort of ease our minds a bit." He stopped and waited as a man who had delivered his message. The old Colonel had risen and taken the paper, and now held it with a firm grasp, as if it might blow away with the rising wind. He did not say a word, but his hand shook a little as he proceeded to fold it carefully, and there was a burning gleam in his deep-set eyes, back under his bushy, gray brows.

"Will you sort of look over it, sir, if you think it's worth while? We was in a sort of hurry and we had to put it down just as we come to it; we didn't have time to pick our ammunition; and it ain't written the best in the world, nohow." He waited again, and the Colonel opened the paper and glanced down at it mechanically. It contained first a roster, headed by the list of six guns, named by name: "Matthew," "Mark," "Luke," and "John," "The Eagle," and "The Cat"; then of the men, beginning with the heading:

"Those Killed."

Then had followed "Those wounded," but this was marked out. Then came a roster of the company when it first entered service; then of those who had joined afterward; then of those who were present now. At the end of all there was this statement, not very well written, nor wholly accurately spelt:

"To Whom it may Concern: We, the above members of the old battery known, etc., of six guns, named, etc., commanded by the said Col. etc., left on the 11th day of April, 1865, have made out this roll of the battery, them as is gone and them as is left, to bury with the guns which the same we bury this night. We're all volunteers, every man; we joined the army at the beginning of the war, and we've stuck through to the end; sometimes we ain't had much to eat, and sometimes we ain't had nothin', but we've fought the best we could 119 battles and skirmishes as near as we can make out in four years, and never lost a gun. Now we're agoin' home. We ain't surrendered; just disbanded, and we pledges ourselves to teach our children to love the South and General Lee; and to come when we're called anywheres an' anytime, so help us God."

There was a dead silence whilst the Colonel read.

" 'Tain't entirely accurite, sir, in one particular," said the sergeant, apologetically; "but we thought it would be playin' in sort o' low

155

down on the Cat if we was to say we lost her unless we could tell about gittin' of her back, and the way she done since, and we didn't have time to do all that." He looked around as if to receive the corroboration of the other men, which they signified by nods and shuffling.

The Colonel said it was all right, and the paper should go into the guns.

"If you please, sir, the guns are all loaded," said the sergeant; "in and about our last charge, too; and we'd like to fire 'em off once more, jist for old times' sake to remember 'em by, if you don't think no harm could come of it?"

The Colonel reflected a moment and said it might be done; they might fire each gun separately as they rolled it over, or might get all ready and fire together, and then roll them over, whichever they wished. This was satisfactory.

The men were then ordered to prepare to march immediately, and withdrew for the purpose. The pickets were called in. In a short time they were ready, horses and all, just as they would have been to march ordinarily, except that the wagons and caissons were packed over in one corner by the camp with the harness hung on poles beside them, and the guns stood in their old places at the breastwork ready to defend the pass. The embers of the sinking camp-fires threw a faint light on them standing so still and silent. The old Colonel took his place, and at a command from him in a somewhat low voice, the men, except a detail left to hold the horses, moved into company-front facing the guns. Not a word was spoken, except the words of command. At the order each detachment went to its gun; the guns were run back and the men with their own hands ran them up on the edge of the perpendicular bluff above the river, where, sheer below, its waters washed its base, as if to face an enemy on the black mountain the other side. The pieces stood ranged in the order in which they had so often stood in battle, and the gray, thin fog rising slowly and silently from the river deep down between the cliffs, and wreathing the mountainside above, might have been the smoke from some unearthly battle fought in the dim pass by ghostly guns, yet posted here in the darkness, manned by phantom gunners, while phantom horses stood behind, lit vaguely up by phantom camp-fires. At the given word the laniards were pulled together, and together as one the six black guns, belching flame and lead, roared their last challenge on the misty night, sending a deadly hail of shot and shell, tearing the trees and splintering the rocks of the farther side, and sending the thunder reverberating through the pass and down the mountain, startling from its slumber the sleeping camp on the hills below, and driving the browsing deer and the prowling mountain-fox in terror up the mountain.

There was silence among the men about the guns for one brief instant and then such a cheer burst forth as had never broken from them even in battle: cheer on cheer, the long, wild, old familiar rebel yell for the guns they had fought with and loved.

The noise had not died away and the men behind were still trying to quiet the frightened horses when the sergeant, the same who had written, received from the hand of the Colonel a long package or roll which contained the records of the battery furnished by the men and by the Colonel himself, securely wrapped to make them water-tight, and it was rammed down the yet warm throat of the nearest gun: the Cat, and then the gun was tamped to the muzzle to make her water-tight, and, like her sisters, was spiked, and her vent tamped tight. All this took but a minute, and the next instant the guns were run up once more to the edge of the cliff; and the men stood by them with their hands still on them. A deadly silence fell on the men, and even the horses behind seemed to feel the spell. There was a long pause in which not a breath was heard from any man, and the soughing of the tree-tops above and the rushing of the rapids below were the only sounds. They seemed to come from far, very far away. Then the Colonel said, quietly, "Let them go, and God be our helper, Amen." There was the noise in the darkness of trampling and scraping on the cliff-top for a second; the sound as of men straining hard together, and then with a pant it ceased all at once, and the men held their breath to hear. One second of utter silence; then one prolonged, deep, resounding splash sending up a great mass of white foam as the brass-pieces together plunged into the dark water below, and then the soughing of the trees and the murmur of the river came again with painful distinctness. It was full ten minutes before the Colonel spoke, though there were other sounds enough in the darkness, and some of the men, as the dark, outstretched bodies showed, were lying on the ground flat on their faces. Then the Colonel gave the command to fall in in the same quiet, grave tone he had used all night. The line fell in, the men getting to their horses and mounting in silence; the Colonel put himself at their head and gave the order of march, and the dark line turned in the darkness

157

crossed the little plateau between the smouldering camp-fires and the spectral caissons with the harness hanging beside them, and slowly entered the dim charcoal-burner's track. Not a word was spoken as they moved off. They might all have been phantoms. Only, the sergeant in the rear, as he crossed the little breastwork which ran along the upper side and marked the boundary of the little camp, half turned and glanced at the dying fires, the low, newly made mounds in the corner, the abandoned caissons, and the empty redoubt, and said, slowly, in a low voice to himself,

"Well, by God!"

THE RETURN OF A PRIVATE

HAMLIN GARLAND

I

The nearer the train drew toward La Crosse, the soberer the little group of "vets" became. On the long way from New Orleans they had beguiled tedium with jokes and friendly chaff; or with planning with elaborate detail what they were going to do now, after the war. A long journey, slowly, irregularly, yet persistently pushing northward. When they entered on Wisconsin Territory they gave a cheer, and another when they reached Madison, but after that they sank into a dumb expectancy. Comrades dropped off at one or two points beyond, until there were only four or five left who were bound for La Crosse County.

Three of them were gaunt and brown, the fourth was gaunt and pale, with signs of fever and ague upon him. One had a great scar down his temple; one limped; and they all had unnaturally large bright eyes, showing emaciation. There were no bands greeting them at the stations, no banks of gayly-dressed ladies waving handkerchiefs and shouting "Bravo!" as they came in on the caboose of a freight train into the towns that had cheered and blared at them on their way to war. As they looked out or stepped upon the platform for a moment, as the train stood at the station, the loafers looked at them indifferently. Their blue coats, dusty and grimy, were too familiar now to excite notice, much less a friendly word. They were the last of the army to return, and the loafers were surfeited with such sights.

The train jogged forward so slowly that it seemed likely to be midnight before they should reach La Crosse. The little squad of "vets" grumbled and swore, but it was no use, the train would not

159

hurry; and as a matter of fact, it was nearly two o'clock when the engine whistled "down brakes."

Most of the group were farmers, living in districts several miles out of the town, and all were poor.

"Now, boys," said Private Smith, he of the fever and ague, "we are landed in La Crosse in the night. We've got to stay somewhere till mornin'. Now I ain't got no two dollars to waste on a hotel. I've got a wife and children, so I'm goin' to roost on a bench, and take the cost of a bed out of my hide."

"Same here," put in one of the other men. "Hide'll grow on again, dollars come hard. It's goin' to be mighty hot skirmishin' to find a dollar these days."

"Don't think they'll be a deputation of citizens waitin' to 'scort us to a hotel, eh?" said another. His sarcasm was too obvious to require an answer.

Smith went on: "Then at daybreak we'll start f'r home, at least I will."

"Well, I'll be dummed if I'll take two dollars out o'*my* hide," one of the younger men said. "I'm goin' to a hotel, ef I don't never lay up a cent."

"That'll do f'r you," said Smith; "but if you had a wife an' three young 'uns dependin' on yeh—"

"Which I ain't, thank the Lord! and don't intend havin' while the court knows itself."

The station was deserted, chill, and dark, as they came into it at exactly a quarter to two in the morning. Lit by the oil lamps that flared a dull red light over the dingy benches, the waiting-room was not an inviting place. The younger man went off to look up a hotel, while the rest remained and prepared to camp down on the floor and benches. Smith was attended to tenderly by the other men, who spread their blankets on the bench for him, and by robbing themselves made quite a comfortable bed, though the narrowness of the bench made his sleeping precarious.

It was chill, though August, and the two men sitting with bowed heads grew stiff with cold and weariness, and were forced to rise now and again, and walk about to warm their stiffened limbs. It didn't occur to them, probably, to contrast their coming home with their going forth, or with the coming home of the generals, colonels, or even captains—but to Private Smith, at any rate, there came a sickness at heart almost deadly, as he lay there on his hard bed and went over his situation.

In the deep of the night, lying on a board in the town where he had enlisted three years ago, all elation and enthusiasm gone out of him, he faced the fact that with the joy of home-coming was mingled the bitter juice of care. He saw himself sick, worn out, taking up the work on his half-cleared farm, the inevitable mortgage standing ready with open jaw to swallow half his earnings. He had given three years of his life for a mere pittance of pay, and now—

Morning dawned at last, slowly, with a pale yellow dome of light rising silently above the bluffs which stand like some huge battlemented castle, just east of the city. Out to the left the great river swept on its massive yet silent way to the south. Jays called across the river from hillside to hillside, through the clear, beautiful air, and hawks began to skim the tops of the hills. The two vets were astir early, but Private Smith had fallen at last into a sleep, and they went out without waking him. He lay on his knapsack, his gaunt face turned toward the ceiling, his hands clasped on his breast, with a curious pathetic effect of weakness and appeal.

An engine switching near woke him at last, and he slowly sat up and stared about. He looked out of the window, and saw that the sun was lightening the hills across the river. He rose and brushed his hair as well as he could, folded his blankets up, and went out to find his companions. They stood gazing silently at the river and at the hills.

"Looks nat'cherl, don't it?" they said, as he came out.

"That's what it does," he replied. "An' it looks good. D'yeh see that peak?" He pointed at a beautiful symmetrical peak, rising like a slightly truncated cone, so high that it seemed the very highest of them all. It was lighted by the morning sun till it glowed like a beacon, and a light scarf of gray morning fog was rolling up its shadowed side.

"My farm's just beyond that. Now, ef I can only ketch a ride, we'll be home by dinnertime."

"I'm talkin' about breakfast," said one of the others.

"I guess it's one more meal o' hardtack f'r me," said Smith.

They foraged around, and finally found a restaurant with a sleepy old German behind the counter, and procured some coffee, which they drank to wash down their hardtack.

"Time'll come," said Smith, holding up a piece by the corner, "when this'll be a curiosity."

"I hope to God it will! I bet I've chawed hardtack enough to shingle every house in the coolly. I've chawed it when my lampers was down, and when they wasn't. I've took it dry, soaked, and mashed. I've had it wormy, musty, sour, and blue-mouldy. I've had it in little bits and big bits; 'fore coffee an' after coffee. I'm ready f'r a change. I'd like t' git hol't jest about now o' some of the hot biscuits my wife c'n make when she lays herself out f'r company."

"Well, if you set there gablin', you'll never see yer wife."

"Come on," said Private Smith. "Wait a moment, boys; less take suthin'. It's on me." He led them to the rusty tin dipper which hung on a nail beside the wooden water-pail, and they grinned and drank. (Things were primitive in La Crosse then.) Then shouldering their blankets and muskets, which they were "taking home to the boys," they struck out on their last march.

"They called that coffee, Jayvy," grumbled one of them, "but it never went by the road where government Jayvy resides. I reckon I know coffee from peas."

They kept together on the road along the turnpike, and up the winding road by the river, which they followed for some miles. The river was very lovely, curving down along its sandy beds, pausing now and then under broad basswood trees, or running in dark, swift, silent currents under tangles of wild grape-vines, and drooping alders, and haw-trees. At one of these lovely spots the three vets sat down on the thick green sward to rest, "on Smith's account." The leaves of the trees were as fresh and green as in June, the jays called cherry greetings to them, and kingfishers darted to and fro, with swooping, noiseless flight.

"I tell yeh, boys, this knocks the swamps of Loueesiana into kingdom come."

"You bet. All they c'n raise down there is snakes, niggers, and p'rticler hell."

"An' fightin' men," put in the older man.

"An' fightin' men. If I had a good hook an' line I'd sneak a pick'rel out o' that pond. Say, remember that time I shot that alligator—"

"I guess we'd better be crawlin' along," interrupted Smith, rising and shouldering his knapsack, with considerable effort, which he tried to hide.

"Say, Smith, lemme give you a lift on that."

"I guess I c'n manage," said Smith, grimly.

" 'Course. But, yeh see, I may not have a chance right off to pay yeh back for the times ye've carried my gun and hull caboodle. Say, now, gimme that gun, anyway."

"All right, if yeh feel like it, Jim," Smith replied, and they trudged along doggedly in the sun, which was getting higher and hotter each half-mile.

"Ain't it queer there ain't no teams comin' along."

"Well, no, seein's it's Sunday."

"By jinks, that's a fact! It *is* Sunday. I'll git home in time f'r dinner, sure. She don't hev dinner usually till about *one* on Sundays." And he fell into a muse, in which he smiled.

"Well, I'll git home jest about six o'clock, jest about when the boys are milkin' the cows," said old Jim Cranby. "I'll step into the barn, an' then I'll say, 'He*a*h! why ain't this milkin' done before this time o' day? An' then won't they yell!" he added, slapping his thigh in great glee.

Smith went on. "I'll jest go up the path. Old Rover'll come down the road to meet me. He won't bark; he'll know me, an' he'll come down waggin' his tail an' showin' his teeth. That's his way of laughin'. An' so I'll walk up to the kitchen door, an' I'll say '*Dinner f'r a hungry man!*' An' then she'll jump up, an'—"

He couldn't go on. His voice choked at the thought of it. Saunders, the third man, hardly uttered a word. He walked silently behind the others. He had lost his wife the first year he was in the army. She died of pneumonia caught in the autumn rains, while working in the fields in his place.

They plodded along till at last they came to a parting of the ways. To the right the road continued up the main valley; to the left it went over the ridge.

"Well, boys," began Smith, as they grounded their muskets and looked away up the valley, "here's where we shake hands. We've marched together a good many miles, an' now I s'pose we're done."

"Yes, I don't think we'll do any more of it f'r a while. I don't want to, I know."

"I hope I'll see yeh, once in a while, boys, to talk over old times."

"Of course," said Saunders, whose voice trembled a little, too. "It ain't *exactly* like dyin'."

"But we'd ought'r go home with you," said the younger man. "You never'll climb that ridge with all them things on yer back."

163

"Oh, I'm all right! Don't worry about me. Every step takes me nearer home, yeh see. Well, good-by, boys."

They shook hands. "Good-by. Good luck!"

"Same to you. Lemme know how you find things at home."

He turned once before they passed out of sight, and waved his cap, and they did the same, and all yelled. Then all marched away with their long, steady, loping, veteran step. The solitary climber in blue walked on for a time, with his mind filled with the kindness of his comrades, and musing upon the many jolly days they had had together in camp and field.

He thought of his chum, Billy Tripp. Poor Billy! A Minie ball fell into his breast one day, fell wailing like a cat, and tore a great ragged hole in his heart. He looked forward to a sad scene with Billy's mother and sweetheart. They would want to know all about it. He tried to recall all that Billy had said, and the particulars of it, but there was little to remember, just that wild wailing sound high in the air, a dull slap, a short, quick, expulsive groan, and the boy lay with his face in the dirt in the ploughed field they were marching across.

That was all. But all the scenes he had since been through had not dimmed the horror, the terror of that moment, when his boy comrade fell, with only a breath between a laugh and a death-groan. Poor handsome Billy! Worth millions of dollars was his young life.

These sombre recollections gave way at length to more cheerful feelings as he began to approach his home coulé. The fields and houses grew familiar, and in one or two he was greeted by people seated in the doorway. But he was in no mood to talk, and pushed on steadily, though he stopped and accepted a drink of milk once at the well-side of a neighbor.

The sun was getting hot on that slope, and his step grew slower, in spite of his iron resolution. He sat down several times to rest. Slowly he crawled up the rough, reddish-brown road, which wound along the hillside, under great trees, through dense groves of jack oaks, with tree-tops far below him on his left hand, and the hills far above him on his right. He crawled along like some minute wingless variety of fly.

He ate some hardtack, sauced with wild berries, when he reached the summit of the ridge, and sat there for some time, looking down into his home coulé.

Sombre, pathetic figure! His wide, round gray eyes gazing down into the beautiful valley, seeing and not seeing, the splendid cloud-shadows sweeping over the western hills and across the green and yellow wheat far below. His head drooped forward on his palm, his shoulders took on a tired stoop, his cheek-bones showed painfully. An observer might have said, "He is looking down upon his own grave."

II

Sunday comes in a Western wheat-harvest with such sweet and sudden relaxation to man and beast that it would be holy for that reason, if for no other. And Sundays are usually fair in harvest-time. As one goes out into the field in the hot morning sunshine, with no sound abroad save the crickets and the indescribably pleasant, silken rustling of the ripened grain, the reaper and the very sheaves in the stubble seem to be resting, dreaming.

Around the house, in the shade of the trees, the men sit, smoking, dozing, or reading the papers, while the women, never resting, move about at the housework. The men eat on Sundays about the same as on other days, and breakfast is no sooner over and out of the way than dinner begins.

But at the Smith farm there were no men dozing or reading. Mrs. Smith was alone with her three children, Mary, nine, Tommy, six, and little Ted, just past four. Her farm, rented to a neighbor, lay at the head of a coulé or narrow gulley, made at some far-off post-glacial period by the vast and angry floods of water which gullied these tremendous furrows in the level prairie—furrows so deep that undisturbed portions of the original level rose like hills on either side,—rose to quite considerable mountains.

The chickens wakened her as usual that Sabbath morning from dreams of her absent husband, from whom she had not heard for weeks. The shadows drifted over the hills, down the slopes, across the wheat, and up the opposite wall in leisurely way, as if, being Sunday, they could "take it easy," also. The fowls clustered about the housewife as she went out into the yard. Fuzzy little chickens swarmed out from the coops where their clucking and perpetually disgruntled mothers tramped about, petulantly thrusting their heads through the spaces between the slats.

A cow called in a deep, musical bass, and a calf answered from a little pen near by, and a pig scurried guiltily out of the cabbages. Seeing all this, seeing the pig in the cabbages, the tangle of grass in the garden, the broken fence which she had mended again and again—the little woman, hardly more than a girl, sat down and cried. The bright Sabbath morning was only a mockery without him!

A few years ago they had bought this farm, paying part, mortgaging the rest in the usual way. Edward Smith was a man of terrible energy. He worked "nights and Sundays," as the saying goes, to clear the farm of its brush and of its insatiate mortgage. In the midst of his herculean struggle came the call for volunteers, and with the grim and unselfish devotion to his country which made the Eagle Brigade able to "whip its weight in wild-cats," he threw down his scythe and his grub-axe, turned his cattle loose, and became a blue-coated cog in a vast machine for killing men, and not thistles. While the millionnaire sent his money to England for safe-keeping, this man, with his girl-wife and three babies, left them on a mortgaged farm, and went away to fight for an idea. It was foolish, but it was sublime for all that.

That was three years before, and the young wife, sitting on the well-curb on this bright Sabbath harvest morning, was righteously rebellious. It seemed to her that she had borne her share of the country's sorrow. Two brothers had been killed, the renter in whose hands her husband had left the farm had proved a villain, one year the farm was without crops, and now the over-ripe grain was waiting the tardy hand of the neighbor who had rented it, and who was cutting his own grain first.

About six weeks before, she had received a letter saying, "We'll be discharged in a little while." But no other word had come from him. She had seen by the papers that his army was being discharged, and from day to day other soldiers slowly percolated in blue streams back into the State and county, but still *her* private did not return.

Each week she had told the children that he was coming, and she had watched the road so long that it had become unconscious, and as she stood at the well, or by the kitchen door, her eyes were fixed unthinkingly on the road that wound down the coulé. Nothing wears on the human soul like waiting. If the stranded mariner, searching the sun-bright seas, could once give up hope of a ship, that horrible grinding on his brain would cease. It was this waiting, hoping, on the edge of despair, that gave Emma Smith no rest.

Neighbors said, with kind intentions. "He's sick, maybe, an' can't start north just yet. He'll come along one o' these days."

"Why don't he write?" was her question, which silenced them all.

This Sunday morning it seemed to her as if she couldn't stand it any longer. The house seemed intolerably lonely. So she dressed the little ones in their best calico dresses and home-made jackets, and closing up the house, set off down the coulé to old Mother Gray's.

"Old Widder Gray" lived at the "mouth of the coolly." She was a widow woman with a large family of stalwart boys and laughing girls. She was the visible incarnation of hospitality and optimistic poverty. With Western open-heartedness she fed every mouth that asked food of her, and worked herself to death as cheerfully as her girls danced in the neighborhood harvest dances.

She waddled down the path to meet Mrs. Smith with a smile on her face that would have made the countenance of a convict expand.

"Oh, you little dears! Come right to yer granny. Gimme a kiss! Come right in, Mis' Smith. How are yeh, anyway? Nice mornin', ain't it? Come in an' set down. Everything's in a clutter, but that won't scare you any."

She led the way into the "best room," a sunny, square room, carpeted with a faded and patched rag carpet, and papered with a horrible white-and-green-striped wall-paper, where a few ghastly effigies of dead members of the family hung in variously-sized oval walnut frames. The house resounded with singing, laughter, whistling, tramping of boots, and scufflings. Half-grown boys came to the door and crooked their fingers at the children, who ran out, and were soon heard in the midst of the fun.

"Don't s'pose you've heard from Ed?" Mrs. Smith shook her head. "He'll turn up some day, when you ain't lookin' for 'm." The good old soul had said that so many times that poor Mrs. Smith derived no comfort from it any longer.

"Liz heard from Al the other day. He's comin' some day this week. Anyhow, they expect him."

"Did he say anything of—"

"No, he didn't," Mrs. Gray admitted. "But then it was only a short letter, anyhow. Al ain't much for ritin,' anyhow. But come out and see my new cheese. I tell yeh, I don't believe I ever had better luck in my life. If Ed should come, I want you should take him a piece of this cheese."

It was beyond human nature to resist the influence of that noisy, hearty, loving household, and in the midst of the singing and laughing the wife forgot her anxiety, for the time at least, and laughed and sang with the rest.

About eleven o'clock a wagon-load more drove up to the door, and Bill Gray, the widow's oldest son, and his whole family from Sand Lake Coulé, piled out amid a good-natured uproar, as characteristic as it was ludicrous. Everyone talked at once, except Bill, who sat in the wagon with his wrists on his knees, a straw in his mouth, and an amused twinkle in his blue eyes.

"Ain't heard nothin' o' Ed, I s'pose?" he asked in a kind of bellow. Mrs. Smith shook her head. Bill, with a delicacy very striking in such a great giant, rolled his quid in his mouth, and said:

"Didn't know but you had. I hear two or three of the Sand Lake boys are comin'. Left New Orleenes some time this week. Didn't write nothin' about Ed, but no news is good news in such cases, mother always says."

"Well, go put out yer team," said Mrs. Gray, "an' go'n bring me in some taters, an', Sim, you go see if you c'n find some corn. Sadie, you put on the water to b'ile. Come now, hustle yer boots, all o' yeh. If I feed this yer crowd, we've got to have some raw materials. If y' think I'm goin' to feed yeh on pie—"

The children went off into the fields, the girls put dinner on to "b'ile," and then went to change their dresses and fix their hair. "Somebody might come," they said.

"Land sakes, *I hope* not! I don't know where in time I'd set 'em, 'less they'd eat at the secont table," Mrs. Gray laughed, in pretended dismay.

The two older boys, who had served their time in the army, lay out on the grass before the house, and whittled and talked desultorily about the war and the crops, and planned buying a threshing-machine. The older girls and Mrs. Smith helped enlarge the table and put on the dishes, talking all the time in that cheery, incoherent, and meaningful way a group of such women have,—a conversation to be taken for its spirit rather than for its letter, though Mrs. Gray at last got the ear of them all and dissertated at length on girls.

"Girls in love ain't no use in the whole blessed week," she said. "Sundays they're a-lookin' down the road, expectin' he'll *come*. Sunday afternoons they can't think o' nothin' else, 'cause he's *here*. Monday mornin's they're sleepy and kind o' dreamy and slimpsy, and good f'r nothin' on Tuesday and Wednesday. Thursday they git absent-minded, an' begin to look off towards Sunday agin, an' mope aroun' and let the dishwater git cold, right under their noses. Friday they break dishes, and go off in the best room an' snivel, an' look out o' the winder. Saturdays they have queer spurts o' workin' like all p'ssessed, an' spurts o' frizzin' their hair. An' Sunday they begin it all over agin."

The girls giggled and blushed all through this tirade from their mother, their broad faces and powerful frames anything but suggestive of lackadaisical sentiment. But Mrs. Smith said:

"Now, Mrs. Gray, I hadn't ought to stay to dinner. You've got—"

"Now you set right down! If any of them girls' beaus comes, they'll have to take what's left, that's all. They ain't s'posed to have much appetite, nohow. No, you're goin' to stay if they starve, an' they ain't no danger o' that."

At one o'clock the long table was piled with boiled potatoes, cords of boiled corn on the cob, squash and pumpkin pies, hot biscuit, sweet pickles, bread and butter, and honey. Then one of the girls took down a conch-shell from a nail, and going to the door blew a long, fine, free blast, that showed there was no weakness of lungs in her ample chest.

Then the children came out of the forest of corn, out of the crick, out of the loft of the barn, and out of the garden. The men shut up their jackknives, and surrounded the horse-trough to souse their faces in the cold, hard water, and in a few moments the table was filled with a merry crowd, and a row of wistful-eyed youngsters circled the kitchen wall, where they stood first on one leg and then on the other, in impatient hunger.

"They come to their feed f'r all the world jest like the pigs when y' holler 'poo—ee!' See 'em scoot!" laughed Mrs. Gray, every wrinkle on her face shining with delight. "Now pitch in, Mrs. Smith," she said, presiding over the table. "You know these men critters. They'll eat every grain of it, if yeh give 'em a chance. I swan, they're made o' India-rubber, their stomachs is, I know it."

"Haf to eat to work," said Bill, gnawing a cob with a swift, circular motion that rivalled a corn-sheller in results.

"More like workin' to eat," put in one of the girls, with a giggle. "More eat 'n' work with you."

"*You* needn't say anything, Net. Any one that'll eat seven ears—"

"I didn't, no such thing. You piled your cobs on my plate."

"That'll do to tell Ed Varney. It won't go down here, where we know yeh."

"Good land! Eat all yeh want! They's plenty more in the fiel's, but I can't afford to give you young 'uns tea. The tea is for us womenfolks, and 'specially f'r Mis' Smith an' Bill's wife. We're agoin' to tell fortunes by it."

One by one the men filled up and shoved back, and one by one the children slipped into their places, and by two o'clock the women alone remained around the débris-covered table, sipping their tea and telling fortunes.

As they got well down to the grounds in the cup, they shook them with a circular motion in the hand, and then turned them bottom-side-up quickly in the saucer, then twirled them three or four times one way, and three or four times the other, during a breathless pause. Then Mrs. Gray lifted the cup, and, gazing into it with profound gravity, pronounced the impending fate.

It must be admitted that, to a critical observer, she had abundant preparation for hitting close to the mark; as when she told the girls that "somebody was coming." "It is a man," she went on gravely. "He is cross-eyed—"

"Oh, you hush!"

"He has red hair, and is death on b'iled corn and hot biscuit."

The others shrieked with delight.

"But he's goin' to get the mitten, that redheaded feller is, for I see a feller comin' up behind him."

"Oh, lemme see, lemme see!" cried Nettie.

"Keep off," said the priestess, with a lofty gesture. "His hair is black. He don't eat so much, and he works more."

The girls exploded in a shriek of laughter, and pounded their sister on the back.

At last came Mrs. Smith's turn, and she was trembling with excitement as Mrs. Gray again composed her jolly face to what she considered a proper solemnity of expression.

"Somebody is comin' to *you*," she said after a long pause. "He's got a musket on his back. He's a soldier. He's almost here. See?"

She pointed at two little tea-stems, which formed a faint suggestion of a man with a musket on his back. He had climbed nearly to the edge of the cup. Mrs. Smith grew pale with excitement. She trembled so she could hardly hold the cup in her hand as she gazed into it.

"It's Ed," cried the old woman. "He's on the way home. Heavens an' earth! There he is now!" She turned and waved her hand out toward the road. They rushed to the door, and looked where she pointed.

A man in a blue coat, with a musket on his back, was toiling slowly up the hill, on the sun-bright, dusty road, toiling slowly, with bent head half hidden by a heavy knapsack. So tired it seemed that walking was indeed a process of falling. So eager to get home he would not stop, would not look aside, but plodded on, amid the cries of the locusts, the welcome of the crickets, and the rustle of the yellow wheat. Getting back to God's country, and his wife and babies!

Laughing, crying, trying to call him and the children at the same time, the little wife, almost hysterical, snatched her hat and ran out into the yard. But the soldier had disappeared over the hill into the hollow beyond, and, by the time she had found the children, he was too far away for her voice to reach him. And besides, she was not sure it was her husband, for he had not turned his head at their shouts. This seemed so strange. Why didn't he stop to rest at his old neighbor's house? Tortured by hope and doubt, she hurried up the coulé as fast as she could push the baby-wagon, the blue-coated figure just ahead pushing steadily, silently forward up the coulé.

When the excited, panting little group came in sight of the gate, they saw the blue-coated figure standing, leaning upon the rough rail fence, his chin on his palms, gazing at the empty house. His knapsack, canteen, blankets, and musket lay upon the dusty grass at his feet.

He was like a man lost in a dream. His wide, hungry eyes devoured the scene. The rough lawn, the little unpainted house, the field of clear yellow wheat behind it, down across which streamed the sun, now almost ready to touch the high hill to the west, the crickets crying merrily, a cat on the fence near by, dreaming, unmindful of the stranger in blue.

How peaceful it all was. O God! How far removed from all camps, hospitals, battle-lines. A little cabin in a Wisconsin coulé, but it was majestic in its peace. How did he ever leave it for those years of tramping, thirsting, killing?

Trembling, weak with emotion, her eyes on the silent figure, Mrs. Smith hurried up to the fence. Her feet made no noise in the dust and grass, and they were close upon him before he knew of them. The oldest boy ran a little ahead. He will never forget that figure, that face. It will always remain as something epic, that return of the private. He fixed his eyes on the pale face, covered with a ragged beard.

171

"Who *are* you, sir?" asked the wife, or, rather, started to ask, for he turned, stood a moment, and then cried:

"Emma!"

"Edward!"

The children stood in a curious row to see their mother kiss this bearded, strange man, the elder girl sobbing sympathetically with her mother. Illness had left the soldier partly deaf, and this added to the strangeness of his manner.

But the boy of six years stood away, even after the girl had recognized her father and kissed him. The man turned then to the baby, and said in a curiously unpaternal tone:

"Come here, my little man; don't you know me?" But the baby backed away under the fence and stood peering at him critically.

"My little man!" What meaning in those words! This baby seemed like some other woman's child, and not the infant he had left in his wife's arms. The war had come between him and his baby—he was only "a strange man, with big eyes, dressed in blue, with mother hanging to his arm, and talking in a loud voice."

"And this is Tom," he said, drawing the oldest boy to him. *"He'll* come and see me. *He* knows his poor old pap when he comes home from the war."

The mother heard the pain and reproach in his voice, and hastened to apologize.

"You've changed so, Ed. He can't know yeh. This is papa, Teddy; come and kiss him—Tom and Mary do. Come, won't you?" But Teddy still peered through the fence with solemn eyes, well out of reach. He resembled a half-wild kitten that hesitates, studying the tones of one's voice.

"I'll fix him," said the soldier, and sat down to undo his knapsack, out of which he drew three enormous and very red apples. After giving one to each of the older children, he said:

"Now I guess he'll come. Eh, my little man? Now come see your pap."

Teddy crept slowly under the fence, assisted by the over-zealous Tommy, and a moment later was kicking and squalling in his father's arms. Then they entered the house, into the sitting-room, poor, bare, art-forsaken little room, too, with its rag-carpet, its square clock, and its two or three chromos and pictures from *Harper's Weekly* pinned about.

"Emma, I'm all tired out," said Private Smith, as he flung himself down on the carpet as he used to do, while his wife brought a pillow to put under his head, and the children stood about, munching their apples.

"Tommy, you run and get me a pan of chips; and Mary, you get the tea-kettle on, and I'll go and make some biscuit."

And the soldier talked. Question after question he poured forth about the crops, the cattle, the renter, the neighbors. He slipped his heavy government brogan shoes off his poor, tired, blistered feet, and lay out with utter, sweet relaxation. He was a free man again, no longer a soldier under command. At supper he stopped once, listened, and smiled. "That's old Spot. I know her voice. I s'pose that's her calf out there in the pen. I can't milk her to-night, though, I'm too tired; but I tell you, I'd like a drink o' her milk. What's become of old Rove?"

"He died last winter. Poisoned, I guess." There was a moment before the husband spoke again, in a voice that trembled a little.

"Poor old feller! He'd a known me a half a mile away. I expected him to come down the hill to meet me. It 'ud 'a' been more like comin' home if I could 'a' seen him comin' down the road an' waggin' his tail, an' laughin' that way he has. I tell yeh, it kin o' took hold o' me to see the blinds down, an' the house shut up."

"But, yeh see, we—we expected you'd write again 'fore you started. And then we thought we'd see you if you *did* come," she hastened to explain.

"Well, I ain't worth a cent on writin'. Besides, it's just as well yeh didn't know when I was comin'. I tell yeh, it sounds good to hear them chickens out there, an' turkeys, an' the crickets. Do you know they don't have just the same kind o' crickets down South. Who's Sam hired 't help cut yer grain?"

"The Ramsey boys."

"Looks like a good crop; but I'm afraid I won't do much gettin' it cut. This cussed fever an' ague has got me down pretty low. I don't know when I'll get red of it. I'll bet I've took twenty-five pounds of quinine, if I've taken a bit. Gimme another biscuit. I tell yeh, they taste good, Emma. I ain't had anything like it—Say, if you'd 'a' heard me braggin' to th' boys about your butter 'n' biscuits, I'll bet your ears 'ud 'a' burnt."

The Private's wife colored with pleasure. "Oh, you're always a-braggin' about your things. Everybody makes good butter."

"Yes; old lady Snyder, for instance."

"Oh, well. she ain't to be mentioned. She's Dutch."

"Or old Mis' Snively. One more cup o' tea, Mary. That's my girl! I'm feeling better already. I just b'lieve the matter with me is, I'm *starved*."

This was a delicious hour, one long to be remembered. They were like lovers again. But their tenderness, like that of a typical American, found utterance in tones, rather than in words. He was praising her when praising her biscuit, and she knew it. They grew soberer when he showed where he had been struck, one ball burning the back of his hand, one cutting away a lock of hair from his temple, and one passing through the calf of his leg. The wife shuddered to think how near she had come to being a soldier's widow. Her waiting no longer seemed hard. This sweet, glorious hour effaced it all.

Then they rose, and all went out into the garden and down to the barn. He stood beside her while she milked old Spot. They began to plan fields and crops for next year. Here was the epic figure which Whitman has in mind, and which he calls the "common American soldier." With the livery of war on his limbs, this man was facing his future, his thoughts holding no scent of battle. Clean, clear-headed, in spite of physical weakness, Edward Smith, Private, turned future-ward with a sublime courage.

His farm was mortgaged, a rascally renter had run away with his machinery, "departing between two days," his children needed clothing, the years were coming upon him, he was sick and emaciated, but his heroic soul did not quail. With the same courage with which he faced his southern march, he entered upon a still more hazardous future.

Oh, that mystic hour! The pale man with big eyes standing there by the well, with his young wife by his side. The vast moon swinging above the eastern peaks; the cattle winding down the pasture-slopes with jangling bells; the crickets singing; the stars blooming out sweet and far and serene; the katydids rhythmically calling; the little turkeys crying querulously, as they settled to roost in the poplar-tree near the open gate. The voices at the well drop lower, the little ones nestle in their father's arms at last, and Teddy falls asleep there.

The common soldier of the American volunteer army had returned. His war with the South was over, and his fight, his daily running fight, with nature and against the injustice of his fellow-men was begun again.

THE VETERAN

STEPHEN CRANE

Out of the low window could be seen three hickory trees placed irregularly in a meadow that was resplendent in spring-time green. Further away, the old dismal belfry of the village church looked over the pines. A horse meditating in the shade of one of the hickories lazily swished his tail. The warm sunshine made an oblong of vivid yellow on the floor of the grocery.

"Could you see the whites of their eyes?" said the man who was seated on a soap-box.

"Nothing of the kind," replied old Henry warmly. "Just a lot of flitting figures, and I let go at where they 'peared to be the thickest. Bang!"

"Mr. Fleming," said the grocer. His deferential voice expressed somehow the old man's exact social weight. "Mr. Fleming, you never was frightened much in them battles, was you?"

The veteran looked down and grinned. Observing his manner the entire group tittered. "Well, I guess I was," he answered finally. "Pretty well scared, sometimes. Why, in my first battle I thought the sky was falling down. I thought the world was coming to an end. You bet I was scared."

Every one laughed. Perhaps it seemed strange and rather wonderful to them that a man should admit the thing, and in the tone of their laughter there was probably more admiration than if old Fleming had declared that he had always been a lion. Moreover, they knew that he had ranked as an orderly sergeant, and so their opinion of his heroism was fixed. None, to be sure, knew how an orderly sergeant ranked, but then it was understood to be somewhere just shy of a

175

major-general's stars. So when old Henry admitted that he had been frightened there was a laugh.

"The trouble was," said the old man, "I thought they were all shooting at me. Yes, sir. I thought every man in the other army was aiming at me in particular and only me. And it seemed so darned unreasonable, you know. I wanted to explain to 'em what an almighty good fellow I was, because I thought then they might quit all trying to hit me. But I couldn't explain, and they kept on being unreasonable—blim!—blam!—bang! So I run!"

Two little triangles of wrinkles appeared at the corners of his eyes. Evidently he appreciated some comedy in this recital. Down near his feet, however, little Jim, his grandson, was visibly horror-stricken. His hands were clasped nervously, and his eyes were wide with astonishment at this terrible scandal, his most magnificent grandfather telling such a thing.

"That was at Chancellorsville. Of course, afterward I got kind of used to it. A man does. Lots of men, though, seem to feel all right from the start. I did, as soon as I 'got on to it,' as they say now, but at first I was pretty flustered. Now, there was young Jim Conklin, old Si Conklin's son—that used to keep the tannery—you none of you recollect him—well, he went into it from the start just as if he was born to it. But with me it was different. I had to get used to it."

When little Jim walked with his grandfather he was in the habit of skipping along on the stone pavement in front of the three stores and the hotel of the town and betting that he could avoid the cracks. But upon this day he walked soberly, with his hand gripping two of his grandfather's fingers. Sometimes he kicked abstractedly at dandelions that curved over the walk. Any one could see that he was much troubled.

"There's Sickle's colt over in the medder, Jimmie," said the old man. "Don't you wish you owned one like him?"

"Um," said the boy, with a strange lack of interest. He continued his reflections. Then finally he ventured: "Grandpa—now—was that true what you was telling those men?"

"What?" asked the grandfather. "What was I telling them?"

"Oh, about your running."

"Why, yes, that was true enough, Jimmie. It was my first fight, and there was an awful lot of noise, you know."

Jimmie seemed dazed that this idol, of its own will, should so totter. His stout boyish idealism was injured.

Presently the grandfather said: "Sickles's colt is going for a drink. Don't you wish you owned Sickles's colt, Jimmie?"

The boy merely answered: "He ain't as nice as our'n." He lapsed then to another moody silence.

One of the hired men, a Swede, desired to drive to the county seat for purposes of his own. The old man loaned a horse and an unwashed buggy. It appeared later that one of the purposes of the Swede was to get drunk.

After quelling some boisterous frolic of the farm-hands and boys in the garret, the old man had that night gone peacefully to sleep when he was aroused by clamoring at the kitchen door. He grabbed his trousers, and they waved out behind as he dashed forward. He could hear the voice of the Swede, screaming and blubbering. He pushed the wooden button, and, as the door flew open, the Swede, a maniac, stumbled inward, chattering, weeping, still screaming, "De barn fire! Fire! Fire! De barn fire! Fire! Fire! Fire!"

There was a swift and indescribable change in the old man. His face ceased instantly to be a face; it became a mask, a grey thing, with horror written about the mouth and eyes. He hoarsely shouted at the foot of the little rickety stairs, and immediately, it seemed, there came down an avalanche of men. No one knew that during this time the old lady had been standing in her night-clothes at the bed room door yelling: "What's th' matter? What's th' matter? What's th' matter?"

When they dashed toward the barn it presented to their eyes its usual appearance, solemn, rather mystic in the black night. The Swede's lantern was overturned at a point some yards in front of the barn doors. It contained a wild conflagration of its own, and even in their excitement some of those who ran felt a gentle secondary vibration of the thrifty part of their minds at sight of this overturned lantern. Under ordinary circumstances it would have been a calamity.

But the cattle in the barn were trampling, trampling, trampling, and above this noise could be heard a humming like the song of innumerable bees. The old man hurled aside the great doors, and a yellow flame leaped out at one corner and sped and wavered frantically up the old grey wall. It was glad, terrible, this single flame, like the wild banner of deadly and triumphant foes.

The motley crowd from the garret had come with all the pails of the farm. They flung themselves upon the well. It was a leisurely old machine, long dwelling in indolence. It was in the habit of giving out water with a sort of reluctance. The men stormed at it, cursed it, but it continued to allow the buckets to be filled only after the wheezy windlass had howled many protest at the mad-handed men.

With his opened knife in his hand old Fleming himself had gone headlong into the barn, where the stifling smoke swirled with the air-currents, and where could be heard in its fulness the terrible chorus of the flames, laden with tones of hate and death, a hymn of wonderful ferocity.

He flung a blanket over an old mare's head, cut the halter close to the manger, led the mare to the door, and fairly kicked her out to safety. He returned with the same blanket and rescured one of the work-horses. He took five horses out, and then came out himself with his clothes bravely on fire. He had no whiskers, and very little hair on his head. They soused five pailfuls of water on him. His eldest son made a clean miss with the sixth pailful because the old man had turned and was running down the decline and around to the basement of the barn where were the stanchions of the cows. Some one noticed at the time that he ran very lamely, as if one of the frenzied horses had smashed his hip.

The cows, with their heads held in the heavy stanchions, had thrown themselves, strangled themselves, tangled themselves; done everything which the ingenuity of their exuberant fear could suggest to them.

Here as at the well the same thing happened to every man save one. Their hands went mad. They became incapable of everything save the power to rush into dangerous situations.

The old man released the cow nearest the door, and she, blind drunk with terror, crashed into the Swede. The Swede had been running to and fro babbling. He carried an empty milk-pail, to which he clung with an unconscious fierce enthusiasm. He shrieked like one lost as he went under the cow's hoofs, and the milk-pail, rolling across the floor, made a flash of silver in the gloom.

Old Fleming took a fork, beat off the cow, and dragged the paralyzed Swede to the open air. When they had rescued all the cows save one, which had so fastened herself that she could not be moved an inch, they returned to the front of the barn and stood sadly, breathing like men who had reached the final point of human effort.

Many people had come running. Someone had even gone to the church, and now, from the distance, rang the tocsin note of the old bell. There was a long flare of crimson on the sky which made remote people speculate as to the whereabouts of the fire.

The long flames sang their drumming chorus in voices of the heaviest bass. The wind whirled clouds of smoke and cinders into the face of the spectators. The form of the old barn was outlined in black amid these masses of orange-hued flames.

And then came this Swede again, crying as one who is the weapon of the sinister fates. "De colts! De colts! You have forgot de colts!"

Old Fleming staggered. It was true; they had forgotten the two colts in the box-stalls at the back of the barn. "Boys," he said, "I must try to get 'em out." They clamored about him then, afraid for him, afraid of what they should see. Then they talked wildly each to each. "Why, it's sure death!" "He would never get out!" "Why, it's suicide for a man to go in there!" Old Fleming stared absent-mindedly at the open doors. "The poor little things," he said. He rushed into the barn.

When the roof fell in, a great funnel of smoke swarmed toward the sky, as if the old man's mighty spirit, released from its body—a little bottle—had swelled like the genie of fable. The smoke was tinted rose-hue from the flames, and perhaps the unutterable midnights of the universe will have no power to daunt the color of this soul.

Two Renegades

O. Henry

In the Gate City of the South the Confederate Veterans were reuniting; and I stood to see them march, beneath the tangled flags of the great conflict, to the hall of their oratory and commemoration.

While the irregular and halting line was passing I made onslaught upon it and dragged forth from the ranks my friend Barnard O'Keefe, who had no right to be there. For he was a Northerner born and bred; and what should he be doing hallooing for the Stars and Bars among those gray and moribund veterans? And why should he be trudging, with his shining, martial, humorous, broad face, among those warriors of a previous and alien generation?

I say I dragged him forth, and held him till the last hickory leg and waving goatee had stumbled past. And then I hustled him out of the crowd into a cool interior; for the Gate City was stirred that day, and the hand-organs wisely eliminated "Marching Through Georgia" from their repertories.

"Now, what deviltry are you up to?" I asked of O'Keefe when there were a table and things in glasses between us.

O'Keefe wiped his heated face and instigated a commotion among the floating ice in his glass before he chose to answer.

"I am assisting at the wake," said he, "of the only nation on earth that ever did me a good turn. As one gentleman to another, I am ratifying and celebrating the foreign policy of the late Jefferson Davis, as fine a statesman as ever settled the financial question of a country. Equal ratio—that was his platform—a barrel of money for a barrel of flour—a pair of $20 bills for a pair of boots—a hatful of currency for a new hat—say, ain't that simple compared with W. J. B.'s little old oxidized plank?"

"What talk is this?" I asked. "Your financial digression is merely a subterfuge. Why were you marching in the ranks of the Confederate Veterans?"

"Because, my lad," answered O'Keefe, "the Confederate Government in its might and power interposed to protect and defend Barnard O'Keefe against immediate and dangerous assassination at the hands of a blood-thirsty foreign country after the United States of America had overruled his appeal for protection, and had instructed Private Secretary Cortelyou to reduce his estimate of the Republican majority for 1905 by one vote."

"Come, Barney," said I, "the Confederate States of America has been out of existence nearly forty years. You do not look older yourself. When was it that the deceased government exerted its foreign policy in your behalf?"

"Four months ago," said O'Keefe promptly. "The infamous foreign power I alluded to is still staggering from the official blow dealt it by Mr. Davis's contraband aggregation of states. That's why you see me cake-walking with the ex-rebs to the illegitimate tune about 'simmon-seeds and cotton. I vote for the Great Father in Washington, but I am not going back on Mars' Jeff. You say the Confederacy has been dead forty years? Well, if it hadn't been for it, I'd have been breathing to-day with soul so dead I couldn't have whispered a single cuss-word about my native land. The O'Keefes are not overburdened with ingratitude."

I must have looked bewildered. "The war was over," I said vacantly, "in—"

O'Keefe laughed loudly, scattering my thoughts.

"Ask old Doc Millikin if the war is over!" he shouted, hugely diverted. "Oh, no! Doc hasn't surrendered yet. And the Confederate States! Well, I just told you they bucked officially and solidly and nationally against a foreign government four months ago and kept me from being shot. Old Jeff's country stepped in and brought me off under its wing while Roosevelt was having a gunboat repainted and waiting for the National Campaign Committee to look up whether I had ever scratched the ticket."

"Isn't there a story in this, Barney?" I asked.

"No," said O'Keefe; "but I'll give you the facts. You know I went down to Panama when this irritation about a canal began. I thought I'd get in on the ground floor. I did, and had to sleep on it, and drink water with little zoos in it; so, of course, I got the Chagres fever. That was in a little town called San Juan on the coast.

"After I got the fever hard enough to kill a Port-au-Prince nigger, I had a relapse in the shape of Doc Millikin.

"There was a doctor to attend a sick man! If Doc Millikin had your case, he made the terrors of death seem like an invitation to a donkey-party. He had the bedside manners of a Piute medicine-man and the soothing presence of a dray loaded with iron bridge-girders. When he laid his hand on your fevered brow you felt like Cap John Smith just before Pocahontas went his bail.

"Well, this old medical outrage floated down to my shack when I sent for him. He was built like a shad, and his eyebrows was black, and his white whiskers trickled down from his chin like milk coming out of a sprinkling-pot. He had a nigger boy along carrying an old tomato-can full of calomel, and a saw.

"Doc felt my pulse, and then he began to mess up some calomel with an agricultural implement that belonged to the trowel class.

" 'I don't want any death-mask made yet, Doc,' I says, 'nor my liver put in a plaster-of-Paris cast. I'm sick; and it's medicine I need, not frescoing.'

" 'You're a blame Yankee, ain't you?' asked Doc, going on mixing up his Portland cement.

" 'I'm from the North,' says I, 'but I'm a plain man, and don't care for mural decorations. When you get the Isthmus all asphalted over with that boll-weevil prescription, would you mind giving me a dose of pain-killer, or a little strychnine on toast to ease up this feeling of unhealthiness that I have got?'

" 'They was all sassy, just like you,' says old Doc, 'but we lowered their temperature considerable. Yes, sir, I reckon we sent a good many of ye over to old *mortuis nisi bonum.* Look at Antietam and Bull Run and Seven Pines and around Nashville! There never was a battle where we didn't lick ye unless you was ten to our one. I knew you were a blame Yankee the minute I laid eyes on you.'

" 'Don't reopen the chasm, Doc,' I begs him. 'Any Yankeeness I may have is geographical; and, as far as I am concerned, a Southerner is as good as a Filipino any day. I'm feeling too bad to argue. Let's have secession without misrepresentation, if you say so; but what I need is more laudanum and less Lundy's Lane. If you've mixing that compound gefloxide of gefloxicum for me, please fill my ears with it before you get around to the battle of Gettysburg, for there is a subject full of talk.'

"By this time Doc Millikin had thrown up a line of fortifications on square pieces of paper; and he says to me: 'Yank, take one of these powders every two hours. They won't kill you. I'll be around again about sundown to see if you're alive.'

"Old Doc's powders knocked the chagres. I stayed in San Juan, and got to knowing him better. He was from Mississippi, and the red-hottest Southerner that ever smelled mint. He made Stonewall Jackson and R. E. Lee look like Abolitionists. He had a family somewhere down near Yazoo City; but he stayed away from the States on account of an uncontrollable liking he had for the absence of a Yankee government. Him and me got as thick personally as the Emperor of Russia and the dove of peace, but sectionally we didn't amalgamate.

" 'Twas a beautiful system of medical practice introduced by old Doc into that isthmus of land. He'd take that bracket-saw and the mild chloride and his hypodermic, and treat anything from yellow fever to a personal friend.

"Besides his other liabilities Doc could play a flute for a minute or two. He was guilty of two tunes—'Dixie' and another one that was mighty close to the 'Suwanee River'—you might say one of its tributaries. He used to come down and sit with me while I was getting well, and aggrieve his flute and say unreconstructed things about the North. You'd have thought the smoke from the first gun at Fort Sumter was still floating around in the air.

"You know that was about the time they staged them property revolutions down there, that wound up in the fifth act with the thrilling canal scene where Uncle Sam has nine curtain-calls holding Miss Panama by the hand, while the bloodhounds keep Senator Morgan treed up in a cocoanut-palm.

"That's the way it wound up; but at first it seemed as if Colombia was going to make Panama look like one of the $3.98 kind, with dents made in it in the factory, like they wear at North Beach fish fries. For mine, I played the straw-hat crowd to win; and they gave me a colonel's commission over a brigade of twenty-seven men in the left wing and second joint of the insurgent army.

"The Colombian troops were awfully rude to us. One day when I had my brigade in a sandy spot, with its shoes off doing a battalion drill by squads, the Government army rushed from behind a bush at us, acting as noisy and disagreeable as they could.

"My troops enfiladed, left-faced, and left the spot. After enticing the enemy for three miles or so we struck a brierpatch and had to sit down. When we were ordered to throw up our toes and surrender we obeyed. Five of my best staff-officers fell, suffering extremely with stone-bruised heels.

"Then and there those Colombians took your friend Barney, sir, stripped him of the insignia of his rank, consisting of a pair of brass knuckles and a canteen of rum, and dragged him before a military court. The presiding general went through the usual legal formalities that sometimes cause a case to hang on the calendar of a South American military court as long as ten minutes. He asked me my age, and then sentenced me to be shot.

"They woke up the court interpreter, an American named Jenks, who was in the rum business and vice versa, and told him to translate the verdict.

"Jenks stretched himself and took a morphine tablet.

" 'You've got to back up against th' 'dobe, old man,' says he to me. 'Three weeks, I believe, you get. Haven't got a chew of fine-cut on you, have you?'

" 'Translate that again, with foot-notes and a glossary,' says I. 'I don't know whether I'm discharged, condemned, or handed over to the Gerry Society.'

" 'Oh,' says Jenks, 'don't you understand? You're to be stood up against a 'dobe wall and shot in two or three weeks—three, I think, they said.'

" 'Would you mind asking 'em which?' says I. 'A week don't amount to much after you are dead, but it seems a real nice long spell while you are alive.'

" 'It's two weeks,' says the interpreter, after inquiring in Spanish of the court. 'Shall I ask 'em again?'

" 'Let be,' says I. 'Let's have a stationary verdict. If I keep on appealing this way they'll have me shot about ten days before I was captured. No, I haven't got any fine-cut.'

"They sends me over to the *calaboza* with a detachment of coloured postal-telegraph boys carrying Enfield rifles, and I am locked up in a kind of brick bakery. The temperature in there was just about the kind mentioned in the cooking recipes that call for a quick oven.

"Then I gives a silver dollar to one of the guards to send for the

United States consul. He comes around in pajamas, with a pair of glasses on his nose and a dozen or two inside of him.

" 'I'm to be shot in two weeks,' says I. 'And although I've made a memorandum of it, I don't seem to get it off my mind. You want to call up Uncle Sam on the cable as quick as you can and get him all worked up about it. Have 'em send the *Kentucky* and the *Kearsage* and the *Oregon* down right away. That'll be about enough battleships; but it wouldn't hurt to have a couple of cruisers, and a torpedo-boat destroyer, too. And—say, if Dewey isn't busy, better have him come along on the fastest one of the fleet.'

" 'Now, see here, O'Keefe,' says the consul, getting the best of a hiccup, 'what do you want to bother the State Department about this matter for?'

" 'Didn't you hear me?' says I; 'I'm to be shot in two weeks. Did you think I said I was going to a lawn-party? And it wouldn't hurt if Roosevelt could get the Japs to send down the *Yellowyamtiskookum* or the *Ogotosingsing* or some other first-class cruisers to help. It would make me feel safer.'

" 'Now, what you want,' says the consul, 'is not to get excited. I'll send you over some chewing tobacco and some banana fritters when I go back. The United States can't interfere in this. You know you were caught insurging against the government, and you're subject to the laws of this country. Tell you the truth, I've had an intimation from the State Department—unofficially, of course—that whenever a soldier of fortune demands a fleet of gunboats in a case of revolutionary *katzenjammer*, I should cut the cable, give him all the tobacco he wants, and after he'd shot take his clothes, if they fit me, for part payment of my salary.'

" 'Consul,' says I to him, 'this is a serious question. You are representing Uncle Sam. This ain't any little international tomfoolery, like a universal peace congress or the christening of the *Shamrock IV.* I'm an American citizen and I demand protection. I demand the Mosquito fleet, and Schley, and the Atlantic squadron, and Bob Evans, and General E. Byrd Grubb, and two or three protocols. What are you going to do about it?'

" 'Nothing doing,' says the consul.

" 'Be off with you, then,' says I, out of patience with him, 'and send me Doc Milliken. Ask Doc to come and see me.'

"Doc comes and looks through the bars at me, surrounded by dirty soldiers, with even my shoes and canteen confiscated, and he looks mightily pleased.

" 'Hello, Yank,' says he, 'getting a little taste of Johnson's Island, now, ain't ye?'

" 'Doc,' says I, 'I've just had an interview with the U. S. consul. I gather from his remarks that I might just as well have been caught selling suspenders in Kishineff under the name of Rosenstein as to be in my present condition. It seems that the only maritime aid I am to receive from the United States is some navy-plug to chew. Doc,' says I, 'can't you suspend hostilities on the slavery question long enough to do something for me?'

" 'It ain't been my habit,' Doc Milliken answers, 'to do any painless dentistry when I find a Yank cutting an eyetooth. So the Stars and Stripes ain't landing any marines to shell the huts of the Colombian cannibals, hey? Oh, say, can you see by the dawn's early light the star-spangled banner has fluked in the fight? What's the matter with the War Department, hey? It's a great thing to be a citizen of a gold-standard nation, ain't it?'

" 'Rub it in, Doc, all you want,' says I. 'I guess we're weak on foreign policy.'

" 'For a Yank,' says Doc, putting on his specs and talking more mild, 'you ain't so bad. If you had come from below the line I reckon I would have liked you right smart. Now since your country has gone back on you, you have to come to the old doctor whose cotton you burned and whose mules you stole and whose niggers you freed to help you. Ain't that so, Yank?'

" 'It is,' says I heartily, 'and let's have a diagnosis of the case right away, for in two weeks' time all you can do is to hold an autopsy and I don't want to be amputated if I can help it.'

" 'Now,' says Doc, business-like, 'it's easy enough for you to get out of this scrape. Money'll do it. You've got to pay a long string of 'em from General Pomposo down to this anthropoid ape guarding your door. About $10,000 will do the trick. Have you got the money?'

" 'Me?' says I. 'I've got one Chili dollar, two *real* pieces, and a *medio*.'

" 'Then if you've any last words, utter 'em,' says that old reb. 'The roster of your financial budget sounds quite much to me like the noise of a requiem.'

" 'Change the treatment,' says I. 'I admit that I'm short. Call a consultation or use radium or smuggle me in some saws or something.'

" 'Yank,' says Doc Millikin, 'I've a good notion to help you. There's only one government in the world that can get you out of this difficulty; and that's the Confederate States of America, the grandest nation that ever existed.'

"Just as you said to me I says to Doc; 'Why, the Confederacy ain't a nation. It's been absolved forty years ago.'

" 'That's a campaign lie,' says Doc. 'She's running along as solid as the Roman Empire. She's the only hope you've got. Now, you, being a Yank, have got to go through with some preliminary obsequies before you can get official aid. You've got to take the oath of allegiance to the Confederate Government. Then I'll guarantee she does all she can for you. What do you say, Yank?—it's your last chance.'

" 'If you're fooling with me, Doc,' I answers, 'you're no better than the United States. But as you say it's the last chance, hurry up and swear me. I always did like corn whisky and 'possum anyhow. I believe I'm half Southerner by nature. I'm willing to try the Ku-Klux in place of the khaki. Get brisk.'

"Doc Millikin thinks awhile, and then he offers me this oath of allegiance to take without any kind of a chaser:

" 'I, Barnard O'Keefe, Yank, being of sound body but a Republican mind, hereby swear to transfer my fealty, respect, and allegiance to the Confederate States of America, and the government thereof in consideration of said government, through its official acts and powers, obtaining my freedom and release from confinement and sentence of death brought about by the exuberance of my Irish proclivities and my general pizeness as a Yank.'

"I repeated these words after Doc, but they seemed to me a kind of hocus-pocus; and I don't believe any life-insurance company in the country would have issued me a policy on the strength of 'em.

"Doc went away saying he would communicate with his government immediately.

"Say—you can imagine how I felt—me to be shot in two weeks and my only hope for help being in a government that's been dead so long that it isn't even remembered except on Decoration Day and when Joe Wheeler signs the voucher for his pay-check. But it was all there was in sight; and somehow I thought Doc Milliken had something up his old alpaca sleeve that wasn't all foolishness.

"Around to the jail comes old Doc again in about a week. I was flea-bitten, a mite sarcastic, and fundamentally hungry.

" 'Any Confederate ironclads in the offing?' I asks. 'Do you notice any sounds resembling the approach of Jeb Stewart's cavalry overland or Stonewall Jackson sneaking up in the rear? If you do, I wish you'd say so.'

" 'It's too soon yet for help to come,' says Doc.

" 'The sooner the better,' says I. 'I don't care if it gets in fully fifteen minutes before I am shot; and if you happen to lay eyes on Beauregard or Albert Sidney Johnston or any of the relief corps, wig-wag 'em to hike along.'

" 'There's been no answer received yet,' says Doc.

" 'Don't forget,' says I, 'that there's only four days more. I don't know how you propose to work this thing, Doc,' I says to him; 'but it seems to me I'd sleep better if you had got a government that was alive and on the map—like Afghanistan or Great Britain, or old man Kruger's kingdom, to take this matter up. I don't mean any disrespect to your Confederate States, but I can't help feeling that my chances of being pulled out of this scrape was decidedly weakened when General Lee surrendered.'

" 'It's your only chance,' said Doc; 'don't quarrel with it. What did your own country do for you?'

"It was only two days before the morning I was to be shot, when Doc Millikin came around again.

" 'All right, Yank,' says he. 'Help's come. The Confederate States of America is going to apply for your release. The representatives of the government arrived on a fruit-steamer last night.'

" 'Bully!' says I—'bully for you, Doc! I suppose it's marines with a Gatling. I'm going to love your country all I can for this.'

" 'Negotiations,' says old Doc, 'will be opened between the two governments at once. You will know later on today if they are successful.'

"About four in the afternoon a soldier in red trousers brings a paper round to the jail, and they unlocks the door and I walks out. The guard at the door bows and I bows, and I steps into the grass and wades around to Doc Millikin's shack.

"Doc was sitting in his hammock playing 'Dixie,' soft and low and out of tune, on his flute. I interrupted him at 'Look away! look away!' and shook his hand for five minutes.

" 'I never thought,' says Doc, taking a chew fretfully, 'that I'd ever try to save any blame Yank's life. But, Mr. O'Keefe, I don't see but what you are entitled to be considered part human, anyhow. I never thought Yanks had any of the rudiments of decorum and laudability about them. I reckon I might have been too aggregative in my tabulation. But it ain't me you want to thank—it's the Confederate States of America.'

" 'And I'm much obliged to 'em,' says I. 'It's a poor man that wouldn't be patriotic with a country that's saved his life. I'll drink to the Stars and Bars whenever there's a flagstaff and a glass convenient. But where,' says I, 'are the rescuing troops? If there was a gun fired or a shell burst, I didn't hear it.'

"Doc Millikin raises up and points out the window with his flute at the banana-steamer loading with fruit.

" 'Yank,' says he, 'there's a steamer that's going to sail in the morning. If I was you, I'd sail on it. The Confederate Government's done all it can for you. There wasn't a gun fired. The negotiations was carried on secretly between the two nations by the purser of that steamer. I got him to do it because I didn't want to appear in it. Twelve thousand dollars was paid to the officials in bribes to let you go.'

" 'Man!' says I, sitting down hard—'twelve thousand—how will I ever—who could have—where did the money come from?'

" 'Yazoo City,' says Doc Millikin: 'I've got a little saved up there. Two barrels full. It looks good to these Colombians. 'Twas Confederate money, every dollar of it. Now do you see why you'd better leave before they try to pass some of it on an expert?'

" 'I do,' says I.

" 'Now let's hear you give the password,' says Doc Millikin.

" 'Hurrah for Jeff Davis!' says I.

" 'Correct,' says Doc. 'And let me tell you something: The next tune I learn on my flute is going to be "Yankee Doodle." I reckon there's some Yanks that are not so pizen. Or, if you was me, would you try "The Red, White, and Blue"?' "

ANCESTORS

FRED CHAPPELL

Harry and Lydie were enduring their third ancestor and finding it a rum go. Not that they were surprised—the first two ancestors had also proved to be enervating specimens—and now they regretted the hour they had joined the Ancestor Program of the Living History Series. Sitting at dinner, fed up with Wade Wordmore, Harry decided to return this curious creature to his congressman, Doy Collingwood, at his local office over in Raleigh, North Carolina.

They were goaded into joining the program by that most destructive of all human urges: the desire for self-improvement. When, as part of the celebration of the one-hundred-fiftieth anniversary of the Civil War, the U.S. Archives and History Division called Harry Beacham and told him that the records showed he had no less than three ancestral relatives who had fought in the great conflict and asked if he'd be interested in meeting these personages, he replied that Yes, of course, he would love to meet them.

What Southerner wouldn't say that?

It is also in the Southern manner to take the marvels of modern technology for granted. The crisp impersonal female voice in the telephone receiver explained that from the merest microscopic section of bone, computers could dredge out of the past not only the physical lineaments of the person whom that bone once held perpendicular but the personality traits too, down to the last little tic and stammer. In their own house Harry and Lydie could engage with three flesh-and-blood examples of history come to life. Of course, it really wasn't flesh, only a sort of protein putty, but it was real blood, right enough. It was pig blood: that was a biochemical necessity.

"Can they talk?" Harry asked and was assured that they spoke,

190

remembered their former lives in sharp detail, and even told jokes—rather faded ones, of course. They also ate, slept, and shaved, were human in every way. "That is the Departmental motto," the voice said. "Engineering Humanity for Historic Purpose."

He asked casually about the cost, and she stated it, and he was pleased but still desired to think just a few days about whether to subscribe to the program.

"That will not be necessary," said the woman's voice. "The arrangements have already been taken care of and your first ancestor is on his way to you. The Archives and History Division of the United States Department of Reality is certain that you will find real satisfaction in your encounters with Living History. Good day, Mr. Butcher."

"Wait a minute," Harry said. "My name is Beacham." But the connection was cut, and when he tried to call back, he was shunted from one office to another and put on hold so often and so long that he gave up in disgust.

So then as far as Harry was concerned, all bets were off. He was a Beacham and no Butcher and proud of it, and if some artificial entity from the Archives Division showed up at his door, he would send the fellow packing.

But he didn't have to do that. Lieutenant Aldershot's papers were in apple-pie order when he presented them with a sharp salute to Lydie. She met him at the front door and was immediately taken with this swarthy brown-eyed man in his butternut uniform and broad-brimmed hat. A battered leather-bound trunk sat on the walk behind him.

"Oh, you must be the ancestor they sent," she said. "Lieutenant Edward Aldershot of the Northern Virginia reporting as ordered, ma'am."

Confused, Lydie colored prettily and looked up and down the lane to see if any of her neighbors here in the Shining Acres development were observing her resplendent visitor. She took the papers he proffered, started to open them, but paused with her fingers on the knotted ribbon and said, "Oh, do come in," and stepped back into the foyer. The lieutenant moved forward briskly, removing his hat just before he stepped over the threshold. "Honey," she called. "Harry, honey. Our ancestor is here."

He came downstairs in no pleasant frame of mind, but then stood silent and wide-eyed before Aldershot, who snapped him a classy

191

respectful salute and declared his name and the name of his army. "I believe the lady will be kind enough to present my papers, sir."

But Harry and Lydie only stood gaping until the lieutenant gestured toward the packet in Lydie's hands. She gave it to Harry, blushing again, and Harry said in a rather stiff tone, trying to hide his astonishment, "Ah yes. Of course. . . . Your papers. . . . Of course."

And for a wonder they were all correct. Here was the letter from History identifying Aldershot and congratulating the Beachams on the opportunity of enjoying his company for three weeks and telling them what a valuable experience they were in for. Then there was Aldershot's birth certificate and a very sketchy outline of his military career and then a family tree in which Harry was relieved to discover not a single Butcher. It was all Beachams and Lawsons and Hollinses and Bredvolds and Aldershots and Harpers as far as the eye could see, all the way to the beginning of the nineteenth century.

"This looks fine," Harry said. "We're glad to have you as one of us."

"I'm proud to hear you say so, sir," the lieutenant said and tore off another healthy salute.

"You don't need to be so formal," Harry told him. "You don't have to salute me or call me sir. We're just friends here."

"That's very kind of you. I'm afraid it may take a little time for me to adjust, sir."

"You'll fit right in," Lydie said. "I'm sure you will."

"Thank you, ma'am," said Aldershot. "I do take tobacco and a little whiskey now and then. I hope you won't mind."

"Oh no. If that's what you did—I mean, if that's what you're used to. Please feel free." A bashful woman, she blushed once more. She had almost said: *If that's what you did when you were alive.* "Harry, you can bring in the lieutenant's trunk, if you don't mind."

The Confederate Officer had too modestly described his pleasures. He did not merely take tobacco, he engorged it, sawing off with his case knife black tarry knuckles of the stuff from a twist he carried in his trousers pocket and chewing belligerently, like a man marching against an opposing brigade. He was a veritable wellpump of tobacco juice, spitting inaccurately not only at the champagne bucket and other utensils the Beachams supplied him as spittoons but at any handy vessel that offered a concavity. The sofa suffered and the rugs, the tablecloths, the lieutenant's bedding and his clothing—his clothing most of all.

In fact, his whole appearance deteriorated rapidly and ruinously. In three days he no longer wore his handsome butternut but had changed into the more familiar uniform of Confederate gray, a uniform which seemed to grow shabbier even as the Beachams gazed upon it. His sprightly black moustache, which Lydie had fancied as complementing his dark eyes perfectly, became first ragged, then shaggy. He would neglect to shave for four days running, and he began to smell of sweat and stale underwear and whiskey.

For he had also understated the power of his thirst. On the first night and always afterward, he never strayed far from the jug and when not actually pouring from it would cast amorous glances in its direction. He drank George Dickel neat or sometimes with sugar water and praised the quality of the bourbon in ardent terms, saying, for example, "If we'd a-had a little more of this at Chancellorsville it would've been a different story." Liquor seemed to affect him little, however; he never lost control of his motor reflexes or slurred his speech.

Yet the quality of his address had changed since that sunny first moment with the Beachams. It was no more *Yes sir* and *No sir* to Harry, but *our friend Harry here* and *Old Buddy* and *Old Hoss*. He still spoke to Lydie as *Ma'am*, but when talking indirectly would refer to her as *our mighty fine little female of the house*. He was never rude or impolite, but his formal manner slipped into an easy camaraderie and then sagged into a careless intimacy. His social graces frayed at about the same rate as his gray uniform, which by the end of the second week was positively tattered.

The lieutenant, though, had not been ordered to the Beacham residence as a dancing master, but as a representative of History which, as the largest division of the Department of Reality, shared much of its parent organization's proud anatomy. And of Living History, Lieutenant Aldershot offered a spectacular cornucopia. The outline of his career that came with him from the government agency barely hinted at the range and length of his fighting experience. He had fought at Vicksburg, Fredericksburg, and Gettysburg; he had survived Shiloh, Antietam, and Richmond; he had been brave at Bull Run, Rich Mountain, Williamsburg, and Cedar Mountain; he had won commendations from Zollicoffer, Beauregard, Johnston, Kirby-Smith, Jackson, and Robert E. Lee. The latter commander he referred to as "General Bobby" and described him as "the finest Southern Gentleman who ever whupped his enemy."

Harry's knowledge of history was by no means as profound as his enthusiasm for it, and he had not found time before Aldershot's arrival to bone up on the battles and campaigns that occurred a century and a half past. Even so, the exploits of the ambeer-spattered and strongly watered lieutenant began to overstretch Harry's credulity. In order to be on all the battlefields he remembered, Aldershot must have spent most of the War on the backs of two dozen swift horses, and to survive the carnage he had witnessed must have kept busy a fretting cohort of guardian angels. Any soldier of such courage, coolness, intelligence, and resourcefulness must have left his name in letters of red blaze in the history books, but Harry could not recall hearing of Aldershot. Of course, it had been some seven years since he had looked at the histories; perhaps he had only forgotten.

For in many ways it was hard to disbelieve the soldier's accounts, he was so particular in detail and so vivid in expression. When telling of some incident that displayed one man's valor or another's timidity, he became brightly animated, and then heated, and would squirm in his chair at the table, sputtering tobacco and gulping bourbon, his eyes wild and bloodshot. He rocked back and forth in the chair as if he were in the saddle, leaping the brushy hurdles at the Battle of Fallen Timber. He broke two chairs that way, and his host supplied him a steel-frame lawn chair brought in from the garage.

He was vivid and particular most of all in his accounts of bloodshed. Although he spoke only plain language, as he averred a soldier should, he so impressed Harry's imagination and Lydie's trepidation that they felt extremely close to the great conflict. In Aldershot's bourbonish sentences they heard the bugles at daybreak, the creak of munitions wagons, the crack of rifles and bellow of cannon, the horses screaming in pain and terror. They saw the fields clouded over with gunsmoke and the hilltop campfires at night and the restless shuffle of pickets on the sunset perimeters. They could smell corn parching and mud waist deep and the stink of latrines and the worse stink of gangrene in the hospital tents.

The lieutenant's accounts of battle went from bloody to chilling to gruesome, and the closeness with which he detailed blows and wounds and killings made the *Iliad* seem vague and pallid. He appeared to take a certain relish in demonstrating on his own body where a Minie ball had gone into a comrade and where it came out and what raw mischief it had caused during its journey. He spoke of shattered teeth and splintered bone and eyes gouged out. When he began to describe the surgeries and amputations, dwelling at great length on the mound of removed body parts at the Fredericksburg field hospital, Lydie pleaded with him to spare her.

"Please," she said. "Perhaps we needn't hear all this part." Her eyes were large and teary in her whitened face and her voice trembled.

"Uh, yes," Harry said. "I think Lydie has a point. Maybe we can skip a few of the gorier details now and then." He too was obviously shaken by what he had heard.

"Well now," Aldershot said, "of course I didn't mean to alarm our mighty fine little female of the house. I hope you'll forgive a plain-spoken soldier, ma'am, one who never learned the orator's art. You're a brave un in my book, for there's many a refined Southern lady who will faint when she hears the true story of things. Especially when I tell how it is to be gutshot."

"Please, Lieutenant," Lydie said. She took three sips of her chardonnay, recovering her composure pretty quickly, but looking with dismay at her plate of stewed pork.

"How about you?" Harry asked. "Were you ever wounded?"

"Me?" Aldershot snorted. "No, not me. I was always one too many for them bluebellies, not that they didn't try plenty hard."

This discussion took place at the end of the second week. At first Aldershot had referred to his ancient opponents as *the enemy* and then changed his term to *the Northern invader*. In the second week, though, it was *bluebellies* every time, and in the third week it was *them goddamn treacherous Yankee bastards*, to which epithet he always appended a parenthetical apology to Lydie:—*saving your presence, ma'am*.

Even that small gesture toward the observance of chivalry seemed to cost him some effort. In the third week the weary Confederate appeared to have aged a decade; his clothes were now only threads and patches, his moustache a straggly bristle, his eyes discolored and dispirited, and his speech disjoined, exhausted, and crumbling. It was clear that remembering had taken too much out of him, that he had tired himself almost past endurance. He had cut down on his tobacco intake, as if the exercise of a chaw drew off too much strength, and had increased his frequency of whiskey, although this spiritous surplus did not enliven his demeanor.

On the eve of his departure, Lieutenant Aldershot begged off telling of the destruction of Atlanta and gave only the most cursory sketch of the surrender at Appomattox. For the first time in three weeks, he retired early to bed.

Next morning he came down late and took only coffee for his breakfast. He had dragged his leather-bound trunk to the front door and stood with his foot propped on it as he bade the Beachams farewell. Gravely they shook hands. When he spoke to Lydie Aldershot, he held his hat over his heart. "Ma'am, your hospitality has been most generous and not something a plain soldier will forget."

Lydie took his hand; she blushed, feeling that she ought to curtsey but not knowing how.

He looked straight into Harry's eyes. "So long, Old Hoss," he said. "It's been mighty fine for me here."

"We've been honored," Harry said. "Believe me."

Then the government van arrived and the driver came to load Aldershot's trunk and they shook hands once more and the lieutenant departed. As they watched him trudging down the front walk, Harry and Lydie were struck silent by the mournful figure he presented, his shoulders slumped, his head thrust forward, and his step a defeated shuffle. When he mounted to the van cab and rode away without waving or looking back, a feeling of deep sadness descended upon them, so that they stood for a minute or two holding each other for comfort and looking into the bright empty morning.

Finally Harry closed the door and turned away. "I don't know about you," he said, "but I feel tired. Tired in my bones."

"Me too," Lydie said. "And I've got to get this house cleaned up. There's tobacco spit everywhere. Everything in the house is splattered."

"I feel like we just lost the war."

"Well, honey, that's exactly what happened."

"I'll tell you what I'm going to do—if you don't mind, I mean. I'm going to call these government History people and tell them not to send the other ancestors. I'm utterly exhausted. I can't imagine how I'd feel after two more visitors like the lieutenant."

"I think you're right," she said. "Do it now."

Harry got on the telephone and dialed a list of bureaucratic numbers, only to find that each and every one gave off a busy signal for hours on end.

So on Monday morning, at ten-thirty on the dot, Private William Harper presented himself at the front door and handed his papers to Lydie with a shy bow. His was a diffident gray uniform that had seen better days, but it was clean and tidy. He was accompanied by no trunk; only a modest, neatly turned bedroll lay at his feet. "Ma'am, I believe you are expecting me?" he said.

Her first impulse was to send him away immediately, but the van must have departed already since it was nowhere in sight, and, anyway, her second stronger impulse was to invite him into the house and feed him. Lieutenant Aldershot must have been in his early forties—though he had looked to be sixty years old when he departed—but Private Harper could hardly have been out of his teens.

He offered her his papers and gave her what he obviously hoped was a winning smile, but he was so young and clear-eyed and shy and apprehensive that his expression was more frightened than cordial.

Lydie's heart went out to him entirely; she took the packet without looking at it, staring almost tenderly upon Harper with his big bright blue eyes and rosy complexion in which the light fuzz was evidence of an infrequent acquaintance with a razor. He was a slight young man, slender and well-formed and with hands as long-fingered and delicate as a pianist's. He seemed troubled by her stare and shifted restlessly in his boots.

"Ma'am," he asked, "have I come to the right house? Maybe I'm supposed to be somewhere else."

"No," Lydie said. "You come right in. This is the place for you."

"I wouldn't want to be a burden," the private said. "Those government people said that you had invited me to come here. I wouldn't want to impose on you."

"We're glad to have you. Don't worry about a thing."

He looked all about him, wonderstruck. "You belong to a mighty grand place. It's hard for me to get used to the houses and everything that people have."

"We feel lucky," Lydie said. "Lots of people are not so well-off." Then, seeing that he could formulate no reply, she stooped and picked up his bedroll. "Please come in. I was just getting ready to make some fresh coffee. You'd like that, wouldn't you?"

"Yes, ma'am."

In the kitchen Private Harper sat at the table and watched moonily every step and gesture Lydie made. His nervousness was subsiding, but he seemed a long way from being at ease. She took care to smile warmly and speak softly, but it was apparent to her from Harper's worshipful gaze that she had already conquered the young man's heart. When she set the coffee before him with the cream pitcher and sugar bowl alongside, he didn't glance down, looking instead into her face. "Now, Private Harper," she said, "drink your coffee. And would you like something to eat? I can make a sandwich or maybe there's a piece of chocolate cake left. You like chocolate cake, don't you?"

"No ma'am. Just the coffee is all I want to wake me up. I was feeling a little bit tired."

"Of course you are," she said. "You finish your coffee and I'll show you to your room and you can get some sleep."

"You're awful kind, ma'am. I won't say no to that."

When the private was tucked away, Lydie telephoned her spouse at his place of business, Harry's Hot-Hit Vidrents, to tell him the news.

He was not happy. "Oh, Lydie," he said. "You were supposed to send him back where he came from. That was our plan."

"I just couldn't," she said. "He's so young. And he was tired out. He's already asleep."

"But we agreed. Don't you remember? We agreed to send him packing."

"Wait till you meet him. Then send him packing. If you can do it, it will be all right with me."

And having met the young man, Harry no more than Lydie could order him away. Harper was so innocent and willing and open-faced that Harry could only feel sympathy for him when he saw what puppy eyes the young man made at his wife. He offered him a drink—Aldershot had overlooked a half bottle of Dickel in a lower cabinet—and was not surprised when the lad refused. "I promised my mother, sir, before I went off to war."

"I see," Harry said, and reflected gravely on the difference between the lieutenant and the private. "But in the army, that must have been a hard promise to keep."

"Oh no, sir. Not when I promised my mother. And to tell the truth, I don't have much taste for liquor."

He did accept a cup of tea, spooning into it as much sugar as would dissolve, and was profusely grateful.

Harry then readied himself with a gin and tonic for another stiff dose of History. "I suppose you must have fought in lots of battles," he said.

Private Harper shook his head sadly. "Only two battles, sir."

"Which were those?"

"Well, I fought at Bethel, sir, and then we were sent down toward Richmond."

"You were at Manassas?" These were place-names that Aldershot had deeply imprinted on the Beacham memory.

"Yes sir."

"And what was that like?"

"Well, sir. . . ." For the first time, Private Harper lifted his eyes and looked directly into Harry's face. His boyish countenance was a study in apologetic confusion as he steadied his teacup on his knee and said, "Well, sir, if you don't mind, I'd rather not talk 'bout that."

"You don't want to talk about Manassas?" Harry asked. Then his surprise disappeared with the force of his realization: Manassas would have been where Private Harper had died.

"I don't like to talk about the war at all, sir."

"I see."

"I know I'm supposed to, but I just can't seem to make myself do it. It opens up old wounds."

"That's all right. I understand."

"No, sir, I don't believe that you do understand. It is too hard for me right now. It opens old wounds."

"That's quite all right. Where are you from originally?"

"Salem, Virginia," Private Harper said. "We had a farm right outside town. I miss that place a great deal."

"I'm sure you do."

"I miss my folks too, sir. Something terrible." And he went on to talk about his life before the war, and his story was so idyllic and engaging that Harry called Lydie from the kitchen to hear it.

The private spoke rhapsodically of such ordinary tasks as planting corn, shoeing horses, repairing wagons, cutting hay, milking cows and so forth; his bright face glowed even friendlier as he spoke of these matters, and as he warmed to his stories his shyness melted and his language became almost lyrical.

He was the only male in a female family, his father having died when Billy was only eleven. He allowed that his mother and three sisters had rather doted on him, but it was obvious to the Beachams that he had no real idea how much they doted. He had not been required to join the army; he had done so only out of a sense of duty and from a fear of the shame he might feel later if he did not join. He had supposed that the colored men attached to the family, Jupiter and Peter—who were not thought of as being slaves—would look after the ladies and take care of the farm. But shortly after Billy went away to war, those two had slipped off and were not heard of again. He had been in the process of applying for permission to return home when the Battle of Manassas befell him.

He seemed to remember mornings fondly, and summer mornings most fondly of all. To wake up to the smell of ham and coffee and biscuits and grits, to look off the front porch into the dew-shiny fields and to see the little creek in the bottom winking with a gleam through the bushes—well, these sights made him feel that Paradise might be something of a letdown when finally at last he disembarked upon that lucent shore. The haze-blue mountains offered deer and partridge, possum and quail, and Billy loved to take his bay mare, Cleopatra, and his father's old long-barreled rifle and hunt on those slopes from morn till midnight.

About that mare he was rapturous. "If I told you how smart Cleo was, and some of the things I've known her to do, you'd think I was straying from the truth," he said. "But I'm not. She really is the best horse in the world, the smartest and the gentlest. Not that she doesn't have a lot of spirit. Why, I believe she had more courage than a bear, but she's as gentle with children as a mammy. And she's the best hunter I know of, bar none."

The Beachams smiled, trying vainly to imagine that Private Harper would deliberately stray from the truth; but it was clear that in regard to his horse his infatuation might fetch him out of the strait path of accuracy without his ever being aware. It seemed that Cleopatra knew where game was to be found up there in the hills and when given her head would unerringly seek out the best cover to shoot deer and fowl of every sort. There never was a horse like her for woodlore. Harry felt his credulity strained when Harper mentioned that she could also sniff out trout in the river and would carry her master to the sweetest fishing holes. And Lydie left unspoken her reservations about Billy's account of Cleo's stamping out a fire and thus saving the Harper farmhouse and barn and the lives of the four of them.

A skeptical expression must have crossed her face, though, because Billy looked at her imploringly and said in the most earnest tone: "Oh, it's true, I assure you it is. You can ask Julie or Annie or my mother. They'll tell you it's gospel truth." Lydie realized then that she must keep her emotions out of her face, that Billy Harper always forgot that his family was sealed away in time past and that he was an orphan in a world of strangers.

He forgot himself so thoroughly when he spoke that his unhappy situation appeared to escape his memory. Yet something was troubling him. As the day went by, he grew restless and his soft volubility began to lapse. Toward the end of the second week, not even questions about Cleopatra could alleviate his distractedness.

On Monday of the third week he spoke his mind. "I know you-all want to hear about the war," he said glumly. "And I know that's what I'm supposed to be telling you. It's just that I can't bear to open up those wounds again. I guess I'd better try, though, since that's what I'm sent here to do."

"You're not supposed to do anything that you don't want to," Harry said. "We haven't been notified that you are required to talk about the war. In fact, we haven't been notified of anything much. I wish I could get a phone call through to those History folks."

"That's right," Lydie said. "I'm tired of hearing about that ugly old war. I'd much rather hear about your mother and sisters and the farm."

All their reassurances would not lighten Billy's darkened spirits. The more they spoke soothing words, the gloomier he became, and they could see that he was steeling himself to broach the subject and they became anxious about him, for his nervousness increased as his determination grew.

When he began to talk, after supper on his third Wednesday, he was obviously desperate. His hands trembled and he kept his eyes trained on the beige patch of living-room carpet in front of his armchair and he spoke in a low mutter. His sentences were jumbled and hard to understand. He was sweating.

"There were onlookers up on the ridges," he said. "We were down in the bottom fields there at Manassas when McDowell brought his

201

troops around. We could see them up there, the spectators, I mean, and I borrowed Jed's glass and took a look and they were drinking wine and laughing and there were ladies in their carriages, and younguns too, setting off firecrackers. So when I handed him his glass back I said, 'I don't believe it's going to be a fight, not with the high society people looking on; I expect that McDowell and General Bee will parley.' And he said, 'No, it'll be a fight, Billy. Can't neither side back off now, we're in too close to each other. McDowell will have to fight here right outside of Washington because Lincoln himself might be up there on a hilltop watching.' But I didn't believe him. I never thought we'd fight that day."

He paused and licked his lips and asked for a glass of water. Lydie brought it from the kitchen, ice cubes tingling, and told the private with meaningful tenderness that he did not need to continue his story.

Harper took the glass and sipped, appearing not to hear her words. He kept his eyes downcast and began again. "At nine in the morning it was already warm and we knew we'd be feeling the heat and then with no warning it started up. Sergeant Roper hadn't no more than told us to brace ourselves because there appeared to be more Yankees here than ants in an anthill when we saw gunsmoke off to our left, a little decline there, and heard the shots and in that very first volley Jed fell down with a ball in the middle of his chest, but before he hit the ground he took another one in his shoulder that near about tore his left arm off. I didn't have a least idea any of them was close enough to get a shot at us. I laid down by Jed and took him in my arms but couldn't do nothing and they made me let him lay and start fighting."

His face had been flushed and sweaty but now was sugar-white and drenched. His eyes wore dark circles, and when he raised them for the first time, caught up as he was in his memories, he seemed not to see Lydie or Harry or anything around him. He was sweating so profusely his uniform was darkening—that was what Lydie thought at first, but then she rose to clutch Harry's arm. Blood was dripping from Harper's sleeve over his wrist and onto the rug.

"So I got on one knee to see what I could and brought my rifle up, but I didn't know what to do. I could tell they were all around us because my comrades were firing at them in every direction but I couldn't spot anything, so much smoke and dust. I saw some muzzle blazes on my right and thought I might shoot, but then maybe that was one of our lines over there. I was a pretty good marksman to go a-hunting, but in a battle I couldn't figure where to aim."

His voice had sunk almost to a whisper, and his tunic and the chair he sat in were soaking with blood. Harry remembered that it would be pig blood and not human, but he was horrified all the same—more disturbed, perhaps, than if it had been Harry's own blood. He looked quickly at Lydie and then rushed to her aid. He knew now what Billy Harper had meant when he said that to talk about the war opened old wounds.

He took his wife by the arm and drew her toward the bedroom. She went along without a murmur, her face drawn and blanched. He could feel her whole body trembling. He helped her to lie down and told her to keep still, not to move; he would take care of everything, he said. It was going to be all right.

But when he returned to the living room, Harper was lying face down on the floor. He had tumbled out of his chair and lay motionless in a thick smelly puddle of brownish blood. Harper knelt to examine him and it was obvious that he was gone, literally drained of life.

Harry telephoned for an ambulance and sat down to think about what to tell the medics when they came. Perhaps they wouldn't accept Private Harper; perhaps they wouldn't regard him as a real human being. To whom could he turn for assistance in that case? He knew better than to call Archives and History; the last time he had called those numbers, a recorded voice informed him that they had all been disconnected. Now he was trying to reach, by mail and telephone and fax machine, his congressman, Representative Doy Collingwood, but so far had received no reply.

When the ambulance came, though, the young paramedics understood the situation immediately and seemed to find it routine. The fellow with the blond-red mustache—he looked like a teenager, Harry thought ruefully—only glanced at the inert figure on the rug before asking, "Civil War?"

"Yes," Harry said. "My God, it was awful. My wife is almost hysterical. This is just terrible."

The fellow nodded. "We get them like this all the time. Faulty parts and sloppy workmanship. Sometimes we'll get four calls a week like this."

"Can't something be done?"

"Have you tried to get in touch with Ark and Hist?"

"With whom?"

"The Archives and History Division . . . in Washington," he asked, then saw Harry's expression. "Never mind, I know. Tell you what, though. I'd better have a look to see if your wife is okay. Where is she?"

Harry showed him the bedroom and stood by while he ministered to Lydie. She murmured her gratitude, but kept her eyes closed. The young medic gave her some pills to take and went with Harry back to the living room. "She'll be all right," he said. "Probably have a couple of rough nights."

The driver had already put down a stretcher and rolled Harry's body over onto it. His eyes were open and a dreadful change had come to his face, a change that was more than death and worse, a change that made Private Harper look as if he'd never been human—in this life or any other.

Harry had to look away. "My God," he said.

"Pretty awful, isn't it?" The medic's response was cheerful, matter-of-fact. "Shoddy stuff, these Ark and Hist sims. But there's some good salvage there, more than you'd think by looking at it."

"What did you call him?" Harry asked. "Simms?"

"Sim. It's a nickname. A simulacrum from the Division of Archives and History. Your tax dollars at work, know what I mean? Sign here," he said, handing Harry a clipboard and a pen. "And here," he said, turning a page. "And here. And here. And here. And here. And here. And here. And here."

The medic had predicted rough nights for Lydie, but she suffered bad days as well and took to her bed. She kept the shades drawn and the lights down and watched chamber music on the vidcube. Harry gave his shop over to the attentions of two assistants and stayed home with his wife, preparing her scanty meals and consoling her and monitoring the installation of the new carpet and choosing a new chair for the living room. Lydie would probably hate the chocolate-colored wingback he'd bought, but that was all right. She could exchange it when she was up and around.

He planned to stay home with her for a week or two—for as long as it took to make certain that the government was sending to the Beacham household no more sims. Harry pronounced the word with an ugly angry hiss; *ssimsss*. He put as much disgust into the sibilants as his teeth could produce, but there was no satisfaction for him.

He was so infuriated and felt so impotent that he began to wish a new specimen would turn up, just so that he could send it away with a message for the people who had dispatched it. He prepared several speeches in his mind, each more savage than the last, each more heartfelt and more eloquent.

He never got to deliver any of them, even though the expected third visitor did, after all, show, a week later than had been stipulated. But he didn't announce himself, didn't knock at the door and present his papers as Aldershot and Harper had done. He just stood in the front yard with his back turned toward the house and gazed at the houses opposite and at the children riding bicycles and chasing balls along the asphalt lanes of Shining acres. Often he would look at the sky, at the puffy cloud masses scooting overhead, and he would take off his big gray hat with the floppy brim and shade his eyes with his hand.

This hat was not of Confederate gray but of a lighter, mineral color, nearly the same gray color as the man's clothing. Nor was his attire military; he wore cotton trousers held up by a broad leather belt and a soft woolen shirt with an open collar. When he removed his hat, shining gray locks fell past his ears and the sunlight imparted to this mass of silver a whitish halo effect. He turned around to look at the Beacham house, and Harry saw that he wore a glorious gray beard, clean and bright and patriarchal, and that his eyes were clear and warm.

Even from where Harry stood inside, the man's gaze was remarkable: calm and trusting and unworried and soothing. When he replaced his hat Harry recognized his gesture as easy and graceful, neither sweeping nor constrained. There was a natural ease about his figure that put Harry's mind at rest. He would still send him away, of course he would, but Harry began to soften the speech he had planned to make, to modify its ferocity and to sweeten a little bit its bitterness.

But when had this fellow arrived? How long had he been standing there, observing the world from his casual viewing point, with his little gray knapsack lying carelessly on the lawn? He might have been there for hours; nothing in his manner would ever betray impatience.

Harry opened the door and called to the man. "Hey you," he said. "Hey you, standing in my yard."

The man turned slowly, presenting his whole figure as if he wished to be taken in from crown to shoe-sole, to be examined and measured for what he was as a physical being. "I am Wade Wordmore," he said, and his voice was full of gentle strength. "I have come a great distance, overstepping time and space; I am the visitor who has been sent."

"Yeah, that's right," Harry said. "The government sent you, right? The History people? They sent you to the Beacham residence, right?"

"That is correct in some measure," said Wade Wordmore. "But I believe there is more to it than that."

"Well, go away," Harry said. "We don't want you. We've had enough—" He didn't finish the sentence he had planned to say; he found that he could not look into Wordmore's gaze and say, *We've had enough of you goddamn sims to last us a lifetime.*

Ssssimssss.

"Gladly I go where I am wanted and unwanted," Wordmore said. "The world is my home, in it I am free to loaf and meditate, every particle is as interesting to me as every other particle, the faces of men and women gladden me as I journey."

"I don't mean for you to wander around like a stray dog," Harry said. "I mean, go back where you came from. Go back to the government."

"But what to me are governments?" the gray man replied. "I, Wade Wordmore, American, untrammeled by boundaries, unfixed as to station, and at my ease in all climes and latitudes, answer to no laws save those my perfect nature (for I know I am perfect, how can a man tall and in pure health be not perfect?), and am powerful to overstep any border."

Here was a stumper. Harry had foreseen that Ark and Hist would send another defective simulacrum, but he had not imagined being put in charge of a bona fide grade-A blue ribbon lunatic. It was clear from Wordmore's manner as he stooped to take up his knapsack and sling it on his shoulder that he was willing to stroll out into a century he knew nothing about, utterly careless about what would happen to him for good or ill. And beyond this privileged residential suburb, Wordmore's adventures would be mostly ill; his strange aspect and wild mode of speech would mark him as an easy victim to chicanery and violence alike.

"Oh, for God's sake," Harry said. There was no help for it. "For God's sake, come in the house."

As Wordmore stepped over the threshold, he removed his floppy hat. But this gesture of deference only served to underscore a casual royalty of presence; he entered Harry's house as if he belonged there not as a guest but by right of ownership. "I am most grateful to you, sir, and to everyone else in the house. White or black, Chinaman or Lascar or Hottentot, they are all equal to me and I bid them good day."

"We're fresh out of those. There's no one here but me and my wife Lydie. She's not feeling well and she's not going to be pleased that I let you come in. I'll have some tall explaining to do."

But Lydie stood already in the hall doorway. She had drawn a bright floral wrapper over her nightgown, yet the cheerful colors only caused her face to look paler and her eyes more darkly encircled. She appeared feverish. "Oh Harry," she said softly, wearily.

"Honey—"

"Among the strong I am strongest," Wordmore said in a resonant steady voice that then quieted almost to a whisper: "Among the weak I am gentlest." He tucked his knapsack under his left arm and went to Lydie and took her hand and drew her forward as if he were leading her onto a ballroom floor. He placed her in the new chocolate-colored wingback chair and smiled upon her benevolently and gave her the full benefit of that gray-eyed gaze so enormous with sympathy.

She responded with a tremulous smile and then leaned back and closed her eyes. "I hope you will be nice to us," she said in a voice as small as the throbbing of a faraway cricket. "We've never harmed anybody, Harry and I. We just wanted to know about his ancestors who fought in the Civil War. I guess that wasn't such a good idea."

"You know," Harry said, "I don't recall hearing about any Wordmores in my family. Are you sure you're related to me?"

"Each man is my brother, every woman my sister," Wordmore stated. "To all I belong equally, disregarding none. In every household I am welcome, being full of health and good will and bearing peaceful tidings for all gathered there."

At these words Lydie opened her eyes, then blinked them rapidly several times. Then she gave Harry one of the most reproachful glances one spouse ever turned upon another.

In a moment, though, she closed her eyes again and nestled into the wingback. Harry could see that she was relaxing, her breathing slowed now and regular. Wordmore emitted a powerful physical aura, an almost visible emanation of peaceful healthful ease. Harry wondered if the man might have served as a physician in the War. Certainly his presence was having a salubrious effect upon Lydie, and Harry decided it would be all right to have Wordmore around for a few hours longer. If he was a madman he was harmless.

"Can I offer you a drink?" Harry asked. "We still have some bourbon left over from an earlier ancestor."

"I drink only pure water from the spring gushing forth," Wordmore replied. "My food is ever of the plainest and most wholesome."

"Tap water is all we've got," Harry said.

"I will take what you offer, I am pleased at every hospitality." He turned his attention to Lydie, placing his delicate freckled hand on her forehead. "You will soon be strong again," he told her. "Rest now and remember the summer days of your youth, the cows lowing at the pasture gate and the thrush singing in the thicket and the haywain rolling over the pebbled road with the boys lying in the hay, their arms in friendship disposed around one another."

Lydie smiled ruefully. "I can't remember anything like that," she said. "I grew up in Chicago. It was mostly traffic and street gangs fighting with knives."

"Remember then your mother," Wordmore said. "Remember her loving smile as over your bed she leant, stroking your hair and murmuring a melody sweet and ancient. Remember her in the kitchen as the steam rose around her and the smell of bread baking and the fruits of the season stewed and sugared, their thick juices oozing."

Lydie opened her eyes and sat forward. "Well, actually," she explained, "my parents divorced when I was five and I didn't see much of either of them after that. Only on holidays when one of them might visit at my convent school."

He was not to be discouraged. "Remember the days of Christmas then, when you and your comrade girls, tender and loving, waited for the gladsome step in the foyer—"

"It's all right," Lydie said firmly. "Really, I don't need to remember anything. I feel much better. I really do."

Harry returned with the ice water and looked curiously at the duo. "What's been going on?" he asked. "What are you two talking about?"

"Mr. Wordmore has been curing me of my ills," Lydie said.

The gray man nodded placidly, even a little smugly. "It is a gift that I have, allotted me graciously at my birth, as it was given to you and you, freely offered to all." He sipped his water.

"To me?" Harry asked. "I don't think I've got any healing powers. Business is my line; I own a little video rental shop."

"Business too is good," Wordmore said. "The accountant weary, arranging his figures at end of day, his eye-shade pulled over his furrowed brow and the lamplight golden on the clean-ruled page, and the manager of stores, the keeper of inventories, his bunched iron keys jangling on his manly thigh—"

"Well, it's not quite like that," Harry said. "I can see what you're getting at, though. You think business is okay, the free enterprise system and all."

"All trades and occupations are equal and worthy, the fisherman gathering in his nets fold on fold, and the hog drover with his long staff and his boots caked with fine delicious muck, and the finder of broken sewer pipes and the emptier of privies—"

"Yes, yes," Harry interrupted. "You mean that it's a good thing everybody has a job to do."

Wordmore smiled warmly and took another sip of water, gently shaking the glass to enjoy the jingle of the ice cubes.

"Maybe it's time we thought about making dinner," Harry said. "I'm not a bad cook. I'm sure Lydie would rather stay and talk to you while I rustle up something to eat."

"Oh no!" she exclaimed. "That would never do. I feel fine. I'll go right in and start on it."

"I wish you wouldn't," Harry said. "You ought to be resting."

"Honey," said Lydie with unmistakable determination, "you're going to be the one to stay here and talk to Mr. Wordmore. I don't care how much I have to cook."

"My food is ever of the plainest," Wordmore intoned. "The brown loaf hearty from the oven, its aromas arising, and the cool water from the mountain spring gushed forth—"

"Right," Lydie said. "I think I understand."

They knew pretty well what to expect at dinner, and Wordmore didn't surprise them, drinking sparely and nibbling vegetables and discoursing in voluminous rolling periods upon any subject that was brought up—except that he never managed to light precisely upon the topic at hand, only somewhere in the scattered vicinity. Yet it was soothing to listen to him: his sentences which at first were so warm and sympathetic and filled with humane feeling and calm loving-kindness lost their intimacy after a while. They seemed to become as impersonal and distant as some large sound of nature: the muffled roar of a far-off waterfall or wind in the mountaintop balsams or sea waves lapping at a pebbled beach. His unpausing talk was not irritating because his good will was unmistakable; neither was it boring because the Beachams soon learned not to listen to it for content and took an absent-minded pleasure in the mere sound of it. Harry thought of it as a kind of verbal Muzak and wondered how Wordmore had been perceived by his contemporaries. They must have found him as strange an example of humankind as Harry and Lydie did.

On the other hand they must have got on well with him. He'd make a good neighbor, surely, because he never had a bad word for anyone. He had no bad words at all, not a smidgen of disapproval for anything, as far as they could discern. If potatoes were mentioned, Wordmore would go a long way in praise of potatoes; if it was bunions, they too were champion elements of the universe, indispensable. Housefly or horsefly, rhododendron or rattlesnake, Messiah or mosquito—they all seemed to hold a high place in the gray man's esteem; to him the world was a better place for containing any and all of them.

He went on so placidly in this vein that Harry couldn't resist testing the limits of his benignity. "Tell me, Mr. Wordmore—"

"Among each and every I am familiar, the old and the young call me by my First-Name," Wordmore said. "The children climb on my lap and push their hands into my beard, laughing."

"Sure, all right. Wade. Tell me, Wade, what was the worst thing you ever saw? The most terrible?"

"Equally terrible and awesome in every part is the world, the lightnings that jab the antipodes, the pismire in its—"

"I mean, personally," Harry explained. "What's the worst thing that ever happened to you?"

He fell silent and meditated. His voice when he spoke was heavy and sorrowful. "It was the Great Conflict," he said, "where I ministered to the spirits of the beautiful young men who lay wounded and sick and dying, their chests all bloody-broken and—"

"Harry!" Lydie cried. "I won't listen to this."

"That's all right," Harry said quickly. "We don't need to hear that part, Wade. I was just wondering what kinds of things you might think were wrong. Bad, I mean."

"Bad I will not say, though it was terrible, the young men so fair and handsome that I wished them hale again and whole that we might walk to the meadows together and there show our love, the Divine Nimbus around our bodies playing—"

"Whoa," Harry said. "Wait a minute now."

"Are you gay?" Lydie asked. She leaned forward, her interest warmly aroused. "I didn't think there used to be gay people. In Civil War times, I mean."

"My spirits are bouyant always, with the breeze lifting, my mind happy and at ease, a deep gaiety overtakes my soul when I behold a bullfrog or termite—"

"No, now. She means—well, *gay*," Harry said. "Are you homosexual?"

"To me sex, the Divine Nimbus, every creature exhales and I partake willingly, my soul gladly joining, my body locked in embrace with All, my—"

"All?" Harry and Lydie spoke in unison.

Wordmore nodded. "All, yes, All, sportively I tender my—"

"Does this include the bullfrog and the termite?" Harry asked.

"Yes," Wordmore said without hesitation. "Why should every creature not enjoy my manliness? Whole and hearty I am Wade Wordmore, American, liking the termite equally with the—"

"Wade, my friend," Harry said. "You old-time fellows sure do give us modern people something to think about. I'd like you to meet my congressman and give him the benefit of some of your ideas. Tomorrow I'm going to drive you over to the state capital and introduce you. How would you like that?" He slipped Lydie a happy wink.

"The orators and statesmen are ever my camaradoes," Wordmore said. "I descry them on the high platform, the pennons of America in the wind around them flying, their lungs in-taking the air, and the words outpouring."

"It's a date then," Harry said. "Pack your knapsack for a long stay. I intend for you and him to become fast friends."

But when they arrived in Raleigh the next day and Harry drove around toward Representative Collingwood's headquarters, he found the streets blocked with cars honking and banging fenders and redfaced policemen trying to create some sort of order and pattern. The sidewalks too were jammed with pedestrians, most of them dressed in the uniform of the Army of the Confederate States of America.

Sssimssss.

"My God," Harry said. He could not have imagined that so many people had subscribed to the Ancestor Program, that so many simulacra had been produced. Looking at the people who were obviously not sims, he saw written on their faces weariness, exasperation, sorrow, horror, guilt, and cruel determination—all the feelings he and Lydie had experienced for the past weeks, the feeling he now felt piercingly with Wordmore sitting beside him, babbling on about the Beautiful Traffic Tangles of America.

Finally a channel opened and he rolled forward, to be stopped by a tired-looking policeman.

Harry thumbed his window down, and the officer leaned in.

"May I see who is with you, sir?"

"This is Wade Wordmore," Harry said. "You'd find it hard to understand how glad he is to meet you."

"I am Wade Wordmore," said the graybeard, "and glad of your company, admiring much the constable as he goes his rounds—"

"Well, I'm glad you like company," the policeman said. "You're going to have plenty of it." He turned his bleared gaze on Harry. "We're shifting all the traffic to the football stadium parking lot, sir, and we're asking everyone to escort their ancestors onto the field."

"Is everybody bringing them in?" Harry asked.

"Yes, sir, almost everyone. It seems like everybody ran out of patience at the same time. They've been coming in like this for three days now."

"I can believe it," Harry said. "What is the History Division going to do with them all?"

"There is no longer a History Division," the policeman said. "In fact, we just got word a while ago that the government has shut down the whole Reality Department."

"They shut down Reality? Why did they do that?"

"They took a poll," the policeman replied. "Nobody wanted it."

"Good Lord," Harry said. "What is going to happen?"

"I don't know, sir, but I'm afraid I'll have to ask you to move along."

"Okay, all right," Harry said. He drove on a few feet, then stopped and called back: "I've got an idea. Why don't we ship all these sims north to the Union states? After all, they're the ones who killed them in the first place."

"I'm afraid that those states have the same problem we do," the policeman said. "Please, sir, do move along. There will be someone at the stadium to give you instructions."

"Okay. Thanks." He rolled the window up and edged the car forward.

Wordmore had fallen silent, looking in open-mouthed wonder at all the cars and the Confederate soldiers streaming by and mothers and children white-faced and weeping and dogs barking and policemen signaling and blowing whistles.

"You know," Harry said, "I just never thought about the Yankees wanting to meet *their* ancestors, but of course they would. It's a natural curiosity. I guess it must have seemed like a good idea to bring all this history back to life, but now look. What are we going to do now?" The station wagon in front of him moved, and Harry inched forward.

"The history of the nation I see instantly before me, as on a plain rolling to the mountains majestic, like a river rolling, the beautiful young men in their uniforms with faces scarce fuzzed with beard—"

But Harry was not listening. His hands tightened on the steering wheel till the knuckles went purple and white. "My God," he said. "We've got all our soldiers back again and the Yankees have got theirs back. War is inevitable. I believe we're going to fight the whole Civil War over again. I'll be damned if I don't."

"—the beautiful young men falling in battle amid smoke of cannon and the sky louring over, the mothers weeping at night and the sweethearts weeping—"

"Oh, shut up, Wordmore. I know how terrible it is. It's too horrible to think about." He remembered Lieutenant Aldershot and Private Harper, and a gritty tight wry little smile crossed his face. "Bluebellies," Harry said. "This time we'll show them."

A Late Encounter
with the Enemy

Flannery O'Connor

General Sash was a hundred and four years old. He lived with his granddaughter, Sally Poker Sash, who was sixty-two years old and who prayed every night on her knees that he would live until her graduation from college. The General didn't give two slaps for her graduation but he never doubted he would live for it. Living had got to be such a habit with him that he couldn't conceive of any other condition. A graduation exercise was not exactly his idea of a good time, even if, as she said, he would be expected to sit on the stage in his uniform. She said there would be a long procession of teachers and students in their robes but that there wouldn't be anything to equal *him* in his uniform. He knew this well enough without her telling him, and as for the damn procession, it could march to hell and back and not cause him a quiver. He liked parades with floats full of Miss Americas and Miss Daytona Beaches and Miss Queen Cotton Products. He didn't have any use for processions and a procession full of schoolteachers was about as deadly as the River Styx to his way of thinking. However, he was willing to sit on the stage in his uniform so that they could see him.

Sally Poker was not as sure as he was that he would live until her graduation. There had not been any perceptible change in him for the last five years, but she had the sense that she might be cheated out of her triumph because she so often was. She had been going to summer school every year for the past twenty because when she started teaching, there were no such things as degrees. In those times, she said, everything was normal but nothing had been normal since she was sixteen, and for the past twenty summers, when she should have been resting, she had had to take a trunk in the burning heat to the state teacher's college; and though when she returned in the fall, she always taught in the exact way she had been taught not to teach, this was a mild revenge that didn't satisfy her sense of justice. She wanted the General at her graduation because she wanted to show what she stood for, or, as she said, "what all was behind her," and was not behind them. This *them* was not anybody in particular. It was just all the upstarts who had turned the world on its head and unsettled the ways of decent living.

She meant to stand on that platform in August with the General sitting in his wheel chair on the stage behind her and she meant to hold her head very high as if she were saying, "See him! See him! My kin, all you upstarts! Glorious upright old man standing for the old traditions! Dignity! Honor! Courage! See him!" One night in her sleep she screamed, "See him! See him!" and turned her head and found him sitting in his wheel chair behind her with a terrible expression on his face and with all his clothes off except the general's hat and she had waked up and had not dared to go back to sleep again that night.

For his part, the General would not have consented even to attend her graduation if she had not promised to see to it that he sit on the stage. He liked to sit on any stage. He considered that he was still a very handsome man. When he had been able to stand up, he had measured five feet four inches of pure game cock. He had white hair that reached to his shoulders behind and he would not wear teeth because he thought his profile was more striking without them. When he put on his full-dress general's uniform, he knew well enough that there was nothing to match him anywhere.

This was not the same uniform he had worn in the War between the States. He had not actually been a general in that war. He had probably been a foot soldier; he didn't remember what he had been; in fact, he didn't remember that war at all. It was like his feet, which hung down now shriveled at the very end of him, without feeling, covered with a blue-gray afghan that Sally Poker had crocheted when she was a little girl. He didn't remember the Spanish-American War in which he had lost a son; he didn't even remember the son. He didn't have any use for history because he never expected to meet it again. To his mind, history was connected with processions and life with parades and he liked parades. People were always asking him if he remembered this or that—a dreary black procession of questions about the past. There was only one event in the past that had any significance for him and that he cared to talk about: that was twelve years ago when he had received the general's uniform and had been in the premiere.

"I was in that preemy they had in Atlanta," he would tell visitors sitting on his front porch. "Surrounded by beautiful guls. It wasn't a thing local about it. It was nothing local about it. Listen here. It was a nashnul event and they had me in it—up onto the stage. There was no bob-tails at it. Every person at it had paid ten dollars to get in and had to wear his tuxseeder. I was in this uniform. A beautiful gul presented me with it that afternoon in a hotel room."

"It was in a suite in the hotel and I was in it too, Papa," Sally Poker would say, winking at the visitors. "You weren't alone with any young lady in a hotel room."

"Was, I'd known what to do," the old General would say with a sharp look and the visitors would scream with laughter. "This Hollywood, California, gul," he'd continue. "She was from Hollywood, California, and didn't have any part in the pitcher. Out there they have so many beautiful guls that they don't need that they call them a extra and they don't use them for nothing but presenting people with things and having their pitchers taken. They took my pitcher with her. No, it was two of them. One on either side and me in the middle with my arms around each of them's waist and their waist ain't any bigger than a half a dollar."

Sally Poker would interrupt again. "It was Mr. Govisky that gave you the uniform, Papa, and he gave me the most exquisite corsage. Really, I wish you could have seen it. It was made with gladiola petals taken off and painted gold and put back together to look like a rose. It was exquisite. I wish you could have seen it, it was . . ."

"It was as big as her head," the General would snarl. "I was tellin it. They gimme this uniform and they gimme this soward and they say, 'Now General, we don't want you to start a war on us. All we want you to do is march right up on that stage when you're innerduced tonight and answer a few questions. Think you can do that?' 'Think I can do it!' I say. 'Listen here. I was doing things before you were born,' and they hollered."

"He was the hit of the show," Sally Poker would say, but she didn't much like to remember the premiere on account of what had happened to her feet at it. She had bought a new dress for the occasion—a long black crepe dinner dress with a rhinestone buckle and a bolero—and a pair of silver slippers to wear with it, because she was supposed to go up on the stage with him to keep him from falling. Everything was arranged for them. A real limousine came at ten minutes to eight and took them to the theater. It drew up under the marquee at exactly the right time, after the big stars and the director and the author and the governor and the mayor and some less important stars. The police kept traffic from jamming and there were ropes to keep the people off who couldn't go. All the people who couldn't go watched them step out of the limousine into the lights. Then they walked down the red and gold foyer and an usherette in a Confederate cap and little short skirt conducted them to their special seats. The audience was already there and a group of UDC members began to clap when they saw the General in his uniform and that started everybody to clap. A few more celebrities came after them and then the doors closed and the lights went down.

A young man with blond wavy hair who said he represented the motion-picture industry came out and began to introduce everybody and each one who was introduced walked up on the stage and said how really happy he was to be here for this great event. The General and his granddaughter were introduced sixteenth on the program. He was introduced as General Tennessee Flintrock Sash of the Confederacy, though Sally Poker had told Mr. Govisky that his name was George Poker Sash and that he had only been a major. She helped him up from his seat but her heart was beating so fast she didn't know whether she'd make it herself.

The old man walked up the aisle slowly with his fierce white head high and his hat held over his heart. The orchestra began to play the Confederate Battle Hymn very softly and the UDC members rose as a group and did not sit down again until the General was on the stage. When he reached the center of the stage with Sally Poker just behind him guiding his elbow, the orchestra burst out in a loud rendition of the Battle Hymn and the old man, with real stage presence, gave a vigorous trembling salute and stood at attention until the last blast had died away. Two of the usherettes in Confederate caps and short skirts held a Confederate and a Union flag crossed behind them.

The General stood in the exact center of the spotlight and it caught a weird moon-shaped slice of Sally Poker—the corsage, the rhinestone buckle and one hand clenched around a white glove and handkerchief. The young man with the blond wavy hair inserted himself into the circle of light and said he was *really* happy to have here tonight for this great event, one, he said, who had fought and bled in the battles they would soon see daringly reacted on the screen, and "Tell me, General," he asked, "how old are you?"

"Niiiiiinnttty-two!" the General screamed.

The young man looked as if this were just about the most impressive thing that had been said all evening. "Ladies and gentlemen," he said, "let's give the General the biggest hand we've got!" and there was applause immediately and the young man indicated to Sally Poker with a motion of his thumb that she could take the old man back to his seat now so that the next person could be introduced; but the General had not finished. He stood immovable in the exact center of the spotlight, his neck thrust forward, his mouth slightly open, and his voracious gray eyes drinking in the glare and the applause. He elbowed his granddaughter roughly away. "How I keep so young," he screeched, "I kiss all the pretty guls!"

This was met with a great din of spontaneous applause and it was at just that instant that Sally Poker looked down at her feet and discovered that in the excitement of getting ready she had forgotten to change her shoes: two brown Girl Scout oxfords protruded from the bottom of her dress. She gave the General a yank and almost ran with him off the stage. He was very angry that he had not got to say how glad he was to be here for this event and on the way back to his seat, he kept saying as loud as he could, "I'm glad to be here at this preemy with all these beautiful guls!" but there was another celebrity going up the other aisle and nobody paid any attention to him. He slept through the picture, muttering fiercely every now and then in his sleep.

Since then, his life had not been very interesting. His feet were completely dead now, his knees worked like old hinges, his kidneys functioned when they would, but his heart persisted doggedly to beat. The past and the future were the same thing to him, one forgotten and the other not remembered; he had no more notion of dying than a cat. Every year on Confederate Memorial Day, he was bundled up and lent to the Capitol City Museum where he was displayed from one to four in a musty room full of old photographs, old uniforms, old artillery, and historic documents. All these were carefully preserved in glass cases so that children would not put their hands on them. He wore his general's uniform from the premiere and sat, with a fixed scowl, inside a small roped area. There was nothing about him to indicate that he was alive except an occasional movement in his milky gray eyes, but once when a bold child touched his sword, his arm shot forward and slapped the hand off in an instant. In the spring when the old homes were opened for pilgrimages, he was invited to wear his uniform and sit in some conspicuous spot and lend atmosphere to the scene. Some of these times he only snarled at the visitors but sometimes he told about the premiere and the beautiful girls.

If he had died before Sally Poker's graduation, she thought she would have died herself. At the beginning of the summer term, even before she knew if she would pass, she told the Dean that her grandfather, General Tennessee Flintrock Sash of the Confederacy, would attend her graduation and that he was a hundred and four years old and that his mind was still clear as a bell. Distinguished visitors were always welcome and could sit on the stage and be introduced. She made arrangements with her nephew, John Wesley Poker Sash, a Boy Scout, to come wheel the General's chair. She thought how sweet it would be to see the old man in his courageous gray and the young boy in his clean khaki—the old and the new, she thought appropriately—they would be behind her on the stage when she received her degree.

Everything went almost exactly as she had planned. In the summer while she was away at school, the General stayed with other relatives and they brought him and John Wesley, the Boy Scout, down to the graduation. A reporter came to the hotel where they stayed and took the General's picture with Sally Poker on one side of him and John Wesley on the other. The General, who had had his picture taken with beautiful girls, didn't think much of this. He had forgotten precisely what kind of event this was he was going to attend but he remembered that he was to wear his uniform and carry the sword.

On the morning of the graduation, Sally Poker had to line up in the academic procession with the B.S.'s in Elementary Education and she couldn't see to getting him on the stage herself—but John Wesley, a fat blond boy of ten with an executive expression, guaranteed to take care of everything. She came in her academic gown to the hotel and dressed the old man in his uniform. He was as frail as a dried spider. "Aren't you just thrilled, Papa?" she asked. "I'm just thrilled to death!"

"Put the soward acrost my lap, damm you," the old man said, "where it'll shine."

She put it there and then stood back looking at him. "You look just grand," she said.

"God damm it," the old man said in a slow monotonous certain tone as if he were saying it to the beating of his heart. "God damm every goddam thing to hell."

"Now, now," she said and left happily to join the procession.

The graduates were lined up behind the Science building and she found her place just as the line started to move. She had not slept much the night before and when she had, she had dreamed of the exercises, murmuring, "See him, see him?" in her sleep but waking up every time just before she turned her head to look at him behind her. The graduates had to walk three blocks in the hot sun in their black wool robes and as she plodded stolidly along she thought that if anyone considered this academic procession something impressive to behold, they need only wait until they saw that old General in his courageous gray and that clean young Boy Scout stoutly wheeling his chair across the stage with the sunlight catching the sword. She imagined that John Wesley had the old man ready now behind the stage.

The black procession wound its way up to the two blocks and started on the main walk leading to the auditorium. The visitors stood on the grass, picking out their graduates. Men were pushing back their hats and wiping their foreheads and women were lifting their dresses slightly from the shoulders to keep them from sticking to their backs. The graduates in their heavy robes looked as if the last beads of ignorance were being sweated out of them. The sun blazed off the fenders of automobiles and beat from the columns of the buildings and pulled the eye from one spot of glare to another. It pulled Sally Poker's toward the big red Coca-Cola machine that had been set up by the side of the auditorium. Here she saw the General parked, scowling and hatless in his chair in the blazing sun while John Wesley, his blouse loose behind, his hip and cheek pressed to the red machine, was drinking a Coca-Cola. She broke from the line and galloped to them and snatched the bottle away. She shook the boy and thrust in his blouse and put the hat on the old man's head. "Now get him in there!" she said, pointing one rigid finger to the side door of the building.

For his part the General felt as if there were a little hole beginning to widen in the top of his head. The boy wheeled him rapidly down a walk and up a ramp and into the building and bumped him over the stage entrance and into position where he had been told and the General glared in front of him at heads that all seemed to flow together and eyes that moved from one face to another. Several figures in black robes came and picked up his hand and shook it. A black procession was flowing up each aisle and forming to stately music in a pool in front of him. The music seemed to be entering his head through the little hole and he thought for a second that the procession would try to enter it too.

He didn't know what procession this was but there was something familiar about it. It must be familiar to him since it had come to meet him, but he didn't like a black procession. Any procession that came to meet him, he thought irritably, ought to have floats with beautiful guls on them like the floats before the preemy. It must be something connected with history like they were always having. He had no use for any of it. What happened then wasn't anything to a man living now and he was living now.

When all the procession had flowed into the black pool, a black figure began orating in front of it. The figure was telling something about history and the General made up his mind he wouldn't listen, but the words kept seeping in through the little hole in his head. He heard his own name mentioned and his chair was shuttled forward roughly and the Boy Scout took a big bow. They called his name and the fat brat bowed. Goddam you, the old man tried to say, get out of my way, I can stand up!—but he was jerked back again before he could get up and take the bow. He supposed the noise they made was for him. If he was over, he didn't intend to listen to any more of it. If it hadn't been for the little hole in the top of his head, none of the words would have got to him. He thought of putting his finger up there into the hole to block them but the hole was a little wider than his finger and it felt as if it were getting deeper.

Another black robe had taken the place of the first one and was talking now and he heard his name mentioned again but they were not talking about him, they were still talking about history. "If we forget our past," the speaker was saying, "we won't remember our future and it will be as well for we won't have one." The General heard some of these words gradually. He had forgotten history and he didn't intend to remember it again. He had forgotten the name and face of his wife and the names and faces of his children or even

221

if he had a wife and children, and he had forgotten the names of places and the places themselves and what had happened at them.

He was considerably irked by the hole in his head. He had not expected to have a hole in his head at this event. It was the slow black music that had put it there and though most of the music had stopped outside, there was still a little of it in the hole, going deeper and moving around in his thoughts, letting the words he heard into the dark places of his brain. He heard the words, Chickamauga, Shiloh, Johnston, Lee, and he knew he was inspiring all these words that meant nothing to him. He wondered if he had been a general at Chickamauga or at Lee. Then he tried to see himself and the horse mounted in the middle of a float full of beautiful girls, being driven slowly through downtown Atlanta. Instead, the old words began to stir in his head as if they were trying to wrench themselves out of place and come to life.

The speaker was through with that war and had gone on to the next one and now he was approaching another and all his words, like the black procession, were vaguely familiar and irritating. There was a long finger of music in the General's head, probing various spots that were words, letting in a little light on the words and helping them to live. The words began to come toward him and he said, Dammit! I ain't going to have it! and he started edging backwards to get out of the way. Then he saw the figure in the black robe sit down and there was a noise and the black pool in front of him began to rumble and to flow toward him from either side to the black slow music, and he said, Stop dammit! I can't do but one thing at a time! He couldn't protect himself from the words and attend to the procession too and the words were coming at him fast. He felt that he was running backwards and the words were coming at him like musket fire, just escaping him but getting nearer and nearer. He turned around and began to run as fast as he could but he found himself running toward the words. He was running into a regular volley of them and meeting them with quick curses. As the music swelled toward him, the entire past opened up on him out of nowhere and he felt his body riddled in a hundred places with sharp stabs of pain and he fell down, returning a curse for every hit. He saw his wife's narrow face looking at him critically through her round gold-rimmed glasses; he saw one of his squinting bald-headed sons; and his mother ran toward him with an anxious look; then a succession of places—Chicamauga, Shiloh, Marthasville—rushed at him as if the past were the only future now and he had to endure it. Then suddenly he saw that the black procession was almost on him. He recognized it, for it had been dogging all his days. He made such a desperate effort to see over it and find out what comes after the past that his hand clenched the sword until the blade touched bone.

The graduates were crossing the stage in a long file to receive their scrolls and shake the president's hand. As Sally Poker, who was near the end, crossed, she glanced at the General and saw him sitting fixed and fierce, his eyes wide open, and she turned her head forward again and held it a perceptible degree higher and received her scroll. Once it was all over and she was out of the auditorium in the sun again, she located her kin and they waited together on a bench in the shade for John Wesley to wheel the old man out. That crafty scout had bumped him out the back way and rolled him at high speed down a flagstone path and was waiting now, with the corpse, in the long line at the Coca-Cola machine.

NOTES ON THE AUTHORS

Ambrose Bierce (1842–1914) was born to poor farmers in Meigs County, Ohio. He worked briefly as a printer's devil before attending Kentucky Military Institute for a year. In 1861, he enlisted in the Union Army and fought with distinction throughout the war. That experience became the source of his 1892 collection, *Tales of Soldiers and Civilians*. After the war, he established a large reputation as a journalist, both on the west coast and in England. Between 1881 and 1906, he published the witty and cynical epigrams and definitions that would become his most popular work, *Devil's Dictionary*. He died mysteriously while covering the Mexican Revolution.

Fred Chappell (1936–   ) was born in Canton, North Carolina, and has taught at the University of North Carolina at Greensboro since 1964. His more than twenty books include novels as well as collections of poetry and of short fiction. Perhaps his most famous works are *The World Between the Eyes* (1971), *River: A Poem* (1975), *Bloodfire* (1978), *Moments of Light* (1980), *Castle Tzingal* (1985), and *I Am One of You Forever* (1985). St Martin's Press published his most recent book, *More Shapes Than One*, in 1991.

Stephen Crane (1871–1900) was born in Newark, New Jersey, the son of a Methodist minister. During a brief period as a student at Syracuse University, he worked as a correspondent for the New York *Tribune* and began writing short fiction. He left Syracuse to live a bohemian life in New York City and to write his first novel, *Maggie, A Girl of the Streets* (1893). In 1895, he gained international fame with the publication of *The Red Badge of Courage*. Crane died in Germany, of tuberculosis, at the age of twenty-eight.

William Faulkner (1897–1962), the South's best-known writer, was born in New Albany, Mississippi, but grew up, and spent most of his adult life, in Oxford. His numerous awards include the Nobel

Prize for literature (1949), National Book Awards for *Collected Stories* (1950) and for *A Fable* (1951), and Pulitzer Prizes for *A Fable* and for *The Reivers* (1963). He died in Byhalia, Mississippi.

Ernest Gaines (1933–   ) was born in Oscar, Louisiana. Though Gaines left the South to attend San Francisco State College and Stanford Universty, he eventually returned to teach creative writing at the University of Southern Louisiana. And he continues to divide his time between San Francisco and his home state. His works are set in rural Louisiana and include five novels: *Catherine Carmier* (1964), *Of Love and Dust* (1967), *The Autobiography of Miss Jane Pittman* (1971), *In My Father's House* (1978), and *A Gathering of Old Men* (1983). *Bloodline* (1968) is a collection of his short stories.

Hamlin Garland (1860–1940) was born near West Salem, Wisconsin, generally the setting of his stories of hard rural life collected in *Main-Travelled Roads* (1891). He continued to depict with power and sympathy the lives of common midwesterners in the nineteenth century in his autobiographical series that included *Son of the Middle Border* (1917), *A Daughter of the Middle Border* (1921), *Trail-Makers of the Middle Border* (1928), and *Roadside Meetings* (1930). Garland was elected to the American Academy of Arts and Letters in 1918.

Ellen Glasgow (1874–1945) was born in Richmond, Virginia, where she spent most of her life and which she frequently took as the setting for her work. She contributed significantly to Southern fiction's transition from the sentimental to the realistic and ironic. Her many works include *The Descendent* (1897), *The Voice of the People* (1900), *The Battle-Ground* (1902), *The Shadowy Third and Other Stories* (1923), *Barren Ground* (1925), *They Stooped to Folly* (1929), *The Sheltered Life* (1932), and *Vein of Iron* (1935). Her autobiography, *The Woman Within*, was not published until 1954, nearly ten years after her death.

Caroline Gordon (1895–1981) was born in Trenton, Kentucky, and began her writing career as a journalist in Chattanooga, Tennessee. Her works of fiction include *Penhally* (1931), *Aleck Maury, Sportsman* (1934), *None Shall Look Back* (1937), *The Garden of Adonis* (1937), *Green Centuries* (1941), *The Women on the Porch* (1944), *The Forest of the South* (1945), *The Strange Children* (1951), *The Malefactors* (1956), and *Old Red and Other Stories* (1963). She taught writing at the Woman's College of the University of North Carolina and at Columbia University. With her husband, Allen Tate, she edited the famous anthology, *The House of Fiction* (1950). Caroline Gordon died in Chiapas, Mexico.

Barry Hannah (1942–   ) was born in Clinton, Mississippi. He attended Mississippi College and the University of Arkansas and has taught writing at Clemson University, Middlebury College, the University of Alabama, the University of Iowa, and the University of Montana-Missoula. He is currently Writer-in-residence at the University of Mississippi in Oxford. *Geronimo Rex* (1972), his first novel, won the William Faulkner Prize and was nominated for a National Book Award. His other novels and collections of stories include *Nightwatchmen* (1973), *Airships* (1978), *Ray* (1980), *The Tennis Handsome* (1983), *Captain Maximus* (1985), *Hey, Jack!* (1987), and *Boomerang* (1989). Houghton Mifflin published Hannah's most recent collection of stories, *Bats Out of Hell*, in 1993.

O. Henry (William Sydney Porter) (1862–1910) was born in Greensboro, North Carolina. At eighteen, he quit school and went to Texas where he worked as a journalist and as a bank teller. A charge of embezzlement eventually brought him a three-year sentence in the Ohio Federal Penitentiary. In 1902 he moved to New York, where, under his pseudonym, he wrote most of his stories. Many of those stories are collected in such volumes as *Cabbages and Kings* (1904), *Heart of the West* (1904), *Roads of Destiny* (1909), and *Rolling Stones* (1912). He moved to North Carolina shortly before his death and is buried in Asheville.

Mary Johnston (1870–1936), the daughter of a Confederate major, was born in Buchanan, Virginia. Severe "nervous disorders" plagued her for much of her life and limited her formal education to three months in an Atlanta school for girls. Her first novel, *Prisoners of Hope*, appeared in 1898. Her second, *To Have and To Hold*, was the best-selling novel of 1900. Among her other books are *The Goddess of Reason* (1907), *The Long Roll* (1911), *The Wanderers* (1917), and *Pioneers of the Old South* (1918). She was active in women's suffrage and helped found the Equal Suffrage League of Virginia. She died at her Virginia home, "Three Hills," and is buried in Richmond.

Jack London (1876–1916) was born illegitimately in San Francisco and grew up in Oakland where he became a voracious reader who rarely went to school. He was a hobo and a sailor before joining the Klondike gold rush. His search for gold was unsuccessful, but it helped him gather material for such novels as *Call of the Wild*

(1903) and *White Fang* (1906). He became a prolific and wealthy writer, but he found little contentment and apparently died a suicide.

Robert Morgan (1933–) was born in Hendersonville, North Carolina, and has taught at Cornell University since 1971. Well known as both poet and fiction writer, his collections include *Blue Valleys* (1989) and *The Mountains Won't Remember Us* (1992). His most recent novel, *The Hinterlands*, was published earlier this year, and another novel, tentatively called *The House by the River*, is expected from Algonquin Press in 1996.

Flannery O'Connor (1925–1964) was born in Savannah, Georgia, but in 1938 moved to Milledgeville, where she spent most of her life. She attended Middle Georgia College there and then went on to the University of Iowa where she received an M.F.A. In 1950, while she was working on her first novel, *Wiseblood* (1952), she discovered that she had disseminated lupus, the disease which had killed her father and would kill her as well. Her second novel is *The Violent Bear It Away* (1960); her two collections of stories are *A Good Man Is Hard to Find* (1955) and *Everything That Rises Must Converge* (1965). Her *Complete Stories* won The National Book Award in 1972.

Thomas Nelson Page (1853–1922) was born in Oakland, Virginia. He attended Washington College while Robert E. Lee was president of the school. He obtained a law degree from the University of Virginia and started a practice in Richmond. His best known short-story collection, *In Ole Virginia*, was published in 1887. In 1893, Page moved to Washington to concentrate on his writing, and during World War I, he went to Italy as United States Ambassador. His books include *Two Little Confederates* (1888), *The Old South: Essays Social and Political* (1892), *Robert E. Lee, The Southerner* (1908), and *Italy and the World War* (1920).

Mark Twain (Samuel L. Clemens) (1835–1910) was born in Florida, Missouri, but grew up in the larger Mississippi River town of Hannibal. He was a steamboat pilot, briefly a Confederate volunteer, a journalist, and an inventor. He gave up these professions, though, to answer "a 'call' to literature, of a low order—i.e. humorous." *Huckleberry Finn* (1885) is no doubt the best known of his many well-known books. It has sold over thirteen million copies and is thus one of the most popular books of all times.